BLOOD
IN THE
SNOW

Seth Sjostrom

*wolfprint*Media

wolfprint, LLC
P.O. Box 801 Camas,
WA, 98607

Copyright ©2013 by Seth Sjostrom

Library of Congress Cataloging-in-Publication Data Library of Congress

Control Number: 2012936550 Sjostrom, Seth.
Blood in the Snow: a thriller / by Seth Sjostrom. - 1st wolfprintMedia digital edition

Trade Paperback

ISBN-13: 978-0-9854389-0-6

1. Sean Kendall (Fictitious character)-Fiction. 2. Terrorism-Ecological-Political- Fiction. 3. Blood Series-Fiction I. Title.

First wolfprintMedia Digital edition 2013. wolfprintMedia is a tademark of wolfprint, LLC.

For information regarding bulk purchases, please contact wolfprint, LLC at sales@wolfprintpublishing.com.

United States of America

Acknowledgements

My deepest appreciation to those who have supported me and my vision. From those who were present at the very moment of inspiration, like my friend and fellow author Ric Conrad. A simple coffee run to a book shop admiring a Jim Brandenburg image was all it took for an entire story to unfold in my head.

To those somewhere in between where ideas evolve from silly notions to earnest endeavors: Tom and Linda Sjostrom for taking me seriously, Michele, Coreena and Jamie for years of caring support. Hayden Sjostrom for inspiring me in ways unmatched by any other earthbound being.

To those who wrought vision to reality: Kathi Hansen for being my angel, co-conspirator, financial advisor, manager and about a hundred other roles whose titles fail to do her justice.

Michelle Stoller for putting her scrutinizing, trusted eyes to my words. John Eley, a wonderful photographer and an even better friend for his moral support and fantastic images.

Tammy Beckwith for ensuring my stabs at book creation were transformed into a viable offering.

For Hayden

One

The young wolf moved swift and light across the frozen ground. Wincing with each step, he favored his injured paw, leaving a conspicuous trail of blood in its wake. The wolf knew he had to keep pushing forward. Whatever had inflicted this injury on him was sure to be tracking him, ready to take advantage of his new weakness. Silently, he moved deeper into the woods, slinking as low to the ground as possible and still able to keep a steady gait.

Higher ground in the range afforded deeper cover in the thick forest, his best chance to escape. His mind reeled, trying to understand where this predator had come from. Outside of the occasional encounter with a mountain lion or a bear, the young wolf did not often feel threatened by any other animal. This incident was different. This new threat kept chasing him. Even when he had come across a grumpy bear, the conflict would quickly resolve as he relented and allowed the bear to go about its business.

He struggled onward, his paw throbbing, his lungs sucking in air. Before being chased, he was the one doing the chasing. Taking advantage of the twilight just before dawn, he had come upon a young pronghorn at the rim of a meadow. He chased the antelope across the open ground and into the neighboring valley, when out of nowhere, something ripped into his paw. Stumbling headlong into the snow, he was confused and frightened. Instinct took over. With great agility, he sprang back on all fours and sprinted toward the nearest grove of trees.

The wolf bounded up the hill, each step coursing pain through his paw, as he made his way toward higher ground. Intent on a thick grove of trees that rose above the valley floor, he fought for refuge. The pack had often used this upper cover to scope out their hunting ground. Using nearly every ounce of energy, he forged his way to the top of the hill.

He panted as he paused to listen and smell the air, searching for a clue that the predator was still on his trail. Unfortunately for him, heading into the brush for concealment also meant heading into the wind, he could not smell anything coming. He started to continue his way deeper up the hillside when a branch snapped behind him. Wheeling around, he saw the enemy he feared. A sound like thunder rang through the valley. The young wolf felt a hot sting rip into his side, shredding his stomach and lungs. In agony, he managed a single pathetic yelp, and his world went black.

Two

With over fifteen years of running operations for the Special Forces, this assignment for the seasoned veteran Tug Gaskill was a piece of cake. After all, the country he was in had lax security, were in the throes of political turmoil and was populated with some of the richest, yet, least informed citizens in the world. No, this operation would be easy. Nonetheless, Tug treated this assignment like any other – with the exacting precision and attention to detail that his years as a Green Beret had taught him.

He had his men practice the scenario, run contingencies, and had developed no less than a half dozen exit strategies for each of his troops. They were ready. As Tug glanced at his watch, he realized that he was ready as well. Giving the 'go' communication into his earpiece, he watched as his men carried out their specific missions.

Under his feet, two men severed the power grid, knocking out the entire area within a five-block radius. At the service entrance bays, four troops ignited their charges, blasting doorway sized holes into the large metal rolling doors. Instantly, the men poured through. On either side of the building, access points were breached. Finally, Tug, with two more men at his flank, rushed towards one of the side entrances, their semi-automatic weapons drawn and ready.

Bursting through the door, Tug found the scene in relative control. His first wave had eliminated half a dozen of the security detail and had the nearby occupants lay prone and face down on the floor. Motioning to the two men who entered with him, "Seal the front entrance." Nodding, the two soldiers moved to the front foyer of the sixteen story building.

Pressing his earpiece, Tug called out, "Teams Three and Four, report."

"Team Four has breached the rear entry. Trip charges have been set to guard the flank. We are heading for the basement."

"Roger that. Team Three?" Tug confirmed.

"Sir, Team Three has met some resistance. We are eliminating the subjects now."

Through the halls of the building, Tug could hear the sound of rapid-fire reports, "Confirm when your area is secure and you are on to the next phase." Checking his watch, he calculated that they would now be behind schedule. They would need to make that time up to meet exfil.

"Sir, this is Team Three, the resistance has been eliminated, we are proceeding to the west stairway."

"Roger that. Skip your objective on the middle floors. Focus on the first three and the top three and move to exfil. Team Two, what is your status?"

"Team two is on the twelfth floor. Our objective is near complete."

"Excellent. Team One, place your charges in the elevator shaft and move out to the rendezvous point," Tug could hear vehicles approaching with their sirens wailing. They needed to move faster if they were going to escape cleanly.

His earpiece crackled. "This is Team Four. The lower level charges have been set. No hostiles. Moving to exfil."

Suddenly, the front lobby was alive with gunfire. Tug sprinted up an adjacent stairway and followed the railing along the mezzanine until he had a view of the front entrance. He watched as several men approached the building, his squad quickly dispatching them. A lull in the surge gave him the opportunity to direct his men to move out. Swinging his Milkor M32 Multiple Grenade Launcher from his back, he lined the sites and progressively peppered the front of the building with six concussive blasts from the devastating Hellhound munitions. The chambers empty, he swung the launcher back behind his shoulders and snatched the Steyr assault rifle he had rested against the banister.

Pressing the transceiver button on his earpiece, he ordered his detail to exfil. Pausing at the stairs, he aimed his gun at the entrance one last time. Smoke and debris still hung in the air, but no additional resistance came through. As his troops caught up with him, they all headed for the North Stairwell. Dropping a load of C-4 armed with a remote detonator on the second floor, they ran the length of the stairwell until they reached the roof.

Placing a small patch of paste-like explosive around the lock, it ignited, and the door swung open. The air was alive with the heavy chop of the awaiting helicopter, already resting on the rooftop. A glance told Tug that he and his detail were the last out of the building. Sprinting across the gravel roof, they dove into the open bay of the chopper and signaled for take-off. Within an instant, the blades picked up torque, and the helicopter was airborne.

From the still open bay, Tug watched as the streets below were filled with the flashing light of emergency vehicles. He could see several security forces enter the same points his team had. At each position, a flash, followed by a brief burst of smoke, signified that the perimeter blasts had been tripped, likely eliminating those that had entered.

As additional crews on the ground surveyed their approach, Tug grabbed the transmitter attached to the M.O.L.L.E. loop on his vest. Flipping open the protective cover, he pushed the red button. First, the basement blew with incredible force. From his vantage, Tug could see the entire building sway on its earthquake protective rollers. Next, each corner where there was a stairwell ignited, sending a barrage of shrapnel rocketing outward. Shards of glass, metal, and concrete leveled nearby structures and massacred the crowd of on-lookers and emergency response personnel that had gathered.

Finally, the rooftop lifted from the structure as the upper story explosives burst to life. The loss of support on the higher floors caused the entire building to shudder and then floor by floor, begin to collapse on itself.

Watching the demolition take place in this methodical fashion, Tug almost felt sorry for the people below. Nearly all of them were innocents caught in a revolutionary war. Many of them had no clue they were in a battle at all. Their families would understand, that was for sure. Tug momentarily wondered if they were eliminating enemies with this strategy or merely creating new ones. Either way, he had done his job. He didn't set the assignments. He just carried them out. He and his team carried this one out well.

Slamming the door to the bay shut, he gave a quick nod of approval as the helicopter raced at top speed, just under the blanket of radar detection into the night sky. As planned, his team entered the scene as ghosts and vanished as ghosts.

Three

Crisp. Clean. Unspoiled. Sean Kendall loved to start the day hiking through the perfectly frosted terrain of Washington's rugged North Cascades. Just as the sun barely peeked over the easternmost crests, he would leave the warmth of his home and escape into a world of solitude and remarkable beauty.

Nestled at the very edge of the North Cascades National Park, the small ranch-style cabin allowed Kendall to walk out of his door and immediately be upon some of the Northwest's most desirable hiking trails. He had fallen in love with his early morning excursions stealing peeks at elk, coyote, or any other of the Park's many inhabitants. Sammy, his Greater Swiss Mountain Dog, faithfully accompanied him on his hikes. The big brown, black, and white painted dog loved to play in the snow. Like his master, he would identify the animals that had been treading through the valley.

The sun on this morning managed to break through the layers of clouds that had masterfully painted the terrain mere hours before. As Sean worked to crest a hill overlooking an expansive meadow, he slowed to admire the vista as the landscape seemed to light up with the morning glow. Leaning his trekking poles against a tree, he snagged a thermos from the side of his pack. Unscrewing the cap, he filled the lid with coffee - still steaming from its protective bottle.

Sipping what was his second cup of the day, he laughed to himself. "Not quite Starbucks, but not bad...." Sean had spent most of his young adult life in Seattle, working as a manager for a large computer corporation. A Starbucks was always within easy reach. He chuckled as he reflected on where his life had taken him - from prominent, polished corporate exec to scruffy-chinned mountaineer. Scarcely over a year ago, he was still fighting Seattle traffic, logging hours each day behind endless taillights. Having had enough, he cashed in his 401k and traded the frantic corporate world for life in the mountains.

He had no clue at the time he had so capriciously accepted a position as a contract negotiator for a group called the Conservancy, that the opportunity would ultimately land him in the beautiful Cascades. Enamored with the organization's approach of merely purchasing land instead of staging protests and other avenues that Sean found rather passive-aggressive, he quickly became quite accomplished, securing several key land deals for the group.

His final project was to purchase a large preserve not far from Mt. Baker. The tract of several hundred acres was home to dozens of pairs of bald eagles who used the salmon runs of the Skagit River to feed on during mating season. The sensitive space just outside of the protection of North Cascades National Park had been eyed for development as a resort and spa. Sean scrambled to broker a deal that would allow the Conservancy to head off the developers and purchase the land themselves.

In return for his services, the organization offered Sean a small tract at the edge of the preserve. He would be allowed to carve the piece into his home and assign him as the preserve steward. As the steward, Sean had the responsibility of caring for the land. He would lead work parties to maintain hiking trails and manage volunteers and youth groups who held summer camps.

When he had time, Sean guided raft trips down the Sauk and Skagit rivers. In the winter, the terrain was nearly all his own to explore - snowshoeing and cross-country skiing throughout the preserve. More often than not, he was left alone to enjoy his retirement in the solace and beauty of the rugged Cascade Range.

A year later, Sean was sipping coffee out of a thermos cap, on the summit of a 4500-foot butte, watching the morning sun dazzle the sea of white-capped peaks that stretched across the horizon as far as he could see. Sean looked down at Sammy, who sat patiently at his master's feet, seemingly taking in the view himself.

Finishing his coffee, Sean returned the thermos to its pocket on the side of his pack, and calling Sammy to attention, shoved off to continue his trek. Traversing the slope, he took in the breathtaking vistas as he drunk in the crisp morning air. As he reached the meadow, he scanned the snow for tracks. While he enjoyed catching glimpses of animals, he usually had to be content with seeing and identifying the traces they left behind. Circling the open field, he found no sign of anything having spoiled the carpet of snow that had fallen in the night. Satisfied with the morning's exercise, he turned to head back up the hill and back towards home. No matter how much he enjoyed the morning rounds, he always looked forward to the hot shower afterward.

Sean paused and adjusted his glove, tugging at the cuff with his teeth. Ready to shove off, he noticed Sammy enthusiastically investigating a patch of snow near the tree line. With curiosity, he hiked over to see what animal had been to the meadow earlier in the morning. As he moved closer, Kendall saw two sets of prints, identifying them as snowshoe tracks. Occasionally, hikers cut through the preserve on long treks in the North Cascade wilderness to visit peaks such as Lookout Mountain and Hidden Lake. "Must have been off to a real early start this morning. Probably some damn poachers," Sean muttered to himself. He didn't mind people hunting deer and elk, but not out of season and on the Preserve grounds. He decided that he would let Adam know. Adam, a friend of Sean's, who ran the local U.S. Fish and Wildlife office.

"What have you got there, Sammy?" Sean looked closer. He noticed something else. A smaller print mixed in with the snowshoe tracks. Sean bent down to identify it. It was larger than a coyote's but similar in shape. "Maybe they had a dog with them," Sean guessed. Then he noticed something unusual about the print. The track was stained inky red in its impression in the snow. The animal had been hurt and appeared to be bleeding from one of its paws. Sean decided to follow the tracks, figuring they were mere hours old, since they treaded atop the night's snow. If the dog was injured, maybe he could help.

"Let's go, boy," Sean called, pushing off. He noticed the bloody spot in the paw print became more pronounced as they followed the trail. Sammy led the way with his nose, following the tracks as they headed up into the tree line. Kendall's concern grew as he saw the animal's paw prints change gait as it tried to take the pressure off of its wound. "I hope these guys brought some first aid gear to tend to their dog," he muttered to himself.

Huffing his way to the crest of a steep hill, Sean pushed his way through low branches. The snowshoe path snaked through the dense growths of holly and evergreens before coming to a stop near a patch of snow that appeared to be the spot of marked activity. Sammy pawed anxiously at the snow, letting out excited little barks. Sean used his pole to brush aside a light layer off the crust that had slid forward. The wintry ground underneath was drenched in blood.

Sean swiveled his head, methodically surveying the area, trying to recreate the scene. He pictured an animal being bowled into the brush, leaving a bloody skid mark in its wake - almost as though a bowling ball barreling down its wooden lane. He studied the hillside. From the bloody patch of bushes, the snowshoe prints continued along the ridgeline. Sammy followed them to the edge; Sean trailed behind, more tentatively than he had before. At the end of the ridge lay a steep gully. Sammy stood at the top, barking and growling towards the basin of the ravine. The prints stopped there. Sean looked over the edge; the snow had been plowed along the side of the gully, a stretch of four feet wide leading to the bottom.

Sean assumed whatever he had been following here, was tossed over the edge. Sean took off his pack and dropped his poles. Slowly and carefully, he made his way over the side. The first few steps provided solid enough footing, the layers of snow had warmed quickly with the early available sunlight, but the next few were harder crust and eventually turned into ice. Sean's foot struggled for traction as the slope steepened, but his boots were no match for the slick ice, and the preserve steward's descent turned into a free fall headfirst towards the creek bed below.

The fall ended with a violent crash through snags of laurel and winterberry, as Sean desperately grabbed at branches to slow the inevitable. His face slammed hard into the turf, his cheekbones digging into what he thought was a mossy log. Relieved that the creek was covered with snow and ice and that the walk home would not be as wet as it could have been, he opened his eyes.

He stood up abruptly, his stomach tightening with what he saw. The log that had stopped his fall with his face wasn't a log after all. An animal was on the ground before him, the snow around its mid-section saturated red with blood. Sean forced himself closer to investigate the wounds. The animal looked like a wolf. It had a gash on his left paw and a gaping hole where its chest used to be. "Poor animal was shot and left to die here," Sean growled, disgusted with the scene. Rage coursed through his veins. Compulsively, he took a last look at the dead wolf, the first Sean had seen in the wild.

Scurrying up the hill, wiping splotches of blood infused frost off of his cheeks, Sean fought for traction up the steep slope. Almost to a point where he could reach an exposed root from the trees above and drag himself up the remaining few feet of the hill, Sean lost his footing and plummeted backward, headfirst back into the ravine. His back jarred against the hill, knocking the wind out of him as he slid back towards the creek bed. Once again, the wolf carcass stopped his fall. This time, with his head ramming into the back of the fallen animal.

Sean's irritation with himself for not taking his ice axe out of the loops in pack temporarily replaced his fury over the dead wolf. With renewed vigor, and disgust, Sean leaped up and again tackled the hill. This attempt was met with a little more success, as he lunged when he reached the spot where he slipped prior and was able to grab the root that he had eyed on his first attempt.

Sammy greeted him at the top, licking at his face and sniffing the wolf blood that had stained his master. Snapping back into his snowshoes, his blood boiling, Sean located the direction of the snowshoe tracks from the ravine. Determined to get some answers, he and Sammy once more chased after the phantom snowshoe tracks.

Sean hiked furiously up the slope, laboring up a steep pitch that demanded he kick out of his snowshoes and tackle the hill with his ice axe in hand to steady himself. He scrambled up the slope until he reached another peak. Beyond the hill was another vast meadow. Sean looked on as the snowshoe tracks spanned across the length of the plateau and into the dense forest beyond. He realized that he would not catch up to the wolf hunters. Not today.

The pack was alarmed and agitated. They were small in numbers, an alpha pair, two young males, a female and two pups that survived the summer and fall. The pack had migrated south to Washington across the Canadian border and into the Skagit Valley in the late fall, their growing family demanding their own province to rule. They found their new territory plentiful with few competing predators to vie against. Now, they huddled in distress over one of the males that strayed on the early morning hunt, chasing a young pronghorn into the lower valley. A tragedy had fallen upon their brother; the group typically hunted as a team, particularly staying close together as they descended into the open country of the valleys below. But the young male, two years old, lost himself in the chase. Now, he was missing, and the pack seemed to know that he was not coming back.

The alpha began the chorus with a low howl, and the rest of the pack joined in. They called out to their missing family member in a final pitch for his unlikely return, the somber sound of genuine concern filling the air.

Sean had pushed himself to get back to his home quickly. He carried his snowshoes up the steps and into the porch. The sun shining through the glass made the tiny room quite warm and welcoming to his chilled bones. Sean tilted his hiking poles against the wall and opened the door to the entryway. In the solitude of the Cascades, he never took care to lock the door when he went on his morning excursions. Few people even knew his home existed. Taking off his pack, he let it fall to the floor with a clunk, the thermos tumbling out of its pocket and rolling to a stop beside the bag. Sammy padded over to investigate, sniffing at the thermos curiously.

Sean grabbed his phone as he filled a glass of fresh water and drained it in several gulps. Dialing Adam's office phone first, he heard the familiar sound of his voicemail. Hanging up, he tried his friend's cell. "This is Adam," boomed the voice after a couple of rings. Sean said hello, and the typical pleasantries before he relayed the morning's events.

"A wolf, huh? Could be… North Cascades Park has been known to be home to a few wolves once in a while. Real shame for one them to be killed," Adam replied to Sean's story.

"Think you could come out and take a look? I'd like to see what we could do to keep this from happening again," Sean said as he put away the contents of his pack.

"Well, I've got a couple hours of work at the office. Why don't you meet me, and we'll head out there before lunch," the Wildlife and Fisheries officer replied.

"Alright, thanks, Adam, see you there," with that, Sean hung up the phone. He turned on the TV and started the water for his shower. The newscaster was retelling the story of a federal building bombing in Colorado that had occurred a few days ago. Smoke still seeped from the rubble of the leveled building. The only new information the FBI had was an anonymous group claiming they did it in protest of the President's latest deal brokered in Asia. The camera panned to the show the families mourning lost loved ones placing bundles of flowers and photographs against a chain-link fence. Sean shook his head, he had fought passionately for his ideals before, but there was a right way to do it. These monsters did not do it the right way. With that parting thought, he returned his attention to the steaming shower that was calling to his cold and weary muscles.

Four

Daryl McKenzie was a big, hulking man. All of the McKenzie boys were. They were a generally quiet family that kept to themselves except for the occasional forays when the boys would head to the taverns. During hunting season, they were especially rowdy. Today, Daryl was on a hunt. He was particularly excited about today's adventure. This was his first hunt with a new client - Tug Gaskill. The McKenzie boys frequently led hunts for people who were either after game that were protected by law or when they wanted help in disregarding the legal limits. Tug was a man who had hunted game all over the world. He was in Washington on a business venture between some of Tug's associates and Daryl's father, Hal. Daryl thought it would be fun to take Tug on an early morning hunt prior to the day's business activities.

Daryl had first seen the wolf pack near Hozomeen Mountain, and over the past several weeks, had tracked their movements south to Mount Terror, following the southwest curve of Ross Lake. Daryl was a proficient hunter and an excellent tracker; he could almost follow the wolf pack in his mind as they made their way to ideal hunting grounds at the edge of the lower valleys. Their father and grandfather taught his brother and him to hunt at an early age. He had remembered his granddad's tales of the wolves terrorizing the ranch and how his grandfather had all but single-handedly exterminated wolves from the entire Skagit Valley. Daryl had never had the opportunity to shoot a wolf himself. Until recently, he hadn't even seen a sign of a wolf in the Cascades. He had hunted nearly every other game animal – bears, cougars, elk, mountain goats, wild turkeys – any animal available to him in Washington. Perhaps it was the stories of Tug's exotic big game adventures, or maybe because it was the irony of the predator turned into prey or just the fact that the government said it was illegal to shoot a wolf made this hunt more appealing. Tug, on the other hand, was excited to test out his new gun on the hunt.

This morning, Daryl figured he would take Tug north of Lookout Mountain to an area near the twisting conduit of Damnation Creek, following the progression that he had been tracking over the past couple of weeks. The hike was a long one, with the depth of snow limiting how far he could take his four-wheel drive. Nevertheless, the two men enjoyed swapping hunting stories as they made their way to the succession of meadows that Daryl was hoping would find them some good targets.

Tug shared with the wide-eyed Daryl of his encounters in Africa hunting rhinos, lions and other exotic game. He told Daryl that a Japanese collector had once offered him over ten thousand dollars to purchase the horn of the rhino that he killed, but Tug decided he would enjoy having the head as a centerpiece for his trophy room more than the ten grand. Daryl reveled in amazement at some of Tug's stories. He had himself, never been out of the United States. The furthest he had traveled was to Montana with his dad on a hunting trip and Idaho for a survival boot camp a family friend put on each year.

Their tales of hunting prowess provided the two men with a pleasant distraction. Making good time, they had benefited from their snowshoes and the cracks of moonlight sneaking through the clouds and spilling onto the snow. The hunters paused as they came to a high ridge that perched above an intersection of three small valleys. This intersection created a bowl-shaped meadow that many animals would channel through on their journeys north and south. Daryl had found this spot to be great for stalking elk and antelope. He had figured this to be a natural hunting spot for the wolves he had been tracking as well. The tree line wrapped around the valley except for a pair of entrances. This made it easy for predators to follow their prey through one of the narrow valleys that dumped into the meadow.

Daryl pulled his tripod chair out of his pack and dug out his binoculars. Tug followed suit. A light flurry of snow drifted down as the men waited patiently, each training their field glasses intently on the meadow below. A forty-minute wait in silence finally afforded the two with the sighting of a young pronghorn antelope. It appeared to be alone as it wandered south through a tributary valley and into the box meadow. Its ears twitched as it strained to test the air for signs of danger.

The young antelope perked its head up suddenly and dashed forward, heading for the southern entrance of the meadow. A black raven flew overhead and circled the valley, monitoring the antics below. From one of the tree-lined slopes bordering the field, a grayish streak leaped onto the valley floor, lunging itself in the direction of the antelope. Daryl nudged Tug and raised his rifle, excitedly squeezing of a round. He looked on sheepishly, hoping his guest wouldn't think him impolite in taking the first shot. He expected redemption in the rest of the pack jumping out of the tree line to join the hunt, as he had observed them before working as a group while he was tracking them.

The shot rang through the valley. The wolf racing toward his prey rolled headlong into the snow. Daryl thought he had gotten off a good shot, but as quickly as the wolf went down, it was back on his feet. Unlike the fleet-footed antelope that raced through the center of the meadow, the wolf turned sharply and sprinted for the tree line. "Damn!" cried Daryl as he positioned himself for another shot, but was surprised by the direction the wolf had chosen.

Tug chuckled and slapped Daryl on the back, "Well, you must have hit it. We'll get him." The hunters grabbed their gear and ran down into the valley. Crossing the meadow, they paused at the spot where the wolf had gone down. They noticed a small spot of blood in the snow. "That will slow him down, let's get after him," Tug said taking the lead. They plodded up the hillside and into the trees as the wolf had. The hill loomed about one hundred feet high. It leveled off for about fifty yards and descended into the next valley. "He might even lead us to the rest of the pack," muttered Tug, trying to sound positive for the dejected young McKenzie boy.

They descended the hill and followed the tracks as they hugged the tree line. The wolf remained out of their line of sight. The tracks paralleled the forest for an additional hundred yards and then climbed the hill toward an area covered more densely with brush and trees. They noticed the paw prints held a more substantial streak of blood as they went, especially where the wolf had to labor up the hill.

Tug's solid instincts took hold, and he suggested that they slow down as they reached the crest of the knoll. He whispered to Daryl, "The wound looks to be opening up more, the wolf might try to tend to it if it feels safe in the brush up ahead." He readied his weapon, an H&K 10mm semi-automatic assault rifle. They took each step carefully. Daryl noticed that about every fifty paces or so, the blood appeared more concentrated; the wolf was pausing to rest, increasingly hindered by his wound.

They neared the top of the hill; Daryl angled towards a tree that provided a blind to peek over without being seen. As he stepped forward, he heard a snap beneath his feet, shattering the silence that had befallen the hunt. "Damn," he cursed to himself, looking down on a branch that lay at his feet. Just as he did so, he spotted the wolf seventy-five yards ahead, only visible through the low branches of Sitka alders. It whipped its head back, looking at Daryl, its ears back showing his fear, despite its muzzle drawn up in a fierce snarl. Flexing, the wolf readied himself to lunge deeper into the brush. An explosion came from behind Daryl, who turned to see Tug nonchalantly firing off a burst round that ripped through the wolf, blowing the animal off of its feet and sliding through the snow. The wolf let out a single, pathetic high-pitched yelp and flopped motionless on the ground.

Tug paused and knelt to retrieve the casings that steamed their way through the snow and to the frozen ground. He looked up at the young McKenzie, who was gawking in awe by the power of the gun and the accuracy of Tug's shot.

The two men walked up to their kill. Daryl looked at the gaping hole that once was the wolf's chest. He had hopes of having it stuffed with its teeth bared; the mess at his feet dispelled that notion. "No sense dragging that thing back with us."

Tug knelt beside the slain wolf for a moment, examining it. "Wiley creature almost got away from you," Tug said with a grin.

"Yeah," Daryl agreed, "I didn't expect the uphill chase. The damn thing was smart and headed for the nearest cover instead of the easiest path. I didn't even get off a second shot."

"I reckon this little baby lived up to its billing. A little much for hunting, I suppose," Tug said, admiring the HK10 in his hand.

"What the heck kind of gun is that?" Daryl asked, examining it.

"It is an assault weapon used for tactical missions. It fires thirty 10mm NATO rounds, good for 500 meters," the Tug replied.

Tug paused for a second and added, "We should discard this carcass somewhere, no need to attract attention to our little fun."

"I haven't seen anyone this far out this winter, and the scavengers'll probably get at it pretty quick, but I suppose you're right. There's a gully just past the ridge over there that eventually runs into Sibley Creek. That ought to be fine," Daryl shrugged.

Silently, the two dragged their kill across the ridgeline that Daryl had described. The steep sides that ran down into the gully provided a slick path to the bottom of the creek. The lifeless wolf flopped, rolled, and then slid out of sight. Proud of their accomplishment, the two hunters headed back for Daryl's pick-up.

Five

Sean climbed into the Jeep and headed toward the office. The drive to the ranger station in Sedro-Wooley was a good forty-five minutes from Sean's house in Marblemount, more with snow on the ground. Yet, he didn't mind, not nearly as much as he used to detest the commute to work each day when he was hostage to corporate life. Of course, his time commitments were his own to keep now, and the scenery was a whole lot more beautiful than the seemingly endless streak of bumpers and taillights in Seattle congestion.

Sedro-Wooley served as the site for the North Cascades National Park headquarters as well as the Mount Baker Ranger Station. Sean had been endowed with a tiny office to perform his volunteer work and help coordinate activities between the conservancy and the parks system. Sean first met Adam Raines, the supervisor of the NCNP Fish and Wildlife District, when he moved out to the region. The boisterous Wildlife officer had heard of the Conservancy and was more than happy to help Sean out with an office in the Park facility. The Conservancy had often worked in cooperation with the park system and the Fish and Wildlife Service on numerous projects over the years. Adam was especially impressed when Sean and the Conservancy stepped in when government bureaucracy was taking too long to acquire the site that nested bald eagles. The organization immediately bought the land, turning it over in a deed to the park for management. Sean and Adam worked closely together to broker the deal and maintain the preserve.

The two fast became friends, sharing countless wilderness adventures - Sean teaching Adam an appreciation for whitewater and Adam sharing his fondness for rock climbing. In the year that Sean lived there, he had been adopted by Adam's wife, Laura, as a member of the family. The couple happily provided the divorcee with a semblance of home during the holidays as most of Sean's family lived on the East coast. His close friendship with Adam had provided Sean with a sense of home after leaving behind his life in Seattle.

"Morning Kendall," the voice boomed as soon as Sean stepped in the door of the Park office. Sean nodded in the direction of his friend Adam.

"Good morning, Sean. You've got a stack of mail in your box," cooed the much softer voice of the receptionist, Paige. Paige, an attractive woman in her late twenties, carried herself with a natural, unassuming appeal with her shoulder-length dark hair and thin glasses that nicely complimented her young face. She did her best to dress in the latest fashions and keep up with the twenty-somethings crowd, though her options for social interaction were limited so far away from the city. She had worked at the park office since she was an AmeriCorps volunteer in college, spending her summers in the office until she graduated and signed on full-time. She had a poorly kept secret crush on Sean since he first stepped into the office, but had never directly confronted him with her desires. A thin thread of hope held in her grasp that the day would come when he was ready to date again, and he would have to look no further than down the hall.

"Thanks, Paige," Kendall replied, and noticing she was sporting a new sweater added, "Another sweater from Christmas?"

"Oh, Sean, you're the first to notice. Yes, it is. Do you like it?" Paige asked as she held her arms out to unveil the entire ensemble for Sean.

"Yeah, it looks great," he replied politely while thinking to himself, "*Oh boy, careful Sean. Paige is sweet, but I don't think you need to encourage her*." Sean didn't quite know how to react to attention from women after his divorce. His lifestyle left him well-toned accented by chiseled facial features offset by dimples and a perpetual boyish grin. Most of the time, his friends would have to point out to him when he caught someone's attention. Paige, on the other hand, flirted with him with the subtlety of clubbing him in the head with a two-by-four. Even he couldn't miss her non-subtle cues.

"Sean, you gonna come in here and tell me more about this wolf of yours?" Adam called from his office.

"Saved by the wildlife cop," Sean muttered to himself. "Yep. I'll be in there in a second. Just going to set my stuff in the office." He dropped his backpack beside his desk and looked at the stack of mail resting in the "in-box". Sifting through it, he recognized the usual government mailings and

Conservancy sealed envelopes from the regional office in Seattle and the national office in Virginia. One item caught his attention. He sighed as he picked up the envelope. The alarm company was still sending him the bills from his ex-wife's address in Seattle. "Oh well, at least I know she's still got the service," he shrugged to himself. Despite their differences, Sean always cared about his ex-wife. The alarm service bill was the last unfinished business from their divorce that had finalized almost two years ago. He tossed the stack into his computer bag and went to find Adam.

Sean found him digging through the bookcases in the small library that housed a microfiche viewer, a copier, and an outdated InFocus projector. "You just looking at the pictures, or are you wanting me to read that to you?"

"Hilarious Kendall. I am looking up Canis Lupis - your grey wolf," Adam handed Sean a book on wolves from the library shelf. "Wanted to get a little more information than I already knew about wolves in Washington. I know that they are a pretty rare sight around here. Recently reintroducing themselves by moving south from Canada into the Okanagan and Pasayten Wildernesses. There is currently an estimate of half a dozen packs in Washington. They don't present much of a threat to people, but ranchers get pretty stressed out about them being anywhere near their livestock. The federal government has employed programs to reimburse them for any losses as a result of a wolf killing livestock, especially in areas like Yellowstone, where they were reintroduced with a little help."

"Have there been wolves as far southwest as North Cascades or Ross Lake National Park?" Sean asked his friend.

"Yeah, they've been spotted as far south as Lake Chelan and as far west as the Mt. Baker. The Park Rangers and the Forest Service document all predatory animal sightings. When a hiker or ranger spots a bear, mountain lion or wolf, there is a hotline to call. The hotline shares information through all service agencies, including the Sheriff's office. We like to know for two reasons. The first is to track the populations of these animals and their range of habitat in the area. The second is so that we can post the appropriate warnings for the campgrounds and hiking trails. Why don't you thumb through that book for a minute, I have a few things to finish up, and we can go take a look at your wolf."

Sean took the book into his office and started skimming through the chapters of relevance. He briefly flipped through the narration of human interaction with wolves. Throughout history, men have feared wolves and wrongfully depicted them as evil beasts that would viciously hunt humans. From storybooks like Little Red Riding Hood to regional folklore, people slandered wolves as a symbol of menace and danger.

Sean learned that hunters, ranchers, and farmers persecuted wolves for years, acting out of fear to exterminate the misunderstood ancestors of man's best friend. Despite their fierce reputation, wolves tended to live quite peacefully with humans. In fact, there has never been a documented case of an attack of a healthy wolf on a human in North America. Despite this fact and the wolf's generally shy and elusive nature, wolf populations have been decimated in the lower forty-eight states. Sean read of specific tales of wolf hunts and studied in horror at pictures of men smiling next to their enormous piles of wolf pelts.

His thoughts turned to wondering who might be out in the woods hunting this time of year. Most of the hunting seasons had expired. He heard of poachers from time to time being caught on illegal hunts in this part of the country. This seemed more like a sport killing. Sean didn't mind hunting when people ate what they killed, but killing for killing sake was a sport that he held in deep contempt. Continuing to thumb through the book, he caught up on more additional wolf facts and their subsequent decline in North America as he waited for his friend.

Thirty minutes had ticked by before Adam stuck his head in Sean's office. Adam was tall like Sean, but held a good fifty pounds on him. He had rugged looks that were softened by an interminable boyish grin. This visage matched his personality as a constant wise-cracker with a sometimes abrasive, though always well-intentioned demeanor. He appeared in the doorway prepared to go, having already strapped on his gear belt with his black forest service Colt .45 nestled in its holster and was pulling on his green Wildlife Service parka. "Ready?" Sean nodded, grabbing his own jacket, and the pair headed for the door.

"You boys be careful out there. We are supposed to see some more snow this afternoon," Paige called to them as they exited the office for the parking lot.

They climbed into Adam's agency sport utility vehicle – a fully equipped truck fitted to handle the arduous northwest territory armed with an accoutrement of brush guards, radio gear, and emergency lights, much like that of a police cruiser. As a Federal Wildlife Officer, Adam had the authority to write tickets and arrest violators of any federal laws predicated by the Department of the Interior, within the boundaries of the national parks, recreation, and wilderness areas, several agencies shared jurisdiction. The Fish and Wildlife officers, the park rangers, and the county sheriffs all worked in concert with one another. Adam was friends with most of them in this area, working from Sedro-Wooley to the Methow Valley, just before

Winthrop. His primary routines did not take him very far from Highway 20, the North Cascades Scenic Highway. However, he had, on occasion, ranged as far north as the Canadian border to support operations throughout the region.

The various law enforcement groups would converge on serious crimes, life-threatening forest fires, and dangerous rescues. There have even been occasions where they have worked with tribal police from neighboring Indian reservations. In fact, Adam had become very close friends with Joe Woodfeathers, a Swinomish police detective, working with him on a search and rescue involving a missing girl from the reservation.

Adam pointed the truck east on Highway 20 and set off for the interior of the North Cascades. The sun still shone in the late winter sky, warding off new snow for the present and allowing the pavement to completely dry, making the morning drive an easy task.

Six

Adam's SUV left the highway and crossed the narrow trestle bridge that marked the start of Cascades River Road. Soon the pavement gave way to rough gravel, bouncing the SUV as it forged ahead. Adam navigated the truck along the tracks that had cut through the snow. Reaching the turn off for Hidden Lake Peak, he shifted into four-wheel drive as he started up the steep, narrow forest service road. Again, Adam followed the tracks left from a previous vehicle. "How far up did you make it in the Jeep?" he asked, rounding a tight curve of the switchback.

"I had to lock it in low when I came up yesterday, but I was able to get all the way to the parking area. The snow gets pretty deep there. This morning I hiked it in from the preserve grounds, through the trail splitting Lookout Mountain and Hidden Lake."

"Pretty mild so far, a lot of years around this time, you can barely get past the 500-foot level," Adam remarked, reflecting on the highly volatile climate of the Cascades.

Soon the men reached the parking area at the base of the trailhead. The underside of the truck scraped across the deep snow as it plowed ahead. Adam maneuvered carefully, not wanting to high-center the vehicle and force them to have to dig their way out when it was time to leave. Satisfied that he had found a spot shallow enough with sufficient traction when they returned, he hopped out of the truck and circled to the hatch to grab his gear. The wildlife officer handed Sean his pack and paused to take in the wintry view of the trailhead. He always felt like winter hikes into the Cascades reminded him of Tolkienesque journeys described in fantasy books. The snowy entrance to the trail seemed to bode an unwelcome countenance forbidding them to continue.

Despite the winter's menacing expression, the hike up the mountain was a particularly pleasant excursion, especially in the summer months. The terrain leading up to Hidden Lake Peak flows through dramatic changes - from the pine bed of the coniferous forest to the lavish green of verdant meadows, to the brilliant floral display of the higher alpine meadows and finally to the exposed rock and glaciers at the summit. In the winter, the area was equally beautiful, with rolling hills of glistening snow transitioning to a sea of countless peaks – each dazzling white pinnacle gleaming in the late winter sun. The views reach their majestic finale when a climber reaches the summit peak or the lookout tower, each straddling a side of the twin peak.

On occasion, forays to Hidden Lake Peak offer interaction with the local wildlife. Overnighters frequently lose food to hoary marmots, nicknamed "camp thieves" - the beaver-like rodents that live along the moderate elevations that lead to the peak. Pikas, tiny, gray animals that resemble chipmunks, can be heard giving away your presence as they chirp out their high pitched warnings. Of course, the larger animals like bear and cougar present hikers with much more rare appearances.

Following the trail, it would have taken the men four hours to climb the mountain and then traverse to the couloirs that led to the valley and creek where Sean found the wolf. Adam, having spent most of his life in the Cascades and the better part of a decade in the central North Cascades, knew the area well. Listening to Sean's story, Adam had a pretty good idea which meadow it was that Sean had first picked up the tracks. Between Lookout Mountain and the northwest side of the Hidden Lake was a section of hills and valleys that flowed into a box meadow. He determined going straight up and over the glacier, while more technical of a climb, would cut their time in half.

"This time of day, on the south side, it's going to be pretty soft. Crampons won't help, but we can use our snowshoes most of the way. We'll have to watch for avalanches, too," Adam warned his friend.

They dug in with their ice axes as they began the climb up the steep slope. Adam went first to cut steps for Sean to follow. The going was slow, and the vertical gain was wearing and tedious, but pressing on, they made good time. Adam was already resting on top of the couloirs when Sean plopped his backpack beside him. He pulled out his water bottle for a long overdue drink. Sean found himself sweating despite the crisp mountain air, topping a scant thirty-two degrees. Adam opened up a Cliff Bar and started munching on it as he tossed a second to Sean. "Two hikes in one day, city boy. I don't need you passing out on me," Adam teased his friend, who was just catching his breath.

Sean ignored him as he looked out at the vista before him. He never did tire of the views in the Cascade Range. To the south and east, Snowking and Glacier Peak dominated the skyline. On clear days, a climber could see Rainer in the distance. Over the ridge and to the north, the Picket Range, Mt. Baker, and Mt. Susan loomed. Taking a swallow of water, he smiled to himself, remembering why he settled down in this remote and beautiful land.

The men finished their snacks and continued their way over the ridge, where they found Sean's tracks from earlier that morning. Sean had been following a trail that led him to where Hidden Lake spilled over the edge of its almost 5,000-foot high basin. It was one of his favorite summertime hikes. It was from that trail that he encountered the tracks in the meadow. Descending the north side of Hidden Lake Peak was a challenge, but less physically demanding than climbing. The two glissaded down the face of the mountain through plush snow, using their ice axes to steer and control their descent. To a layman, glissading looked more like child's play than a controlled climbing technique, and to many climbers, it represented a fun respite amid an arduous hike. Sean loved sliding down the mountain, on more adventurous climbs, he would sometimes haul up a short pair of skis, but today, the seat of his pants provided his quick travel down the mountain face.

Just as Adam had guessed, they immediately happened on to the meadow where Sean discovered the tracks. Adam knelt to investigate. "Looks like it could be a wolf. Notice the pattern. There isn't a separate track for the left and right paws. They use this method of stepping in their own tracks to ease winter travel. They each follow single file so they do not tip off prey how many wolves there are in the pack. I'll admit, this does appear to be a wolf's tracks, it's tough to tell for sure, though. They don't look any different than the print of a large dog," Adam pointed to the pattern in the snow and compared it to a nearby mark left by Sammy.

Following the tracks, as Sean had earlier, Adam was curious about the spot where the tracks stopped abruptly into a square of plowed snow and then started again almost ninety degrees toward the hill and brush. It was in the next couple of sets of tracks that the blood began to reveal itself. Once more, Adam knelt to take a closer look. "From what you've told me, I'd guess that the wolf hurt its paw back near the disrupted snow. Either a trap or it got shot and then took off for the nearest cover it could find, which was up this hill."

"Ahhhh," Adam looked to the right of the wolf tracks and spotted the snowshoe track of the hunters. He followed them with his eyes as far as he could. "You see up there on that ridge just north of the meadow? That was likely where they set up, might have seen hoofed animals use this valley as a conduit north and south. Good spot," Adam, himself a hunter, admiring the positioning used by the shooter. His father had introduced him to hunting as a child, but had also taught him a strict code of ethics as well. He knew that for future generations to enjoy the tradition, the animals and habitats would have to be maintained with prudence.

"Easy there, Davey Crocket. I never could understand how you could shoot a deer with those big brown eyes batting at you. I'll stick to hunting with a camera," Sean declared defiantly. He preferred to keep a sizable can of pepper spray holstered to his side in lieu of a gun when venturing into areas renowned for bear sightings. Adam urged him to at least carry a firearm when he hiked alone, taking Sean to the shooting range on numerous occasions and was surprised that his friend had proven himself to be quite a good shot. Nevertheless, Sean maintained his philosophy that being on the animal's turf, it was his responsibility to avoid conflict.

"Well, while you're yapping about your camera, why don't you put it to use by snapping a couple of pics of the track with blood in it. The poachers probably parked at Lookout Mountain trailhead or Marble Creek Campground," Adam shrugged as he continued to scan the area.

Sean complied and started taking pictures. When he had taken the shots that Adam had asked for, he returned the camera to his pack and slipped his shoulders back into the straps. "From here, the tracks go up the hill and then into the brush on the next ridge."

As they began to push up the hill, Adam looked at the hunter's tracks. "Red Feather," confirming Sean's suspicions. The men didn't say much when they first reached the spot where Sean had uncovered the patch of blood mixed in the disturbed snow. Adam pushed around it with his ice axe. "This is where they caught up to it. He stopped for a second in this brush, probably tried to catch a scent, was too late to react." The Wildlife Officer got up from the spot and moved back to the crest of the hill. Staring at the tracks, he looked for a sign where the hunter may have set himself to take a shot. He poked around with his ice axe looking for a gun casing but came up empty.

Meanwhile, Sean was taking more pictures. He photographed the blood saturated snow and the crest of the hill where Adam was searching. He kept his camera out and followed the tracks to the ravine. Adam caught up. "So, this is where it was dumped, huh?"

"Yeah, down at the bottom. Careful, the hill is pretty slick," Sean warned his friend.

"City boy, I'm a trained professional," rolling his eyes, Adam began his descent. The snow on the top half of the ridge was soft from the morning's sun, Adam's foot sinking several inches with each step. A little more than halfway down, Adam's plunging left foot had only penetrated an inch of soft snow before hitting the slick ice underneath. Expecting the same traction he found at the start of his descent, he was already bringing his right foot around to step. Just like Sean had earlier that morning, Adam plunged headlong into the ravine. Hands instinctively in front of his face, the wildlife officer slid on his belly down the steep slope until his hands slammed into a cold, wet, sticky mound of fur.

"Jeez!" he bounded up, looking at what broke his fall.

"I'd give you an eight for that beauty. Probably deserved a nine, but you *are* a professional, after all," Sean called from above.

"Very funny. You wanna get your skinny butt down here and take some photos of this while I get a closer look," Adam grumbled as he wiped his messy hands off on his Gore Tex pants. He reached into his light pack and pulled out some latex gloves along with a small plastic jar and a pair of tweezers.

Sean gingerly made his way down the slope, using the point of his ice axe to penetrate the ice to retain his balance. He once again dug out the camera and started taking pictures as his friend had requested.

Adam inspected the gaping wound of the wolf. A grapefruit-sized section of the animal's abdomen was missing. "Well, it's definitely a wolf. That is one nasty hole. Not anything you'd normally see from any hunting rifle used for animals around here. That would stop a grizzly in its tracks. Probably overkill for a grizz, too. I was going to fish around with the tweezers for a bullet or fragments, but looking at this, I think they probably pierced right through and out again."

"So, what now?" Sean asked, not thrilled with seeing this sight for a second time.

"I think I'll call Shayne and have him bring out one of his snowmobiles and bring the wolf back for an autopsy." With that, Adam plucked his radio out of its sheath on his belt. Shayne Matthews was one of the Park Rangers from neighboring Rockport. He was good friends with Adam and Sean. He asked the deputy on duty to relay a message for Shayne to meet them with a snowmobile.

Adam laid out a black trash bag with the opening wide. With his gloved hands, he grabbed the paws of the wolf hog-tie fashion and lifted the half-frozen and stiff from the early stages of *rigor mortis* wolf off of the snow. "Don't suppose you'd hold the bag open?"

"Rather not," Sean admitted, but grimacing, he hooked the blade of his ice axe into a corner of the plastic bag and held it wide.

Adam plunked the dead wolf into the sack and smirked at Sean, "My dad would have been so ashamed of you. He made me help with his hunting spoils when I was five. I probably couldn't count how many elk and deer I have skinned."

"Once you're past fingers and toes, you're pretty screwed, huh? Anyways, I'll take my food out of a plastic wrapper, thanks," Sean replied unabashedly. He picked up Adam's pack and slung it over his right shoulder while his own rested on his left. Adam was free to hoist the bag holding the rigid wolf. They began to make their way down the mountainside to the entrance of the meadow that paralleled Nehalem Creek.

Making their way through the ravine, Sean and Adam followed the bank of the icy creek. Pushing through deep sections of snow, they labored to force a robust pace. Making good time, Sean suddenly stopped. Adam followed his friend's eyes as they combed the slope up ahead. "See something?" the wildlife officer asked.

"I'm not sure," Sean admitted. Curiosity fueling a heightened pace; he moved ahead of his friend to a bend in the trail. As he rounded the corner, a flurry of wings flashed in front of him as a dozen crows took flight. His eyes lighting on the ground, Sean spied something sticking out of a significant snowdrift. Making a beeline for the mound, he quickly realized what he saw - a leg of a deer, raw and picked in places to the bone by the crows that fled when he approached. As he inspected the mound, his stomach twisted. A few feet from the deer was the body of a dog. Next to it, another deer. By the time Adam rounded the corner and joined him, Sean counted four deer and two dogs.

"What the...," Adam gasped.

"You tell me," Sean whispered.

"Two, three...five deer. Three dogs, and that is just those near the surface," Adam counted. Poking around with Sean's ice axe, he added the carcass of another deer. Studying the wounds on the animals, he found they were from high caliber weapons. "Let's get out of here. We have a bonafide poaching ring on our hands. Nice sleuthing there civilian," Adam patted his friend on his back, gritting his teeth

. Most of the trail sloping downward, they made good time to the intersection where they were to meet Shayne Matthews, the park ranger. They only had to wait fifteen minutes before they heard the approaching sound of a two-stroke engine. Shayne's snowmobile soon crested the trail from Marble Creek Campground. He slowed the vehicle to a stop near the feet of his friends. "A wolf, huh? Too bad, it's nice for the park to have these guys making a comeback. Hunters?" the ranger asked.

"Probably, it's just… the size of the wound is ridiculous. Not what you would expect from any hunters around here. This thing would bring down the biggest game in Africa with ease," Adam remarked. "I was hoping that you could take it into town. I'll swing around later with the truck. I'd like to send it to the forensics lab in Olympia for some analysis. As it is, I can only guess what kind of weapon was used to kill this little guy."

"No problem. We can use the bungee cords to strap it to the back," Shayne agreed.

"Why don't we hike back to the truck and we'll meet up with you in Marble Mount and grab a burger. Then we'll take the wolf off of your hands."

With his instructions, the young park ranger started up his snowmobile and took off back down the trail that he had taken to meet them. "Only you could think of a burger after seeing this," Sean remarked as they began their return hike to Adam's SUV.

"Trust me, after the hike back over Hidden Lake Peak, you'll be ready to eat a whole buffalo when we get to town," Adam grinned at his friend.

Seven

The park ranger's SUV was already parked outside the Buffalo Run restaurant when Sean and Adam arrived. The snowmobile rested on the trailer behind the truck, the dead wolf covered by a blue tarp strapped to the back unceremoniously covered in a layer of fresh snow. Adam brought his own SUV to a stop beside the ranger's truck. Looking through the windshield up at the sky, he observed the morning sun had given way to dark, late-winter clouds, and as the two men got out of the truck, the chill of the wind provided a rude greeting.

Entering the restaurant, they were instantly welcomed by a friendly and familiar hostess, "Afternoon boys, Shayne's got a table right over there. I'll get some coffee for you."

"Hot cocoa for me. I've had my fill of coffee for the day," Sean called after the hostess and found his seat at the table.

"What took you guys so long? Six thousand nine hundred vertical feet and eight miles, half of it downhill, a Boy Scout could have beaten you," grinned Shayne.

"Hey, that was my second trip up there for the day, cut me some slack. Besides, I was slowed down by bigfoot there," Sean pointed to Adam.

Coming to his own defense, the Fish and Wildlife Officer retorted, "You might have speed and stamina, but you have the skill of a city boy. Still, you did all right for a privileged softy such as yourself."

"Alright, boys, before you start arm wrestling, here are your drinks," the waitress cut in. She smiled and took their orders—three buffalo burgers with fries, except for Sean, who asked for broccoli and carrots with his burger.

"So what did you think of that bullet hole? Didn't look like anything caused by a hunting rifle," Adam asked.

"No, I don't think it was a hunting rifle at all. Looked almost more like an assault rifle. It was high-powered and high-caliber," Shayne answered.

"Yeah, I was thinking a 10-mil, or bigger. The exit wound was not what you would expect from a hunter's kill. The through-hole was huge, like that of a .44 caliber round shot, but higher velocity. While it cut a large opening through the wolf, it did so cleanly. A .44 Magnum, for example, would enter small and leave big due to its mass and therefore slowed delivery. Whatever was shot there had the impact of a .44, but the velocity of .22 or 9 millimeter. It entered big, left big, and cut clean. We should think about bringing Hall in on this. They won't want the wolf in their lab, I'll take care of that, but I'll bring him up to speed and share the data," added Adam, speaking of the local Sheriff's Deputy who was a close friend of theirs.

"Great, the food's here," Shayne changed subjects eagerly as their waitress came around the corner with their plates.

"Ugh. I had just gotten my appetite before you guys got back into conversations about exit wounds," Sean snapped, as he made room for his plate on the table.

"I take it ol' Sean here will not be taking part in any of our hunts this year?" Shayne asked as he poured A-1 sauce over his buffalo burger.

"Naw. I've had to listen to him bellyache ever since he dragged me out to the wolf. He'd probably set off warning shots to frighten off the elk before we'd ever get a chance to bag 'em," replied the wildlife officer.

Ignoring them, Sean tended to his burger, trying to figure out what the motive was for the wolf shooting. Ultimately, he resigned that it was out of mere sport. Ever since wolves made their return to Washington, ranchers had warned that they better not affect their livestock. From time to time, he would hear of cougars being shot for fear of their encroachment on ranches and suburbs, even though the shy animals rarely made an appearance in either of those human areas. He assumed this was the case of an overzealous hunter with a new toy.

"Why toss the wolf into the creek?" Sean asked.

"Probably didn't think about the consequences of their actions and afterward figured better safe than sorry. There aren't too many people out in that part of the forest, especially this time of year. They just got unlucky that they tracked the wolf to a spot near the preserve," Shayne answered. "I'm more concerned about the weapon. It seems like military to me. I wonder if your hunters stole them or picked them up on the black market."

"Well, I'll get forensics to give us an idea of what gun was used. From there, I doubt we will see anything more like this out there. Like we said, probably just some idiot trying out a new toy," Adam said as he pushed empty plate forward. He looked up at Sean, "You ready to head back to the office? Some of us have work to do."

Daryl and Tug joined the rest of the McKenzie family and his father's associates around the breakfast table. "Thought you boys would be bringing back breakfast," Hal, the McKenzie patriarch, asked.

"Naw, I took Tug on a hunt I've been putting together for a few weeks," Daryl answered.

"Not the wolves, I wanted in on that," Jeb complained. Then his eyes brightened, "Did you get 'em?"

"Yeah, we got one, or at least Tug did. Nearly blew the damn thing in half," Daryl giggled excitedly.

"You didn't use the H&K?" Hal McKenzie, the Washington leader of the Greys, groaned.

His grandfather had been an original member of a group of rogues called the Greys. It comprised of similarly minded countrymen who were increasingly unhappy with the growing regulations passed down from the federal government and even more displeased with the displacement of "American jobs" to foreigners. The McKenzie's grandfather, Lucius, was the current figurehead leader of the ragtag group's Washington force, with the elder's declining health; Hal had taken over the group's true leadership reins. Over the last decade, part of the group had broken off and established a compound in the mountains of Idaho. An unsophisticated training facility assembled where they would train the kids in Idaho and Washington on military tactics and the use of weapons, dreaming one day the next civil war would come. Despite their impassioned intentions, they rarely did anything more destructive than harassing local law enforcement officers and people that failed to see things their way.

A second portion of the group splintered away, taking a more diplomatic approach, actually getting a handful of officials elected to various offices, a few actually representing rural counties across the United States in Congress.

Several members of the splinter groups had worked over the past few years, trying to reunite the two factions. The leadership realized that the one group's political ties and resources combined with the other's willingness to risk life and limb to fight for the cause could be an enterprising union. They were becoming especially concerned over the growing trend of United Nations interests trumping those of the United States. The ever increasing power of the One World Organization further diffused U.S. influence. To reconcile the groups and rectify specific issues, they brought in a military tactics expert, Tug, and Senator Timothy Small's aide, Jerry Rhinehart, from Idaho – each representing a separate set of assets – all sharing the same common goal.

"Boys, it is time that the Greys get some respect. The gawddamn government is going too far these days. Their talks of globalization, free trade with every damn pathetic country out there are just plain dangerous. It just means more money in their pockets and less for the everyday hard-working Americans like us. We need to gather our forces. The time to act is finally drawing near. I know we have talked about this for years, but now we have the power actually to do something about it. This here is Jerry Rhinehart. Rhinehart is the top aide for Idaho senator and member of the Idaho faction of the Greys, Timothy Small. The nation-wide diplomatic faction that broke off years ago is seeking a reunion. They have tried things their way for years, and now they are prepared to do things our way, with their support," the grisly old Greys leader shared with the group.

"Why now?" Daryl asked.

"Well, there is a big bill coming up this month. They are going to expand the power of the One World Organization. We need to prevent that from happening. Their objective is to concede to international land-use laws allowing the UN to act as an enforcement agency. Can you imagine other governments telling us what we can and can't hunt or fish or farm whatever and wherever we want? It's bad enough our own government tries to tell us what to do, the last thing we need is some foreigners making the rules," piped in congressional aide Jerry Rhinehart.

"I thought that's what you and your group were supposed to be preventing," Hal asked pointedly.

"It was, it is. It's just with the recent economic events the rest of Congress is trying to help fat cat business to make more money by expanding the free trade zones. But I can't for the life of me, figure out how the granola movement has had such an impact. I don't know who can rationalize taking away a man's living in favor of some damn bird or hunk of trees, but there they are," Rhinehart replied.

"What are we going to do about this?" Jeb McKenzie blurted out, almost yelling.

"I'm glad you asked Jeb. You know the war games and training you have attended out at the compound each summer?" Rhinehart asked.

"Of course, Daddy took Daryl and me out there since we each turned five," Jeb answered excitedly.

"Well, it's about time we took all that learning and training and put it to use. Ol' Our organization has some serious concerns over a big convention that is going to take place in Seattle in one week. It's short notice, but the One World Organization big wigs want to get together so they can get their plans to Congress before they vote. We don't have a lot of time, and we need to act fast. We must make ourselves heard at that convention. You hear about that federal building bombing in Colorado? Leveled the whole damn thing. Tug led that mission. He took a portion of the Greys that is established in Colorado and took care of that building, a bunch of the federal government with it. Our most successful operation ever. We were hoping they would get the message, but now we are going after the leaders of the organization. Nearly the whole damn bunch will be at the convention. We have some preliminary plans, but we need to make sure we are ready to execute," Rhinehart continued.

"What can we do to help?" Daryl blurted.

"You and your brother are to work with Tug to make sure our brethren in Idaho and Washington are ready to act. We will have some last-minute training based on our plans. Then, you will lead the Greys' next mission!" Rhinehart exclaimed.

"When do we start?" Jeb asked.

Tug leaned across the table, "We started this morning." He kicked a crate next to the table and nodded to the youngest McKenzie to open it up.

Jeb pried the lid free from the box. Inside were a dozen military assault rifles. He lifted one out in amazement. He had never held a weapon that powerful. This was much more than the hodge-podge of old and outdated guns he had trained with in Idaho. He had some nice hunting rifles, but nothing like these assault rifles. He looked at Daryl, even more irritated about not being included in the morning's hunt.

Tug grinned at Daryl's younger brother. "We need to round up the troops and make sure you are all trained on those. We need to bone up on assault tactics and then practice the scenario. We have the troops from Idaho en route and your dad has summoned the remaining Washington brothers to join us."

"Boys, you are about to make history. Your grandfather and I have been building this legacy for years. The Greys are about to rise up. These damn politicians and foreigners, friggin' tree-hugging liberals…all of 'em are about to be put in their place," Hal boomed, spitting a wad of tobacco into the narrow opening of an empty beer bottle.

Lucius McKenzie looked at Rhinehart approvingly. The new civil war was about to begin.

Eight

The trip back to the office was slow. Snow began to pile up on the roads, making for slick driving. Occasionally, Adam would stop to check on a car or pickup that had slid off the road and offer his assistance. By the time they had arrived, the forty-minute trip had become almost an hour and a half.

They kicked the snow off of their boots and entered the light stained timber building. They received the typical greeting from Paige, with, of course, the bachelor Sean garnering most of her attention. Adam nudged him, never missing an opportunity to rib his friend.

"What's the weather report, Paige?" the Fish and Wildlife Officer asked.

"All over the board for the week. A little more snow for the next couple of hours, then warming up for the next couple of days. Once you get the idea that spring might just not be far off, another big front will come through," the receptionist replied. She turned to Sean, "You look cold and tired. Can I get you some hot tea or anything?"

Sean paused and nodded. "Yeah, actually a cup of tea sounds great!" he admitted and hustled toward his office. He wanted to look up the experiences of areas where wolves were reintroduced and how the authorities managed public sentiment. Firing up his computer, he logged onto the internet.

Paige quickly came bouncing in with a mug billowing steam, "Here Sean, green tea, with just a touch of honey."

"Thanks Paige, I appreciate it," Sean said, as he cupped the warm mug in his hands. The heat worked its way into his skin, warding off any chill he had absorbed while outside.

"What are you working on?" the receptionist asked.

"I wanted to look up areas of the country where wolves have been reintroduced. I am curious to see how public perception was before, during, and after the presence of the wolves," Sean replied.

"You know, my aunt and uncle live in Wyoming. They have a big ranch out there. When the government wanted to bring wolves back to Yellowstone, they were pretty upset about it. They attended several town meetings where the program was rolled out. They were guaranteed that livestock losses would be compensated. They were also reassured that wolves would not pose a major threat to any serious ranch encroachment," Paige said.

"Did that help?" Sean asked.

"No, not really. Everyone was pretty skeptical. They didn't believe the government would keep their end of the bargain, and they didn't believe that the wolves wouldn't pose a problem. I guess like a lot of things, the fear of the unknown was a powerful thing, in this case, the fear of the wolves in their backyard," Paige answered, leaning back in the chair opposite of Sean's.

"How did things turn out?" Sean asked.

"Well, it was pretty messy at first. The local ranchers protested quite a bit. One even hunted down and killed a wolf that was inserted into the park. Several more wolves were killed in the vicinity of area ranches," Paige replied.

"Isn't that illegal?" Sean asked.

"Yeah, the rancher who killed the wolf in the park was arrested and ultimately had to pay a fine. The other incidents were passed over as the ranchers claimed the wolves posed a threat to their livestock. Several claims were processed for livestock that were killed. A lot of them only assumed to be by a wolf, though many of them were not proven. The government compensated them anyways. Eventually, the local authorities were trained to identify what actually killed the sheep, and the number of claims fell. Most of the deaths were the result of domestic dogs or cougars, not wolves," the young receptionist responded.

"Here's a site. It reports that after the introduction at Yellowstone, a study showed that less than 3% of livestock losses in the surrounding areas occurred from any wolf involvement. Most were from disease and weather. Attacks from other predators, including bears and cats far outnumbered that of wolves," Sean read.

"Yeah, that's pretty much what my aunt and uncle said. The few proven wolf attacks in their area were on sick or injured sheep that were likely to struggle through the winter and die anyway," Paige said, "So there are really wolves back in Washington, huh?"

"Yes. Actually, they have been here and even down in eastern Oregon for a few years. Numbers are only estimates, and they are pretty small. A handful of packs in either state at best," Sean answered.

"Well, I think it's great," the receptionist said. She leaned in close to Sean, her full eyelashes beating like the wings of a hummingbird. "What can we do to help them?"

"Well, we are going to find out. First, we need to track down who it was. Hopefully, we can identify the weapon that was used. Aside from that, the work that we do to educate people is the best we can do," Sean replied.

"Well, if you need anything, you let me know," Paige said softly.

"I will, Paige," Sean chuckled as the receptionist walked back to her desk. Sean had consistently fended off the often subtle and occasionally not so subtle flirting from his young colleague. He couldn't help but to feel a little flattered, but he never reciprocated, at least not wittingly.

The room was filled with smoke as the cigars were stoked and enjoyed by the men sitting in leather-clad wingback chairs. Senator Timothy Small sat across from the Democratic National Committee chair. Harold Billings, who smiled at Small and flicked the ash from his cigar into the ashtray stamped with the Senatorial emblem. He looked every bit the part of a politician adorned a dark, pin-striped three-piece suit. His hair and mustache were whitening; he wore a knowing look and spoke with confidence. "So, things are finally in place?" he growled questioningly.

"Yes. I have my best manhandling the arrangements himself. We are using the same mercenary that we employed for the Colorado job," the senator replied.

"There can be no blowback on us Small. Are you sure sending one of your guys is the right thing?" the Texas protégé asked.

"Rhinehart can handle himself. He is a good man. He has been my aide through all of my campaigns, running my bid for the open chair seat. He understands the need for discretion. Gaskill is the only one that I would consider a wildcard in all of this. While he did work in Colorado, how can anyone fully trust a mercenary? " Small said.

"Then I suggest you keep your boy under control. We have a lot riding on this. This legislation stands to undermine everything that this country represents. The two-party system is at risk. With both the Democrats and the Republicans talking tough and riding the middle line has worked for a long time. The people are getting restless. We have lost three seats to the green party. You have lost two yourself to the libertarians. I don't need to tell you that further erosion will stand to cause some real problems for both of us," Billings warned.

"No arguments here, Harold. Look, you and I will never agree on the direction of this country, but I think we both know it can't be fractured by a third or fourth party gaining any additional traction," Small replied.

"And there we agree."

"Are you ready for what comes next? Once we start down this path, there is no turning back," Small asked.

"Colorado was the first step on the ledge. We are already in this. Let's finish it," Billings growled. "We can't afford failure."

"We won't fail. Things have just become a little more difficult these days. With President Marshall at the helm, he has bolstered a lot of support for bipartisan bills that move the dial on the Free Trade Organization. Giving up too much control to other countries and organizations is just plain dangerous, for both of us," the Republican senator replied coolly.

His democratic counterpart looked up at Small, "Then maybe therein lies the answer…," he swirled his Scotch and picked up his head, smiling, "If this thing in Seattle fails and this vote goes through, maybe dealing directly with Marshall is the answer."

"You mean….the president….," Small stammered.

"Whatever it takes," Billings said and then abruptly smiled in a drastic 180-degree turn, "So, when all of this is done, what do you say we meet up and do some hunting? I can show you some spots that my Daddy showed me years ago - some of the best damn hunting in the world."

"Yeah, sure, Harold. Let's get this matter under hold, first," Small agreed, his voice giving way to his discomfort with how the conversation had progressed.

"That's what I like about you, Small, you always focus on the business," Billings laughed and put his hand on Small's shoulder as he stood up preparing to leave, "Don't worry old boy, you have my utmost faith you will get this thing done. We will worry later about repercussions. Just keep your mercenary, this Tug Gaskill, under control."

Small sat in his capitol mall office, staring out his window. He knew that he had placed himself in league with some unscrupulous individuals, each with their own agenda. The last place he wanted to end up was in the crossfire of these men should the plan unravel.

His life had finally taken shape the way he had wanted. He had his ranch in Idaho. His daughter was enrolled in an Ivy League School. His wife wore the role of political spouse to perfection. He even got to travel around the country on the taxpayers' dime to satisfy his wanton improprieties. But all of this came at a price. A price he could not afford if his plans did not take shape as he had designed.

Nine

S ean spent the afternoon the way he often did, playing with Sammy, tending to the various Conservancy business items of the day, and squeezing in some exercise. Whatever melancholy or stress that would set in, a good workout and his favorite music pumping through his headset would generally cure it. Sean found keeping himself lean and fit while living in the North Cascade, a relatively easy task. Whether it was rock climbing, mountain climbing, or running whitewater, he always played hard.

As he finished his daily chores, the daylight's brief stay was already coming to an end as the sun worked its way beyond the horizon. A glance at his watch told him it was time to prepare dinner. He opened the refrigerator and leaned on the door. Sammy walked over to see if he would receive a snack. Sean sighed. He did not want to eat at home tonight. He thought about calling Adam or Shayne. Shayne would be with his wife. Adam would stay in Sedro-Wooley on a weeknight like this. "Hmm, I guess I'm on my own tonight, buddy," Sean said to Sammy. He grabbed a beer and set off for the shower, thinking to himself that he would go to the local cantina for a burger and catch a hockey game on the TV if it was on.

Sean pulled the Jeep onto Highway Twenty towards town. Just down the street from the Buffalo Gap restaurant, where he an Adam met Shayne for lunch, was the Last Chance Saloon. Its claim to fame spelled out on a letter board in front of the bar – "Last Tavern for 65 Miles". Sean parked and walked into the dingy little bar. He was instantly hit with a blast of warmth and spirited voices as he opened the door. The fire in the fireplace was roaring, and a collection of townspeople scattered. Some were eating dinner; some were at the bar describing their hunting stories; others were playing darts towards the back of the room. Sean picked a spot at the bar. As usual, he selected a seat at the corner that was next to another empty seat. This spot gave him a view of the room, but kept his relatively shy nature in check from sitting down next to someone he didn't know. Not that there were many people in this town that Sean didn't know, the combined population of each community within reach of the saloon was less than a few hundred.

Wally, the bartender, asked Sean what he could get for him. Sean asked for a pint of a microbrew from Sedro-Wooley. Glancing at the chalkboard above the rows of liquor bottles, he read that the special was a pork chop served with macaroni and cheese.The idea of comfort food sounded just right for his disposition.

As Wally slid him his beer, Sean asked if there were any games on. "Naw, missed 'em, all of the good games were on the east coast, so we're just letting the jukebox play tonight." An old country song was wailing on the dusty jukebox in the corner of the room.

"Pretty good crowd tonight," Sean said as even more people were filtering into the bar.

"Yeah, tomorrow's a holiday for some of the folks. Course you wouldn't know you're retired, right?" Wally laughed. Sean just shrugged and sipped his beer. He scanned the room. Coming to the bar alone always felt like such a blend of warmth being around others and yet strangely lonely. He allowed his gaze to circle the bar. The tavern was small. The bar itself was just a few steps inside of the room. Two old pool tables filled a majority of the rear of the room, their felt faded and worn down the center. A pair of dartboards hung on the wall leading towards the restrooms. Pockmarks dotted the adjacent wood-paneled walls courtesy of years of stray shots. Beside the bar was a big rustic fireplace, that along with some candles on the few tables, Sean felt, gave the bar it's only character. From the outside, the bar was not very welcoming. A few barely running vehicles sat rusting in the driveway, and the forlorn structure of the bar itself presented a very foreboding visage.

Wally brought out Sean's dinner, and he motioned for another beer. Sean quickly settled into his pork chops and mac & cheese. "Not bad," he thought to himself. He used to cook for his wife and got quite good at it before the divorce. Since he had been on his own, it just never made sense to cook anymore. He would throw some burgers or steaks on the grill a couple of times of week, the rest of the time, he would resort to microwaved quesadillas or tuna fish sandwiches.

Sean hardly noticed when someone had sat next to him. His mind was preoccupied running over the day's events as he devoured the rest of his food. It wasn't until he pushed away his plate and grabbed for his fresh beer that he had realized the bar had filled up around him. Sean noticed next to him was a couple of the guys who had been playing darts. He overheard them bragging to Wally that they had come to town to clean up on elk hunting near Mount Baker.

The man two seats over was asking a young lady that Sean had never seen before, if he could buy her a drink. She was beautiful, startling so to be at the little local bar in the dead of winter. She had ocean-blue eyes that sparkled, dancing magically in the firelight. Her auburn hair intertwined with streaks of brown lacing down to her shoulders. Her face had a heart shape that was complimented by soft, full, enticing lips. Her smooth skin and cheeks were rosy from being out in the chilly air. Apparently, she refused the many drink invitations, because the man's voice became almost pleading. Sean glanced over; he saw that she already had a relatively full glass of red wine in front of her. The hunter was not taking no for an answer. He grabbed her arm and nudged his friend with a grin. "I'm the finest thing you'll find in this town, little lady," he declared, still hanging on to her arm. The girl tried to pull away, but the man held even tighter.

"Ouch, you're hurting me," she gasped as she tried again to yank her arm away.

Sean had quietly slipped out of his seat and walked past the man sitting next to him and positioned himself between the hunter holding the girl's arm and her bar stool. "I think that's enough, pal. She is not interested," he said, putting his arm between the body of the girl and the hunter.

"Buddy, this is none of your business," the man said, getting up out of his stool, still holding the girl's arm. He was a big man, about Sean's height, but outweighing him by a good fifty pounds.

"I do not want to get into this with you, but you've got to leave her alone," Sean replied coolly, noticing the guy's friend slipping out of his stool. He was closer to Sean's size and weight.

"So *you're* gonna tell *me* what I can or can't do?" the bully of a man grumbled, giving the girl's arm a slight twist, causing her to let out a shriek.

In a flash, Sean grabbed the man's wrist with his left hand and twisted, the hunter reflexively let go of the girl's arm. Sean followed through with his right hand, slamming his palm into the elbow of the hunter's twisted arm. A horrible sound filled the room as the tendons in the joint ripped out of position, and the bones surrounding the elbow shattered into various pieces. The hunter's arm fell limp, Sean, hearing the sound felt his stomach tumble, almost throwing up his dinner. The man let out a pain-induced bellow, but was still able to bring his big left fist into the side of Sean's head. Fortunately, Sean was already turning his head to see what the man's compatriot was doing, allowing the blow to graze him, and spared the full force.

Despite the weakened connection, the shot was powerful enough to knock Sean back a step. He saw the second man rushing around from behind his friend. Sean used the momentum of being knocked back by the blow he received, to position himself for a perfect kick to the second man's midsection, causing him to expel all of the air in his lungs and fall back onto the floor. The first man enraged with his useless limb, recovered enough to push Sean back with his good arm. The force of the heavier man's shove nearly knocked Sean to the floor. He stumbled over the stool that was now vacated by the assaulted woman. Sean caught himself as the hunter was preparing to lunge for him. The barstool wobbled from Sean's hip propelling into it. Sean kicked at it with his left foot, catching his ankle on a rung. He lifted his foot into a little kick and flipped the stool upside down, grabbing the leg as it toppled. In a fluid motion, Sean swooped it up over his shoulder, slamming it down on the charging man just as he was about to ram his body into Sean. The stool came down, Sean swinging it like an axe into the man's right shoulder. The man screamed in pain as the top of the wooden stool crashed down on him. Sean toppled back from the impact, recovering, he brought the stool around in the other direction, delivering a crushing blow into the hunter's already severely painful arm. The man fell to the floor in a loud thump, wailing in pain.

The second man, back on his feet, recovered from the kick to the midsection, had been right behind his big friend. Leaping over his buddy, he caught Sean in the face with a right hook. Sean stumbled back and hit the wall. He had nowhere to go and was out of tricks, dazed from the blow to the head. He felt hands grabbing his collar and tried to shake off the haze so that he could defend himself. He was confident that he would suffer another strike before he could collect himself. That blow never came, and the hands released from his collar. His assailant was jerked away as Wally, and a tavern regular grabbed the man's arms and pulled him back.

Sean blinked, his left eye starting to swell, "Thanks guys," he said feebly, bending over to catch his breath and collect himself.

Wally and the local pulled the bully out of harm's way, pushing him into a chair. The locals watched over him as Wally tended to the big man on the floor who was sitting up looking at his dead arm and then shooting glances full of rage over at Sean.

"Making friends, eh Sean?" Wally asked, helping the hunter to his feet and ushering him over to a chair by his friend.

Just then, Jim Hall, the East County Sheriff, came barging through the door. He surveyed the room, eyeing Sean, who was still leaning against the wall and then at the two out-of-towners, one of which looked much worse for wear. "Alright, Wally, what happened here?"

"Well, when I came out from the kitchen, I saw our friend, Sean here, clubbing that feller there with one of my bar stools, and that one there ready to make up for it by slugging Sean in the eye. Red here, tells me it started with the big one harassing some lady. City-slicker Sean decided to defend her honor, apparently by snapping that one's elbow into a handful of pieces," Wally replied, pointing towards the offending aggressors as he relayed his story.

"Yeah, the big guy was squeezing the lady's arm and looked like he had hurt her when Sean reacted," the man named Red added, pulling on his suspenders slung over his red and black flannel shirt. The Highway 20 snowplow driver cleared the stretch for thirty years, a staple at the tavern.

"Well, I guess he got what was coming to him. Do you want to press charges?" Jim asked, flipping his small leather-bound notebook shut.

"Nah, as long as these fellers stay clear of my bar, and Sean doesn't make a habit of playing hero. Looked like he was about to lose round two," Wally declared.

"Alright boys, you heard him. You guys come in here again, or harass anyone in this county. You will be booked, that goes for messing with Sean there. As for you, Sean, try and leave the law enforcement to me," Jim said and then added, " You need a ride into the medical clinic? Have to go to Sedro this time of night." He asked the two hunters.

"No, I'll get him there," grumbled the second man.

"Good, then get out of here," Jim said and watched the two men slink out of the bar. He remained on the porch of the bar until they pulled onto the highway, making sure they didn't get into any mischief on the way. The beat-up Ford pick-up squealed its tires on the pavement as it left.

"So, where is this girl?" Jim asked, glancing around the bar. Wally and Sean scanned the room, stunned. The attractive woman who had garnered the undesired attention of the hunters vanished.

"She must have snuck out when all the ruckus started. Couldn't blame her, I guess," Sean replied, rubbing his eye. Wally handed him a fresh beer and a pack of frozen peas his cook had retrieved from the kitchen.

"She sure was purdy. Didn't see her come in with anyone," Wally said thoughtfully and turned to the Sheriff's deputy, "You off duty, Jim?"

"Yeah, I was on my way home when I heard the call. I figured I was the closest to come down and respond. Buy me a beer Sean?" he grinned as slid into the bar stool.

"No problem."

"Aw, forget it, these are on the house," Wally said and slid a beer to the off duty sheriff's deputy. "So where did you learn to do that, Sean? That guy's arm looked pretty messed up, and he was a pretty big guy, too."

"I guess Adam taught me that one. When he was in the military, he learned that move to get an assailant to drop a weapon. It just kind of clicked, didn't have time to think, really," Sean replied meekly. "Sorry about your chair. Any damage?"

"No, this is good solid wood. Guess, that hunter fella found that out," Wally scoffed.

"Have you ever seen that girl before? I wonder if she is staying at Clark's?" Sean asked speaking of Clark's Cabins, a series of rental units in town, made famous for its hundreds of bunnies that ran loose on the premises.

"Nope, not too many places to hide around here, though. If she stays, we'll probably see her around. Not many people pass through this time of year. The highway is often closed at Diablo Dam until the road clears up at the pass," Jim replied.

"Hmm. Oh well, guess it doesn't matter much. So, I am glad it was you who responded. I am not too sure Buddy likes me very much. If he came, he would have thrown me in jail just for the fun of it," Sean said, sipping his beer. Buddy Ray was one of the other deputies serving Skagit County. He never quite warmed up to Sean and always cast an odd disapproving stare when they ran into each other.

"Aw, Buddy's alright. He's just a good 'ol boy. He means well, just not used to your kind of folk around here. No hunting, that's just odd to some of these guys. It's Red and Wally you should be thankful for, sounds like they might have saved you a match to your black eye," the Sheriff's Deputy laughed.

"Yeah, you're right. I had my hands full," Sean said thoughtfully, his mind wandering to the woman with the auburn hair.

Senator Timothy Small put his glass of port on the desk and reached for the phone. As he picked it up, he was both nervous and excited about the information he was about to receive. He looked over at his cohort and smiled. Harold Billings was sitting in the luxurious leather chair across the desk from him, enjoying an imported cigar. "This is Small."

"Senator. I met with the Greys guys here in Washington. They are a little rough but motivated. Tug thinks he can work with them. He has McKenzie's boys following him around like lost puppies. All he has to do is wow them with his big game stories, and they idolize him," said Jerry Rhinehart over the phone.

"You think this can be pulled off cleanly? I need this one, but not if it can be traced back to me, Jer," replied the senator.

"Jerry, this is Harold. You know we have a lot riding on this. I think this is the one we pull out all the stops on. If you and Tug need resources, I am prepared to back this operation fully," Billings stated, cutting the senator off.

"Thank you, sir. Tug is going to assess the situation at the convention site this week. He will work with Joe Lyndon to review the troops here. They come in bright and early tomorrow. Lyndon is a guy he picked up after the Colorado job. Supposed to be a crack military security specialist. Was in the Marines for a while and became disenchanted with the armed forces being used for political purposes he didn't subscribe to."

"Do you trust him?" Small asked his aide.

"I do if Tug does. Tug is a little rough around the edges, but he is good," Rhinehart answered.

"What about the alignment of the factions, do they seem to buy it?" Billings asked, smoke from his cigar blowing up over his head.

"Appear to. I guess it will work out for us either way. If things go well, there really is a reunion that might lead somewhere. If not, they are made out as the blame, and we were never there," Rhinehart replied.

"That is the plan. Good work, Jerry. Keep us posted. Make sure you call from the scrambled cell phone. If someone does get wise, we don't need a poor phone connection to link us," Small said.

"No problem, boss. I'll check in again tomorrow." With that, Rhinehart hung up the phone and put it into his briefcase.

"What about Hiroshi? Have you had any luck with him?" Small asked. Hiroshi Hasegawa was a Japanese importer who had gathered several business partners together and were looking for an American connection to help thwart the efforts of World Trade Agreements that would pose harsher restrictions and penalties on illicit trade. He hooked up with Harold Billings at a convention in Las Vegas. Harold sought him out, knowing one of his committees was after him for violating environmental treaties.

"Are you kidding? I have to beat him off with a stick. He keeps wanting to go to Washington himself. It seems he has a pension for animal parts. Supposed to be better than Viagra in his country," Billings replied.

"He wants to go there, then, let's try to get him there. His investment could be a boon to the organization. When people start looking for who financed that rag-a-muffin group in Washington, he might be a good place for them to look if we position him properly," said Small.

"Well, hopefully, it won't come to that. While our contingencies make these folks expendable, it would be far better to keep them around for future ventures. In the meantime, have Tug meet up with Hasegawa and keep him entertained."

"Good. I know if you sign off on the committee recommendations, it would severely cripple his, uhh, import business. I think he will play along," Small concluded.

"Could be good for both of us to have another fall guy on the line in case things get a bit hairy," Billings offered as he clenched his cigar in teeth.

Ten

Sean woke up to the soft pink glow of sunshine, sneaking its way through his window blinds. He rubbed his chin gingerly. His jaw still ached from the previous evening. He thought that it was odd that his jaw opposite from the impact of the big redneck's fist was the one hurting the most. He choked down some ibuprofen and looked in the mirror. His chin red, but didn't appear bruised. The swelling around his eye had all but completely gone away. He was fortunate to have just a shadow of a bruise to remind of the evening's melee. He walked down to the kitchen and started to make some coffee. He didn't feel like his usual routine this morning. With a sudden inspiration, he decided he would forego his morning hike and venture into town for an espresso coffee instead.

He hastily ran water through his hair, gargled some mouthwash, and headed for the door. The day had turned out to be very temperate for the time of year. The sun was out, and a light, fresh layer of light snow had fallen on the ground. The roads were clear as the morning sun was quickly heating the blacktop above freezing. Sean wheeled his Jeep on to the road and headed towards town. The northwest, home to Starbuck's and Coffee People, the leaders of the espresso revolution, even afforded the quiet village of Marblemount a small selection of stands and shops. Sean chose to stop at a little espresso shop, and fruit stand in Rockport, near Sauk Mountain. Sauk Mountain was one of his favorite jaunts. In the summer, a windy drive up an old logging switchback took hikers to the base of the trail. From there, Sean could make it to the top of the 5400-foot mountain in less than forty minutes. For most of the winter, the road was impassable, and several extra miles added to the hike. Once on top of Sauk Mountain, hikers are rewarded with a magnificent view of countless peaks, including some of the best vistas of Mount Baker. Sauk Mountain itself is an attractive mountain with several saw-tooth peaks lining the top ridge. On the north side of the summit, an alpine lake sits about halfway down the slope. To the delight of early hikers, many animals can be seen in the area, mule deer, marmots, ptarmigan, and occasionally, black bears. In the summer, the hike is so pleasant and quick; Sean would often take his breakfast up there and catch the sunrise.

This particular morning, Sean's focused on his daily caffeine intake. The coffee shop was a small, quaint log cabin in the front of Pershing's Farm. Some of the area's wares such as fruit, vegetables, and honey lined the shelves. Fresh baked goods and, of course, steaming coffee brought in most of the visitors first thing in the morning. This morning was no exception. Sean parked his Jeep in the narrow driveway off of Highway 20. There were already several vehicles in the parking lot. Walking up to the porch, Sean stared at Sauk Mountain in the background. Snow had blanketed the whole mountain. It seemed to glow as the sun had just begun to peak over the southeast face. The squeak of a hinge interrupted the interlude.

The door to the coffee shop opened up as a group of customers exited, sipping their hot lattes and mochas. Sean held the door for them and nodded a good morning. One of the customers caught Sean's eye as she was sipping her coffee. Her head was down, not allowing him a reliable glance. He paused and turned; there was something about her. His eyes fell onto the spray of auburn hair that spilled from her ball cap. She walked down the steps of the porch and turned back to the door. Her eyes caught him, staring back. It was the woman from the bar. She wore a light gray sweater that made her blue eyes incredibly soft in the morning sunlight. Her face looked fresh and vibrant in the crisp morning air. Sean's mind stuttered, not providing him proper instructions. He just stood there for a moment holding the door, half in and half out of the little coffee shop. The woman looked equally unsure of what her next step should be. Their eyes just fixed on one another. Finally, she let a slight smile escape her lips and continued towards her car.

Sean smiled back, remaining in the doorway of the shop. He started to go towards her car, but shook off the idea and shimmied inside the little coffee stand. The woman watched him as she started her car and began to back up towards the highway. Sean, now inside the shop, stopped halfway to the counter. He paused and then suddenly dashed for the door. Bounding down the steps towards where her car was parked, his mind began filling with random words that he was trying to string into an intelligible sequence. By the time he landed off of the final step, Sean watched her car drive away, east on the highway. "Damn it, Sean," he mumbled to himself, thumping his fist into his forehead. His eyes followed the taillights until they disappeared around the curve, leaving only the light cloud of dust from the gravel parking lot to settle behind. Dejected, he walked back into the coffee shop.

"Forget something?" Jessica, the young barista, asked from behind the counter.

"No, I …uh, just thought I needed something," Sean stammered, his mind still not clear and functioning at full speed. He felt compelled to find out more about the mysterious woman. What was her story? Where was she staying? She was beautiful, Sean admitted to himself. He couldn't stop thinking about her eyes. They sparkled when she smiled. It seemed like there was such depth in them. He shook himself, "Get a grip, Sean."

He ordered his coffee and a breakfast bar from the baked goods rack. He turned back to the counter and grabbed a water bottle. "Let me get one of these, too." He gave the girl some change. He walked out on the porch. It was still chilly out, but the morning sun felt good on his face as it fought through the fresh air. He leaned on the railing, studying Sauk Mountain while he drank his latte and ate his breakfast bar. The morning was so beautiful. He felt compelled to hike up the trail.

When he finished his coffee and breakfast, he got back in his Jeep. He turned up the road that led to the Sauk Mountain trailhead. With the fresh snow, he would be limited to getting only a couple miles up and would have to walk the rest of the way. He locked the Jeep into 4-wheel drive low as the big tires began to slip, especially in and out of the steep hairpin turns of the switchback-logging road providing the toughest stretch. The Jeep plowed on, Sean carefully playing the clutch out as he rounded the corners. A couple of miles up the road, the snow was deep enough that Sean reluctantly concluded that driving on would be treacherous. He pulled the Jeep into a tributary road and parked. The snow was too deep on this seldom-used offshoot. Sean made sure he parked level and kicked the snow away from the tires so it would be easier to get out when he came back down the hill.

Grabbing a small daypack that he kept in the Jeep, he prepared for his hike. His daypack was always stored in his Jeep, stocked with essentials for such an impulsive ramble. It contained a pair of binoculars, a small first aid kit, a camera, and a few other amenities like food and water. With a second thought, he also grabbed his snowshoes and strapped them on. He started up the slope. He usually would follow the switchback road, but he decided he would cut straight up the hill through the forest. The steep vertical slope was more challenging, but he figured he would make better time nonetheless.

He trudged through the soft snow, cutting a path through the trees. Occasionally, he would notice mule deer tracks cutting across the snow. The terrain he was cutting through was very rough and uneven; the snow hiding the pits and bumps. He would intermittently post hole through a deep patch of snow, causing him to lose his balance, forcing him to pull his foot out and find a firmer spot to recover.

It took him about forty-five minutes to reach the parking lot of the Sauk Mountain trail about 4000 feet up the hill. From this vantage, he got a tremendous wide-open view of the snow-covered peaks of the lower North Cascades. Mountains such as Snow King, Hidden Lake Peak and Lookout Mountain were visible, as well as much of the Skagit Valley.

Sean paused to catch his breath and take in the view. He reached in his pack and took a swallow of his water before moving on. He passed the small outhouse at the start of the trail. In the summer, the path was an easy, safe jaunt that would accommodate even the most novice of hikers. With its relentless switchbacks snaking up the face of the mountain, each section of trail terraced on top of the other in an expansive sub-alpine meadow. It was a favorite among tourists. In the winter, the story was much different. The trail was lost in the snow, the contour of the terraces becoming indistinguishable slopes that only varied in the amount of snow that settled on them. The slope of the face itself was prone to small avalanches, making winter ascents increasingly dangerous. Sean elected to traverse the trail up to where the meadow bordered the forest.

Leaving the trail in favor of the protective pines, Sean entered the domain of the bears, deer, and other fauna that made the dense stands home. This made the hike arduous, but the snowpack was lighter under the canopy of the tall fir trees, and he was less likely to encounter an avalanche. Sean snaked his way through the forest, making his own switchback up the steep slope. Occasionally he would see footprints from deer that had crashed down the hillside with incredible agility.

When Sean finally reached timberline, the sun was fully exposed on the ridge that led to the top of Sauk Mountain and the small picnic area that looked over Sauk Lake. The ridgeline was packed with snow. In the warm morning sun, it was beginning to soften. Sean took a reading from his watch; it was already forty degrees. He took his jacket off and tied it around his waist. The two layers of shirts that remained were more than enough in the sun after a tough uphill climb. Sean spotted two ptarmigan on the peak of Sauk Mountain, unique alpine birds that were nearly as plump as chickens.

They were pure white in their winter plumage. Next to the bald eagles that nested along highway 20 in the winter months, the awkward ptarmigan were the official bird of the North Cascades. Carefully, Sean perched on a rock that overlooked the lake to the north and Skagit valley and southerly North Cascade mountains to the south. Here he pulled his water back out again and took a swig as he soaked in the morning sun and the incredible view.

He turned his attention to the little lake to the north. Sauk Lake was an alpine pool that nestled about halfway down the mountain's north face. Many of the animals that took residence in the area of Sauk would use the lake as a watering hole as they traversed the slope. Some animals made the journey over or around Sauk to reach the Skagit River, just on the other side of Highway 20. The salmon spawning season provided exceptional wildlife viewing. Bears and eagles took full advantage of the Pacific Northwest salmon runs. Sean looked beyond the lake; a shadow caught his eye in the valley below. "Couldn't be," Sean muttered to himself. He reached in his pack and dug out his field binoculars.

"I'll be darned," Sean trained the binoculars on the shadow below. A black bear was groggily bumbling about, sniffing the mountain air. It was still pretty early for bears to break hibernation. While this day had turned out exceptionally mild, there were still a few blasts of winter that would hit the Cascades before spring would officially arrive. Knowing bears were not particularly friendly when they first woke up, Sean figured he should start heading down the slope and to the trail. The bear's den was likely close, and he wasn't sure how it would react, especially if it had yearlings.

Sean knew that black bears, in general, rarely posed a threat to people. As long as they don't feel cornered or you stand between them and their offspring, they will leave you alone. Sean usually packed bear spray, a small one in a hip holster and a big can fastened to his pack.

Deftly, he glided back down the ridge toward his trail of footsteps leading back down the south side of the mountain. He paused as he reached a clearing that opened up to the east. Something that direction caught his eye, a brief flash in the distance. He trained his eyes east, towards Damnation Peak. There it was again, this time a series of orange strobes. "What the heck is that?" he asked himself. He refocused his binoculars. Scanning the ridges to the west, he failed to find the source. Whatever the strange flashes were, they were gone. "Hmm," Sean dismissed the odd apparitions and headed down the mountain.

Jeb, not wanting to be outdone by his brother Daryl, set out for his own morning hunt with their esteemed guest. He didn't get as early a start as he wanted, because Tug was on the phone with Rhinehart. He mentioned something about an investor from Japan coming in that afternoon. He had pleaded with Tug to bring along the H&K MP 10 semi-automatic assault rifles. These were powerful assault weapons. They were lightweight, primarily made of fiberglass and plastic. He took Tug to one of his favorite hunting grounds near Damnation Peak, north of the area where the Tug and Daryl had gone, and deeper into the wilderness. Mule deer and elk were plentiful in this area. They had even hunted bobcats and in the spring and summer black bear and the occasional grizzly. He wanted to find out what this new toy could do. He also figured if he got some practice with it, he could get the jump on his older brother and impress the elders.

Tug, while personally reluctant to go out with the younger McKenzie, he thought it would be good to see what Jeb was made of, one on one. He had also been instructed to show an investor a good time. He figured this would be a good recon trip. After the previous day's excursion, he was even more reluctant to bring one of the assault weapons; Daryl promised to move even further away from civilization and winter outdoor enthusiasts. The warming of the snow made traveling much more tedious. With every other step, one of them would sink up to their hips in snow. This constant post-holing made for a dreary and tiring hike. They finally set up on a ridge overlooking Damnation Peak and the Diobsud Buttes. The valley below crisscrossed with creeks. Animals of all sizes would follow the stream for water access as well as a navigation.

Jeb took out his scope and started scanning the valley below. He had hoped to find game as exciting as the wolf that Darryl ran across the previous morning. He had a plan to ensure that it would happen. He didn't share it with Tug. Instead, he set Tug up on a ridge just northwest of Damnation Peak. "Ah'll be just over the next ridge. Ah'll be up high, so if you see something low, it'll be a clear shot," Jeb told his guest. He bounded down the slope with a grin. His new toy, the assault rifle, in his grasp.

He approached the next ridge with care. Jeb knew there was a bear den in the nook of downed trees and rock outcroppings. He crept up to the alcove. In the fall, he had tracked a bear that had taken refuge in the nook. The nearby trees provided some protection. Positioned right in the middle of mule deer country, the spring and the length of summer held an endless supply of berries affording a delicious bounty until the anticipated salmon runs in the fall. With the entrance facing south, the daily sun warmed the den. It also meant that if the bear wanted to leave the shelter before the thaw, his task would be made simpler.

Jeb retrieved his collapsible axe and clicked it into its fully assembled position. With one final breath, he chipped away at the den entrance. A few mild days left the snow, underneath the initial layer of crust, quite soft. In short order, he had managed a hole that poked all of the way through to the musty, black chamber of the den. He pulled out his LED light and peaked in. He saw the mass of brown fur that he had anticipated. A cinnamon-colored bear had selected this spot for the winter. Jeb set his pack down carefully. Sifting through the first few of layers, pushing aside a sandwich wrapped in foil and an extra layer of clothing. Finding the right tool, he placed it in his left hand while he cocked it with his right. Unsure if this was going to work and if it was, what the net result would be, he slung his pack back over his shoulder and leaned his assault rifle against his leg. He wanted a quick retreat if necessary. Steadily, he raised the flare gun to point the barrel into the den. He bit his lip for a moment and squeezed the trigger, sending a blast into the hole.

The den was ablaze with light, following the concussive discharge. The mother bear awakened abruptly and confused. Her heart raced wildly against her chest as she spun around the cave. She bellowed and gnashed her teeth to warn what mysterious assailant was attacking her and her cubs. The light from the flare rendered her sleepy, maladjusted eyes useless. She feared the den was no longer safe and scooped her rustling cubs up to their feet with her massive paws. The big mother bear then burst through the light snow-covered entrance to get away from the intense burning light that lay in the back of the cave. The snow from the entrance felt good against her sore, abused eyes. Every glance encircled with halos; she fought to make out vague shapes.

She looked back to the big brown masses resembling her cubs that had followed her out onto the snow. She swung back the other direction. Her vision blurred, but she could smell danger. In a fury of rage, fur, and claws, she tore after the scent. She had no idea the risk that she was facing, but knew she had to face whatever was before them to protect her cubs. Instinct had taken over, leaving fear, pain, and worry at the doorstep of her den.

Jeb waited for the bear to break through the entrance to the cave. He hid behind a tree that had fallen in the nearby grove. He wasn't sure what the bear's reaction would be. The answer to that question did not take long. He heard a loud bellowing roar from the cave. A few seconds later, a furious and disoriented black bear came crashing through the thin layer of snow which covered the entrance. A large female bear was lashing about wildly in all directions. Jeb watched silently in curiosity and amusement. He realized that the bear was having trouble seeing.

The bear paused in its thrashing and fury to sniff the air. She lifted her snout straight toward the sky, maximizing all of her senses to find and locate danger to her and her cubs. They, too, struggled to adjust to the light. They relied on the grunts and groans of their mother to decide what to do next. As yearlings, they were almost two-thirds of her size. The summer would be the last summer under her care, a critical season for maturing and understanding this strange and dangerous world.

The bear appeared to catch Jeb's scent and recognized him as a potential danger to her offspring. He moved from his perch behind the fallen alder. The mother bear picked up his form, though her eyes were still quite clouded. Without hesitation, she charged off in his direction.

Jeb took off on a mad dash across the slushy ground. He knew the angry bear would be in tow. The hunter hoped that an early awakening, blinded by the flash from the flare and struggling to adjust to the sunlight, would give him enough advantage to lead her into the clearing where he had positioned Tug. He had a seventy-five-yard head start from his position. The distance he had to travel was just around the bend. The bear, acting on acute instinct, was able to make a surprisingly sharp path towards Jeb. He began to worry that he had underestimated the bear's ability to recover from hibernation. What he didn't know was that the mild weather had the bear's system priming for recovery and an early springtime awakening without his help.

He rounded the bend, flagging his arms wildly in the air. He had hoped of signaling to Tug that he was out of position while continuing to attract the bear to his direction and Tug's line of sight. It appeared to be valid on both accounts. The bear careened around the corner with more speed and agility than ever. The mother bear had made up enough ground to close within 30 yards of Jeb, a distance well within her kill range.

The bear was wild in her fury. She thrashed about in every direction, trying desperately to pick up some trace of danger. She finally calmed down enough to focus on a different sense. At this moment, her sense of smell was her best ally. Instinct seemed to take over and offer her direction. The rude awakening and struggling to adjust to daylight after several months of sleep, left her vision and hearing suspect at best. She lifted high on her back haunches and stuck her snout into the air. She quickly picked up a strange smell. Instinct pronounced that this new smell represented an imminent danger to her and her cubs. Without hesitation, she took off toward this scent.

As she proceeded forward, she spied movement from behind a fallen tree. She could not make out the shape definitely, but she could detect the mass of motion. She followed this apparition down the hill towards the clearing that spit two ridges, following an alpine creek.

Steadily, she was closed in on her unknown assailant, as the figure started up the hill on the near side of the clearing, her rage intensified. With each step forward of her massive legs, she came closer to what instinct told her she had to rid for the welfare of her cubs. She closed within ten yards of the creature, which was finally starting to come into focus in her adjusting eyes. She raised her front paws for one last sprint to face her enemy when her left knee exploded in pain. She crumbled down on the snow, slamming into the hill with her front shoulder. She bellowed in unspeakable agony and fear. She knew she must get up to save her cubs, but was unable to make her leg move within her command. In unrelenting pain, she kicked with her right leg and pawed furiously with her front paws. She could smell danger in front of her and could hear the crunching of snow behind her. The threat was approaching from both sides.

Jeb turned his trek uphill. This placed him at significant risk as his pace slowed dramatically while the mother bear's speed would remain unchecked. As he strained forward, he could hear her footsteps closing in – she was only a few yards away. Jeb made a couple of diagonal lunges up the slope before he heard the blast from the ridge on the other side of the clearing. He turned back to see the massive bear collapse in a heap onto the snow, her momentum carrying her into the base of the hill. She was less than a few yards away from the fool-hearty McKenzie boy when she fell. Jeb looked back at her. Her knee shattered in fragments of bone and tissue. Her lower leg barely tethered in place by a few strands of tendon. She tried in vain to get up and chase after Jeb, but her injured leg was useless. She bellowed in low groans and growls as she clawed at the snow for traction, but was only able to spin helplessly on the ground.

Tug walked casually up to the scene. Jeb appeared shaken from the chase being closer than he had expected. The bear continued spinning and screaming on the ground at their feet. A mass of her fur, tissue, and blood splattered on the hillside, just past her huge body.

"Well, gawddamn. That was close. I thought she was gonna get me. Nice shot, but did ya have to wait so long?" Jeb asked his new hero and added, "You gonna finish her off?"

"No, Jeb. I have a better idea. I have a client coming in this afternoon. He is a big fan of hunting, and I think we can show him a good time. He has a pension for bear paws and gall bladders," he said calmly, staring at the frightened animal still reeling in immense pain. "I think she'll live, at least as long as we need to bring our client out. That injury will slow her down pretty good."

"Well, I guess that makes sense. You know, Daryl and I set up hunts all the time where one of us leads a party, and the other release an animal from a cage we have hidden in the woods. If the client is a real city slicker, we sometimes even drug the animal to make sure our customers get off a shot and have a good time."

"Good, then you'll understand my plan. By the way, the client I am referring to will pay a thousand dollars for the paws and innards," Tug told Jeb, still keeping an eye on the bear who was starting to collect herself.

"Wow. Well, mama bear has two cubs. Guess we got a right nice amount of dough to be made," Jeb replied.

"If you do a good job, I'll let you and Daryl have the money for the cubs. This man who is coming in is one of the financiers of our mission. I'm counting on you boys," Tug said, his voice sounding like that of a parent promising their child ice cream if they behaved.

Tug laughed as his tone was effective in reaching the young McKenzie. Jeb eagerly shook his head and promised that they would not let him down. "So, where did you find that bear, anyway?" Tug asked curiously.

"I knew where its den was. I shot a flare in there and just waited for her to come out. She sure was pissed, boy," Jeb replied excitedly.

Tug just smiled to himself. In his own mind, he concluded, "These boys sure aren't bright, but they are easily motivated."

Eleven

The mother bear finally began to calm down. The creatures that had attacked her were gone and she could hear the cries from her frightened cubs from the nearby ridge. They were hiding under cover of the brush as she had taught them. They only crept out after she called to them, letting them know that the danger had passed. Despite the terrible pain, she hoisted herself up on her three intact legs. She knew she had to get to her cubs and steer them to safer ground. She took her first tentative step, her injured leg, dangling from a few remaining strands of leg remained, dragged along the ground. She collapsed again in horrible pain. She tried again, putting more pressure on her non-injured side, trying to prevent the leg from dragging.

Her cubs looked on anxiously, not understanding what happened. They were used to their mother handling every encounter that they witnessed in their short lives without contention. Nor had they ever seen their mother in such agony. She hobbled to her cubs. As she nuzzled their black and brown faces, they inspected her wound. Her injury was so severe that the body autonomically cut off the flow of blood to her left leg. The amazing feature of animal physiology kept her alive, at least for the time being.

As her smallest cub sniffed her leg, his mother batted at him with her paw and let out a bellow. She did not want their help with her wound. She was not about to let anything touch her there. Once the trio had collected themselves, they muzzled happily, enjoying confidence together. The mother knew she had to get them away from there and find a new safe shelter. She would search for a stand of fir trees with low-lying branches to bed while her injury healed. Their progress would be plodding, as movement had become an enormous undertaking for the mother bear. The pain was excruciating, but instinct told her, they had no choice. Their slim chance for survival hung on her getting them to safety.

Sean hesitated at the steps of the office. He rubbed his jaw and winced at the reflection in the window. His eye was still showing vague signs of yellowing at the site of the bruise from the previous evening's skirmish. Nonetheless, he turned the knob and entered the Fish and Wildlife Service office.

In seconds, Paige bounded up from her chair. "Good morning Sean," she sang. He turned slightly, hiding his slightly blackened eye.

"Morning, Paige," Sean muttered, making a beeline for his office.

"Rough night?" the young receptionist asked.

"You can say that," Sean replied and asked, "Is Adam in?"

"He was. He should be back any minute. Sure, you're okay?" Paige asked.

"Yeah, why?"

"You just sound kind of funny," Paige said as she poked her head in Sean's doorway. She had been following him unbeknownst to him. "Oh my goodness…," she gasped, throwing her hands up to her face. Sean looked up, his face twisted in mild irritation and disappointment in having to explain the previous evening's events to Paige.

"Yes?" he offered a sly response as if nothing was wrong. "Oh, the eye. I …uhh… walked into a door?"

"No, unh uh, not buying it," the receptionist smirked, shaking her head.

Just then, the door to the office opened up. The heavy footsteps of Adam chorused through the office. His face appeared above Paige's shoulder, "What the hell happened to you?"

"Well, since you're both here, I can get through this story once," Sean answered and went on to relay the incident at the bar the previous night.

"So, what about this *girl*?" Paige asked in a demanding tone. Adam and Sean exchanged glances.

"I don't know. She just disappeared," Sean said, not willing to go into running into her on his way to coffee.

"Sounds like you made pretty quick work of that guy, well at least until the second one nearly took your head off. Still, I'm proud you, buddy," Adam smiled.

"Oh Adam, I think it sounds rather chivalrous. Can I do anything for you, Sean?" Paige asked earnestly.

"Well, actually, I *could* use a couple of Advil," Sean replied as Paige dashed to her desk and returned quickly with two pills and a glass of water.

"Thanks, Paige," Sean accepted the ibuprofen. He heard the phone ring in the next room, relieved that Paige would need to leave his office and retreat to her desk.

"So a couple of rednecks stirring up trouble. What were you thinking?" Adam laughed at his friend.

"I guess I wasn't. I just can't deal with guys messing with women like that," Sean replied meekly.

"So…this girl?" Adam asked, grinning.

"I guess she *was* attractive. Something about her eyes. And her smile…" Sean nodded, his voice trailing away to absorb the picture in his mind. "I ran into her this morning."

"You did? What did you say?" Adam asked eagerly.

"Well…nothing. I didn't know what to say. I started after her, but I was too late. She was already driving away," Sean admitted to his friend.

"Aw, man. You can think, or not think and jump two guys, but you wimp out with a girl. What are we going to do with you, Kendall?" Adam laughed.

"Alright, so what have you found out about the wolf?" Sean asked, quickly changing the subject.

"Well, forensics has just received the carcass. A preliminary look suggests maybe a military weapon. Large caliber and high power. Smooth casing. Huge, but cut through like butter. They'll try and ID the exact weapon. Jim says his people are interested. They even contacted the base at Fort Lewis to give them a heads up. They asked about any recent weapons shortages or heists, but it happens more often than you might think. There is a robust black market for military weapons. If you want it, you can get it—stuff from Israel, Russia, wherever," the Fish and Wildlife Officer replied.

"Why the wolf?" Sean asked.

"Who knows. Somebody was probably just wanting to play with a new toy. They likely would have shot the first thing to cross their path," Adam shrugged.

"Is there anything that we can do?" Sean asked.

"Well, wolves *are* protected by federal law. If we catch the hunters, they'll probably pay a fine and could do a minimal prison sentence. If the weapons turn out to be illegal, we have a much bigger case. That, of course, would then fall under the jurisdiction of the Alcohol, Tobacco and Firearms Bureau," the Federal officer answered.

"Well, let me know what you find out. Busy day for you?" Sean asked.

"Just the usual. I need to patrol the logging roads and parking lots, making sure that hunters have their licenses and that they stay within their limits. I'll keep a lookout for any unusual high-powered guns. I should probably get back out there. Want to come?" Adam asked.

"No, thanks. I'm going to get in a workout after I get some stuff done around here," Sean said.

"Alright, buddy. Careful with nurse Paige out there. She's on the prowl," the officer laughed and left the office.

Sean tidied up his area, placed the calls that he needed, and wrapped up his brief workday. Most of the time, he didn't need to come to the office, but being in the company of his friends made him feel like his days were a little more purposeful. The Conservancy echelon wanted to show Sean some appreciation for his efforts and decided to offer him a piece of property adjacent to the preserve and asked him if he would manage it. Sean eagerly accepted their offer and moved him and Sammy out to the Cascades.

He clicked off his light and grabbed his jacket, heading out of the office. He passed by Paige's desk, thinking that had made a clean escape.

"Done for the day?" the voice sang from behind him.

He turned to face the administrative assistant, "Yep."

"You take care of that eye. Stay away from those damsels in distress," Paige smiled.

Sean grinned in spite of himself, "Oh, I'll try. I'm not sure they are reserving a spot for me at the round table."

"I think Arthur himself would be honored. Then again, if your white horse ever came riding up to me, I'm not sure I would disappear on you," Paige said, a devilish look splashed across her face.

"I'll keep that in mind should I see you tied to a railroad track or stuck up in a castle dungeon somewhere," Sean said, "Have a good day, Paige." He strode out of the office and into the mild afternoon.

The young administrative assistant watched as Sean walked out to his Jeep and drove away. She loved her job, but there were not a lot of eligible bachelors in the North Cascades. Paige smiled to herself. She was sure even among a city full of men, she might seek out the kind, rugged Mr. Kendall.

Twelve

Congressional Aide Jerry Rhinehart, returned from SeaTac airport, a good four-hour drive from the McKenzie homestead. He was sent to pick up the Japanese investor, Hishiro Hasegawa. The foreign traveler was asking Rhinehart endless questions about hunting in northern Washington. Jerry did his best to answer Hasegawa's questions and keep his interest peaked in his visit. As he wheeled the rented late model SUV on to the long dirt drive of the McKenzie's, he could see Tug and the brothers loading their gear into the old crew cab four-wheel-drive pick-up. "Looks like they're ready for you, Hishiro."

"I am very excited to join the hunt," the Japanese businessman added.

Hal McKenzie approached the SUV and greeted the man. "Welcome to Washington. The boys and Mr. Gaskill are ready for you," Hal said. While the investor's money was welcome and they were technically fighting for the same cause – keeping the two countries' economies separate - he was not pleased having to be hospitable to any man of color. His dad, Lucius, wouldn't even come out of the house with the man on the ranch grounds.

Jeb and Daryl were too blinded with dollar signs in their eyes to care about entertaining the businessman from Japan. They were excited to get to the hunt. They took Hasegawa's hunting gear out of the SUV and tossed them in the bed of the truck. Tug jumped in the back seat with Hishiro while the boys climbed into the front seats. With scarcely little time for Hasegawa to catch his breath, they set forth toward the Damnation Creek trail that Jeb had taken Tug to earlier that day. He just hoped the bear was still alive.

Tug kept the conversation light. He entertained his guest with many of the same tales that he had shared with the boys since his arrival. Hasegawa hung on every word as Tug talked of rhinos, tigers, and elephants from his well-traveled resume. The brothers tried adding their own adventures in the northwest, though they felt belittled next to Tug's stories. The Japanese freight magnate described his collection of taxidermied art. Hides, heads, and petrified animals of all sorts adorned his museum-like study. Some he had killed himself, but many he had purchased.

They arrived at the trailhead in short time, considering the season. Most of the snow on the old gravel roads they took had turned to slush, and the beefy truck had little difficulty handling the terrain. Jeb had butterflies in his stomach. He was excited about the hunt. He was already spending the portion that he would grab from the bounty that Hishiro would pay for the bear parts.

Hishiro, himself, was as exuberant as a schoolboy. He did not know what lie before him. The group had not let on that the bear had already been shot. They didn't even tell him that they were necessarily hunting for bear. Tug, in the seat next to him, was holding his cool-as-steel exposure. He was here because he had a job to do. He would feign excitement to get more access to the weapons in Hasegawa's possession.

The four-wheel-drive pulled up to a stop. Mud and snow had caked on the wheel wells of the big truck. The doors opened, and the four men jumped out of the vehicle and grabbed their gear. Hishiro looked around at the peaks of the mighty Cascades in awe. The landscape was like nothing he had seen before. This rugged and natural beauty of the land takes away the breath of many a visitor, and it was true for Hasegawa. With all of their gear assembled, they began the march after their prey.

Jeb and Tug took off on a line towards where they had left the bear reeling in pain. Daryl and Hishiro huffed behind. The group entered the valley as Tug and Jeb had earlier that morning. Tug motioned for them to lay low on the ridge where he set up previously. He pulled out his scope and surveyed the clearing. He spotted the area where the bear went down. He could see the bear's trail up the slope. He suggested that Jeb and Daryl scout up that direction while he took Hasegawa further south into the clearing. His rationale was two-fold. The late winter sun would set soon behind the mountain peaks. He knew they had to move quickly. He also wanted to keep the morning's wounding of the bear quiet to his guest. Let Hasegawa have some fun. They could celebrate his hunting prowess later that evening.

The bear family had moved further up into the foothills of Damnation Peak. The mother bear had become numb to the pain, focusing on getting her cubs to a place of safety. She was able to find a group of fir trees that would provide temporary shelter. Her instinct was to keep moving further, but she was nearing exhaustion. The cubs returned to normal as their mother, though hobbled, was acting as they expected. She lay down behind a snowdrift that had formed around one of the trees. Her cubs huddled in next to her.

While not ideal, the soft branches of the firs and the wintry boundary of the drift afforded fair protection from the elements. The mother bear's weary body demanding rest, she cuddled with her yearlings. Soon the trio of bears was sound asleep.

She had been in a deep slumber for several hours when her mothering instincts detected danger. She grunted, lifting her big head into the air. She listened to every sound. The low howl of the wind, the melting snow falling off of the trees, the heavy breathing of her sleeping cubs; she tried desperately to differentiate between normal sounds and those that did not fit in. There it was! She heard it - the sound that woke her so rudely from sleep. She hoisted herself up out of the snowdrift, sticking her snout into the air. She tried to catch a scent, but couldn't; yet she knew danger was out there. She growled at her cubs. They jolted into attention, waking up out of their sleep. The tone in her warning sent them stumbling out of the drift. She snapped at them with her powerful jaws, something she had seldom ever done. She sensed that she had to face this enemy on her own. She had to let her cubs know that trouble was near. They heeded her warning and started further up the slope.

She watched them briefly, satisfied they that would comply with her strict instructions, and headed in the direction of the disturbing noise. She strode forward carefully, trying to keep her weight off of the injured leg. Sleep had provided a much-needed rejuvenation of energy, but it did not help the throbbing and aching. Putting aside her agonizing pain, she focused on eliminating the danger that threatened her cubs.

Jeb and Daryl nearly tumbled down the slope. Jeb motioned where the bear had fallen. With the extent of the bear's injuries, Tug had figured the bear could struggle a mile away from the scene at best. Daryl looked at the yard sale of fur and blood at the base of the hill. It reminded him of the site where the wolf had been killed. He figured Tug used the same weapon, probably with the same ease and skill as he had the previous day. In concert, the two seasoned hunters trudged on. The tracks left by the bear were evident and easy to follow. The extra weight on the bear's right side and the left leg dragging through the soft snow created a very well-marked trail.

They followed the bear's tracks straight up the slope. As they reached the top of the first ridge, they noticed her cubs joined the mother bear's tracks. The brothers grinned. They picked up their hand-held radios and let Tug and Hishiro know that they found the trail of a bear.

"Well, Hishiro, you will be welcomed into the northwest by one of our biggest predators," Tug said as they checked their weapons. For this hunt, Tug had mandated that the crew armed with only conventional hunting rifles for this trip. That and his .44 that he kept strapped to his hip. He had a pretty good idea where they might find the bear. He also hoped that he could count on Daryl and Jeb to get the bear to react. They turned west and headed up the slope. He would lead Hishiro on a diagonal course to rendezvous with the brothers. Tug cleverly chose a route that would cut down on time and veer clear of the morning's wounding of the bear. He didn't want to let on that this was a canned hunt. He wanted to milk every bit of pleasure from this adventure for the influential investor.

He checked his watch. He figured they had about two hours before it would be dark. They would have to move with speed if they were to make this happen today.

The mother bear didn't know what she was going to face. She paused briefly, finding concealment behind a boulder. She listened carefully, hearing the faint sound of crunching in the distance. The wind was beginning to shift direction, and the scent of man had just barely tickled her nostrils. She moved forward, wanting to put herself in between the men and her cubs. Her injured leg touched the ground sending pain shooting through her entire left side. The threat of danger and the reminder of her pain sent her into a rage. She charged headlong in the direction of the men.

Jeb and Daryl saw the bear's form emerge on the next ridge. She was a mere fifty yards away. Their radios beeped, and Tug's voice told them that they were in sight. The two brothers got up and ran in the direction of the businessman from Japan. They could now hear the bear crashing down the slope behind them, closing the distance. As the bear reached the middle of the hill, they heard the first shot from Hasegawa. The bear bellowed loudly, sounding almost remorseful. The impact of the blast caught the bear in her left shoulder, causing her to stumble back. She kept her composure and turned away from the brothers and towards where the shot fired. Daryl steadied himself and fired a shot into her opposite shoulder. The shot rocked the bear onto her back, again letting out an echoing howl. Relentlessly, she forced herself back up and spun towards Daryl. Another shot fired, again from Hasegawa. The bullet pierced into the back of the mother black bear, embedding into her spine. She fell on to her side, paralyzed, her limbs frozen in position.

Jeb raised his gun for a kill shot, but Hishiro motioned him off. He raced up to the bear and dropped his pack. "The power of the bear is greatest if it is still alive." The bear twisted on the ground, helplessly slashing with her jaws. The injury to her spine retarded her movement. Only her large head retained mobility. Hasegawa dug in his pack and produced a long, savage dagger. Its ivory handle intricately carved, the shape of a dragon etched on both sides.

The boys watched as the Hishiro quietly went about his preparations. The mother bear looked around the scene wildly, desperate to regain movement in her body. Her deep brown eyes filled with rage and fear. She could do nothing but wait for her attackers to kill her and end her pain, but her agony would get worse before it would get better.

The Japanese man quickly knelt, the dagger held with the point facing downward in his fist. With one vicious stroke, he cut into the bear's left paw. He sawed at the flesh with the wicked blade until it the paw was sliced entirely off at the wrist, blood spilling in torrents onto the slushy ground. The bear, snorting through her nose, thought of her cubs, all she wanted to do was rid her babies of these monsters. Her body just wouldn't respond.

Hasegawa continued, meticulously he went to each limb and continued to perform the procedure, putting each paw he collected into a drawstring silk satchel. Finally, he drove the dagger straight into the bear's side, just above her hip, slicing a deep gash. He traced a small rectangle and began digging through the muscles in her stomach and retrieved a fist-sized organ. The bear's growling and snorting continued, though the growls began to resemble sad little moans. She lie there completely defenseless, blood oozing for her belly. The Japanese game hunter held up the organ, blood dripping off of it - the coveted gall bladder. He placed it into a final satchel.

Tug was already up the hillside, searching for the cubs. He found the snowdrift which the bear had used for her nap but could see no trace of the offspring. The hike to the bear had taken him longer than he thought. He almost admired the resiliency of the bear. She covered good ground on three limbs before they caught up to her. He checked his watch. They would not have time for the cubs today, returning to the group. The McKenzies were reliving the attack and laughing at the bear's helplessness. Jeb and Daryl took turns taunting the bear, sticking their noses in front of her big, agonized brown eyes. Hasegawa was gleefully packing his treasures carefully away.

When Tug told them they had to call it a night, they were disappointed in hearing that they would not be able to go after the cubs. They tried to argue, but Tug remained firm. He placed a boot on the bear's shoulder; her eyes stared at him in vain. Without an iota of expression, he rolled her onto her stomach with his foot and walked away.

The cubs retreated up the slopes toward Damnation Peak. They did not venture far, remaining just inside of the dense forest of firs. They could hear the sounds of thunder in the distance. They were confused as to what they should do next. They had relied on their mother's urgings for all of their short lives. When the sounds had stopped, and the forest became silent, they began to make their way back down the hill cautiously. Their senses were frantically trying to detect danger as they pushed on. Their powers of instinct had been developing in their mother's care. Now without her guidance, they tried to emulate her cautious testing of the air as they proceeded. Shrieking as they found their mother at the base of the hill, they were thrilled; they bounded down the mountain to her side.

They were puzzled with the scene; she did not get up to greet them. There was no nuzzling, all that she offered them was a half-hearted groan. Her heart rate was slowing, loss of blood and shock were easing her towards death. Her cubs sniffed her muzzle, their little bleats and moans begging for her response. She could only moan back and stare at them with her sad, weary brown eyes.

Throughout the night, the cubs kept their vigil at their mother's side as she slowly bled to death. At the morning's light, they awakened. They sniffed their mother's snout. It was cold and lifeless. They did not understand. They sniffed at the blood on the ground, not realizing that the life of their mother escaped through those red trails. They begged for acknowledgment from their mother, but received no response. They whimpered and snuggled close to her, waiting for her to wake up. She never would.

The four hunters returned from their excursion near Damnation Peak. Hasegawa was pleased with his bounty. The silk bags containing the bear paws and gall bladder were placed in sealed plastic pouches and put in an ice chest. The boys had told him about the cubs, and he was already planning his next trip. He pulled ten more silk bags out of his luggage in anticipation of eight more bear paws and two more gall bladders.

Tug walked into the farmhouse and hunted down Jerry Rhinehart, the congressional aide. He found him tapping the keys on a laptop computer.

Cursing as he hit the backspace several times to fix mistakes. He looked up to see the tactical mercenary looking down at him. "Tug, yer back. Any luck?"

"Yes, I think our Asian friend had a good time. He got his parts, the freak. He is very enthusiastic about getting back out there. The boys saw her with some cubs," Tug replied.

"Good, good. That will have to wait until tomorrow. We have work to do," Rhinehart said. "D-day is in less than a week. The men are assembling. They arrived late this afternoon, while you were on your hunt." He paused for a second and added, "Is there going to be enough time to get this bunch in shape for the job?"

"Good enough. We will position to get out quick and quiet. If some of these backwoods goons don't quite make it, our faction will remain clear of the aftermath. That's the plan," Tug said in a whisper, looking over his shoulder, ensuring none of the McKenzie household followed him around the corner.

"The shipment came in. The supplies are in the old barn in the back of the house. Having Hasegawa's connection with the freight has worked out well. I had the men set up camp in the woods behind the barn. They are all pretty excited - quite rough around the edges, though. It's like having a dozen Jebs and Daryls out there, more than a little frightening. One of them hurt themselves hunting yesterday. Broke his arm. Figure he'll be in lookout detail," Rhinehart filled in the military leader.

"Is Lyndon here?"

"Yep. He's in debriefing the elders. I think they are optimistic that the two groups are going to unite strongly. They are looking at this coup to be the catalyst of a bigger, stronger union. Of course, all Small and I care is that the greenies and open-trade folks get the message. What these groups do after that, I could care less," Rhinehart added.

Tug went into the den where he found his tactical partner, Joe Lyndon. The McKenzies and Joe were drinking Miller Genuine Draft, discussing the job in Colorado. They relived how smooth Tug and their men pulled off that attack. They were confident that with their oversight of this operation, the Seattle plan would also be a success. Rhinehart had hoped that their support with the McKenzies would unite the party in Colorado with the contingents in Idaho and Washington.

"Tug, you're back," Lyndon extended his hand. He caught up with Tug in Colorado, just before the federal building bombing. They had shared mutual contacts working as mercenaries in Central America. Tug thought with this job's more prominent profile and tight planning schedule, not to mention coordinating this bunch of rogues, he would be of a great help here in Washington.

"I'm glad you could make it. I think I am going to need your help," Tug said, shaking his hand.

"Yeah, this group sure seems to have the motivation, we just have to teach them enough skills to pull this off and get out," Lyndon replied. "When do we start?"

"Right now. You settled in?"

"Yeah, I pitched a tent out near the cavalry. Figured working from within would inspire some respect and camaraderie," Lyndon added.

Tug nodded in approval and motioned for them to meet and greet their little army. The two men walked out to the clearing in the woods behind the barn. A grizzled group of men were sitting on top of the several large crates in the barn, drinking beer and swapping stories. There were representatives from Idaho and Washington. Their voices grew excited and then quieted to silence as the two men from the house approached. Behind the two strike team leaders were Hal and Lucius McKenzie, Hiroshi Hasegawa, and Jerry Rhinehart.

"Gentlemen, you have been brought here for a monumental task. We are joining brothers who have been divided for far too long. We are gracious for the hospitality provided by the McKenzies. We are thrilled that we have a contingent of folks from Idaho. Along with the Washington crew, the old Greys are becoming the power we knew it could be. We have the political backing," Rhinehart said with a motion that emphasized his presence, "We have the financial backing with Mr. Hasegawa and another financier who could not be here. We have the military backing of Tug and Joe, who you will get to know quite well over the next few days. Boys, the time to take arms and act is upon us. The Greys are going to make their mark. The world will hear us. Lucius..." Rhinehart turned to his host. He held his hand out, gesturing for the elder statesman to make a few remarks.

The old McKenzie patriarch stepped up beside Rhinehart. "The Greys have long stood for the freedoms of Americans. *Real* Americans. We have a common interest today with Mr. Hasegawa because we want the same thing. Keeping America and Japan separate. We don't need the dang government telling us what to do. We damn sure don't need someone else's country telling us what and where we can hunt, how to do our business, and make our laws." He cleared his throat and sat down on a crate, his feeble body tiring out from standing and the torrent of pent up emotion released with their new initiative. Hal stood up to take his place.

"Boys, we are going to war. Next week, a group of tree huggin', Euro lovin', flowers behind their ear pansies are going to drive their Volvo's up to Seattle. They are going to sit down with lawmakers, and them types to convince them the world needs one economy. One set of laws. They are going to start with advancin' this One World Organization bull. They are going to make the Endangered Species Act ratified across the countries. Some tree huggin' geek in Canada will tell us we can't shoot a goose or log our own property. We are gonna send a message. We are gonna tell the world, *show* the world, we mean business. We are going to keep *our* America!" Hal shouted, spit spraying into the air. The crowd of camouflage clothed men let out whoops and cheers.

"Over the next few days, Tug here is gonna take you rag-tag batch of scum and turn you into a machine. This machine will march into Seattle and take out the entire delegation. We will stop their meeting. We will exterminate these politicking vermin. We will erase their message and send our own," Hal said, motioning to Tug and Joe.

"Men, the next few days are going to be tough. Joe will teach the fundamentals of the weaponry and some basic duck, cover, and get the hell out of dodge maneuvers. I will teach you the layout of the target zone in Seattle. You will know all of the access routes in and out of the block as well as the city. You will understand every bit of your part of the mission. You will be precise in our re-enactments over the next few days. Your lives will depend on it. Know this. If anyone gets left behind, if anyone gets caught, you *are alone*. We do not know you. We never knew you. Joe and I will be snipers in the wings. If you get caught, you will find one of our bullets in the back of your head. Captures cannot, and *will* not, be tolerated," Tug warned the group, sizing them up. He looked at the clipboard in his hands. Hal listed the dozen men, including the McKenzie boys, matching their strengths. They had a lot of work to do. But he also knew this motley crew of rednecks served as little more than a set of pawns for this mission. Ultimately, he figured a tap to the head of each one of them was the best method of clean up when the job was finished.

Thirteen

S ean shook his head. He stood at the mirror, dripping wet. His towel hung around his neck. Decision time. Sweats, pizza and the game on TV, or back to the bar. What did he think was going to happen? He looked closer in the mirror, his right eye ringed by various colors, none of them handsome. "The heck with it," he mumbled to himself. Sammy looked up at his owner, one eyebrow raised. "Yeah, I'm talking to myself. If I go, you have to stay here." The Swissie looked at him quizzically. Sean rubbed his dog's head and continued getting ready.

A half-hour later, he pulled his Jeep into the tavern driveway. He parked on the grass next to one of the immobile vehicles that served as rusting sculptures on the lot. Sean hopped out of the Jeep. His boots met the ground with a splash. The snow melted, replaced by a garnish of grass poking through in its place.

He stepped into the bar; instinct caused him to scan the room for the hunters that were in there the night before. The coast was clear. The lady from the night before wasn't there either. "Well, if it isn't the knight in shining armor. Black Butte Porter?" came the voice from behind the bar.

"Sure. I promise, no flying furniture tonight," Sean replied meekly, sitting at the bar. He looked up, glad to see the hockey game on - Colorado versus Los Angeles. "Should be a good game. Ever since the trade, the rivalry has been pretty hot."

"Yeah, but I am afraid with you around, it might look like a hockey game had broken out in here," Wally teased his customer.

"Very funny. What's good tonight?" Sean asked.

"The beer, and…the view…," Wally said, his voice trailing as he looked past Sean's shoulder.

Sean turned to see the woman from last night, standing in the doorway. The light from the lamppost outside made her look almost dreamlike in the entryway. Only her silhouette was visible in the glow, appearing as cherub emerging from the sky. Even buried under layers of winter clothes, she was captivating. Her shoulder-length hair flowed in the breeze against her neck, seemingly in slow motion as she came into the room. Her eyes locked with Sean's. They both paused and stared for what seemed an awkwardly long time. She slowly walked up to him, her expression soft, yet determined. Sean could not tell what her body language and visage were telling him.

"Hi," her voice warm and soft. Standing in front of Sean sat very tall on the barstool, making them the same height. Her eyes looked directly at him as she spoke, a crooked, almost shy smile crossed her face, "I was hoping I would find you here."

"You, um, want a seat?" Sean asked, motioning to his right.

"I'm fine for now," she enjoyed the equal height, and the freedom of standing made her feel more confident. "I want to apologize for last night. I didn't know what to do. The next thing I know, my feet were taking me out the door. I guess I was embarrassed," both of her hands lightly grasping Sean by the crooks of each arm.

"I want to thank you for what you did last night. It was really sweet. I mean, I *can* take care of myself. But still…it was nice. Oh, look at your eye…," she continued, letting go of Sean's arm and softly touching the bruise under his eye. Her touch was so delicate, barely grazing the skin on Sean's face. It felt unusually good, making him uncomfortable, yet intrigued.

"It's no big deal. I just couldn't sit anymore and listen to that guy act that way to you. That was you this morning, wasn't it?" Sean asked, shifting gears.

"Yes. Again, I didn't know what to say. It took me a second to realize it was you, by then, you had already gone inside," she replied, shrugging her shoulders.

"I'm Sean, by the way," he said, extending his hand.

"I'm Miranda. Miranda Shaw," She took his hand. It was strong, yet warm and soft. She guessed he was not a rancher or a forester, more of what she would have figured for the typical young inhabitant of the North Cascades.

"Can I get you something to drink?" Sean asked.

"No, but I'll get you *your* next drink," she said, slipping into the seat he had offered her moments ago.

"Wally, an energy drink and vodka, and pinot…?" he said, his face looked at Miranda questioningly.

"Yes, how did you know?"

Sean's face held a twisted smile, looking shy, and yet mischievous at the same time. "I guess I noticed from last night. I am a big pinot fan, myself. Doesn't always go with the gourmet crowd around here. I'm pretty sure I am the only reason this place has any wine that doesn't come out of a jug with a twist top."

"This place doesn't have a lot of wine drinkin' around here. Just city-boy," Wally said, placing their drinks on the bar in front of them.

"City boy?" Miranda asked, her eyes raised in curiosity.

"Yeah, from Seattle. Been out here for almost a year now," Sean replied.

"On your own?" Miranda asked, glancing at his left hand and quickly back to her brandy snifter that was serving as a wine glass.

"Just me and my dog Sam. Sammy is pretty much all the family I've got," Sean answered.

"Oh. Sounds lonely," Miranda commented.

"I like to look at it as serene," Sean smiled thoughtfully.

"I see. A loner *and* a ladies' man," Miranda smiled and then shifted gears before Sean could react, "How is your hand? You gave that one guy quite a beating."

"It's fine. Sorry about that, guess I kind of switched into survival mode. If Wally and Red hadn't pulled off the second guy, I might have gotten it worse," Sean replied modestly.

"I'm sorry," Miranda said, looking at him, her blue eyes sparkling in the firelight of the dimly lit bar. She smiled and added, "Do you always play the hero? Get a lot of damsels that need rescue around here?"

"No and no. I just can't stand how some guys treat women. Like I said, I guess I just reacted," Sean replied, swirling his drink in the thick bar glass.

"Well, it was charming. I am glad you aren't too worse for wear. Shame, too…" Miranda trailed off.

"What's a shame?" Sean asked, his eyebrows raised.

"Uh…kind of a cute face," she replied, her cheeks showing just a hint of blushing, as she looked at the different colors that underlined Sean's eye. She realized she was staring and suddenly became very interested in her drink.

"Cute, huh?" Sean asked, not about to let that one go.

"So, what are you doing out here?" Miranda asked, trying to change the subject.

"Having a drink, watching the hockey game," he replied glibly.

"No, I mean in the middle of the North Cascades. You don't really fit in," Miranda said, ignoring Sean's attempt to play coy.

"I helped an organization protect a big plot of land along the Skagit River. When I decided to leave corporate life, I decided to oversee taking care of the land myself," Sean answered.

"Not running away from anything?" she asked, trying not to be too pointed.

"No, and not *anyone*, either. I just wanted a break. Play in the rivers and mountains out here for a while," Sean said and then asked, "How about you? I haven't seen you around here."

"Oh, I live in Anacortes. I am out here for a couple of weeks helping take care of my Grandma Helen. She lives out east of Diablo. She has taken ill, and I had some time off, so I figured I would pitch in. Give me some time to spend with that part of the family," Miranda replied, her eyes never leaving his.

Sean realized that was why he had never seen her. He didn't know many folks from that side of the pass. "That's nice of you. So…why come *here*, specifically? Soaking up the local color?"

"No, I just, well, I love my relatives, but in short spurts. This bar was the only place open when I came into town last night," Miranda replied almost apologetically.

"I get it," Sean answered casually, putting his empty glass on the bar. Miranda nodded to Wally, and two more drinks slid in front of them. "So, what do you do for fun?"

"I love being on the ocean. Any chance I get, I am in a boat or the water. I love animals. I read a lot. Oh, and I hang out in backwoods bars trying to get good-looking men in trouble," she smiled.

"Yeah, I have seen you in action. You're good at it," Sean smiled back.

Miranda moved a little closer. Sean could smell the perfume on her neck. He could almost feel the heat from her body as she leaned in. He felt tiny beads of sweat begin to form on his forehead.

"How about you," Miranda asked, her voice almost a whisper.

"Well, you may have picked up, I like the mountains, rivers, animals…like you, I've spent a fair amount of time on the ocean. Used to be a pretty good surfer 'back in the day'," Sean answered.

"That would be fun to watch," Miranda said with a broad smile across her soft, sweet face. "What did you say you did for a living?"

"I didn't. I used to manage a company in Seattle. I cashed in some stock, moved out here not too long ago," Sean answered.

"Not sure I can imagine you all suited up with a briefcase," Miranda said, eying him.

"Well, it wasn't that bad. I made it fun. I had to do something with my life," Sean replied.

"Did you go to school for that?" Miranda asked.

"Not for that specifically, but I got a full-ride baseball scholarship at Southern Cal," Sean answered.

"Baseball, huh? I guess I can see that. Explains the beer commercial machismo you displayed last night," Miranda quipped.

"I wasn't exactly the type to rush the mound, but thanks. Once I graduated, I played in Tacoma for the Mariners farm club for a couple of years. I completed my Master's Degree by the time I realized I was not going to be a pro ball player and had to get a grown-up job for a while," Sean said, not returning Miranda's jabs. "So how about you. What do you do besides start bar brawls?"

"I am a marine biologist. I am studying whale migration and population in the Pacific Northwest," Miranda replied.

"You count whales for a living? If I knew I'd get paid to swill beer on a boat all day, I would have chosen that career path," Sean joked.

"It's not all fun and games. The weather on the coast can be downright brutal," Miranda contested.

"I can imagine. Do you work with a team or by yourself? I imagine that could get kind of lonely," Sean asked.

Miranda raised an eyebrow, "You live in the woods with your dog, closest town miles away population of maybe ten."

"Touché," Sean conceded.

As their banter continued, they had slowly inched towards each other, until their foreheads were just inches apart. Miranda froze. She kept her lips remaining inches away from his, the heat of his breath mixing with her own. Sean stayed there for a few seconds, looking at her, just past her lips and nose, together so close, staring at her pale blue eyes.

Then he backed off and calmly returned to the conversation. "I guess we have a bit in common," Sean suggested.

"I suppose we do," Miranda replies softly.

"I would love to show you around. It really is a magical place. Right now, with the snow, it is so peaceful and quiet. In the summer, it is alive with green and the forest's visitors taking advantage of the river," Sean said.

After a brief argument, Miranda paid the bill by threatening to make a scene if Sean didn't concede. Sean figured last night's ruckus was enough commotion in the bar for one week. The two put their coats on and in what seemed like slow motion, made their way to the door. Sean walked Miranda to her car. They faced each other. Sean felt his heart race. He had no idea what to do. He wanted to kiss her. He wanted to stay and learn more about her.

Sean reached down and grabbed Miranda's hands. He looked deeply into her eyes. Miranda looked up at him in anticipation. "Miranda…" Sean started, still unsure of what words would come out of his mouth, "I, uh, really enjoyed talking to you tonight. Why don't you come over tomorrow? Breakfast or dinner…?"

"Dinner," Miranda replied, "I need to help my aunt and grandmother tomorrow. They have some guests; I can help with the food and keeping up the house. I can break away tomorrow evening, say...seven?"

Sean agreed and gave her his phone number. They hesitated for a moment, each holding on to their share of the paper with the number on it. He thought for a moment to kiss her. Their foreheads touched briefly. They remained for several seconds, looking at each other's eyes until he abruptly backed off. He flashed a huge smile at her. "Goodnight, Miranda Shaw. See you tomorrow," Sean turned and began crunching his way through the snow to his Jeep.

"Goodnight," Miranda called back softly. She took a big sigh, watched him walk away, and climbed into her car.

Sean paused and watched as she drove off. He stood standing outside of the driver's door of the Jeep. He wasn't sure whether he should curse himself or give himself a high-five. There was something about this woman. When their foreheads touched, the feeling that coursed through him was almost magical – tingling and warm. He pulled his collar up; the night's wind was colder than it had been all day. He looked up at the stars. A cloudbank rolled in, consuming them in its path, obscuring many of the twinkling lights. He sighed despite himself and climbed into his Jeep. As he wheeled onto the road, he realized that he never ate dinner. He had not even seen the score of the game since early in the first period. "Oh well," he thought to himself. He would grab a protein bar at home and catch Sports Center on the television.

Fourteen

Sean awoke the next morning with Sammy nudging his nose against his master's face. Sean turned away from his enthusiastic, furry alarm clock. "Alright, Sammy," he mumbled and swung his leg out from the bed and put his feet on the cold, hardwood floor. He looked outside - the day appeared very gray. Dark clouds had moved in overnight, spelling more snow for the range. He made his way to the coffeemaker and gathered his gear while his daily vice of caffeine was brewing. He loved the smell of fresh coffee in the morning.

He checked the digital thermometer that sat on the kitchen windowsill. Twenty-nine degrees. He grabbed his thermals and donned his waterproof outer layers. He filled up his thermos, whistled for Sammy, and the two-headed out the door. Sean opened the door to the Jeep. He tossed his pack in the back and let Sammy jump onto the passenger seat. Sammy was always ready for a morning hike. The muscular dog would march proudly alongside his master, soaking in every bit of praise he could garner.

Sean thought that they would head northeast of North Cascades Highway. He was curious about the flashes that he saw the other day from Sauk Mountain. He figured they came from an area not far from Damnation Peak. He had his snowshoes and his cross-country skis today. If the terrain were amenable, he would try skiing to see how far he could into the Diablo wilderness. He found a wayside to park his Jeep. The big wheels of the SUV plowed through several inches of snow and ice that had formed from the slush freezing overnight. He found the trailhead, and he and Sammy made their way up the steep slope. Sean reveled in the cold mountain air and solitude. The cold was almost burning his lungs as he took a deep breath - crisp, pure mountain air.

His mind was still full of last night. He felt his heart pound, just by thinking of Miranda. He couldn't erase the feeling that overcame him when their foreheads touched, their mouths and lips inches from one another. He could so clearly picture those ice-blue eyes. His mind so far away from his current task, he nearly tripped over a fallen branch. For the time being, he decided he had better put his mind to rest, despite being excited about seeing her again this evening. He hadn't been on a date since his divorce. He couldn't understand why this felt so natural. Shaking his head clear, he adjusted his pack and looked after his dog.

They had been on the trail for some time, Sean's thermos of coffee was nearly empty, and Sammy's fur had collected a mass of frozen snow along the way. The Greater Swiss Mountain Dog didn't mind as he frolicked happily in the snow with his best friend. They were one ridge removed from the base of Mount Diablo when Sammy suddenly became agitated. The big dog let out a low growl from his throat, not at all menacing, but concerned with whatever his senses were telling him. Sean watched as Sammy bounded up the hill. The dog was very intent on following his nose. Sammy's actions began to appear as they had two mornings prior when they found the wolf. Sean did his best to keep pace with the dog.

As Sammy peaked the hill and looked over into the next valley, his hair stood up on his back, his tail rigid. Sean was right on his tracks. He wasn't sure what he was looking at, at first. Resting on the base of the next hill was a big black mass. Sammy looked at his master and continued down the mountain. As they crossed the meadow, Sean scanned the ridges, alert to any movement or disturbance. The dog reached the black mass first. Sammy was furiously sniffing the ground and very cautiously sneaking up to the ball of fur to drink in every bit of the scent.

Sean felt his throat tighten. He held back a choke when he was able to see what lie before him. A big, beautiful black bear lie motionless on the frozen ground. Blood was splattered all over the snow surrounding the bear. Each of its four paws had been hacked off and were missing. Sean noticed a mass of blood that was trailing from its midsection. Fortunately, the cold snap that arrived the night before had prevented significant decomposition. While Sean was sure the scent was overpowering to Sammy, he was at least spared the wretched smell of death. Sammy continued circling the bear. Curious and concerned, he was continually looking back at Sean for assurance.

Surveying the area, Sean found two smaller sets of paw prints covering the scene. He pulled out his binoculars and tried to locate anything in the direction of what appeared to be the latest sets of prints. "Cubs, she had cubs," Sean said to himself, Sammy's ears perking up at his owner's voice. Sean did not see any sets of human prints trailing those of the cubs.

Sean hastily hiked to a spot, high on the ridge where he was able to get the slightest reception on his cell phone. For the second time this week, he phoned his friend, wildlife officer Adam Raines.

The McKenzie compound was ablaze with activity. The dozen men, leaders not included, had wolfed down eggs, sausage, and hash browns whipped up by the McKenzie women. They had all assembled in the old, patched up barn. Tug and Joe Lyndon sauntered up to the band of rebels. They instructed the men to load several crates in the bed of a Sno-Cat that had a flatbed and canopy on the back. When all of the gear was properly stowed aboard, the men jumped into the bed of the Cat, using the crates as benches. Tug and Joe grabbed the seats in the cab and drove the tank-like winter craft deep into the Cascade wilderness.

After a cold and bumpy forty-minute ride, the Sno-Cat came to a stop. The men piled out, the last two dragging the crates to the edge of the bed, while the rest of the men paired up to hoist the containers on the ground. Tug and Joe nodded in approval, seeing this rough bunch operate in teamwork without being ordered, as a positive start.

Tug assembled the crew as Joe walked into the woods, stopping at intervals of one hundred yards to place targets. Tug described the weapons enclosed in the crates. He briefly told of their history, what battles they were used in along with some basic instructions. When he finished, he tossed the gun he was using as a prop to Daryl and nodded to the rest of the group to grab their own. They rushed to the crates, practically knocking each other over to get their hands on one of the powerful weapons. Tug casually walked to the cab of the truck and produced two large, black, hard-sided cases. He opened one of them up, and began assembling his personal long-range sniper rifle.

Joe returned from placing the targets and, like Tug, began assembling his sniper rifle. The men lined up, facing the ten targets placed in one hundred yard increments. Daryl was the first to get his crack at firing the weapon. His first pull of the trigger sent the gun flying back into his shoulder, pain seared through his entire right side as the report was far more potent than any he had felt before. The target remained unscathed. The men around him laughed. Daryl flipped the switch on the side of the gun and again squeezed the trigger.

The weapon, in automatic mode, sent a shower of bullets into the trees, nicking the number three, five, and six targets, as well landing rounds in several unmarked trees and sending a spray of snow from unimpeded bullets into the air. A pile of casings steamed in the snow at his feet.

"Well, men. At least Daryl demonstrated the power of this weapon. Fortunately for you, on this mission, accuracy is not necessarily vital. You took out more unmarked trees than you did ones with targets. As far as I am concerned, the convention next Friday is open season. I do expect you to be sharp enough to not take each other out along the way, however," Tug declared and nonchalantly hoisted his weapon up to his shoulder. In one motion, as he brought the rifle up, he fired two rounds. Both bullets whizzed through the air, neatly embedding themselves into the center of the number ten target, one thousand yards away.

Joe took Daryl's weapon from him and switched it to burst mode. In similar fashion to Tug, he used one fluid motion as he brought the gun up and squeezed the trigger ten times. A trio of slugs landed in the target of each tree. The men were in awe of their two instructors. The accuracy and ease in which they had used their weapons was impressive. One by one, the men took turns firing on the targets. They tried several positions- kneeling, prone, standing, and braced on a berm. As the men poured through their shells, they increased in their skill of handling the weapons. After each man had their go at shooting in manual mode, Tug stopped them.

"Good job, men. You have shown progress. For some of you," Tug said, tapping a clipboard, "You will be assigned specific targets. The rest of you will own a variety of assignments. Some of you will be back up to aid removal. Some of you will be cleaners. If things get out of hand, your job will be to take out all of the major entrances. Two of you will be code fire. This is what we are here for. Your job will be to use those over there," he said, pointing two unopened crates. The men looked on intently.

"Joe, you take these eight over there. Work on the targets, the removal tasks, and back up. I want you four with me. You will be the cleaners and code fire personnel," he motioned for Daryl, Jeb, and four other men to follow him. "Daryl, you will be in charge of the cleaners."

"Cleaners?" Daryl asked with a twisted expression on his face, tobacco juice spurting out onto his chin. Just then, a second Sno-Cat churned up the old logging road. Hal, Jerry Rhinehart, and Hishiro Hasegawa stepped out of the cab. The men appeared almost comical in their disparate attire. Hal had on a big camouflage hunting jacket, Rhinehart, a long wool trench coat with a scarf, neatly tossed around the lapels, and Hasegawa was stuffed in a dark parka, complete with a fur-lined hood that he raised into place.

"You're just in time for a little demonstration," Tug said, grabbing Daryl's weapon. He switched the assault rifle into automatic mode and pulled the trigger. A steady spray of bullets spewed into the woods, a hundred yards away. The sounds "crack, crack, crack" resonated through the meadow as lead burrowed into the belly of the tree, wood shrapnel splintering into the air. The top of the big fur leaned and then toppled to the ground.

The students watched as Tug cleanly sawed the tree in half with the assault rifle. Hasegawa and Hal McKenzie looked impressed. The other men waited with their mouths wide open. "Daryl, fetch me that case over there," Tug demanded. Daryl snapped to attention and did as he was instructed.

Tug unsnapped the latches of the case and produced a tube with a handle protruding from its center. He grabbed a cylindrical shaped object from the case and slid it into the tube. He adjusted the site, looked behind him, squared up, and pulled the trigger. A blast exploded from the tube and the cylinder rocketed towards a giant fir tree in the distance. The rocket slammed into the tree with tremendous impact, creating an explosion that rocked the meadow. The tree disintegrated into a shower of needles, bark and twigs, leaving only a charred stump with a spire of smoke swirling up from the base of the felled tree.

Fifteen

Adam showed up to the scene on his snowmobile with another in chase. Adam had called National Parks Ranger, Shayne Matthews, to join him. Sammy rushed up to the two, receiving a pat on his head from Adam. "Thanks for coming, guys," Sean said, his two friends staring at the pawless carcass of the bear.

"I've seen this before, unfortunately," Shayne said, inspecting the bear's wounds. "Pretty common for poachers to try and get bear parts to sell on the Asian black market."

"Is it illegal?" Sean asked.

"Yeah, hunting out of season, a mother with cubs and this type of mutilation are considered inhumane. It honestly doesn't carry a lot of jail time, just some fines and a revocation of a hunting license, not that whoever did this probably even has one," Shayne replied. He had Adam help roll the bear onto her side. A gaping rectangular hole ripped into her midsection. "See this? The blood flow patterned in this way is a sign that the bear was still alive when she was cut open. Probably to get at her gall bladder. Supposed to promote virility," Shayne said, pointing to the pattern of blood loss, indicating that the bear was allowed to bleed to death, suffering immeasurably in the process.

"Looks like shot in three points - back, right and left knee. Took her down slow, eventually paralyzing her, but kept her alive for the removal of parts. This is some sick stuff," Adam said, noting the arrangement of what appeared to be bullet wounds. "Any sign of the cubs?"

"No, while I waited for you guys, I hiked up that ridge. Their paw prints seemed most fresh in that direction. I didn't see any of the hunter's tracks that way, either," Sean answered, pointing to a ridgeline that swept along the side of Damnation Peak.

"Good, we might have a chance to catch up with them. Finding them might be their only hope for survival. Think Sammy will help us?" Shayne asked, taking the last of his photos for evidence.

"I think Sammy would love to," Sean remarked.

The three men and the Greater Swiss Mountain dog made their way up the trail. The tracks of the bear cubs led up the ridge that skirted Damnation Peak and headed for the Picket Range - a series of consecutive peaks that framed a stunning view of the Northern Cascades. They had gone past the base of the mountain and neared the brush, when Sammy suddenly stopped in his tracks. He let out a soft warning growl, letting the group know something was ahead. The men slunk down, and Sean ordered Sammy to sit and be silent.

Sean pulled out his field glasses, studying the terrain. Then he saw it, movement in the brush. He stopped his scan and focused on a bush that had moved about a hundred yards ahead. He motioned to the other two men and handed his binoculars to them, each taking a turn.

"That's one of 'em," Shayne said, handing the field glasses back. "The other should be close. Under these circumstances, they will stay right by each other's side."

Sean confirmed his suspicion, as he returned the binoculars to his eyes, he saw the light brown snout of a second cub. "What do we do?"

"Well, I came prepared," Shayne said, taking his pack off and producing a rifle stored in two pieces. He screwed them together, making sure that both chambers were loaded and adjusted his sights. He zeroed in on the first cub and squeezed the trigger. The cub yelped and bounded into the brush. The second cub had reared up and faced the men. Just as he was about turn and follow his sibling, Shayne fired a second shot, catching this one in the chest. This cub, too, let out a yelp and high-tailed into the brush. "Adam, why don't you head back and snag one of the snowmobiles. You can follow the ravine down there and rendezvous with us down the slope of the next ridge. Sean and Sammy can come with me and track down the cubs. They shouldn't get far."

The cubs had spent most of the day at their mother's side. As her body grew colder, instinct took over for the cubs – it was time for them to move on. In great despair, they abandoned their fallen mother, following the path that she had been leading, further up the slopes, deeper into the wilderness. They ambled along the trail their mother had chosen before her horrific death - the Picket Range, a remarkable, yet challenging to reach section of the Cascades. The travel was slow, occasionally stopping to eat winterberries along the way, frolic with each other and then return to the task of heading for remote wilderness.

As the cubs reached the high ridge of Diablo Peak, the shifting wind delivered a new scent. It was a scent similar to that of their mother's killer – the smell of man. They doubled their speed along the ridge, trying to reach the safety of the more dense brush.

The female cub found a patch of firs like the one that their mother had taken refuge in to rest. Following her mom's lead, she took to rest in the soft grove of firs. Her brother settled in beside her. They took respite in this little patch of asylum, anxiously anticipating what was going to happen to them.

Their brief wait met with yet another scent – a mix of man and wolf. The sister cub carefully rolled over and faced the direction of this new smell. She edged closer to the bush concealing her. She couldn't see the danger, but she could sense it. Peering further out beyond the protective cover, she tried to catch sight of what was before them.

A pop sounded from a distance and was followed by piercing pain in her side. Frightened, she bolted further into the woods. Her brother, bewildered by the actions of his sister reared up over the limb that was blocking his view. Another pop, and he too met with a sharp pain in his chest. He let out a frightened yelp and took after his sister. He met her in the woods. She was sluggish, scared, and losing control of her limbs. Her front legs gave out, sending her face-first into the snow. Rising, she took a few more steps only to fall again. Slowly, she lifted her head, looked at her brother, and bowed into the soft snow as her world melted into inky blackness.

The male cub looked at his sister in bewilderment. Like his mother, his sister was lying in a motionless heap. He sniffed at her, lost his balance, and fell on top of his sibling. He rolled off of her and stood up weakly. He staggered back, crashing through a small laurel bush. Instinct screamed at him to move on, but his body would not cooperate. His thoughts grew increasingly fuzzy. A tunnel appeared about him, the darkness taking over, drawing him in until his world too, finally went black.

Sammy led the charge with Sean and Shayne following close behind. Sammy's nose laced with ice crystals from putting his snout into the footprints of the cubs and then lifting his head to follow the trail. It did not take long to find the first cub. The female lay out cold. Shayne knelt and checked the cub for breathing. Placing the back of an ungloved hand to her nose, he felt the slightest breath of warm air. Locating the dart that he had loaded into the gun, he removed it from the bear's side. Shayne repeated the same procedure with the male cub.

Sammy spent his time sniffing each cub, curiosity taking hold. Sean knelt beside each cub, stealing the opportunity of the rare instance actually to touch a wild bear. The cub's fur was a little coarse, like that of the winter fur of a sled dog. Multiple layers acted to protect the bear from the cold and the wet elements of the season. Sean looked at these innocent creatures who lost their mother. Despite edging towards adolescence, the cubs would have benefited greatly by having their mother nearby for one last season.

A few minutes later, Sean heard the snowmobile closing in from a distance. Shayne placed muzzles on each of the bear cubs. He checked their pupils. Satisfied that they would be out long enough to get them into the cages in the back of the Park Ranger pick-up, he flashed Sean the thumbs-up sign.

Sean grabbed the rear paws of the first cub while Shayne took the front. They hoisted the cub into the air and then slowly made their way down into the ravine where Adam readied the stretcher hitched to the back of the snowmobile. They gingerly set the cub on the board and headed back for the male. Adam worked a rope into a series of knots and secured the bear cub to the stretcher. A few minutes later, Sean and Shayne returned with the second cub. They helped secure him to the aluminum-framed canvas stretcher, and they made their way back to the truck.

The eyes of the male bear had just begun to twitch as they placed him in a wire cage in the back of the pick-up, signs that the effects of tranquilizers were waning. They worked quickly to get his sister into her matching cage. Satisfied that the bears were locked securely into their crates, the men and the mountain dog set off for town.

Sixteen

Shayne and Adam brought the cubs to Sedro-Wooley to await transport to an animal rehabilitation center that would check them for injuries and decide if they could make it back into the wild, or if they would require living out their lives at a rescue preserve.

Sean shed his hiking clothes and enjoyed a warm, rejuvenating shower. Re-outfitted, in more fashionable street attire, he strode into the living room, stopping to pat Sammy affectionately on the head. Leaving his faithful dog to mind the house, Sean climbed into his Jeep to make a run into town in preparation for dinner that evening.

His first stop was the Cascadian View restaurant. He opened the door and waved at the waitress, who was busy cleaning tables, preparing them for the impending dinner crowd. "Is Nicole in?" he asked her.

"Yeah, I'll go get her," the waitress grinned. She put down the towel she was using to clean off the tables and pushed her way into the kitchen. Sean heard her whisper a little too loudly, "Nicole! He's here!"

"Who's here?" he heard the voice from inside the kitchen call back.

"Him! The guy with the wine!" the waitress answered.

"Sean?" the voice called again, coming closer to the door to the dining room.

"Yeah, *Sean*," the waitress replied in a loud whisper. She reappeared into the dining room, grinning at Sean. "She's coming."

"Thanks," Sean smiled back, his hands in his pockets, assuming the shy pose that he generally adopted in the presence of female attention.

"Sean?" the restaurateur said, coming through the swinging doors. She patted herself down to eliminate any debris or wrinkles in her clothes from working in the kitchen.

"Hi, Nicole. How are you?" Sean asked.

"Oh, good. You know, it is pretty slow this time of year. Some folks come from Seattle and make a special trip out here. Of course, last month, the Skagit Valley Eagle Festival kept us busy. How have you been? You look great," Nicole replied, her attractive face showing the slightest bit of color in her cheeks.

"Good. I have been doing a lot of hiking. Sammy gets a little cranky when I don't get him out," Sean replied.

"You spoil him. It doesn't take many walks in the wilderness of the Cascades to develop a thirst for more, though. What brings you in? Need some wine?" Nicole asked, her smile showing off hints of dimples in her cheeks.

"Yeah, I am thinking of cooking some Mahi tonight. Thought I would grab some Pinot," Sean said.

"Oh, have guests? Gris or Noir," Nicole asked, a hint of jealous curiosity in her voice.

"Both actually. Gris with dinner, Noir just to have on hand," Sean replied.

"Ok, I'll be right back," she quickly disappeared through another door that led to the wine cellar.

Sean was left to wait, his high energy causing him to fidget as he looked around the empty restaurant. Occasionally the beaming waitress would bounce by wearing an expression as though she was baring a great secret. Sean just politely smiled back as the young girl tended to her dinner preparations.

Nicole reappeared a couple of minutes later with two bottles in hand.

"I know you like the Drouhin from Oregon for the red. I thought you might like to try a Washington Pinot Gris," she said, handing him the two bottles of wine.

"Sounds good to me. I don't know what I'd do without you," Sean smiled, thanking her and paying for the wine.

It was true, without Nicole and her restaurant, Sean would never get the wine that he had become accustomed to in his days of entertaining in the city. It was a gamble to open a restaurant of any real caliber so far off of the beaten path, but the community rallied around each one, helping them through the leaner times. Sean had always refused Nicole's offers for discounts on the bottles that he would purchase.

"Just one thing," Nicole asked, her face pursed in an impishly inquisitive pose, freezing Sean as he neared the door, "when are you going to make *me* dinner, Sean?"

Sean turned to the endearing restaurateur and looked into her eyes for a moment. He flashed her his patented smile and without a word, leaned against the door and made his exit. As the door closed behind him, Sean hustled to his Jeep. He liked Nicole, but had never endeavored to ask her out. He rationalized that he needed more time after the divorce, or the right excuse to make it easy. The truth was that keeping their relationship plutonic kept the pressure off of him from moving his life forward in that realm. Why, then, was it so natural for him to invite Miranda to dinner? Whatever the reason, he knew that he had to hurry to get everything ready for the evening. He couldn't remember putting this much effort into a dinner, and for an inexplicable reason, he was indeed very excited.

Sean's next stop was the local grocery store. He had called ahead for them to bring in some *Mahi Mahi* from Seattle, his favorite fish. They had no trouble having some trucked out. He paused as he entered the store; something was lying in the back of his mind that he had to do. The light bulb went off in his head - Adam was going to meet him at his place to share what forensics had found so far. Sean decided to grab a six-pack of beer for them to enjoy while they talked.

He hurried back to the cooler of the small general store. Two large men in camouflage pants and flannel shirts were piling cases of beer into each other's arms. "When do we get to go back out there?" one of them asked anxiously.

"I dunno. Tug said maybe this evening. Maybe tomorrow night. A night hunt, with infrared scopes and everything," the other said.

"You mean like the ones we seen on the TV?" the first man said.

"Yeah, like that, I guess," said the second one.

"Oh, man. It can't be tonight. They said we was strategizin'. He was gonna show us a video and go over some drafts of the plan."

"Aw, you're right. Come on stack one more on. That oughta be enough," the man said with the fourth case of beer layered in his outstretched arms. "Ah, heck, grab two more." The two men took their stockpile of beer to the front counter.

Sean swore that he had seen them before, either around town or in the tavern. He was curious what they were talking about. A hunt? "Back out there?" He stopped and watched them go to the counter and pay. Two more men joined them. One of them had his arm in a sling. Sean peered cautiously around the aisle. He recognized the two men from the skirmish at the tavern. He didn't want to be embroiled in another incident -not this evening. Still, he was drawn to learn more about the two hunters.

As the men paid for their beer, they shuffled their way to the door. Sean ducked back behind one of the aisle end caps. He waited a moment and then followed the aisle towards the door. Peering through the door of the grocery store, he saw three of the men lower the tailgate of a big, raised truck and slide the cases of beer into the bed. He tried to look closer and catch the license plate number. But it was caked with mud, and he couldn't quite make it out.

"What the hell are *you* staring at?" Sean heard a gruff voice from behind and a big hand coming down on his shoulder.

"Ah, man," Sean cursed to himself and spun around to face the man behind him.

"*You?*" the man barked, his face red and twisted in surprise to Sean, looking back at him. His right arm was wrapped tightly in a white sling. The man clasped a pack of beef jerky clumsily in fingers that were dangling out of the white gauze.

"Look, buddy, I think we had enough the other night," Sean said, trying to neutralize the situation. Despite his best attempts, he couldn't resist his mouth opening for a parting comment, "How's the arm?"

"You little puke!" the man growled, dropping his jerky to the ground and lunging at Sean with his good arm.

He swung wildly at Sean's face. Adeptly, Sean leaned back as the man's big fist flew through the air straight at him. He caught the fist with his right hand and leveled his knee into the man's mid-section. The hunter let out a deep gasp and crumpled to the ground. Sean grabbed him by the collar and pulled him away from the doorway and behind a rack of magazines. "Look, pal. I am not in the mood for this. I'll gladly snap your other arm if you want me too, otherwise go back to your friends out there and go about your business," Sean said in a low, even tone to his would-be assailant.

"What's going on over there?" a voice called from the big green truck. Sean released the man's collar and gently shoved him towards the door, worried that he would have three more angry goons to confront.

Fortunately, the big man was too embarrassed to have been manhandled by Sean - who was a good fifty pounds lighter than him - for a second time. "Nothing, I, uh, just forgot something!" He shot Sean a menacing look and walked to the truck. Sean knelt and picked up the package of jerky the man had just bought. Impishly, his eyes widened into a wicked smile, opening the package and selecting a big piece of the teriyaki-flavored meat. He grinned as he watched the truck drive away and took an overdramatized bite. The big hunter just stared in fury as he glared out of his window at Sean, who was enjoying his left behind snack.

Sean returned to his house and had just finished putting his groceries away when he heard Sammy bark, alerting him that a vehicle had rumbled up the driveway. Adam had arrived. "Come on in!" Sean called as he heard the heavy footsteps on the porch steps. The door opened. Sammy came bouncing into the room, followed by Adam, Jim Hall, and Shayne Matthews.

"Brought the guys with me," Adam declared the obvious.

"No problem, I'll grab some beers, we can sit in the patio," Sean said, grabbing four beers between his fingers. He walked into his patio. It was a small room wholly sealed with glass panels for the winter, what light was available made the place a surprisingly bright and warm spot to relax in. In the summer, he could remove the glass and replace them with screens to enjoy the shortened but remarkably pleasant days. Sammy followed the men into the patio and nestled down on a rug in the middle of the room.

"Found out some interesting stuff," Adam began. "Shayne, you want me to start?"

"Sure," Shayne replied, taking a swig of his amber-colored beer.

"Well, the boys from Olympia tried to get what they could from the wolf. Not much left. The hunters were smart enough to pick up the casings, so I had no comparative for them. They did agree that the bullet entry and exit wounds look like a high-powered assault rifle—something with big rounds or maybe multiples fired in a very tight grouping. The entry caused some shrapnel from the bullet to disperse deeper into the body cavity. Looks a lot like new military, maybe U.S. maybe not, but military nonetheless. I passed the information on to Jim," the Fish and Wildlife Officer declared.

"Yeah, I found out that there have been half a dozen reports of weapons missing throughout several western states in the last couple of months. Two of them had reports of foreign weapons confiscated or weapons seized overseas. One was in Colorado. Stolen from a National Guard outfit outside of Pueblo. The other was in the Port of Seattle. A military shipment brought in on a civilian ocean tanker. It was traced back to a legitimate container logistics company in Japan. The ships show up one less container than were recorded arrive for inventory. The point is, the weapons could have come from anywhere," Jim said, taking a sip of his beer.

"What do we do from here?" Sean asked, disappointed in little new information discovered.

"Well, we keep our eyes and ears open in case something comes up. Outside of that, this type of thing doesn't command much attention from the higher authorities. We don't have proof that there is anything more than simple poaching going on. Adam and Shayne have a little more to do with the enforcement of these matters. Probably warrant extra patrols and whatnot," Jim replied.

"Right. We can put in requests for a few more heads to patrol the usual hunting spots. Beyond that, it is a lot of luck trying to catch guys like this," Adam added.

"Speaking of eyes and ears open. I was at the market today, picking some stuff up for tonight; I overheard some guys talking about hunting. They said something like they wish they could get back out there, but someone else was making them wait. They mentioned a night hunt. Oh, and then, I ran into my old friend from the other night - the gentleman from the bar. He tried to go after me again, so I inserted my knee into his intestine," Sean filled his friends in.

"What did the guy look like?" Shayne asked.

"Well, big and dumb. They used poor language. Wore camo pants and flannel shirts," Sean replied, shrugging his shoulders.

"Big guys? How big? Like the guy the other night?" Shayne asked.

"No, bigger. They drove a big jacked-up Chevy crew cab pick-up. Had two rebel flag license plates in the back window," Sean answered.

Sean's friend shot each other glances. "Sounds like the McKenzie boys," Adam told him.

"The McKenzie boys?" Sean asked.

"Yeah, big, rednecky boys. Live in the middle of nowhere out east of Diablo. Come into town from time to time. They have been busted for a few hunting violations. Their grandfather has tried to stir up things over a few fringe political ideas in years past. I understand he is pretty racist, but overall pretty harmless. The boys would, on occasion, start a bar brawl or two, especially around hunting season, but heck, even you do that," Adam replied with a smirk.

"The guy I had the run-in with was leaving in the same truck with them," Sean said, ignoring Adam's dig.

"Hmmm. Something to keep our eyes on," Adam agreed. "So what happened with the guy from the tavern?"

"I threatened to break his other arm. Of course, that was after giving him the knee enema. He finally appreciated my viewpoint and just moseyed on," Sean said, looking at the clock perched on his mantle and added insistently, "Well, gentlemen, I'd love to chat more about big burly rednecks, but I have a, um, a *date* to prepare for."

"Oh, really? Anyone we know?" Shayne asked.

"No, I don't think so," Sean replied meekly.

"Hmmm. The girl from the other night, maybe? The damsel in distress, huh? The least she could do for that lovely shiner of yours," Adam jabbed at his friend.

"Or is it Nicole? I think she had the hots for you, Sean. She didn't believe you drank that much wine. Oh, and the girl from the office," Shayne joined Adam.

"Don't forget the waitress from the Buffalo Run," Jim added curiously.

"Alright, alright. Just go. I promise I won't tell you anything about it!" Sean said, urging his guests to leave, playfully using his hands to shoo them towards the door.

"Aw c'mon. Some of us married guys need to live vicariously through the resident bachelor. You're gonna tell me, right buddy?" Adam asked, landing a light punch in the side of Sean's rib.

"Not one word," Sean said, giving him a shove back, clearing him out of the doorway. "Bye, guys!"

His friends piled out of the house and toward Adam's SUV. They were still jawing about Sean's romantic possibilities at the door was closed behind them. Sean turned to the kitchen and hastily began making preparations for his dinner date. Sammy watched him in bewilderment as the bachelor dashed about erratically straightening up the house. He finally ended his frenetic tirade by scooping the four empty beer bottles up and stowing them in the recycling bin. Satisfied with a quick scan around the house, he hurried off for the shower.

Seventeen

Miranda followed Sean's directions carefully. A light snow had begun to fall, but her light-duty SUV handled the roads with ease. She found the driveway and pulled in next to Sean's Jeep. Grabbing a bag from the passenger seat, she walked up the stone pathway to the front door of the house. She heard a resounding "woof" from inside the house accompanied by the patter of paws on the hardwood floor. She gently knocked on the door, which swung opened just as soon as her fingers grazed the wood.

"Hi, did you find it okay?" Sean's smiling face asked her, as he held the door for her. Sammy sat patiently, his tail anxiously swooshing on the floor, hoping for a pat on the head.

"Yes, it was no problem. This must be Sammy," Miranda said, rubbing the Swissie's head with her gloved hand.

"Yep, that's my boy. Sammy, go lay by the fire," Sean said. Sammy obediently got up and went into the living room and lie down on a small rug that rested near the fireplace. "Can I take that from you?"

"Sure," Miranda said, handing him a tall, brown bag. Sean grabbed it, feeling through the paper that it was a bottle of wine.

"Would you like me to open it?" he asked, heading for the kitchen.

"Please – sort of reparations from the other evening, I hope you like it. There are not too many choices in this town," she said.

"Yeah, I know, I had to make a special arrangement with the owner from the Cascadian View to have some brought in," Sean replied. He took the bottle out of the paper sack, recognizing it as an award winner from Oregon. "Nice choice," he called. He gently pulled on the wine tool as the slightest "pop" heralded the cork leaving the mouth of the bottle. He quickly filled two glasses and turned to find Miranda standing right behind him.

"Thank you. Can I help with dinner?" Miranda asked her eyes raised inquisitively.

"No. If you want some entertainment, you can have a seat and watch. You can be thankful it's not your kitchen. I'm a decent cook, but, uh…I'm kind of on the frantic side," Sean admitted.

"Ah, the guy who cooks with every burner on high and exhausts every pot and pan in the kitchen?" she asked him with a sly grin.

"That's me. Have you been peeking in my windows?" he asked, throwing a handful of fettuccine noodles into a pot of boiling water.

"No, but not a bad idea…" she said with a little laugh and walked over to the sliding glass doors of the living room. "Nice place. I love the view."

Sean looked up and watched her reflection in the window. She stood with her arms crossed, wine glass dangling gently from her fingers.

"Kind of makes living way out her well worth it," Sean admitted.

Miranda spun around to face him, "I think it's not the only thing worth coming out here for."

"Uh, I'll check the fish," Sean said, his face immediately flushing a deep crimson red. "Almost done," he said to himself, though out loud. He walked over to his tiny dining room table. It was already set with two place settings. He lit two tall candles and returned to the kitchen.

"Smells, good. You cook all the time?" Miranda asked.

"This is probably the first time I have cooked in about a year, unless tossing some slabs of meat on the grill counts," Sean replied.

"Well, I feel special," Miranda cooed.

"We'll see. My cooking might change your mind about that," Sean grinned. He placed the two plates on the table and sat down next to her.

"Wow, this looks great. Thank you."

Sean smiled at his guest; he couldn't resist the draw of her eyes. The flame dancing from the candles caused them to light up brilliantly.

Miranda hoisted her wine glass, "To the last true gentleman."

Sean raised his glass, allowing it to clink against hers, "To a beautiful damsel gently," he started and then smiled and added, "Who *could* take care of herself, of course."

"Of course," she smiled, her blue eyes twinkling.

They sat for a while, quietly enjoying their food. Occasionally, they would exchange glances at each other. Miranda accidentally allowed a stray noodle to slip off her fork, leaving a trace of alfredo sauce on her nose. Sean leaned over and gently wiped at it with his finger. Miranda put her fork down. She leaned over to him, her slender fingers wrapping softly around Sean's neck. Her lips met his for the first time, soft and pure. Their eyes locked on one another's. Sean felt like the flame from the candle was an inferno. He felt color rush through him, flooding his cheeks. He wanted to kiss her more, but just smiled and casually sunk back into his chair.

"I'm glad you like it," he said.

"Oh, I do," Miranda said earnestly with a grin. "You're quite a good cook, Mr. Kendall."

They finished their meals, and Sean hastily picked up the plates and put them in the kitchen. He grabbed two clean glasses and another bottle of wine.

"Would you like to sit by the fire?" he asked, motioning Miranda towards the living room. She nodded, making her way to the rock fireplace. Sammy followed, settling at her feet. Sean tossed two new logs onto the fire and poured Miranda a fresh glass of wine.

"So, got any good whale counting stories?" Sean asked with a smirk.

"Yeah, I think it was the one where the whale ate the baseball player," she teased back.

"Sounds exciting. What happened to the baseball player?" Sean asked.

"He was rescued by a lovely whale watching princess," Miranda giggled, batting her eyes.

"I like that," Sean grinned.

He fought for another witty comment, but instead, leaned in to kiss her. Their lips met, soft at first. They pressed closer and closer until Sean turned his head ever so slightly. They kissed sweetly. Miranda wrapped her arms around Sean's neck. Sean cupped her chin with gentle hands. They remained this way, drinking in the feeling of being close for the first time. Sean felt like the world slipped away, leaving only this beautiful woman at the end of its ever-tightening tunnel.

Miranda finally pushed him away. Her eyes locked on his. "What was that about?" she asked, her voice barely above a whisper.

"You tell me. I was just trying to shut you up," Sean said straight-faced, and then cracked a sly grin out of the corner of his mouth. He felt a sensation begin to well up in his stomach that he had not felt in years.

"Hmm. I kind of liked it, Mr. Kendall. Is there more where that came from?" Miranda smiled.

"I hope so," Sean replied softly.

Eighteen

The McKenzie brothers, Tug Gaskill and Hishiro Hasegawa, combed the trail that led to the ridge to Diablo Peak. They decided they could carve out some time to try and get the bear cubs. They knew time was of the essence if they were to capture them. Walking through the dark, their night-vision goggles cast the scene in different shades of monochromatic green. Snow had begun falling all around them, the reflective surface of the wintry ground adding light to their vision, almost making the field of view too bright for the high tech devices. Quickly, they reached the spot where they had killed the bear. Daunted, they found several new footprints at the scene, despite the fresh falling snow was working to obscure them.

"Damn!" Tug cursed. He followed the footprints up the ridge. He looked closer and found the prints of the bear cubs.

"More hunters?" Daryl asked.

"Maybe, at any rate, I doubt that we are going to get the cubs," Tug replied.

The men continued along the trail just the same until they reached a point in the path where the sets of prints led into a grove of trees. Jeb recognized two indentations in the snow, "One bear fell here, the other there."

"Looks like it. Let's follow the trail out," Tug agreed, urging the group to keep a rapid pace.

The men hiked into the ravine and found the snowmobile tracks. "Looks like a drag. Probably shot the cubs up there and placed them on a skiff towed behind a snowmobile to get them out of here. Probably sellin' the parts themselves," Daryl groaned disappointedly, almost as though a child who did not get his way.

"I don't know, it does look like the cubs felled here, but I don't see any signs of gunshot wounding," Tug said, digging around one of the indentations. He was about to stand back up when he saw something. He bent down to pick it up. He held it up in the light. "A tranquilizer dart, boys. It looks like we got some do-gooders on our hands. Well, Hishiro, no baby grizzly Viagra for you today. Let's see what else we can find." Slightly dejected, the crestfallen men made their way up the next ridge and scanned the horizon for a new target.

Sean and Miranda had all but finished a glassful Pinot, sharing stories of their backgrounds and history. The two swapped highly edited life stories, Sean lightly treading on his divorce, Miranda admitted to having been engaged but had broken it off.

They swapped college stories, both having been athletes. They walked through how their lives had brought them to where they are.

"So what about your family out here?" he asked.

"Oh, honestly, I know they are a little rough around the edges, but they are family. Grandma Helen and Aunt May would come to visit my family in Anacortes every once in a while. I guess my uncle and cousins would have these huge hunting fests with their buddies and send the women away for the week. We were supposed to be doing that this week, but Grandma Helen being ill and all, we had to stay here. I don't think my grandfather and uncle were thrilled with it, but that's the way it goes," Miranda said, shrugging her shoulders.

"Well, I am glad you are here. I kind of wish we met under different circumstances, but I guess things happen for a reason," Sean said, spinning the wine around the bowl of his glass.

"I guess they do, hero," Miranda smiled and then looked at her watch, "I should be getting back."

"Yeah, you okay to drive? You want me to take you home?" Sean asked.

"You *are* sweet. No, I'll be fine," Miranda said, getting up from the couch. The night had consumed many hours, and it had gotten late, but the flood of adrenaline that seared through her fended off the fatigue.

Sean got up to walk her out. He felt her hand graze his. He opened up his palm as she laced her fingers into his. Reaching the door, he paused to help her with her coat. "Looks like it has been snowing most of the time you were here."

"It's pretty, I love the snow," she said, looking up at him, smiling with the purity of a child. They reached her car. She pulled him close, grabbing the collar of his shirt. They shared a gentle, sweet kiss, and she got into her SUV. "Maybe I can call you tomorrow?"

"Sure, you've got my cell number. I'd like it if you called," Sean agreed. He watched Miranda shut her car door and back her way down his long, winding driveway.

Walking back to his house, Sammy trailed behind him. Sean burst with elation from the evening. He had not had such a good time talking with any woman like he had this night with Miranda since his marriage soured. Sean picked up the glasses from the evening and blew out the candles. As the smoked weaved its way up into the air, Sean smiled at himself - she wanted to see him tomorrow. This wonderful interlude wasn't over yet.

Nineteen

A horrible sound erupted in the night. Snow and debris scattered in pieces of shrapnel darting throughout the cave. The blinding flash of light and screams from strange animals seemed to come from everywhere. The bear could hear footsteps of unseen assailants dancing around him, confusion and terror preventing him from taking appropriate action. He pushed his way up, twisting around, desperately trying to get his bearings. Another explosion and his life ended horrifically, the high caliber bullet piercing his skull, exploding against the shallow cave wall that had protected him against the elements. In the same ceremonious fashion as the female bear, the Japanese investor and hunter pounced on him and collected his trophies in his little silk purple sacks. The edge of the jagged ivory-handled knife was carving easily through the thick flesh, until the purple satchel was filled. The blade sat beside the brutalized bear, sticky with fresh blood.

"Good work, boys," Tug said, admiring how this small team of bandits went about sacking the cave. The signs in the area had been consistent with bear traffic - the broken branches, the marked tree from scratching away itches, the decayed droppings told the men that there was a good chance that this little rock outcropping might hold another sleeping bear. Tug thought it would be an excellent time to practice some of the assault tactics that he and Joe were teaching them by attacking the cave.

He directed the McKenzie boys to take opposite diagonal lines to the cave from their cover positions. He handed Daryl a small explosive, shaped like a discus used in track and field events. Giving Jeb his high-powered MP5 assault weapon, he sent the hunters turned mercenary apprentices on their way. Jogging from tree to tree, they zigzagged their way to the cave, each flanking either side of the entrance. Daryl pulled the pin and pushed the trigger on the incendiary device, tossing it into the mouth of the cave. The boys took off their night vision goggles, counted to five, and stormed the cave. They found a just awakened, blind, and defenseless adult male black bear. Jeb turned his body into the cave and pulled the trigger of his weapon, opening fire. The high-powered gun let off a blast that knocked Jeb back slightly. The shot went straight toward the head of the bear, shattering its skull, killing it instantly.

The bear dropped to the ground with a crash. The boys grinned proudly, excited that their instructor was pleased. Hasegawa hurriedly ran up to the bear and began hacking his delicacies for the market back home. Since he had already had the remains of the other kill for his own personal pleasure, this one would be pure profit. Tug remained stoic, his cold expression unchanging as the ivory-handled knife wielded by the Japanese investor plunged into the bear.

The smoke hung in the air as the senator mulled over his position on the upcoming events. He questioned whether teaming up with Tug Gaskill on multiple projects was the right decision. He also wondered if having his aide, Jerry Rhinehart, so involved in the plans, put a traceable link back to his office in play.

He gently gnawed on the end of his cigar. "Jerry, that little twit. He would allow himself to take the fall before his senator got into trouble," Small was pretty sure about that. But the stakes for "pretty sures" were getting a little too high. Still, dealing with those bumpkins in Washington, he had to be sure someone was adequately monitoring the situation. He would keep a close eye on this one. No breadcrumbs could be left behind to trail back to Washington, not after their plans unfold next week.

A puff of smoke circled upward as Small sighed. His entire career hung on this operation being successful and untraceable. Rhinehart was a good right-hand man, but he was not worth the failure of Small's future administration. This country was going to get back to its historic glory during the cold war, and he was going to be leading the charge.

He looked at the picture hanging on the wall beside his desk. He was shaking hands with the president in the oval office. He savored the cigar between his teeth, envisioning himself settled back in the chair that sat directly behind the famous desk that had been the scene of many addresses to the country, how he longed to be the one appointed to that seat. Too many years of political correctness had softened this once great nation – too many weak influences made America a mockery. No, he was going to correct all of that.

First, he had to prove himself to the financial backers that would provide the economic prowess for his campaign. They were eager to see him make a strong impact. A strong impact they were about to get.

Twenty

Sean dismissed his usual hike for an early start to the office. Despite his better judgment, he agreed to meet Paige out for coffee, but first, he wanted to check in with Adam. The drive west on Highway Twenty was a pleasant one. The road had a light dusting of snow on it, but traction was solid. The view that greeted him as he traveled down the road was as magical as ever. The leafless branches painted white with snow against the dramatic backdrop of the Cascade peaks with Mt. Baker as the centerpiece was awe-inspiring. Occasionally, a bald eagle would soar overhead, looking for breakfast along the Skagit River. With little traffic to contend with, Sean wheeled the Jeep into the Sedro-Wooley Ranger Station in short time.

Seeing Paige wasn't at her desk, he strolled on into his office.

"You're in early," a voice called from Adam's office.

Sean grabbed his stack of mail and headed for the voice that was calling to him. "Morning," Sean said, plopping into the chair across from Adam's desk.

"How are you doing? You look tired," Adam told his friend with one eyebrow raised.

"I didn't get my coffee yet this morning, told Paige I'd meet her in a bit," Sean groaned.

"Hey, speaking of dates, how was last night?" Adam asked, a wide grin across his face.

"Said I wouldn't tell," Sean drawled, sleepily, crumpling a piece of junk mail and tossing it at his friend, grazing his temple. "So, what have you heard on our poachers?" Sean asked, quickly steering the subject away from his date with Miranda.

"Well, I think we are on our own, for now, at least. We don't have that much manpower in the winter months. The Feds don't send agents for a few poachers and unsubstantiated claims of possible stolen weapons. They will rely on me, Shayne, and Jim to find something more concrete. Admittedly, I didn't like the tone I got from the HQ in Seattle," Adam told him.

"So, in the meantime, some guys get to go around destroying animals with military weapons?" Sean asked.

"Well, no. Forensics might come up with something. If we can pull in the ATF, they have a lot more clout. In the meantime, I have been scheduling extra patrols along the logging roads known to be access points for hunters. So have Shayne and Jim," Adam sympathized, "It honestly doesn't feel like a poaching ring. Too few incidents. Usually, poachers want a haul. This looks like some guys getting their kicks with some dangerous toys."

"Well, let me know what I can do to help," Sean said.

"For starters, you can quit tripping over dead animals," Adam grinned at his friend.

Sean rolled his eyes and returned to his pile of mail at his desk. He was waiting for a reply to his grant request to erect a viewing platform on the Skagit River. Tourists arrive in droves for the Bald Eagle Festival, and the platform would give them a safe access point for them to view the birds and other wildlife that come to take advantage of the salmon run. He was also hoping that he would make the cut for a lottery run down the Rogue River this year. He bought a new raft at the end of last season, and he was itching to take it out on a technical stretch of whitewater. Finding neither such correspondence in his mail, he thumped the pile of envelopes back onto the desk and headed out for his coffee date.

Sean pulled into the little café in Sedro-Wooley. He parked the Jeep and hopped out. A brisk breeze pronounced a very cool and crisp morning; Sean pulled his collar up to avoid the chill against his neck.

He entered the café and instantly met with the wonderful aroma of freshly brewed coffee and the whirring of a machine frothing foam for lattes. He saw that Paige was already at her desk. She waved to him, smiling. Sean walked up to her. "Morning, Paige. What can I get for you?"

"I'll take something tall, strong, and sweet," the young receptionist said with a grin.

"Vanilla Latte it is," Sean said, rolling his eyes.

"Make it, Caramel, thanks."

Sean walked up and placed their orders. Returning, he sat down across from Paige. She immediately launched into conversation, "So, Sean. What is this I hear about a *woman*?"

"Ugh, I can't do anything around here," Sean groaned.

"Was it a *date*?" Paige persisted, looking at Sean through her little round glasses.

"Well, it *was* dinner. People need to eat, right?" Sean said.

"I don't remember getting an invitation to dinner," Paige continued her rant.

Sean heard their order called; he wasted no time leaping up out of his seat to get their coffees. He walked to the counter and fisted the two drinks that he ordered. "Here you go," he said, handing her tall paper cup full of hot milk and coffee. "I just had dinner. We talked..."

"The girl from the tavern, right? The one who got you into the fight," Paige pressed, trying to soak up every bit of information from the enigma that she saw as Sean.

"She didn't get me in the fight, it just..." Sean started before he was cut off.

"Oh, Sean, relax. I'm just messing with you. You're so easy to twist," Paige said, and then in a softer, more excited voice, "So tell me about her. Do you like her?"

"Yeah, I guess. I mean, I don't know that much about her. I just felt so comfortable talking to her. I felt like I could have talked to her all night. You know how sarcastic I can be - she has fun with it. She just turns and it right back at me," Sean told Paige.

"Are you going to see her again?" Paige asked.

"I hope so, I really don't know," he admitted. Wanting desperately to change the subject, "So how are things with you? Are you still seeing the guy from Canada?"

"Off and on. He's nice and all. He just isn't everything that I am looking for. The distance thing doesn't help, either. We are supposed to go skiing next weekend on the north side of Baker. It should be fun. Wanna come?" Paige asked, a hint of hope in the tone of her voice.

"I don't know, got a lot going on. You've heard us talking about the wolf and the bear incidents?" Sean asked.

"Yeah, that stinks. I got to see the cubs. They're so adorable. They looked so scared, though," Paige replied.

"They took them down near Seattle to Northwest Trek. They are going to evaluate whether or not they can be rehabilitated and set back into the wild," Sean said. "So, things are going well then with the man from the land of round bacon?"

"Good enough. Not that I wouldn't change things if the right situation came along..." Paige said, looking at Sean, trying to peer into his eyes that seemed to be looking everywhere but at her.

"Well, you're young still. Just have fun, and if things are meant to be then all will work out," Sean consoled. He did care about Paige. He also knew there was no way he should enter into any kind of relationship with her. They were in very different parts of their lives. He swished his coffee cup; no more liquid splashed around the sides, "Well, are you ready?"

"Yeah, I guess I should get back to mind the shop. I don't have the luxury of choosing if and when I work," Paige agreed, jealousy dripping off her tongue. "I'm going to use the restroom, wait for me?" Sean nodded, and the girl hurried off to the ladies' room.

Sean waited by the door. He stooped to read the headlines of the morning paper. Investigators had still not determined who was responsible for the federal building bombing in Colorado, though the list of groups admitting to it began to rain in. Sean just shook his head. He was about to give up on the paper and stand back up, when he overheard two men in the booth next to him talking.

"So how far is this place? I just want to pick it up. We're looking at a hundred bucks apiece for picking the run. What is it? Bear parts - liver and stuff? It's supposed to give them a real rise - disgusting. I can't believe what those people pay for that stuff," one man said.

"Yeah, he said Liberty Bell would take us another hour and forty minutes, maybe more with snow," the other man said.

"Why out that far?" the first man asked.

"I don't know. I just follow instructions; besides, we're paid by the mileage. We'll take it easy. Snow will help to keep fewer people out that way. You about ready?"

Sean's attention to the conversation snapped when a voice called from behind him, "Hey stranger, you going to buy that, or just read it off the shelf?"

Sean stood up, his mind was on satisfying his curiosity about the men, but turned his attention to the woman behind him. Paige stood grinning as big as ever. Sean couldn't help but appreciate her energetic, happy-go-lucky nature. Paige grabbed his arm, "So, I know you're a taken man and all, but I was hoping you would walk me to my car."

Sean held the door for her as they walked out. His head darting around, he didn't see which way the men went. "Are you going back to the office?" Paige asked.

"No, I, uh, I've got something to do," he said, still looking around the parking lot.

"Well, thanks for the coffee," the receptionist said, noting that her friend's attention suddenly seemed to be elsewhere.

"Anytime, Paige," Sean replied distractedly. He climbed into his Jeep. He wasn't sure if it meant anything - parts, talking about male potency and Japan…but he figured he would check it out. He pulled east on Highway Twenty, towards Liberty Bell Mountain.

Hishiro Hasegawa called his Seattle contacts the night before. He knew Tug would not approve of a rendezvous, so he arranged for the McKenzie boys to slip out before the day's training session with him. He wanted to get the bear parts en route to Japan. He knew he would get big favors in Japan for these gifts. He offered the boys a hundred dollars apiece to take him to a rendezvous point. He also paid two dockworkers from a port north of Seattle to come and retrieve the packages.

They didn't have to travel far from the McKenzie homestead to reach the Liberty Bell parking lot. The secluded location would allow them to slip back before they were noticed missing. The boys just couldn't resist the easy money. They pulled in and parked next to a tree at the far end of the lot. Hishiro lit a cigarette and took a drag. He blew the smoke out slowly through the crack in the window. He checked his watch. The delivery van was five minutes late. Snow continued to drift down gently. Another minute passed, and headlights suddenly cut through the snowflakes. Hasegawa jumped out of the truck and lowered the tailgate. The McKenzie boys remained in the vehicle with the engine running, enjoying the warm air blowing out of the vents.

A grey delivery van pulled up next to the big green four by four. Two men climbed out and joined Hasegawa. They exchanged pleasantries. Hasegawa pulled an ebony box to the edge of the tailgate. He gave the men instructions on how to package the contents and ship them out on his next freighter to Japan. Handing each of them an envelope, they were about to shake hands when another set of headlights pierced through the snow. The McKenzies' called for Hasegawa to high tail it back in the truck. Hishiro, clambering, had barely gotten a leg in the cab when Daryl's foot hit the accelerator, launching the powerful vehicle forward.

Sean traveled ahead without knowing what he might find, but the mysterious conversation beckoned him east towards the popular Liberty Bell trailhead anyway. Not much traffic made its way that far east during the winter months. The pass was known as a treacherous stretch of road during inclement weather. This made the conversation at the café convincingly peculiar. The destination, parts – it all probably meant nothing, yet part of him thought that maybe he should have clued Adam in before he ventured out on his own.

As he rounded the bend, passing the sign for the Liberty Bell Mountain/Blue Lake trailhead, he surveyed the site and turned into the parking lot. Spying two vehicles parked toward the back of the lot under the boughs of a tall fir tree, his string of thoughts concluded abruptly. He drank in the scenario quickly, trying to assume his next action. Two men were waddling from the bed of a pick-up truck towards the back of a gray minivan, toting a small crate the size of a picnic cooler. Sean wheeled the Jeep up next to the van, still unsure of what his move would be. With a burst of inspiration, he grabbed his map of the North Cascades and hopped out.

"Hey, guys…," he called to the men approaching the van, waving his map in front of him. "Man, all this snow, I think I'm way off track…" His ruse was quickly interrupted by the sound of spinning of tires across the snow-covered ground. He glanced up to see a pair of headlights swinging around the van, heading straight for him. Sean moved in an instant to duck out of the way, but the corner of the truck caught his hip, flinging him helplessly onto the frozen ground of the parking lot. His head bounced on the icy gravel as his vision and thoughts transitioned from a fragmented haze to complete darkness.

"Son of a…" Daryl cried, recognizing Sean from the store the previous day. He didn't want them to be identified, knowing Tug would be furious. He called to Hishiro to jump in the truck. As soon as the cab door opened, he slammed his right foot on the gas pedal, aiming straight for the man who had gotten out of the Jeep. He saw the man look up and try to spin out of the way, but the intruder was not fast enough. The occupants of the truck heard the satisfying "thunk" as the front of the vehicle hit its target. The paper the man was holding flew into the air and drifted down like a giant snowflake, as the man himself was tossed violently in the air to land hard on the ground, lying motionless in a lump. Without slowing down for a moment, Daryl drove hurriedly onto the highway, the truck fishtailing as it fought for traction between the parking lot and the road. In his rearview mirror, he saw the cargo van careening hastily in pursuit, exiting the trailhead parking lot.

"Oh man, I think you killed that guy," Jeb stuttered, his heart pounding in his chest.

"It was the only thing that popped up in my head. I didn't want that guy to identify us," Daryl stammered.

"I don't think you have to worry about that now, brother," Jeb jabbed back in response.

Hasegawa just kept looking back through the rear window. All he saw was the cargo van behind him. No other headlights appeared on the road as they sped along. "You boys are crazy, I guess I'd rather be working with you than against you," the Japanese businessman declared. Not new to violence himself, Hasegawa smiled to himself. The McKenzies were perfect pawns in which to carry out his business – naive, easily motivated, and when action was called for, they reacted with the calm and rationale of an enraged bull.

Tug was waiting for them as the McKenzies and Hasegawa returned to the compound, "Boys, where ya been? Hunting?"

Jeb, reacting, thinking Tug was sore about not being invited, "Nah, we was just delivering the bear parts. Woulda been fine if it weren't..." He stopped short, his older brother kicking him in the shin.

"If it weren't for *what*?" the mercenary mission leader demanded, seeing Daryl react to his brother.

"Well, some guy showed up. I, uh, I sort of ran him over with the truck," Daryl stammered, scraping the toe of his boot across the ground.

"You did what? You insolent fool! 'I sort of ran over someone.' How do you 'sort of' run over someone? Did I authorize you idiots to go anywhere?" Tug grabbed the large McKenzie boy by the collar and pulled him in closer, causing Daryl to stoop, "I need your damn attention on this mission. I don't need you guys running around, stirring up a bunch of hornet's nests. You inbred, backwoods... get out of my sight!" Tug shouted and turned impatiently towards the Japanese magnate, "Mr. Hasegawa, I need to speak to you!"

"Mr. Gaskill, it was..." Hasegawa started.

"Shut up! Listen here. I don't care about any of your sideline interests. I was told to humor you with our hunts. I will not have you jeopardize *my* mission. I can almost not blame those dumb hillbillies, but you should know better! I appreciate your funds to help carry out this mission, but if you want it to be successful, you stay the hell out of my way and let me run this operation without your interference. You got it?" Tug snarled, and then his visage softened, "So, what's with this guy? Is he going to be an issue?"

"Mr. Gaskill, I do not think the man will be a problem. If he lives, he had very little time to see anyone or anything. The snow was very thick in the pass. He had barely been able to glance at the truck when Daryl ran him down. I apologize," Hasegawa conceded.

"Tug!" the men heard a voice call from the den, it was Rhinehart, Senator Small's aide. "We have a telecon!"

"Mr. Hasegawa, please excuse me, oh, and leave my men alone!" Tug declared, pushing his way past the Japanese investor. He found the room that Rhinehart was in and closed the door behind him. The aide readied the speakerphone.

"Sir, Mr. Gaskill has joined us," he told Senator Small.

"Tug! How is progress?" the voice boomed over the phone.

"We'll pull it off. We may have an issue, though," Tug reported evenly.

"Oh?" the senator's voice called.

"It seems our investor friend couldn't keep his nose clean. He had those damn redneck boys take him to trade some bear parts. There was an incident. Someone showed up at the meet, and the older McKenzie freaked out and ran the person down. Doubtful it'll be traced to us, but who the hell knows," Tug continued.

"Hmm. Let's think about this," the senator stated calmly into the phone, "This could be advantageous. Those dolts in the woods there and the foreign businessman call attention to themselves, and yet we keep this office clear of implication. I think this could be a good thing. In your plans, you think you can do more to shine attention on them?"

"Make them take the fall? As easily as dominoes, Mr. Small," Tug replied.

"Good then. Let's see that that happens. Rhinehart, I need every individual who has seen you terminated at the end of this mission. Otherwise, your involvement with this office is over. You'll have to finance your early retirement. You had better start thinking of which jungle you would like to call your home, should things go awry. Anyways, keep me informed. And by all means, keep this office clean, gentlemen," Small said and hung up his end of the phone.

"Got more work to do," Tug barked at Rhinehart, springing from his chair and heading out to find his squad of hillbillies.

Sean fought his way to regaining consciousness. He was freezing, and his head was killing him. The light from the sun's rays filtering through the white clouds and reflecting off of the snow was blinding. Lifting his head, he noticed a trail of blood following, as it dripped from his bottom lip into a little pool on the ground where his face had been. He spat, sending a wad of blood spattering on the ground.

Wearily, he sat up, moving each of his limbs gingerly, making sure each one of them functioned as they should. They all appeared to be operational, but none without a great deal of pain, particularly his left knee. He looked at his leg, a tear in his pants and blood staining the perimeter of the hole, indicated the source of his pain. Inside the split, he saw a good-sized gash in his knee, the same knee that had contributed to the shortening of his baseball career.

He sat there, shivering in the cold, still trying to collect his thoughts. He glanced around the parking lot, noting that it was empty, except for his Jeep. His vehicle was as he had left it, still running. The wipers were sweeping the windshield while the headlights sliced through the falling flakes of snow. He groaned and pushed himself to his feet.

Gingerly, Sean shook his head, trying to banish the dizziness and haze that dominated his senses; each movement only served to make his head pound even worse. Slowly, he began the cold walk to his warm car. Favoring his left leg slightly, Sean managed to hobble his way to the door. Using the frame of the Jeep to take the weight off his sore limbs, he popped into the warm vehicle. He sat back in the driver seat and laid back his head.

The heat coming from the Jeep's climate control system was rewarding, forcing away the chill from his sore bones. Looking in the mirror, he reassessed his injuries. He had a cut on his forehead, and blood was still oozing from his mouth. Sticky red fluid soaked his.

Reaching into the glove box, he grabbed two Advil. Pounding them in his mouth, he swallowed. The little orange dots could not work fast enough for Sean. Casting the bottle aside, he collected himself and grabbed the wheel of the Jeep. He dabbed at his wounds with a napkin left in the cup holder from one of the week's many coffees. Angrily, he was determined to see if he could catch up with either of the vehicles. Shifting the Jeep into gear, he left the parking lot in a spray of snow and gravel.

Tug rejoined the men out by the barn. "Daryl, Jeb – get over here," he motioned for the two brothers to join him. "So, tell me about this guy you hit. Do you think he was there by accident?"

"I think I saw in him in town. He's a local, I'm fairly certain—some transplant pretty boy. I thought I saw him messin' with Jenkins the other day," Daryl told him.

"Hmm. Could be our do-gooder that nabbed the cubs. If he's alive, he could be trouble. We need to find out and send him a message," Tug said, the cigar clenched between his teeth circling as he sublimated about the situation.

"Yessir, sorry fer..." Daryl started.

"Sorry doesn't do us any good now, boy. Just focus on the mission," Tug declared. "Let's get to work."

He returned the men to their training exercises. The groups were decidedly sharper at carrying out their selected duties, pleasing Tug and Joe. It seemed as though they were progressing quickly. When they had a minute away from the group, Joe asked Tug, "What about this 'do-gooder'? The last thing we need is someone poking their heads around this."

"I agree. I think we need to contain that tonight," Tug replied.

"You think they really might have killed that man?" Joe asked.

"Maybe. I don't really care. Either way has its advantages and disadvantages. We'll send out a small team tonight to check it out. Let's finish up, call in the troops." Tug called the men. He asked Daryl, Jeb, and two other men, Jenkins, the man with the broken arm, and his slender friend Bud to join him and Joe. They sat on hay bales in the barn and leaned in as they addressed the men.

"Sounds like we might have a little trouble from town. I don't need trouble right now. You four have seen the man. It seems like he is poking his nose where it doesn't belong. Probably the same man who got to the bear cubs. Maybe a hunter who wants part of your action, I don't know, I don't care. I need him out of the way. If you didn't kill him at your little meeting today, I prefer you just deliver a warning. I would rather have him too scared to take a leak, never mind even thinking about talking to the police. If we can prevent him from talking, or at least delay him talking, we have less of a problem than the state police called out to investigate a hit and run homicide. We need this done tonight, quick and quiet like. You McKenzie boys, you're known around town, your discretion is especially crucial. You two – Jenkins and Bud – I need you two to sniff around town and see if he is still alive. If he is, you make sure that under no uncertain terms, he understands that he is a target, and opening his damn mouth *will* get him killed," Tug told the men, his face looking very concerned.

"What should we do cap'n?" Jeb asked.

"Find out who he is. Find out where he goes. Find out who is close to him. To get to someone, threaten those he cares about," Joe Lyndon spoke up, looking at the group thoughtfully. Tug glanced at Joe, nodding his approval at Joe's interjection.

"Will do, Mr. Lyndon," Jeb replied.

"Ah'll send him a message alright," Jenkins declared menacingly, shaking his good hand.

It wasn't until Sean had nearly reached the town of Diablo itself, when he saw the taillights of the van. It parked along a pull-out, so one of the anxious, stressed out delivery men could relieve themselves. Through the windshield, he could see the surprise on the driver's face to see the red Jeep coming his direction.

As Sean sped closer to the van, the suspect vehicle roared to life, the driver turning the wheel, aiming right at Sean's Jeep. Cranking the wheel and stomping on the gas, the Jeep pulled ahead, darting to the right, just missing the oncoming van. The van shot through the parking lot and onto the road.

Sean spun the Jeep around, playing out the clutch and sending the Jeep back onto the highway. He quickly caught up to the All-Wheel Drive minivan. He followed it down the twisting roads of the pass. Without warning, the minivan locked up its brakes. Sean slammed on his own, and downshifted sharply. He turned the wheel, narrowly avoiding the rear bumper of the van. The Jeep fought for traction, losing to a patch of ice and sending it sliding wildly toward a snowbank. The skid plate of the well-outfitted four-by-four took the brunt of the blow, but the harsh impact stalled the vehicle. Sean looked on helplessly as the van took off. Sean started up the car and tried again to take chase, but the Jeep's wheels wouldn't catch traction.

He hopped out and studied the deep snow of the ditch where he landed. Despite the Jeep's high clearance, it had high centered, the body resting with the tires helplessly lifted off the ground. "Ugh!" Sean cursed, kicking at the snow under the four-wheel drive.

Relenting to the setback, Sean opened the hatch and grabbed his foldable camp shovel and went to work. After a few minutes of digging, he climbed back in the Jeep and tried it. The back wheels slipped, but he felt the front hubs engage, and the Jeep dug for traction. He heard the crunching of snow, and the small SUV climbed back onto the highway.

Sean knew trying to catch up to the men at this point was fruitless, so he drove a bit more cautiously towards town. In the midst of the chaos of flying sheet metal and skidding tires, Sean recalled seeing an insignia on the van. It was a Japanese symbol with the Port of Seattle written in black block letters immediately underneath it. Disappointed that was all his adventure would yield, he decided to call what he had into Adam when his cell phone showed coverage.

Relieved at returning to civilization, Sean made his way back through town, his handful of Advil having no apparent effect on his throbbing head and frustrated to have lost the men in the van, his spirits hung low. His cell phone finally beeped, alerting that it again had coverage. He quickly snatched it up and dialed Adam's number. In haste, he relayed the incident at Liberty Bell Mountain. Adam was quick to chastise him for going out there on his own.

"Well, I thought I might lose them if I didn't stay on them. I figured I had to take a risk and get out there quick," Sean said.

"And how'd that work for you?" Adam asked over the phone.

"I'm about shy a pint of blood, I have a killer headache, and I am pretty sure there is a tattoo of someone's license plate on my forehead," Sean admitted meekly.

"Well, at least we can use that license plate embossed on your feeble head to track down whoever ran you over," Adam joked, then added, "Seriously, were you able to identify anything?"

"Not really, I know that it was a truck that hit me, but it all happened so fast. The snow was coming down pretty hard, too. All I could distinctly see was a set of headlights coming at me and the sound of exhaust and spinning tires. I did get a good look at the other vehicle. It was a gray cargo van. It had a Japanese symbol on it and the Port of Seattle written in block letters on the doors," Sean replied.

"That gives us *something* to go on. How are you feeling?" Adam asked.

"I'll live. Just need this headache to go away," Sean answered, his voice declaring his suffering.

"Hang in there, buddy. I'll have Jim run down the lead on the van and see what he comes up with. Try to quit playing hero for a while, okay?" with that, Adam hung up the phone.

Sean had barely clicked off the phone with Adam very long when it lit up, ringing. "Hello?"

"Hi, Sean. What would you say if a woman wanted to buy *you* dinner?" the voice said on the other line, it was Miranda.

"Is she cute?" Sean asked, grinning, trying to think his way through the throbbing pain and his woozy head, thrilled that Miranda had taken the initiative to call him. As much as he wanted to see her again, he sure wasn't going to be the one chasing her down.

"Oh, I think you'll like her," Miranda cooed.

"Sure, I guess," Sean said, feigning ambivalence.

"Oh, and one other thing...I'll need to borrow your bathroom later, though, I'm gonna be packing my toothbrush," she purred in a teasing voice.

"Uhm...uh," Sean stammered.

Miranda laughed, "Not for what you think, big fella. I'm not that kind of girl. I was told this restaurant in town was great, but they use a ton of garlic. I thought we might want to freshen up afterward."

"Oh, right, that's what I assumed you meant," Sean said.

"I'll see you, say around, seven again?"

"Sure. Why don't you just come to my house and we'll go from there," Sean said, hanging up the phone a broad smile spreading across his face. He glanced at his reflection in the rearview mirror and groaned, "Oh, that's nice." His face now had a gash on his forehead and a cut on his lip to match his finally healing black eye.

When Sean got home, he tended to his wounds as best he could. Pulling off his shirt, he studied his war-torn body. He had a patchwork of bruises all over his midsection. Removing his torn, blood-soaked pants, he poured hydrogen peroxide on his knee, watching the white fizz doing diligent work on his wound. When he was satisfied that he cleaned it thoroughly, he wrapped a bandage tightly around his leg. He rinsed his mouth with a cup full of the peroxide, spitting out a wad of blood that had been welling up inside. Finally, he dabbed at his forehead with an antiseptic soaked handful of gauze, wincing with each poke as sharp stabs of pain screamed out at him until they finally subsided into the dull throb of a concussive headache. Studying himself in the mirror, he sighed, "Great, buddy, great."

Looking over to the doorway, he saw Sammy quietly staring at him in apparent curiosity. "What's up, pal? I know I look like hell." Sammy crept close and sniffed his master's bandaged knee, letting out a sympathetic whine. Sean ambled into the kitchen and grabbed a glass of water, Sammy staying close at his heels. Sean plopped on the sofa, and the big Swissie put his head in Sean's lap. The tired and beaten man stretched out relaxed, scratching his dog's head. He tossed a leftover painkiller that he had from his last knee flare-up down his throat and chased it down with the beer. A hand on his loyal companion, it wasn't long before he leaned his head back and melted into a deep, dark sleep.

Sean popped his head up with a jolt, pain searing his temples and pounding at his head. The doorbell rang, followed by a persistent knocking at the door. Sean pushed himself up, slightly disoriented, he looked around the dark room. Switching on a light, he glanced at the clock. The knocking continued with Sammy holding sentry in front of the door. "Oh, no!" Recollection found its way through Sean's groggy head – Miranda was coming over for dinner. Sean bounced up off the couch. He groaned, with his hand on his head, the quick movement intensified the dull pain in his throbbing head.

"I'm coming!" Sean called. He hurried to the door. Pausing before opening it, he assessed his appearance. He grimaced at his disheveled clothing, having thrown on an old pair of jogging shorts and T-shirt after tending to his wounds when he got home. Reluctantly, he put his hand on the doorknob and gave it a yank. The door opened to a beautiful and smiling Miranda. She stood on the porch, a vision in a sleek black dress that was draped by an elegant wool coat. Her dog, Charlie, pushed through and sniffed his new friend, the Swiss Mountain Dog.

"Oh my God," Miranda said with a gasp, her hand covering her mouth in alarm. "What happened to you?" she said, stepping inside the house.

"I, uh, I'm sorry I'm not ready. I didn't mean for you to see me this ragged. I guess I fell asleep on the couch," Sean said, his voice giving away his weariness. He sheepishly ran his fingers through his mussed hair.

"Fell asleep, or passed out after suffering a concussion? I don't want to be the one to tell you, but you don't look so well," Miranda said, carefully surveying Sean. "You're bleeding through your bandage. Let's take care of this," she said and started towards Sean's bathroom. She paused briefly in her duties to kneel and pat an expectant Sammy on the head.

"Sit!" Miranda commanded sternly, pointing to the toilet seat. Sean obediently sat down as the two dogs looked on in what Sean swore was amusement. "What happened?" Miranda asked as she took the bandage off from around Sean's knee.

"Well, I was in Sedro-Wooley having coffee this morning. I overheard some guys talking about making some sort of exchange that sounded suspicious, so I followed their lead out to Liberty Bell Mountain," he started.

"By yourself," Miranda cut in, disapproving.

"By myself," he admitted and continued, "Anyways, I got there, barely took a couple of steps out of the Jeep and a truck tore across the parking lot. I tried to get out of the way. I guess I didn't."

"Oh, my God! Did you call the police? Do you need to go to a hospital? We shouldn't go out tonight. Maybe we should just stay in and baby you. You look like you could benefit from some TLC," Miranda rambled with animated concern she finished re-cleaning Sean's knee and was now checking his forehead.

"No. You came all the way out here, the dress..." Sean started his pride wavering.

"Hush, it can wait," Miranda replied harshly.

"No, I'll be alright. I'll take a quick shower, and I'll be good to go," Sean said, starting to get up. "I think we still have some wine left..."

"I know where the kitchen is, I'll get it myself," Miranda barked back and ordered, "you go sit back down on the couch."

"Make yourself at home. I'll be right out. I am going to clean up real quick," Sean insisted and went to take his shower despair Miranda's urging.

When he got out, he found Miranda sitting on the sofa, petting Sammy. Sean had thrown on a nice pair of slacks over his re-bandaged knee and a pressed black button-down shirt. "Well, you cleaned up nice," Miranda said approvingly from the sofa and smirked, "Ooh, you smell better too!"

"Thanks. You look great, by the way. Are you ready to go?" he asked his date. He looked at her favorably. Her black dress swayed softly as she moved. Her hair was up in the back, and earrings hung down dancing in the light. Sean was delighted to share his evening with this woman.

"I still think we should stay. I'm not convinced you shouldn't see a doctor," Miranda frowned.

"Nonsense, that power nap was all that I needed. Really, I feel great. Come on, let's go. I *insist*," Sean said, his voice pointed in, belying his stubbornness.

"Argh," Miranda huffed, "You are so obstinate. I suppose there is no arguing with you. Alright. I let the dogs out while you were in the shower, they should be good to go for a couple of hours," Miranda smiled and got up from the sofa. "You two be good," she turned to the dogs, and they headed for the door.

She smiled as Sean took her arm and held the door for her. She was being treated so well by this woodsman; it was a manner that she had thought was a long-forgotten trait in men. For however long it was going to last, she was going to enjoy every moment of it.

The McKenzie brothers, Jenkins and Bud, had already investigated the parking lot at Liberty Bell. Finding the lot empty, they drove into Marblemount. Not knowing whether to be relieved or disappointed at the vacant trailhead, they were determined to find the annoying man from town.

They didn't know exactly how to find him - they didn't know his name, but if he were still in the area, they would track him down. They drove slowly by the tavern; the Jeep they were searching for was not parked outside. Continuing their search through town, they were cautious not to ask too many questions, but they were hoping to get lucky, just by circling the town. It wasn't long before that very luck did find them. Buying road treats at a gas station, they saw a red Jeep drive by heading into town. Excitedly, they piled into the crew cab pick-up and tore off after the suspect Jeep.

Maintaining a safe distance behind the red four-wheel drive, they were careful not to draw unnecessary attention to themselves. As the Jeep pulled into the restaurant parking lot, they stared as they drove by. Daryl pulled the truck into the next driveway, an electrical substation. It was only a few hundred yards away from the restaurant that the Jeep had turned. "Let's split up," the older brother said. "You guys got the best look at him. You check out the restaurant. Call us on the radio, and we'll come up in the truck."

Jenkins and Bud strolled through the crunching snow of the substation towards the restaurant. Walking casually into the parking lot, they took a good look at the Jeep. Bud reported into the radio that it looked like the same one that was at Liberty Bell.

They decided to take a peek into the windows of the restaurant. Jenkins snuck behind a bush outside one of the large picture windows while Bud kept watch. Peering over the sill, he saw several diners in the restaurant enjoying meals at dimly lit tables. He saw a hostess seat Sean and a woman. Jenkins frowned as he studied the woman, thinking that he recognized her. "Nah, you think you remember every hot girl," he thought to himself, "Wait a minute, I *know* her, she's the broad from the other night!" He motioned to Bud with a "thumbs up". It was their man. Bud radioed excitedly to the brothers to bring the truck.

The McKenzies had been sitting impatiently in the pickup, talking about the rapidly approaching day that they would get to put all of their training to use. Daryl grinned and flipped his empty beer can out of the window as he started up the truck. He wheeled the vehicle down the street and into the restaurant parking lot. The brothers hopped out, joining the two men who had been waiting for them. They huddled to discuss their plan, sending Bud to the bed of the pick-up. The conspirator jogged over to the Jeep lugging a heavy black trash bag. Hastily, he dumped the contents of the sack on the hood of the four by four. Retrieving a vial of liquid from his coat pocket, he wrote on the windshield in erratic block letters: "Mind Your Bizness".

Daryl slunk away from the group; he wanted to see the man again, to be sure it was the guy that he had run down. He snuck up to the window and peered inside. "What the…". He called his brother to join him at the window. Jeb jogged up beside Daryl and squatted, looking into the restaurant dining room.

"What's this happy horse poop?" he exclaimed.

A very courteous Nicole led Sean and Miranda to their table. The restauranteur was dressed surprisingly elegant for an area where jeans were the protocol. Nicole shot Sean an approving glance of his appearance, at least until she noticed the cut on his forehead. "Rough day, Sean?" she asked.

"You can say that. Nicole, this is Miranda, Miranda, this is Nicole. Nicole is a bright light of culture in this town," Sean said, introducing the two women.

The women exchanged pleasantries. Nicole handed each of them a menu and described the specials for the evening. "Can I select a Pinot for you two?" Nicole asked. Sean agreed and the restaurateur left them to search her wine cellar.

"Nice place. Nicole seems sweet," Miranda added and then offered up meekly, "So, I have a confession to make…"

"Oh?" Sean said, almost nervous about what bomb would be dropped on him.

"Well, last night, I was ragging on you so hard about being a jock at Southern Cal. Well, I kind of put myself through school through sports, too. I was just having so much fun picking on you that I didn't want to add fuel to your fire," Miranda confessed with a grin.

"Oh?" Sean raised a curious brow.

"I was a swimmer. And a pretty good one, too," she admitted smiling.

"I'll bet you were. What did you specialize in?" Sean asked, with interest.

"Freestyle, butterfly, breaststroke – you name it," Miranda said proudly. Sean could see that it was important to her.

"See, sports can be a vital part life," Sean commented, "Well, we're even then. I played baseball, you swam."

"Two peas in a pod," Miranda produced a warm smile.

Nicole came over to see if they were ready. Sean admitted that they hadn't even looked at the menus. The restaurateur smiled politely and walked away. Sean began reviewing the evening's offerings.

"She has a crush on you, you know," Miranda said, grinning at Sean.

"Nah, she is just nice. I am probably her best customer," Sean replied.

"My, aren't we the naïve one…" Miranda started, but her thoughts were interrupted with the front door bursting open. A large man entered, with another equally large man trailing close behind. They both made a beeline for their table.

Sean looked up, "Oh great." He recognized them as the men with the big green truck – the guys that Adam had identified as the McKenzie brothers.

Miranda turned to see who had come in.

"What are you doing?" big Daryl McKenzie bellowed.

Sean realized that the man was looking past him with a look of disgust across his face. Sean jumped up out of his chair. "Gentlemen, let's take this outside," he said, putting his hand against Daryl's chest, holding him back.

"Miranda!" the second man called to Sean's dinner date.

Sean instantly furrowed his eyebrows in bewilderment. These men know Miranda? The three men were at a temporary impasse. They all stood facing each other, the McKenzies wearing scowls on their faces. Miranda stood up and positioned herself between the three testosterone-filled egos.

"Miranda, what are you doin' with this pretty boy?" Daryl demanded.

"Daryl, what I do with my time is my own to decide. Sean has been very nice to me. He defended me at the tavern a few nights ago. He is very much a gentleman," Miranda informed her cousin.

"Very much a pansy," Jeb snorted.

"Jeb, stop it," Miranda said.

"Guys, *outside*," Sean said sternly, wanting to take all of this attention out of Nicole's restaurant. Fortunately, the men relented without more provocation, the dining room full of patrons sat motionless in silence, watching the intrusion.

The four stormed out into the chilly night, stood just outside the entrance of the restaurant. "Guys..." Miranda started, but the men were not listening. In the shadows, Jenkins and Bud began to realize that this woman, the woman that Jenkins had been hitting on at the bar, was related to the McKenzies'. Not wanting to land on their wrong side and be fingered by her, they kept to the shadows, eagerly anticipating the McKenzies pummeling their common foe.

"You stay away from our cousin," Jeb shouted, jabbing a finger in the air at Sean.

"Cousin?" Sean asked.

"Yes, Sean, this is Daryl and Jeb..." Miranda started but was once again cut off.

"Look, I don't want any trouble, I don't know what your problem is, but...," Sean tried to diffuse the situation, but all he got in response was Daryl's big fist connecting with his chin. Sean staggered back, knocking into the light pole. Jeb stepped in and grabbed Sean by the collar, rearing back to deliver his own blow.

"Jeb! Stop it! Leave him alone!" Miranda demanded, tugging on Jeb's big arm. Jeb tried to yank his arm away from his cousin. Sean took advantage of the distraction and pushed him hard in his chest with both hands causing the big McKenzie boy to stumble back. Sean snapped to a defensive posture, ready to face the boys.

"But, Miranda, he..." Jeb began.

"He nothing! He has been nothing but nice to me. We are going to go back to our evening, have a nice dinner there and you boys are going home. *Now*!" Miranda said in a harsh tone. She put her arm around Sean. "Are you okay?" she asked him, looking at his chin, it had been graced with a crimson mark at the site where her cousin's fist had landed.

"I'm fine," Sean growled, glaring at his two assailants.

"Go!" Miranda said, pushing her cousin in the direction of his truck.

Daryl hesitated, but finally relented and walked towards his truck. His brother looked at Sean and then at Miranda and then dejectedly followed his brother.

Assured that her cousins minded her, she turned back to Sean. "I'm sorry about that. Trouble seems to follow me when I am with you. Come on, let's go back inside," Miranda said, pulling Sean near her, herding him back towards the restaurant entryway.

Sean looked over his shoulder at the two men retreating to their vehicle. His heart was still racing from the incident. He struggled between wanting to get even for getting slugged and keeping the peace for Miranda's sake. The tension in his arm was met with a more solid grip from Miranda to keep him heading back to the restaurant and away from her cousins. More than anything, Sean wanted answers. When they returned to their seats, Nicole came over to the table.

"What was that about? Do you need me to call the police?" she asked the two.

"I'm not quite sure," Sean said, "But no, I don't think the police need to be brought in for this, probably just a misunderstanding. I am sorry for the disturbance." He shot Miranda a quick look, letting her cousins off of the hook.

Her return glance showed her appreciation. "That's okay. I have been toying with the idea of adding a dinner show. Let's call this a pilot run – no harm, no foul. Well, I brought you a great Pinot. I think you'll like it," Nicole said, gently patting Sean's shoulder. She presented the bottle and tried to get her guests settled back into enjoying their dining experience.

When she left, Sean turned his attention to Miranda. "So, what was that all about?"

"I was kind of hoping you could tell me. As you now know, those two boys are my cousins," Miranda said, exasperated. "They can be a little overprotective, I guess. I am so sorry. They are a little country and backward, but they usually mean well."

"They didn't seem too well meant out there," Sean said, rubbing his chin. "I have seen them before. They were with the guys who were messing with you at the tavern, the night we met."

"Are you sure?" Miranda asked, unbelievingly.

"Yeah, I'm sure. They drove away in that big green pick-up. I remember the rebel flags on it," Sean told his date.

"Yeah, they're pretty special, huh," Miranda said, sarcastically. "I can't believe they were with those guys."

"You haven't seen them before?" Sean asked.

"No, just the family has been around the house. They have had a few visitors, but they stayed in the barn and camp out in the pasture. Hunting buddies, I think. Funny, though, they met with a Japanese guy in the driveway. They take clients on hunts; he must have been one."

"A Japanese guy?" Sean asked. His mind was reeling. He almost felt dizzy. Flashbacks of the parking lot at Liberty Bell Mountain flitted through his mind. He thought he saw a Japanese man get into a vehicle, a truck - the truck that ran him over. Japanese…the writing on the minivan – it was Japanese characters. The clues were trying to take shape in his head.

"Yeah, I have seen him around a couple times lately. Unusual for my uncle. He generally doesn't like anyone– he can be pretty prejudiced. Not one of the better qualities exuded by my family," Miranda conceded.

"But, they *are* family," Sean said, shaking his head.

"Ah, those dreadful family secrets," she lamented.

"We've all got 'em," Sean admitted. "Miranda, I, uh – is it possible your cousins might be mixed up in something."

"What do you mean? Like I said, they are a little backward, but they wouldn't hurt a flea. Well, unless you happen to have big horns and can be mounted on a wall," Miranda said, laughing.

"Well, I think that is what this is all about – hunting. There might be a connection with them and the bear. Maybe even the wolf. In fact, it may have been *their* truck that ran me over," Sean said.

"No way. I'm sorry Sean, I just can't believe that they would do that," Miranda declared defiantly.

"How can you be sure?" Sean asked.

"Because they are my family. I think I would know them better than you," Miranda snapped back defensively.

"Look, I don't mean to offend you, but something funny is going on around here, and I am telling you that there is a possibility that your cousins are involved, if not them, then perhaps their friends," Sean said, his voice sounding very even and calm.

"Well, if they *are* my cousins' friends, I might buy that, but if I am telling you, Daryl and Jeb are not involved in anything shady," Miranda contested, her voice too coming across a little more calmly.

"Well, nothing we can do about it tonight, let's try and enjoy our dinner," Sean said, picking up his menu. He sensed the resistance wasn't going to go away.

"What would you say if we got it to go?" Miranda said, smiling. "I think the fun has been pretty much sucked out of the meal here."

Sean agreed. They placed their orders, but they did not get out of the restaurant without one last argument ensuing—this one over who got to pay the bill. Miranda won by reminding him of her cousin's chin-check. She figured the least she could do was to buy dinner.

Nicole brought out their meals and slipped the re-corked bottle of wine into a paper sack. Sean again apologized for the incident and held the door open for Miranda to head out. They walked through the falling snow. Sean scanned the parking lot instinctively. The way his week had been, he felt he had to look over his shoulder constantly. Not detecting any threats to him or Miranda, they proceeded to the Jeep. Miranda let out a horrified shriek when she saw his SUV. Thrusting himself in front of her, Sean shielded her with his body from the sight. Perched on his Jeep, was a bloody, severed bear head displayed on the hood of his four-wheel drive. Red letters from what appeared to be blood spelled "Mind Your Business" oozed down his windshield.

"Nice," Sean muttered, shaking his head. He pulled his cell out and dialed Jim Matthews, the Sheriff's Deputy. He told him what had happened and asked if he wanted to see. Jim was close by, so he agreed to come and check out the scene.

Miranda had walked away and stood on the porch of the restaurant. She looked up at Sean as he approached, "I suppose you want to blame this on my cousins too?"

"I didn't say that," Sean said glibly, though that was precisely what he was thinking. "How do you suppose they knew you were here?"

"I don't know. It is not like this is a big town. Maybe their friends came here to decorate your truck, and they saw me in the restaurant," Miranda replied, her voice cracked a little, showing that she was still visibly disturbed.

"Or maybe they came here together, took a peek through the windows, and to their surprise, the guy that broke their friend's arm was sharing a bottle of wine with their cousin," Sean said.

"Whatever. You don't know that. Maybe a friend of theirs did see me with you. It could be a coincidence. You don't seem to be making a lot of friends lately," Miranda replied. She tried not to let the little smirk escape as she kept her visage of disgust and irritation.

"You seem to bring trouble into my life at every turn," Sean replied curtly. His timing was perfect. The Sherriff's Deputy arrived with his lights sweeping the parking lot, distracting the couple before Miranda could return volley with her reply.

Jim climbed out of his SUV, and Sean introduced him to Miranda. Jim shook her hand and smiled as the trio made their way to Sean's Jeep. The deputy looked around the Jeep with a keen eye.

"Looks like you aren't making a lot of friends lately, Sean," Jim told his friend. Miranda scoffed and shot Sean a look as the deputy dittoed her remark. The policeman looked closely where contact might have been made against the surface of the vehicle. He shone his flashlight at a couple of spots, pointing out a few smudges to Sean. "See here – gloves. A smudge, but no prints." He took out a small digital camera and took some pictures of the morose scene. After making a few notes, he began collecting the physical evidence off of the Jeep.

"I'm afraid that is all we can do tonight. I'll send this stuff to the lab for processing, but I will admit, I don't expect much from it. Maybe if we had the rest of the body, we could try and match the bullet with the wounds from the wolf, but a severed head and some blood isn't going to lead to much of a trail I'm afraid. Try and stay out of trouble, okay, Sean?" the officer took a bag out of his 4x4 police vehicle and used his gloved hand to place the bear head in it. He tossed Sean a bottle of window cleaner and a couple of paper towels. Sean went to work, vigorously cleaning his windshield.

The ride to Sean's house was quiet. Each passenger had been being tormented by a barrage of thoughts running through their heads, and the night's events had long shattered any of the positive vibes that had been building over the evening. When they arrived at the house, they found two thrilled dogs to greet them. Once they had received their share of pats and coos, Sean let them out into the yard. The dogs ran into the night, joyfully chasing each other.

Sean and Miranda looked at each other. Neither knew how or if they should salvage the evening. Sean broke the silence, "I understand if you are ready to go home."

"Well, this evening has certainly not gone well. But…I have to tell you, I am *starving*," Miranda replied, and for the first time since her cousins arrived at the restaurant, cracked an honest smile.

"We might as well eat. Do you want some of this wine?" Sean asked, holding the brown paper shrouded bottle in his grasp.

"More than ever," Miranda gasped.

Sean poured two glasses of wine and squatted in front of the fireplace as they ate their to-go meals. The tension of the evening eroded into the enjoyment of the warm fire, fine northwest cuisine, and silky red wine. Eventually, the conversation grew from comments on the food and wine to sharing more stories about their past, how they grew up, what they wanted for their future. Their cardboard boxes of food emptied, Sean tossed another log on the fire. He was beginning to warm up to the point where he was again enjoying this woman's company.

"Oh, the dogs," Miranda alerted. She bolted up to let the dogs in. "Say, Sean, what's the story with Sammy? How did you get him?" she asked, hitting a subject that she knew they both appreciated.

"Sammy is awesome. I got him when I was in Seattle. I volunteered on a disaster relief task force for the ASPCA. I was part of a team that responded to a big flood at the coast. I found a Greater Swiss Mountain Dog that had just had puppies. They were stuck on the roof of a building that was half underwater. When I arrived, two of the pups had slipped off of the metal roof into the water. I jumped in after them and dragged them to the boat. I got them into the little Zodiac raft and then went back to get the mother and the rest of the pups. When I found the owners, they were so relieved, they offered one of the puppies to me," Sean told her.

"Wow, you *really* are a boy scout, aren't you," Miranda laughed.

"How about you, where did you get Charlie?" Sean asked.

"Uhh, I got custody of Charlie. He was given to me and my ex-fiancé by my grandmother. She was a very special woman..." she drifted off, deep in thought.

"Was?" Sean asked.

"Oh," Miranda said, snapping out of her thought. "She passed away not long before we broke up. I think she was a big part of why I stuck in there as long as I did with him. She was always so positive and supportive. I guess I was hoping her sense of family and general zeal for people would rub off on him, it never did. My grandmother is one of many reasons why Charlie is so special to me," she looked over at the chocolate lab.

"He is a good boy," Sean said. Both dogs hearing 'Good boy' thumped their tails enthusiastically against the floor.

"So what about you and your ex-wife?" she asked.

"We parted okay. I don't know what happened, we just kind of grew apart. Probably shouldn't have been married to start. I suppose we clung onto something that wasn't there," Sean said thoughtfully.

"Has there been anyone since?" Miranda asked softly.

"No. Spending time with you is as close as I have come," Sean said, a shy smile spreading across his face.

"I'll take that as a compliment, Mr. Kendall," Miranda replied, leaning over to kiss him. Her lips were so close; he felt every whisper. She pushed their dinner plates out of the way and crawled next to him. She kissed him gently.

Smiling, he pulled her close, burying into her hair, enjoying her scent. She purred as they embraced, enjoying each other's warmth and soaking in the evening.

Resting her head on Sean's shoulder, Miranda nuzzled next to him.

"I'm glad you're here," Sean said softly.

"Me too," Miranda whispered.

Twenty One

The wolf pack had ventured deeper into the wilderness, arching west of the previous day's location. They had never found their lost brother, but they did find his bloody trail. Together, they mourned him through the days that followed. The alpha's instinct drove the pack further undercover, to the foothills southwest of the Picket Range. The wolves had to relearn their roles in the hunt, missing their beloved member. With no competing packs in the region, they only had to share the Cascades with mountain lions and the occasional grumpy bear that came out of hibernation. This made their task of establishing their territory an easier one. Finding food was their primary struggle. The wolves worked as a team catching rabbits, small deer, and elk. As they ventured further south, they found an abundance of prey at their disposal.

The alpha led his pack with caution; he knew something was out in the woods, something dangerous. With cautious restraint, he followed a scent, the scent of several young animals. He got excited and let out the yip that told the other wolves that the hunt was on. Forging through the snow, he led the pack towards this wonderful scent; a meal was at hand. They reached the end of the woods and stopped near a clearing to collect themselves and survey the scene. A group of lambs were huddled together at the opposite end of the field. They circled the clearing, staying within the protective cover of the forest. As the pack rounded the meadow, reaching the closest grove of trees to their prey, the unfortunate stock of lambs. Crouching low to the ground, the wolves moved carefully, staying upwind of their presumptive meal.

The alpha studied the area with his keen senses. He could not detect any other predators in the vicinity of the meadow. The eldest female circled to the southernmost flank, the beta male to the north. The remaining female stayed back undercover, caring for the two pups. The alpha slunk low and started straight on towards the young sheep. The juvenile animals saw him and started their chorus of desperate bleats. They had little room to move in their small corral. They shimmied to the left, towards the female wolf. The youngest lamb was in the middle of the herd; her only form of protection. From the southern flank, the female charged into the corral.

The attack was perfect, as if concerted from a military command, they divided the herd into a manageable objective. The alpha soared into the enclosure, isolating half of the lambs. The male on the northern flank joined the other wolves, and they had successfully cornered the youngest of the sheep in the flock. The female plunged through and caught the young sheep on the leg, the alpha leaped forward and grabbed the lamb by the throat, crushing its windpipe and severing its carotid artery. His powerful jaws dragged the lamb out of the corral and into the safety of the woods. The other wolves fell in behind the alpha, protecting him as he carried their meal to the refuge of the forest.

Following another morning of training, Tug relented to allow the men a respite of rest. They were days from the mission. He needed them to be sharp. Daryl and Jeb wanted to take Hasegawa on another hunt to make up for the loss of the cubs. The previous evening, when they were in town looking for Sean, they heard from one of the employees in the convenience store that some ranchers north of Marblemount had reported an attack on sheep. The ranchers has assumed a mountain lion was the culprit. The convenience store clerk said he thought it might have been a wolf. Another customer claimed to have seen one in the area.

Daryl thought that considering where the wolves were last tracked, that they might make a wider sweep to the south. He figured they would try to continue towards the Skagit River, but then divert further south from where the other wolf had been shot. Consulting with his brother, they agreed on an angle to locate the pack, and Hasegawa readily agreed to join them. They began their approach on the ridge that sat behind the ranch where the attack on the sheep occurred. They carefully combed the area for tracks and signs that the wolf pack had indeed been there.

It was Jeb who got lucky. He went to the base of the ridge and found a single line of tracks through the snow. The prints were linear, single file. The wolves following their front paw with the same spot with their rear. The wolf following would retrace the previous wolf's tracks, concealing how many wolves might be in the pack. Jeb let out a whoop and called to the others. The trail careened to the south, around a vast clearing. Their hopes were confirmed, only a few hundred yards from the clearing, nestled in the trees, was a well-cleaned carcass of a lamb. From there, however, it was difficult to discern where the tracks led.

Hasegawa and Daryl joined him. From the spot of the devoured lamb, they spread out and searched for more signs of the wolf pack. Following an imaginary line across the terrain, they seem to have found the path that the pack had been taking. Daryl instructed the men to hike up the ridge. They proceeded with caution as they neared the valley behind Sauk Mountain. They would have to be careful, if the trek took them any further south, they would be too close to civilization to shoot. The crack of the guns would be heard in the next valley, and they could tip off to the authorities. Undaunted, the men pursued their prey with vigor and lust. Hasegawa imagined the storied, cunning American beast stuffed and displayed in his study. The efforts would be worth the wait if they would be lucky enough to catch the pack.

Sean woke up slowly, groaning as he looked at the clock. Rolling over, he let out another groan, every muscle and bone in his body ached. Looking down at his bare chest, it looked like a checkerboard of bruises and scratches. With each movement, his head pounded ruthlessly. His head was killing him. Mixing the concussion with red wine was probably not a great idea, he concluded. Sammy lie next to the bed, looking up as if his master would hit the snooze button. Sean decided the dog must have been worn out from playing with Charlie, not to get up before him. The dog's eyes were still shut, but Sean saw his tail softly thumping on the floor.

"Come on, buddy," Sean said, "If I can get up, you can get up." He grabbed a t-shirt and sat up. Carefully stepping over his dog as he shuffled towards the bathroom, each step causing his legs and back to throb. He found the bottle of Advil, tossed a couple of pills in his mouth, and stuck his head under the faucet to chase them down. He wiped the excess water off of his face and headed for the kitchen. He made a beeline for the coffee maker and slunk onto his leather sofa. Sammy followed him into the living room and lay down on the floor next to the couch.

The two wine glasses on the floor next to the fireplace reminded Sean of the previous evening. He smiled. He was starting to like this woman, despite the trouble that seemed to follow her. A part of him didn't want to like her, but she appeared infectious to him. He loved the way she could volley back and forth with him; they laughed so hard together. With his latest round of injuries, she was sweet and nurturing to him.

He heard the coffee stop dripping into the pot and pushed himself up to retrieve a cup. Sammy followed dutifully behind. He seemed as sleepy as his owner. Sean took a sip of the hot fluid; it felt good going down. He looked through the glass windows of his sunroom to see light snow was falling outside. Yawning, he began planning his day. He was determined to find out who sent him that sick warning on his Jeep. The hunters from the bar were his primary suspects, but he couldn't let go of the growing possibility that Miranda's cousins were involved.

The hunting party made their way along the craggy ridge. Without tracking the wolves and lying patiently in wait, or without an immense amount of luck, even seeing a wolf was an infrequent event. Now in four days, Daryl hoped to run into a wolf for the second time and snare a trophy for the Japanese magnate. They weren't without subtenant knowledge. Due to the accounts from the ranchers and Tug and Daryl's previous exploits, they had a pretty good idea of where the wolves have been. The soft snow provided a clean trail giving the men a stable path to follow. The weapons the hunters carried could fire from a great distance with accuracy. They stacked the deck well, reducing fate's decision in their encountering the wolves on this particular hunt.

As the men crested the peak of the ridge, Daryl held his arm out, motioning to the others to halt. They hunkered down behind a large, snow-covered rock. Daryl retrieved his field glasses and trained them on the area below. Following the trail of single file paw prints as they crossed the meadow to a small grove of trees in the belly of an otherwise open valley. The forest almost looked like a small island in the wintry sea of white. Daryl couldn't be sure, but it appeared as though the prints penetrated this little stand of trees, and then vanished. Jeb and Hasegawa joined Daryl with their binoculars.

"Yes! I see them!" Hasegawa declared in an excited whisper. "There, in the grove, beside the rock. I saw the yellow eyes!"

"Good job, Mr. Hasegawa!" Daryl said. "Okay, fellas. We're about two hundred yards out. Let's see if we can't get a little closer." He surveyed the ridge, sighting a ravine that led down to a ledge a hundred feet above the valley floor. It would enable them an advantageous position looking down into the valley. He led, urging the group to keep quiet as they carefully made their way to the strategic location.

Daryl pointed to the ledge, and allowed Hasegawa and Jeb to pass. He stopped to tie his wet shoelace. Biting the fingertips of his gloves, he pulled them off of his hands. He watched as Jeb was the first to reach the ledge, setting up in firing position towards the small cluster of trees. Hasegawa knelt beside him. Daryl's cold, wet hands fumbled with the gloves as he tried in vain to complete the loop he was working. The gun resting against his knee teetered and fell down the ravine with a series of silence-shattering clanks.

The first wolf shot out of the grove at the sound of the falling gun. Jeb quickly fired his weapon at the blurry shape of the wolf. The wolf hit the ground hard, sprawling, heading into the snow. Another wolf ran out behind the first, following an identical path. Hasegawa fired his weapon, missing with his first shot. He fired several more times, each bullet trailing after the wolf that eventually disappeared into the thick trees leading north into the Cascade wilderness. The first wolf pushed his way up to make a desperate attempt at flight, but Jeb fired a second shot from his rifle. The bullet caught the wolf in the throat, dropping it to the ground instantly, its tongue dangling out of its mouth as its lungs bellowed for air for the last time.

By the time Daryl joined the men, the remaining wolves fled in the opposite direction of the ridge, out of sight and out of range. "Nuts!" he cursed, upset at alarming the pack and not being in position to get a shot off.

Hasegawa had made it clear to the men that if they were lucky enough to shoot a wolf, he wanted to bring it back and have a taxidermist prepare it for his trophy room. He would pay the boys a handsome reward if they were successful. That was all the incentive the McKenzie boys needed to ensure Hasegawa his prize. The men carefully made their way down the ravine to the valley floor. Daryl still hoped to see another wolf, but he would not be so lucky. Still, he was excited about Hasegawa's reward money, and another opportunity to further the extermination of these predators that his grandfather had instilled in him as soulless, wasteful beasts.

The wolves made their way to a tight grove of trees. It was an advantageous position for them, offering a protective stand where the wolves could smell the scent of any animals that made their way through the valley. The dense foliage provided cover for them, allowing the wolves to lie in wait for a young pronghorn or mule deer to pass by. Settling down to rest, they prepared for the evening's hunt when they were disturbed by the clatter from midway up the ridgeline.

The young female was startled. She saw the alpha leap to all fours and stand rigid. She assumed he intended to lead a charge into the forest surrounding the valley. Reacting, she lunged into the meadow, making four long strides before she was caught in the midsection with the first ball of steel, plunging her headfirst into the snow. She felt weak, but hearing a second shot, she pushed herself forward. Another shot rang through the valley, the wolf bolted with all of her might to propel herself away from danger, but heard yet another blast. This would be the last sound that she would hear as a second ball of steel ripped through her throat, slicing through an artery in a painful explosion of flesh and steel.

The alpha pair shielded the pups, hovering over them. They started to follow their siblings but were stopped cold by the sharp growls of the alphas. The pack leader knew that cover was their best ally. The sounds were coming from high on the ridge. They would avoid the distance between the cover and the rim and head for the forest by slipping out of the backside of the grove. The alpha first, the pups followed, nudged by the female as they quietly stole into the safe passage of the nearby thick stand of trees.

The hunters made their triumphant return to the McKenzie homestead. They found the crew industriously loading trucks and Sno-Cats with gear. Tug and Joe waved them over. "Boys, I know I gave you the day off, but we decided that it was time to move off of the homestead. We are going to move our entire operation to the training compound. We stay in the bunkers and pitch tents for the gear. Get all of your stuff and pack it in the bed of the truck. We move out in thirty minutes," Tug mandated. The boys helped Hasegawa unload the carcass. With years of practice, they skillfully strung Hishiro's wolf on a rack that the boys and their dad used for bleeding deer and elk. Hishiro took his ivory-handled knife and cut a slit in the belly of the wolf, draining the blood from its lifeless body. Taking one last look back at their coveted trophy, they ran off to retrieve their gear.

"Think they are ready?" Joe asked doubtfully.

"As much as they're gonna be," Tug shrugged. "Be better if Hasegawa didn't take the brothers off as his personal playmates and hunting guides. We don't have time for that, and it has scared up a lot of trouble."

"Trouble? Like that do-gooder snooping around at Diablo?" Lyndon asked.

"Exactly. Who knows what else? They seem to attract trouble. They sent the guy in Marblemount a little message, though. We'll see if that did the trick. If not..." Tug started.

"If not?" Joe questioned.

"If not, we take care of it permanently. The mission is in two days. We need to be quiet until then. After that, the McKenzies and Hasegawa can attract all the attention to themselves that they want," Tug said with a sardonic laugh.

Joe nodded in understanding as he watched the boys scurry out of the barn with their army surplus crew bags and toss them into the bed of one of the Cats. Satisfied the troops were sufficiently stocked, Tug gave the signal to crank the engines, and the rebel squad moved out.

Harold Billings, a thirty-year politician, Senator Timothy Small, and Jerry Rhinehart, Small's assistant, met in the Senator's office. Rhinehart had left Washington for the District of Columbia that morning. He was eager to get out of the area and away from the compound. He wanted to distance himself from the upcoming fray. Only Tug and Joe knew of his connection with Small and Billings. Hasegawa knew he was in league with a player in politics, but he did not know who, and they were determined to keep it that way.

The men had assembled to review the mission's progress. "So essentially, the Green Party, the Tea Party and the libertarians are getting together to seek legislation to ensure they have access to elections on par with us. The majority of the political supporters and lobbyists are gonna be in Seattle in two days?" Billings asked.

"Yessir, ninety-percent of the supporting vote on the new resolution will be isolated in one location. Fish in a barrel," Small said boastfully. "We have got them right where we want them."

"And you got Hasegawa to front the cash?" Billings asked.

"Who cares about his money. We have the weapons that his freighter was carrying. The men have been training with them for the last several days," Small replied with a smile. "The question is, what do we do with him when it's over?"

"Hmmm. Can we trust him?" Rhinehart asked.

"We don't have to trust him. We have his fingerprints on the murder weapons," Small cooed.

"Then we will have to take care of that loose end when the time comes. Along with the McKenzies and their backwoods friends from your own Idaho, Small," Billings added pointedly.

"The plans are already constructed. Gaskill knows that no one can be left behind to share what they know. No one can be captured. He will use them and fry them himself," Small replied.

"And you trust him?" Billings asked.

"You can never fully trust a guy like Tug Gaskill, but you can bet on them doing what is right for their own preservation, and leaving no trace keeps him alive as much as it does us," Rhinehart answered.

"Excellent. You know, this can slam the door on any upstart parties. If they get any more traction by the next election, we may never be able to save our system. Everything both sides have fought for will be in jeopardy. It will give us enough time to solidify our position with the American public and put all of this chaos to rest once and for all," Small concluded.

"Amen, gentleman, Amen," Billings said, raising his Scotch highball glass into the air.

Sean left the house. His sore bones and muscles were slowly beginning to loosen up. His grave demeanor gave away his aim; he was on a mission. Despite Miranda's pleading about her cousins, he was sure that they were responsible for the warning left on his Jeep. He was increasingly convinced that they were responsible for running him down. He wanted some answers. Adam and Shayne were busy running down the Japanese freight company angle. Sean was determined to extract answers from the McKenzies himself.

He drove into town, and starting with the Post Office. Sean asked the townspeople what they knew about the McKenzies. He found the postal clerk sorting through letters and asked the man if he knew anything about the family. The old clerk took off his cap and wiped his brow with his sleeve. Looking thoughtfully at Sean, he told him that they came in once in a while to pick up their mail. They never had anything delivered out to their house. As far as he knew, no one in town had ever been out there. Their homestead was supposed to be somewhere east of Diablo, deep in the woods. They were a very eccentric family, but that was pretty much all he knew about them.

Sean thanked the post clerk and moved on. He continued posing questions around town and received a similar story in each location. People in this town knew of the McKenzies, but never saw much of them or knew a lot about them. Old Lucius McKenzie used to stir up a fuss many years ago, with his intolerant rantings that both democrats and republicans were killing the country and should be ousted from the area. Most of the community ignored him and his ramblings, discounting the old man as a kook. Frustrated, Sean figured he would have to rely on Shayne to dig something up or get information directly from Miranda, if she was willing – which he doubted. She didn't seem very pleased with his line of inquiry implicating her cousins. He wasn't even sure if he would see her again.

The boys got a call from the convenience store clerk. Daryl received the call just as he was running out of the house to catch up with the caravan out to the new training site. He and Jeb had hunted with him in previous seasons. The clerk told him that one of the locals was in asking about them. Daryl asked if it was a city slicker looking boy, tall and thin, drove a red Jeep. The clerk confirmed each of the descriptors, and they hung up the phone. The convoy to the training barracks was ready to depart. The boys scrambled to reach their crew. Their minds churned, they knew they had to teach this guy a lesson – messing up their hunt, messing with their cousin, and now, snooping around on them. Daryl's blood boiled, they must do something about it.

Tug was just giving the signal for the last truck to move out. Daryl hastily alerted Tug to the phone call. "This is what I was talking about! This is the attention we don't need! Is there anyone who knows where the barracks are?" Tug asked.

"No, sir. It's a secret family spot," Jeb said, joining Tug and his brother.

"I don't need anyone snooping around. Does this man have any connection that can lead him out to the training site?"

The boys were reluctant to admit that Sean had been spending time with their cousin. Jeb finally admitted it. He knew there would be worse repercussions if he didn't. "Uh, he knows Miranda," he admitted.

"Your cousin? The girl I have seen around the house?" Tug asked incredulously.

"Yessir. She won't be no problem. She's family," Daryl chimed in, trying to assure his mentor.

"If it's a she and she knows this irritating man, then she *is* a problem," Tug snorted. He called Bud and Jenkins to the room and apprised them of the situation. "Find her. Before you come to the compound, you find her."

Tug looked at his watch. He had the training back underway. He wanted to get the crew set up at the compound before sundown. They could train in the evening. Tug scratched his head and finally decided to send two men to locate the McKenzie cousin and shut her up. If they ran across this "pretty boy", they would make sure that he was in no condition to talk either. He didn't trust the McKenzies to be effective in dealing with their family member, so he ordered the boys to join the others at the compound immediately. Tug reasoned that the other men would carry out their duties without regard to family loyalty.

Bud and Jenkins returned to the McKenzie house and sought out Bonnie McKenzie, "Ma'am?" Bud called out to the McKenzie mother. She came around the corner, she had an apron on and was drying a plate a well-used dishtowel.

"Yes, dear?" she called back.

"You seen Miranda, Daryl asked me to give her a message?" he asked.

"Oh, she went to town. She has been so good spending her days with Daryl and Jeb's grandmother and me. I thought she could use a break," Mrs. McKenzie said, and then whispered, "I think she found a man in town. Did you want to leave the message with me?"

The two thugs winced at the thought of the nuisance with Miranda. She was apparently off to see him again. They would wreck that little romance. The men thanked Mrs. McKenzie and about-faced to begin walking out of the house. The McKenzie Matriarch called, "Are you boys going into the woods to play those games?" But the men did not reply. They had work to do.

Miranda called Sean on his cell phone. She was already on Highway Twenty heading west. Her phone clicked into coverage and the number dialed. "Hey, Miranda! I was just thinking about you," the voice from the end of the line answered.

"Really, good thoughts?" Miranda smiled into her phone.

"Absolutely," Sean replied. Even over the phone, Miranda could tell Sean was grinning.

"How are you feeling? I was thinking I could come down for a little TLC," she said.

"Hmmm, I think I could use some of that," Sean said, still smiling.

"Who said it was for you? A girl needs some too, you know," Miranda teased.

"Yeah, come on down," Sean agreed.

"I'm already on my way."

Miranda arrived at Sean's riverfront home and parked her SUV. She had barely opened the door, and Charlie jumped out to find his friend. Sean heard them pull up and was ready for them. He opened the door, and Sammy ran out to greet Charlie and Miranda. Miranda hugged Sean as he led her into the house, the dogs followed happily behind.

"You want some cocoa or coffee?" Sean asked as they entered the living room. Miranda agreed to some cocoa and sat on the sofa, watching the snowdrift slowly to the ground through the large windows of the living room. Sean had a fire burning in the fireplace delivering pleasant crackling and popping noises into the living room. He joined her on the couch, and Miranda leaned over to give him a warm kiss.

"What's on your mind, Sean?" Miranda asked as she pulled back and studied his face.

"What do you mean?" he offered aloofly.

"I can tell. You have that look," she replied sternly.

"I guess I wear my heart on my sleeve, huh?" Sean admitted. "Well, I need to talk to you. It's about your cousins…."

"Sean, I have told you. They are not the ones who ran you down. They couldn't be, they are not like that. I don't agree with how they live and think all the time, but they are not murderers," Miranda protested.

"Maybe not, but I do think that they are poachers. The bear head last night…"

Miranda cut Sean off again, "We don't know that was them. It may have been a coincidence."

"Like them hanging out with the guys from the bar?" Sean retorted back.

"That's not fair!" Miranda was getting upset.

"What do you mean not fair? I know they are your family, but…"

"This was a mistake," Miranda replied, turning away.

"Miranda…" Sean didn't know how to get the information he needed without setting her off.

"Sean, if you want to know something about my family Sean, just come out and ask me," Miranda declared, turning to him, her hands on her hips.

"I need to know if they've been out hunting the past few days? What are they doing with the Asian man?" he asked.

Miranda stared at him, an ice-cold expression hung on her face, "I don't know and I don't see how any of this makes any sort of difference."

They sat quietly for a moment. Sean was furiously trying to think of the right thing to say. Miranda was preoccupied, reviewing the facts, trying to figure out whether she was trying to prove Sean right or wrong. Her stomach felt sick. Inside her head, she knew the possibility existed that her family was involved, and she *did* like this man, but he was in no position to question the people that she had known all her life. Abruptly, she decided that she had to err on the side of family loyalty. She stood up from the couch, "Thank you for the cocoa, but I think I should be going."

The dark mood was broken suddenly by the dog's reactions. Sammy's ears perked up, followed by Charlie's. Sammy let out a low growl and then a bark. He got up and ran to the door, Charlie followed. Sammy let out several warning barks. "What got into him?" Sean asked. He thought he had heard the rumble of a truck, but it didn't come down the driveway. He opened the door and the two dogs ran out to investigate. He surveyed his front lawn, but still didn't see anything. He turned to try and encourage Miranda to stay to talk things out. He gently touched her shoulder and looked at her calmly.

He was just about to speak when the dogs resumed their barking. Their tirade made Sean curious and instinctively tensed up. The manner in which they were barking conveyed an unusual tone. As quick as the barking began, it stopped just as suddenly. A horrible yelp from the front yard filled the air. Sean sprang down the hall to check on the dogs. He heard a sickening thump at his doorstep as he hurried down the hallway. He rushed to the front door and yanked it open. There was Charlie, limp on the doormat, his tongue drooping out of his mouth, blood covering his brown fur. The chocolate lab was struggling to take in breaths. He let out a quiet little whimper, the last sound that would escape him as his lungs slowed to a stop.

Miranda ran up behind Sean. She felt all of the blood in her body drain to her feet, almost passing out at the vision in front of her. "No! Charlie!" she cried. She moved forward, but Sean urged her back inside the house.

Sean had barely taken a step out on to the porch before he felt something hard hit him on the back of the head. As he dropped to his knees, another crushing blow railed into the back of his skull, forcing his body to hunch over, his forehead slamming to an abrupt rest on the cold concrete. Sean struggled to gather himself. A steel-toed boot delivered a vicious kick into his stomach. Expelling a bellyful full of air, he fought for consciousness as more blows were delivered.

Miranda pushed through the door and saw Sean doubled over. She shrieked as she saw two men trading kicks into his side, blood beginning to stream from the corners of Sean's mouth, painting the ground. Miranda recognized the men as the ones from the tavern. One wore his arm in a sling and, in his free hand, menaced a tire iron. The two men looked up at Miranda and paused in their beating of Sean.

"Hello, pretty," the man named Jenkins gave a toothy grin in her direction.

"Leave him alone!" she cried, running through the doorway and onto the porch.

Jenkins held up the tire iron, threatening to strike Sean in the head, freezing Miranda in place. "You and your boyfriend behave little girl." He rolled Sean over with his foot, grabbing Miranda's chin with his good hand as he did so.

Bud grinned at his friend, momentarily taking Sean for granted. Sean took advantage of the opportunity and hooked his leg into Bud's. With a mighty tug, he brought the large man to the ground. As Bud landed, Sean swung his elbow, delivering a punishing blow to his face. The hunter grabbed his nose and howled. Jenkins shoved Miranda to the floor and turned his attention back to Sean. Already up on his knees, Sean launched himself into Jenkins' midsection, plowing his assailant into the doorframe of the house, knocking the wind out of him. Jenkins let out a gasp trying to collect his breath. Bud recovered from the blast to his nose and hurled himself at Sean. Sean kicked out with his right foot, catching Bud square in the jaw, causing him to stumble back onto the dead Labrador retriever. Sean clasped his hands together and brought them down in a fierce chop on the back of Jenkins' neck. As the man fell to the ground, he met with the heal of Sean's shoeless foot catching him square in the face.

Seeing the melee and his master in trouble, Sammy came roaring up and leaped on Bud, tearing at him viciously. Bud screamed wildly, trying to avoid the gnashing teeth of the angry and protective dog. The hunter swung his arm up, hitting Sammy in the head with the butt of his revolver. The big dog let out a yelp and rolled onto the ground. Miranda collected herself and grabbed Sean's phone, calling 911. Bud, hearing her make the call, launched himself to his feet. Snatching the tire iron from the ground, he swung it wildly at Sean. Reassessing their position, he grabbed Jenkins by the collar and dragged him away from the porch. Sammy shook off his haze, getting up to his feet and began chasing after the men. Bud whipped his pistol out and aimed it haphazardly in the direction of Sammy. Sean let out a sharp whistle, and as the big dog was taught, he immediately dropped to his belly and froze. A second whistle sent him running back to his master as a pair of bullets raced by and impacted the snow a mere handful of yards away.

"If you keep snooping, we'll be back for the girl," Bud threatened, calling out to Sean and Miranda as he pulled his partner away from the scene. To ensure that they were not going to be chased after, he fired a parting shot in the direction of the doorway, a bullet piercing into the side of the house. Sean ducked and crawled into the foyer, dragging Sammy with him, slamming the door behind them. He peered out of the side window and watched Bud and Jenkins complete their retreat across his lawn towards the road.

In the safety of the house, Sean ran to see if Miranda was okay. He wiped a smear of blood from his mouth and found her in the kitchen. He saw her hanging up the phone. "I called the police, they are on their way," she said shakily.

Sean squeezed her, "Good. Are you okay?"

Miranda nodded weakly, "How about you? I am not sure your poor head needed any more trauma."

"I'll be okay. I'm, um, sorry about Charlie," he said, looking into her watery eyes. Her breathing was irregular, trying to hold in the sobs.

"I think you have a concussion, Sean. Let's get you taken care of," Miranda replied, avoiding the subject as she studied Sean's dilated eyes, gently dabbing at Sean's mouth with a paper towel. Once again, she went to work nursing Sean's wounds.

When she had him cleaned up, and all open injuries addressed, Miranda asked, "What is going on? Why would they do that to Charlie? Why would they attack us."

"I don't know for sure. They think we know too much about what they are up to and want to keep us quiet, I guess. That or they are trying to get revenge for the other night. I am trying to piece it all together. I swear I saw a green truck through the trees," Sean said.

"A green truck. Are you sure?"

"Am I sure it was your cousins'?" Sean asked back, looking at her expectantly.

"There are a lot of green trucks. I just don't know..." she didn't know what to believe. Miranda didn't know who to trust – this man she barely knew, or her flesh and blood - she agreed in silence that she would confront her family herself.

"Where do they live, Miranda?" Sean asked.

"I'll take care of it," she said sternly, her eyes welling up with tears. "Are you going to be okay? I'll call you later," she said flatly, grabbing her keys.

"I don't think you should go anywhere, Miranda, we were just attacked and shot at," Sean pleaded desperately.

"I am going to my family's house. I'll be okay," Miranda snapped and marched off to ask her cousins about Charlie and the attackers. She breezed by and left Sean and Sammy to watch her make a hasty exit. The big dog looked up at his owner as if to share his master's concern and inability to reason with the strong will of the auburn-haired woman.

Jim arrived quickly at Sean's house. He pulled his police SUV into Sean's driveway and passed Miranda as she wheeled her vehicle out onto the road. He got to the porch and looked down at the chocolate lab. He scribbled on his note pad and mumbled to himself, "A shot to the head from close range. Looks like a .44." Sean opened the door to see the deputy assessing the situation.

"What is going on, Sean? This is way more serious than a bunch of angry poachers," Jim said.

"It appears that way. It was the guys from the other night at the tavern," Sean replied.

"You think that is what this is all about?" asked the young Sheriff's Deputy.

"I don't know, maybe," Sean shrugged in a very non-committal way. "But I would say this is a little over the top." Sean pointed to where the bullet from Bud's gun impregnated the siding of his house.

"Yeah, I'd say this moves our charming lads into the felony category. So, if the dogs were out in the yard, did you hear the shot?" Jim asked.

"I think they used a silencer. When they shot into the wall, all I heard was a noise similar to that of a high-powered air gun," Sean reported.

"*Silencer*? What is a hunter doing with a gun with a silencer?" Jim asked, scratching his head, "Where do you suppose they went?"

"I have a suspicion," Sean started, "The McKenzie brothers that you and Adam told me about. As it turns out, the girl I met is their cousin."

"You're kidding? I didn't know they had family that was outside of their home, or gene pool for that matter," Jim laughed.

"Yeah, I have seen them with the tavern guys, too. Miranda says she has not seen them around the McKenzie's house, but I saw them drive away together the other day. And I think I saw the same green pick-up out on the road. May have been the same people who tried to run me down," Sean said.

"Hmm, poaching can be big business. Some of the country folks don't like to have their business messed with. But this is serious," Jim replied.

"What about the Japanese freight company – did you find out anything?" Sean asked.

"Still looking into that. Hasegawa Enterprises own it. Old Japanese money. Big time family business since the late forties. Nothing turned up yet. We have asked the Port Authority to look out for that van and try to investigate any possible links to the poaching trade," Jim replied, and then looked sullenly at the lifeless chocolate lab, "I guess I can bag this one. I'll take the slug out of the wall and take it to the lab. You got something to help pry that out?"

Sean nodded and jogged off to find a screwdriver and pair of needle-nose pliers. He returned quickly and began chipping away at his siding to extract the bullet. Shayne started to remove the body of the lab when Sean stopped him. "Would it be okay if I keep Charlie here for Miranda. I think maybe she would prefer to have him buried instead of him being sliced open in a lab. Can we assume the bullet in him will match the bullet in the wall?" Sean asked as he was finally was able to dig the bullet from the wood siding of the house and handed it to Jim, holding it in the teeth of the pliers.

Jim agreed, but only if he could get the bullet out of the lab first. Snapping on a pair of gloves, he used the needle-nose pliers to burrow into the wound in Charlie's head. Triumphantly, he extracted the bullet that ended the dog's life. The deputy dropped the fragment into an evidence bag and turned to Sean, "I'll take this stuff into the lab and go pay a visit to the McKenzies. I think it is time that I see what is going on over there. You need me to get you some medical attention?"

"No, I'll be fine. Just let me know what you find out," Sean said, picking up a clean corner of his welcome mat. Blood from the dog was splattered all over it, Sean walked to the trashcan and with a wrinkled nose, dropped the straw mat into the container.

Miranda was vacillating wildly between fury and distress. She drove her SUV through the light falling snow with rage-filled purpose. She wanted to know if her cousins had anything to do with what happened at Sean's. She didn't know who to believe. While her parents raised her very differently from her relatives, she did grow up spending the summers and holidays with them. Despite their differences, she cared for them deeply. She wheeled her SUV into the driveway and wiped away her tears with her gloved hands. When she felt like she collected herself, she marched into the house. Her aunt greeted her in the kitchen. "How's grandma?" Miranda asked.

"I think she's doing better. The house will be much quieter, as well. The men that your uncle has been working with have all left. I think the boys are off on one of their hunting trips," Mrs. McKenzie said.

"The boys aren't around?" Miranda asked, her mouth twisted in a perturbed grimace.

"No, dear, like I said, they are off on their hunt," Miranda's Aunt replied.

"Is Uncle around?" Miranda asked.

"Yes, I think so. Check his workshop. He's been out there all day fiddling with something," the aging McKenzie woman said.

Miranda spun away from her aunt and headed outside to find her uncle. She walked into the barn and crossed over to the workshop area. There, she saw Lucius and Hal studying something intently on the bench. Hal looked up, seeing her coming. He and the old McKenzie patriarch leaned over, considering some sort of a map. Hal hastily crumpled it up in a wad and tossed it in the corner of the workbench. "Hi hon, what can I do you fer?" he said with a nervous smile.

"Do you know where the boys are?" Miranda asked impatiently.

"They are on a hunting trip, deep in the woods. They will be gone for days," Grandpa Lucius answered.

"Have they been in town at all today?" Miranda continued her questioning.

"No, darlin', they left for the hunt first thing this morning. Something we can do for you?" Hal asked with a grin.

"It's just...have they hunted any wolf or a bear recently?" she asked.

"Why, that'd be illegal. Lucius and I have taught the boys right," Hal drawled.

"Well, how about clients? Have they been on any hunts with anyone lately?" Miranda pressed on.

The two elder statesmen shot each other glances, "Why all the questions, Miranda? You know the boys. They keep to themselves. Now we're trying to finish up a little project. You run along, and don't worry about your cousins. They ain't up to no good," Hal assured her.

"Thanks, uncle," Miranda said and walked out of the barn. Uncle Hal was always her favorite growing up. She remembered playing on his lap after family dinners, him protecting her when the boys got rambunctious. He even taught her how to fish. While she knew her family had some odd political views, she loved them for their warm and welcoming personalities. Still, she couldn't argue that something seemed strange over the past week around the homestead. She was curious about what they were studying. She undoubtedly picked up an odd vibe from her uncle. She also knew that they had bragged in the past about their illegal hunts; it would certainly not be out of character for them to be participating in less than appropriate hunts. Maybe Sean was right. She looked back and saw her uncle shove the document in a bag and then toss the bag into a feed barrel and secure the lid. Hal and Lucius sauntered towards the house, as the women were calling them in for supper.

Miranda peeled to the left as she exited the barn, jogging to the corner and ducking out of view. She stood upright and pressed herself against the wall of the shop. Waiting for the men to enter the house. As they went inside and the screen door slowly closed into place, she crept back into the barn.

Miranda made her way to the workbench, her eyes scanned the area, unable to detect anything out of place. She looked over to the feed barrel. It sat in a dusty corner under a giant rebel flag that distastefully adorned the wall. Miranda pried open the seal, letting the lid slide onto the floor. Inside was a sack stuffed with papers. She pulled the sack out and emptied the contents onto the workbench. Inside was a detailed street map of Seattle, crumpled into a ball. Reaching into, she pulled out the next document. It looked like a small copy of a blueprint. Studying the manuscript closer, she noted that it depicted one large room of a building outlined in red with all exits and windows highlighted in yellow. She frowned, it meant nothing to her., yet she was puzzled why her uncle would have it.

She peered more in-depth into the barrel again. In the bottom, lay an old, dusty book. Picking it up, she read that it was titled "The Code of the Greys". She opened the weathered tome. On the inset page was a picture of two young men in camouflage, proudly brandishing rifles. She squinted, looking closer. One of the men was her grandfather - Lucius McKenzie.

Twenty Two

"Miranda! What are you doin' in here?" Lucius McKenzie called out from the doorway of the shop.

"I, uh, was looking for some tools. Charlie died today, I was going to make him a little cross," Miranda stuttered, trying to think calmly.

"Sorry to hear that, good dog that Charlie. I see you found some of our stuff," Lucius pointed.

"Oh this, I didn't know what it was," Miranda said, trying to come across innocent, letting the map drift back down to the workbench.

"Well, I might as well tell ya. Hal and I was fixin' a surprise for your Grandma. Our fiftieth wedding anniversary is upon us, and we thought we would take her into the city. We ain't been there in years," Lucius lied. "Maybe you could help us. Do you think she would like that? Maybe a big bash with one of them fancy ice sculptures, the whole works. Do it up real nice."

"Uh, yeah, sure," Miranda smiled. "So that is what the map was for, makes sense, I guess," she said to herself.

"You'll keep this our little secret?" Lucius asked his granddaughter, both of his eyebrows raised in a rather mischievous manner.

"Of course, Grandpa," Miranda replied and slowly started towards the entrance of the barn.

"Where are you off to now?" Lucius asked, hoping he and Hal could return to going over the plans. They had hopes of studying Tug's work so that they could pass their learnings on within the Greys.

"Oh, I'm going to head back into town for a while. Say, Grandpa? Do you know two guys who have been hanging out with Daryl and Jeb, one of them has his arm in a sling?" Miranda asked.

"Nah, unh uh. Sorry, ain't seen no one like that. I was here when the boys took off today, too. Just the two of them," Lucius replied.

Miranda made her exit and headed for her car. She was hoping to catch up with Sean. She was so shaken up over Charlie, that she felt like she left things with him unsettled. She knew that Sean believes her cousins are in trouble, but she couldn't resist hoping that he had merely strung together coincidences. Now her uncle and grandfather were casting doubt on her thoughts. "Was Sean, right? Maybe her family didn't know what their friends have been up to. That must be it," she resigned to herself.

Jim drove east towards Diablo. He passed through the little town and kept on the highway as it rounded the pass. The snow had begun falling harder, casting its wintry spell on the spectacular backdrop. He wasn't sure where the McKenzie place was. They were self-sufficient for utilities and didn't require much interaction with the community or its services. He wasn't even sure how or if they communicated with the outside world. Old police reports he had found at the station afforded him a vague idea where the McKenzie homestead might be. The hard falling snow elevated his challenge.

He drove on, his windshield wipers clearing away the snow as swiftly as they could. There was no address, no mailbox to assist him in finding his destination. He tried to determine the correct turnoff by counting mileage. He watched the odometer spin as he cruised forward. According to the report, the turnoff to the McKenzie homestead should be just ahead. He slowed the police SUV down. Off to the right, he caught a glimpse of an opening in the brush, he gently applied the brakes, trying to avoid skidding in the icy conditions.

Jim slowed to turn around when he saw it, a narrow corridor hidden among one of the many twists in the highway. Fresh tire tracks snaked down a constricted path that led deep into the brush. The Sheriff's deputy eased the SUV onto the crude four-wheel-drive road putting the vehicle into gear as the tires spun in the deep snow. The road was so narrow, that tree limbs scraped along both sides of the SUV. The rough terrain was rough and jostled his body vigorously as he made his way into the woods. He couldn't believe these people lived out here.

Taking a peek at his odometer, he was already a mile and a half in off of Highway Twenty. He began to suspect that he hadn't selected the right road after all. The tracks that he followed were likely just those from a hunter's four-wheel-drive vehicle. Stopping the truck, he looked around, trying to discern any signs of a homestead. Seeing nothing but dense forest, he decided to head back to the highway. With no room to turn his vehicle around, he relented to keep driving into the wilderness until he found a suitable space to make a U-turn.

The odometer kept clicking along, reminding him how deep he was penetrating the deep backcountry. It wasn't until he was at mile five when he finally saw an opening in the rough road wide enough that he could turn around in. He slowed the big SUV down as it bounced along. Pulling to a stop, not he paused to check his senses. He rolled his window down to try and confirm the noise. Cocking his ear, he heard a sound reminiscent of a gunfire report in the distance.

Grabbing his police issue shotgun, he climbed out of the truck. In the distance, he could hear gunfire ricocheting through the forest in steady, rapid reports. "Holy cow, that sounds like semi-automatic," he said to himself. He leaned back in the truck and tried his radio – nothing. He was out of range this deep in the mountainous forest.

Hesitating for a moment, he decided he would leave his truck and take a quick look around. Carefully, he stepped into the woods, trying to remain in the cover of the trees and low-lying brush as he began to circle the clearing. He crept through the dense underbrush. The deputy stopped; he saw something just ahead of him. Focusing on the object, he began to recognize its shape - a Sno-Cat, covered in green and white netting – camouflaged neatly amidst the wintry landscape. He walked around it slowly. He saw another vehicle parked nearby, covered with the same mesh.

The gunfire continued, only a short distance away - several weapons discharged rapid-fire. Jim pushed further along the circumference of the clearing, hugging the tree line. Creeping from trunk to trunk, he crept closer to bringing the open space into view. Masked by the gunfire, Jim didn't hear the green pick-up pull up behind his police cruiser. He didn't hear the men search for him, as he listened to the constant barrage of weapons as he closed in. The deputy pressed on taking great care with each step towards the sounds. Cresting a short hill, he finally saw a camp, a row of tents and four permanent bunkers covered with snow, only crude doors revealing that a manmade structure nestled in the hill's bosom. Beyond the fortifications, he saw about a dozen men. Most were holding assault weapons as two other men walked around them, appearing as though they were giving instruction and pointers.

Jim paused, deciding what his next move should be. He realized that the safest course would be to drive back to Highway Twenty until his radio would receive reception. He started to turn, but stopped short - feeling the cold of steel pressed against his neck. He closed his eyes momentarily, a shiver running down his spine – Jim knew he was in trouble.

"Just stay right there, officer. Bud, grab his shotgun and hip-holstered .45," Jenkins, the man with an arm in a sling, said, keeping his handgun securely trained on the deputy.

Bud walked up to Jim and snatched his shotgun away. Jenkins kept his Winchester hunting rifle pressed against the deputy's neck. Bud popped the snap on the officer's holster and slid out the county issue .45.

"Move it," Jenkins said, nudging Jim forward with his rifle. Reluctantly, the deputy stepped forward, and the three men marched their way between the bunkers and out to the makeshift firing range.

All eyes fell on the men as, one by one, the mercenaries practicing their live-fire drills ceased their exercises. Tug saw the trio and turned to face them. For the first time that any of the men could remember, Tug looked uneasy. It only lasted a brief moment as the hardened mercenary snapped into action. He halted the training and motioned for Joe to come over.

"We found him snooping around the Cats," Jenkins said, giving Jim a shove with his gun. "What do we do with him?"

"First, we find out what he's doing here," Tug said gruffly.

Joe stepped up and tossed some cord to Bud, "Tie him up." Bud put down the weapons he confiscated from the Sheriff's Deputy and did as instructed.

"So, *deputy*, what are you doing out here?" Tug asked the county police officer.

Jim remained silent. Tug just nodded his head. He drew back and slammed his fist into Jim's stomach. The deputy's knees buckled, forcing Bud and Joe to hold him up.

"Let's try this again. What are you doing out here?" Tug growled.

Again, Jim remained silent. "I don't have time for this," he tossed Joe his gun. "Kill him."

"Don't you think we should wait and see if anyone comes after him?" Joe asked, not even readying his gun for firing.

"Not getting soft on me, are you Joe?" Tug asked, his eyebrow raised as he cocked his head.

"No, it is just, I don't want a bunch of feds crawling around here looking for him," Joe replied.

"Hmmm, maybe you're right," Tug agreed, as he studied the deputy's .45. "Why don't you lock him in the last bunker."

Joe almost seemed relieved. He grabbed the crook of Jim's arm and spun him around roughly towards the nearest bunker. In one fluid motion, Tug swung the Sheriff's Deputy's weapon and pulled the trigger. A bullet flew out of the handgun and burrowed into the back of Jim's skull. Slipping out of Joe's grip, the officer fell face-first into the snow.

Joe turned around, stunned, his face splattered with the deputy's blood, "I thought we were going to lock him up!"

Tug just laughed and sneered, "Joe, who are you really? I ask you to step up to the plate just once, and you turn pale on me. You know the rules, Joe. When someone knows too much, they are always a greater liability alive than dead." He swung Jim's gun in Joe's direction. "Let's see how this is going to go. He surprised you, you two-shot it out, and as luck would have it, you're both good shots. Nah, I shot him in the back of the head, that won't work. Ah, hell, I'll just kill you and figure it out later." Tug squeezed his finger back on the trigger, firing the gun for the second time.

Joe could feel the bullet whiz past his head and imbed itself harmlessly in the bunker behind him. Tug laughed. "Just kidding, I know it was just a difference in opinion. I need you on this one, Joe. Your help with this band of hooligans is essential, but when I tell you to kill someone, you had better do it. The next time anyone questions my command on this assignment, I *will* put a bullet through him. Alright. We have less than forty-eight hours. People are going to be looking for this man. We need to divert their attention. I need two men, one to drive his police vehicle to the site where the first wolf was killed, the other man plays escort and assists with hauling the body. He was following a lead and lost radio contact, and then he got lost in the storm. Leave his vehicle there. We'll get the manhunt away from here. As long as it takes more than forty-eight hours to find him, I really don't care."

Tug selected two men and sent them on their way. He gathered the rest of the trainees and returned them to running through their assigned drills. Monday was the eve of the mission. He would run through the computer simulation with the group a couple of more times. He had to ensure that they were in position for maximum impact. Tug had himself and Joe ready for quick removal and sniper locations for take-out if eliminating the entire squad became necessary. Then again, the more he thought about it, he and Joe as the only survivors of the mission was the only viable option.

Twenty Three

Sean put Charlie into a body bag that he got from Jim. It was one of the most challenging tasks that he had ever had to do. He carried the stiff body of the chocolate lab into his shed and shut the door. He turned away from the closed doors and sighed. What was going on around here? Sean needed someone to tell him where the McKenzies lived. Someone around here had to know them. The convenience store clerk! He had gone fishing and hunting with the McKenzies. He knew more than he was telling.

Sean got into the Jeep and backed it down his driveway. The Jeep was still rolling backward when Sean jammed it into first gear, causing snow and gravel to spray out as he hurried down the road. Moments later, he pulled into the convenience store parking lot. He recognized the old pick-up parked along the side of the building as the vehicle from earlier. The same clerk was still on duty. Hopping out of the Jeep, Sean strode into the store. "Jack. It's Jack, isn't it?" Sean asked, approaching the man abruptly. The rage he was feeling must have been apparent on his face.

"Yeah, look, man, I don't know what they did, I just told them you were asking around that's all," the clerk stammered, holding his hands up in front of him as he backed away.

"What? You *called* the McKenzies? Told them, I was…" the light bulb was slowly coming on for Sean. The men were working with the McKenzies. It was after they heard Sean was asking about them that the rednecks from the bar came to his house.

"Oh, let me tell you what they did," Sean said, sliding across the counter that was separating him from the clerk. "They came to my house. They killed my friend's dog. They dumped his dead body on my doorstep. They hit me in the head with a tire iron. They shot at me. They threatened an innocent *woman*," Sean informed him, snarling.

He took a quick scan of the area, snatching a jack handle that was left on the corner of the counter; he clenched it tightly in his fist. Wielding the weighty piece of steel in the air, "You ever been hit with a tire iron, *Jack*? It would probably feel like getting hit with this!" Sean slammed the jack handle down on the counter with a loud bang, shaking everything nearby. The store clerk leaned further back, away from Sean.

"Look, man, I'm sorry! I didn't know…" the clerk started.

"All you need is to tell me where the McKenzie boys live. You've been out there, right, Jack?" Sean growled at the store clerk. He was still wielding the jack handle menacingly. He was well within striking distance of the trembling clerk.

The clerk went pale and warm urine seeped its way down the front of his pants. He finally spit out, "The ranch is east, past Diablo, just before Washington Pass. It is hard to find. If you go too far, you'll end up down a long old four-wheel-drive path. We used to go hunting out there. I…I'm sorry, buddy."

Satisfied, Sean tossed the jack handle down. He placed two hands on the counter and vaulted over it. As his feet hit the floor, and he pushed the door to the store open, the clerk called out, "I'll kick your butt next time!"

Sean paused with one hand on the door. He turned and looked at the young man who walked around the corner of the counter. Sean's face was cold and purposeful, but then brightened into an evil, crooked grin, "Hey Jack, you might want to change your pants." Nonchalantly, he continued pushing open the door and walked out to the parking lot as the clerk looked down at the wet trail that led to his shoes. Mortified, he just bowed his head and slunk back behind the counter.

Sean hurried to his Jeep. Just as he opened the door, he heard brakes skidding to a stop in the road. He looked up to see Miranda's SUV pulling into the convenience store parking lot. Driving up to where he was standing, Miranda leaned her head out of the window, "I thought that was your Jeep."

"Yeah, how are you holding up?" Sean asked, his face displaying his concern.

"I'm okay. Where are you headed?" Miranda queried.

"Uh, well, I was just going to see your cousins. I was worried about you," Sean admitted.

"Sean, I told you that my family wasn't involved. I just spoke to them, and there is a rational explanation that clears things up, well, some of them at least. Can we just go back to your house and take care of Charlie?" Miranda asked softly.

Sean hesitated, his momentum had him all charged up to finally get answers from the McKenzie brothers. At the same time, he did understand Miranda wanting to lay Charlie fitfully to rest. "Alright," he conceded. He climbed into his Jeep, and Miranda followed him to his house.

"You sure you're ready for this?" Sean asked her as they got out of their vehicles.

"Yeah, do you mind if we just find a spot close by? It is so peaceful here," Miranda asked, taking the serenity of Sean's home, "He would have loved living at a place like this."

"I don't mind. We'll make sure you can visit Charlie anytime you want," Sean said. Together, they walked the perimeter of Sean's property, looking for just the right spot. They settled on a peaceful nook not far from the river next to a little tree that seemed appropriate for Charlie. Miranda forced a slight smile and turned away. Sean nodded and went to grab some tools. He entered the shed and selected the necessary items to chip through the cold ground, but he paused as he looked at the black bag that held the chocolate lab. He certainly could not understand how anyone could shoot a dog in cold blood like that. Charlie would just as soon lick you to death as pose any real threat. He was sure the McKenzie boys were behind it – a cruel act imposed on their cousin. Sighing, Sean grabbed his tools and walked out to the spot they had selected. He found Miranda there as he had left her, her arms crossed, crying.

"I'm sorry," Miranda sniffed, trying to straighten up.

"Nonsense," he said softly, giving her a strong and comforting hug. "Why don't you go inside and take care of Sammy while I do this?"

"No, I'll stay. Should we bring Sammy out?"

"Not until we're done," Sean replied. With her insistence on remaining at his side as he prepared her dog's grave, he began clearing away the snow from the ground. His task was not a pleasant one. He was sad and furious about having to bury Charlie. Moreover, he felt guilty that this incident happened because of him and at his home, no less. He stepped down hard on the shovel; it hit the hard winter ground with a loud "chink". His mind wandered as he worked. He wondered why the men would threaten

Miranda, that didn't make sense to him. He figured the McKenzie boys were pissed about him seeing their cousin, but they should be threatening *him*. The shovel was barely chipping away at the frozen ground. He shuffled off to the shed to grab his pickaxe. He would need it to break up the icy soil.

Sean's mind continued reviewing the facts of the past couple of days. What did the men not want Miranda to tell him? About poaching? He heaved the pick to the ground after he had successfully broken out a four-foot-wide basin. He had at least whittled away enough of the top layer, that he was able to trade for the shovel. He broke the silence and polled Miranda, "What do you think is going on? I can see these guys, your cousins, whoever, not being real happy about us being together, but why threaten you? Why do this to Charlie?"

"I don't know, Sean. It doesn't make any sense. I went to the house. Grandpa said the boys had been gone all day on the first of a multi-day hunting trip. Their friends, too. I asked him about the men that came here, and he said he had never seen the guy with the sling," Miranda said, hoping that her Grandfather's word was strong enough evidence.

"The guy at the convenience store. He called your family to tell them that I was asking about them, suddenly guys are showing up at my doorstep. They shoot Charlie and thump me with a tire iron," Sean recounted, take a moment to lean on the handle of the shovel o he could look at Miranda directly.

"All because I am seeing you?" Miranda asked, sullenly watching Sean dig out a grave for her chocolate lab.

"That is what I don't get. I think I stumbled onto a poaching ring. I know I can't be sure, but your family might be mixed up in it," Sean said. "The Japanese man you saw visiting at the house. What do you know about him?"

"Not much. Some businessman, I guess. It sounded like he was going to do some hunting with my cousins. That's about it. Why?" Miranda asked.

"Well, I swear when I got run down, the Japanese man was there. The van that was in the parking lot had some sort of Asian writing on it. I know that the bear I found in the woods had its gall bladder and paws removed – a popular delicacy in certain cultures used for medicinal purposes. I think that he was there to arrange for the delivery of those bear parts. You say your cousins took him hunting, well, I think that is what they were after. They could have taken him to the exchange, freaked out when they saw me, and ran me down," Sean theorized as he went back to work on the grave.

"Sean, you don't know that. My cousin may have taken him hunting; that is what they do. But attempted murder…I'm sorry, but you are barking up the wrong tree," Miranda snapped, turning away.

"Come on, Miranda. The facts are starting to pile up, and each time I turn around, they are in some way connected to your family. I know it's not what you want to hear, but that is the truth," Sean replied firmly.

The air hung heavy in the silence that followed their discourse. Sean diligently pressed on with his unpleasant task. Miranda brooded in her internal conflict. She couldn't shake off the fact that Sean might be right, but she was unwilling to admit that out loud. After all, she had just met Sean, and her loyalties had to remain with her family. Guilty until proven innocent – the American justice system had prevailed with that ideal for years, why should it not ring true in her mind? She stared across the Skagit River as if the answers would sweep down the turbulent waters towards her. The currents denied her the response that she needed.

Sean finally carved out a hole that he felt was satisfactory. The time had come, a morbid, sad end to the conversation that was creating thick tension between the two. Sean lifted the black polybag and gently lowered it into the grave. Miranda placed one of Charlie's favorite toys in with the bag. They took one sullen moment to say goodbye to Charlie for the last time before he would be forever offered to the earth. Miranda shook her head slowly, and Sean began refilling the hole with dirt. He found the first shovelful extraordinarily challenging to pour over the body of the dog. It seemed almost disrespectful in its finality of life on earth. Miranda, who had been holding herself stoically, began to cry uncontrollably.

Sean continued to sift spade after spade of dirt into place. When he finished, he left Miranda and the mound of overturned dirt to mourn in peace. He returned his tools to the shed and stopped by his workbench. Picking up a section of the picket-shaped garden fence, he snapped off a couple of the pieces and, with a couple of nails, fashioned a white cross with the wooden slats that he had freed from their moorings. Slowly, he made his way across his yard and softly palmed Miranda's shoulder, giving it a slight squeeze. She leaned her head on his shoulder and wiped her cheeks with her hands. Sean held her for a moment and then kneeled to place the cross on the mound. Once again, he let go of her and let her have some time at the site to herself. He went back into the house and put some water in his kettle to boil.

Sammy joined Sean and nuzzled his leg. The big dog dutifully followed his master around the house, his mannerism sullen as if mirroring how his two human companions felt. Sean went to the window and silently watched Miranda. She stood above the grave, her head in her hands, shivering in the cold. Wiping her tears on her sleeve, she turned towards the house. Sean backed away from the window and went into the kitchen. Grabbing two cups and filled them with cocoa. He reached above the cabinet and pulled down a bottle of Raspberry Schnapps to add to the concoction.

Miranda walked into the kitchen. She was holding her arms close to her body, still trying to shrug off the cold. "Drink this," Sean said, holding out the cup of cocoa. Miranda accepted the hot mug and brought it to her lips. The warm liquid felt good as it warmed her from the inside out. Sean tenderly led her to the sofa by the fireplace to warm up, "Hanging in there?"

"I'll be alright. Charlie is…was like…," she started and began crying. Sean grabbed her cup as Miranda started to shake. He set the mug down and held her tight.

"Like family, I know," Sean said, his voice calm and soothing. Miranda nestled closer in his arms. Sean stroked her back, trying to comfort her. They sat contently immersed in profound silence, until Miranda eventually fell asleep in his arms.

Twenty Four

The two men that Tug assigned to dispose of Jim's body drove hastily down Highway Twenty. They were eager to complete their mission as swiftly as possible, as one man was driving the Sheriff's vehicle, and if they got caught, the entire operation would be in jeopardy. They made their way to the turn-off for the Hidden Lake Peak Trailhead. The road became increasingly steep, and each vehicle had to be locked into low four-wheel drive to maintain traction. Reaching the clearing, they were relieved to find no traces of late winter hikers or hunters at the trailhead. Without hesitation, the men grabbed the body of the Sheriff's Deputy and made their way up the trail. The snow had begun falling hard, increasing their desire to make it back to camp swiftly.

Their instructions were to carry the body as high up the trail as possible and find a deep ravine to toss the body into, preferably an alpine lake or crevasse. The men knew that a hike too far up the mountain in these conditions would take entirely too long. Lugging the dead weight of the deputy up the slope, they were motivated to find a spot quickly. They surveyed the area. The terrain to the east sloped off dramatically. It was well off of the trail, and nearly invisible this time of year. They picked Jim's body up and hauled him to the edge of the mountain. With a concerted motion, they heaved the stiff corpse off the side of the face. They watched in delight as the body twisted and rolled its way into a deep crevice.

Satisfied, the men watched as the dead deputy sunk into a deep trough of snow, leaving most of the body covered. With more snow falling, it would not take long for any trace of the police officer would completely disappear, as well as erase their tracks that they left behind. Not precisely what Tug had asked of them, but it would do the trick, they thought.

Hurriedly, they returned to the parking lot and jumped into the four-wheel-drive truck, leaving the deputy's SUV behind. The idea was that the young patrolman had returned to the area to investigate the poaching incident and wandered off trail. With any luck, a search for him would divert most of the law enforcement resources in the region. Even with the efforts of a search team, the body could lay buried until the late spring thaw. The squad of radical mercenaries would be long gone. Only the wake of their destruction left behind.

Miranda slept for about an hour, when she finally lifted her head from Sean's chest and through sleepy eyes, looked up at him groggily. "How long have I been out?" she yawned.

"Just a little while," Sean whispered his reply.

"Oh, you poor thing," Miranda stated, "You are so sweet to me." She sat up and looked up at Sean intently.

"Oh, so you're back to liking me," Sean said softly.

"I like *you*. I'm just not in love with some of the ideas you have. You have been more than kind," Miranda responded.

"Nah, I'm just doing what any guy would," Sean scoffed.

"No, at least not any of the guys I've known," Miranda corrected him. "So, what now? What is your next step?"

"I don't know. I haven't felt like I have gotten anywhere with the authorities. They just don't have a lot of jurisdiction over these things, I guess," Sean replied. "I really would like to ask your cousins a few questions. At least find out about their friends."

"Well, even if you went out there, you wouldn't find them right now. They are off on an extended hunting trip. Who knows when they'll get back," Miranda answered, glad to have a built-in excuse for not rehashing that argument with him right now.

"I might try a different angle, the diplomatic approach. I have a friend in Seattle who I want to pay a visit. I think I might get closer to some of the answers we are after, like why Adam isn't getting any of the help that he has requested," Sean said.

"It looks like it is snowing pretty hard. Are you sure you should drive to Seattle right now?" Miranda said, looking out the big window overlooking the yard and the river.

"Yeah, the Jeep can handle it. If I leave now, I could be back before it is too late," Sean said.

"This might sound a little forward, but do you mind if I stay here tonight? Most of my family is off hunting. Grandma and Aunt Helen go to bed so early, I don't want to be alone tonight," Miranda asked, her voice sounding sad.

"No problem. Just remember, those guys know where I live. Regardless of whether or not they are in league with your family, they don't seem to mind targeting you in their threats. In fact, with the last round of excitement, it almost seemed as though you were the target. Are you going to feel safe here alone?" Sean asked her.

"Yeah, I have Sammy. I just won't let him out. You'll have to hurry home," Miranda smiled. It was the first smile Sean had seen from her in several hours.

"I will," Sean replied. "Do you want to go home and grab some stuff? I'll give you a spare key. You can come over whenever you want. Are you sure you'll be okay?"

"Thanks, Sean, I appreciate it," Miranda said, her voice catching a cold edge to it.

"Look, I'm just trying to help. Just in case you change your mind...," Sean dug in his kitchen junk drawer to find his extra key and handed it to Miranda. He gathered his gloves and keys and started for the door.

"You be careful out there," Miranda said and placed a soft kiss on his cheek.

"I will. Stay safe yourself. If you need anything, all of the local numbers are in that little book by the phone," Sean said, pointing to the kitchen counter and headed out of the door.

Miranda called to Sammy and patted the seat to let the big dog know he should jump into her truck. With her travel companion settled next to her, she maneuvered the SUV out of the driveway. Charlie's death shook her. She wasn't sure who or what to believe. Sean swore that her cousins were mixed up with those guys. Nothing was making sense. She knows her cousins wouldn't hurt her or Charlie, so they couldn't be in league with the hunters form the bar. She pulled into the long driveway of the McKenzie homestead. As she let Sammy out, he ran furiously around the yard sniffing all of the traces of Charlie his nose could conger up.

Miranda went into the old, weathered house of her relatives. She checked on her aunt and her grandmother. They were sitting in the living room drinking tea. She stopped long enough to exchange a few pleasantries and scampered to her room to collect her things. She paused on her way out. Her grandmother was already asleep in the chair, a twisted mass of yarn and knitting needles resting in her lap.

"Aunt Helen, when is Grandma's anniversary bash? I want to make sure I am in town for it," Miranda whispered as she queried her aunt.

The McKenzie mother looked at her with a quizzical look, "What are you talking about?"

"You know, for their fiftieth," Miranda said.

"Fiftieth? They've been married for fifty-four years. And their anniversary isn't until November," Helen McKenzie said.

"What? Oh…" Miranda stuttered, "I, uh, must have been thinking something else."

"Going somewhere?" her aunt asked, spying at the overnight bag that Miranda had hastily thrown together.

"Yes, I am going to Sean's. Something terrible happened today," she admitted.

"Oh, what dear?" her Aunt cooed.

"Charlie died. Sean helped me with him," tears started to well up in Miranda's eyes, her voice choked.

"Oh, Miranda," Mrs. McKenzie rose to hug her niece, "How? What happened?"

"He was shot, probably a stray bullet from a hunter…" her voice trailed off, she didn't want to get into a long conversation with her aunt.

"If only everyone were as responsible as Daryl and Jeb," Mrs. McKenzie scolded no one in particular.

"Yeah, Aunt Helen, if only," Miranda replied, almost under her breath.

Hal McKenzie stormed into the house, "Miranda, who's dog is that running around my yard?"

"Oh, that's my friend's. He went to Seattle. I told him I would watch Sammy for him. Cute, isn't he?"

"He's alright, least he's a real dog, not some damn floor mop some people call dogs. Still can't beat a good hound…" Hal grumbled as he reached in the refrigerator for a pitcher of iced tea.

"Is he staying in Seattle? It's going to be icy tonight," Mrs. McKenzie said.

"He'll be back. He is just visiting an old friend. Someone he used to know when he worked with the government," Miranda replied. She was hoping Sean would get back early. The North Cascades Highway could get very dangerous when winter weather hit.

"Government, the government is all a bunch of crooks running this country into the ground. What kinda hooligan are you running around with? You shouldn't see him. He's trouble!" Hal barked at his niece.

"Oh Hal, leave her alone," Helen McKenzie ordered her husband.

"I'm going to take off guys, I'll see you later," Miranda said, giving each one of them a kiss. She walked over to her grandmother and covered her shoulders with the very withered and frayed blanket that had slipped into her lap. Miranda grabbed her bag and made her way out the door. She scratched Sammy behind the ears as she started up her SUV.

As she drove down the long and bumpy McKenzie driveway, heading for Sean's house, her mind was spinning and sorting through everything that she and Sean have faced. She was adamant about her family not being involved in all of the trouble that had been developing. But why did her grandfather and uncle lie to her about the building drawing and map? More things that just didn't make sense added to a growing list of facts that were beginning to overwhelm her assurance of her family's innocence.

Hal shuffled off for his den. He reached in the file cabinet drawer and grabbed the secured radio Tug gave him. "This isn't a good time. What do you need? This channel is for emergencies only!" Tug's voice declared over the radio, annoyed that his work was broken up by one of the foolish McKenzie tribe.

"It's that guy from Marblemount. The one, you guys, were talkin' about when the boys took that Japanese fellow to Liberty Bell. He's going to Seattle to talk to a 'friend' in the government. I have a bad feeling about that. I just thought you should know. He left probably an hour ago. Supposed to be back sometime this evening," Hal McKenzie reported.

"Hmmm, good work, Hal. This might just be the opportunity to exterminate the pest that keeps buzzing around. How did you happen to get this information?" Tug asked, rubbing his chin.

"Oh, just one of the folks from town. We aren't completely hermits out here," Hal scoffed, not wanting to share the fact that his own niece could be the one bringing trouble into the plan.

"Good enough. Keep your ears posted for anything else that comes up. Otherwise, just leave these boys out here to me," Tug signed off with the

McKenzie father. He thought to himself; he needed to get this guy out of the way. He radioed to the two men he sent to dispose of Jim. They reported that they had delivered the package and were heading back to the training camp. He diverted them for one more task. This time they would make sure that the little do-gooder nuisance got the message – by shutting him up permanently.

Twenty Five

Sean peered through his windshield as the little wipers on the flat sheet of glass did their best to keep up. The snow had begun falling steadily, drastically reducing visibility on the roads. The transition from winter to spring had brought very erratic weather to the region. "Guess the groundhog saw his shadow," he muttered to himself. He was glad that his friend had agreed to meet him north of Seattle in Burlington. That would save him quite a bit of driving time.

Rachel York was a good friend of Sean's. Bouncing between Olympia, Seattle and the District of Columbia, she managed the northwest for the Department of Interior. A good part of her job was balancing the interests of the lobbyists from all sides. She had to entertain the notions of radical conservationists on the left and staunch business interests on the right. Sean had worked with her on several projects for the Conservancy, becoming friends during their frequent negotiations. Sean always appreciated her straight-forward nature, a rarity in the political setting.

Rachel was tall, had long black hair, and embellished her presence by wearing the most current in fashionable clothing. She carried herself with the perfect blend of femininity and power, allowing her to command as much respect as she did second glances. The Assistant Regional Director for the Department of Interior was a force to be reckoned with - a shrewd businesswoman, but never one to yield on her principles.

Sean strode into the café that they had agreed on. The little bell above the door announced his arrival, getting the autonomic response of the patrons' eyes greeting him. He saw that Rachel was already there, nestled in a table that sat along the wall. Her friendly smile instantly gave Sean a sense of comfort in his longtime ally. She was as Sean had remembered her, a remarkably elegant and attractive woman that exuded a poised strength and confidence. She stood to hug Sean, revealing a sleek grey dress that was cloaked by her long, white wool coat.

"I've missed you," Rachel said, squeezing Sean tightly.

"Hi Rachel, how've you been?" Sean asked, giving her a slight squeeze back.

"Oh, you know this racquet. Trying to separate the bull from what's real. It seems to get a little more difficult every day," Rachel replied, "You look great. How have you been?"

"Until recently, I would say I have been pleasantly bored. As you can see from my eye, I have found a bit of adventure in my serene little world," Sean said, pointing to his black eye that was starting to heal, the dark purple had relented to a pale yellow.

"I thought you had a little shiner," Rachel smiled and shrugged, adding, "Kind of cute that way."

"Thanks," Sean said, his eyes gave way to a subtle roll, the only indication that the offbeat compliment made him slightly uncomfortable. The waitress came over and asked to get them some drinks and took their orders.

"So what's going on Sean, you sounded so troubled over the phone?" Rachel asked.

"Well, the best I can figure is, I stumbled into some sort of a poaching ring. I am still trying to piece it all together; I was hoping you would help me out there. Were you able to get any of the info that I requested?'

"Yeah, some. I am still trying to get more. The freight company you asked me about belongs to the Hasegawa family. They own a series of vessels and distribution sites that run between Japan, the U.S., and Africa. The D.O.I. has some information on them because they have been busted several times for trafficking articles protected under the Endangered Species Act. I was able to dig up something interesting, though. The Hasegawa family has been prominent in Japan, fighting against their inclusion in the singing of the One World Free Trade Treaty imposing international laws under the act. They led a group of importers in proposing a retraction of Japan's agreement in the act. They were not successful. What was really interesting was some business owners in the United States, and even a few politicians had tried to offer their support for the trade group in Japan," Rachel shared with Sean.

"Anyone from Washington?" Sean asked with interest.

"No, the closest was a senator from neighboring Idaho and a senator from Colorado. The guy from Idaho was Republican Senator Timothy Small. He's not your typical conservative. Generally pretty quiet, but he did pop up on this Japan thing. He has been hammered in the past for some insensitive statements. He votes anti-big government and anti-environmental, pretty much anti-everything. He has been in opposition of the FTO and other free-trade agreements, but overall quietly assumes the party line. I don't see him as being a part of any criminal activity, though," Rachel said.

"The other guy?" Sean probed.

"Harold Billings - an old, old-time democrat. Part of the machine. Instrumental in DNC for decades. The old guard of politics. Typically voted pro-NAFTA, pro One World, pro-UN...until recently when he made some cautionary statements to his own party," Rachel replied.

"How about big-business, who were the representatives who supported Hasegawa's cause?" Sean asked.

"A whole variety of folks. Industries from oil, steel, weapons manufacturing, textiles..." Rachel started, she flipped through the pages of a manila file folder, scanning the lists of business support.

"I get it. How about poaching? Have you ever run across any poachers using military-type weapons?" Sean asked, switching gears.

"It happens randomly. Usually not a poaching ring, blasting an animal to pieces is not generally a way to increase profit," Rachel said.

"Hmm. A couple of the animals near the preserve have been blown to bits, while others killed for parts. I witnessed an exchange with the freight company's delivery truck. It was with some hunters from out my way. I am pretty sure a Japanese man was there too. I saw him right before a jacked-up four-by ran me over," Sean filled her in.

"Did this happen to be the man?" she asked, handing Sean a photo from her file.

Sean looked at the picture and returned his mind to the afternoon, where he was run down. The man in the photo did resemble the man who was in the parking lot that day, but he couldn't be sure. It was pretty much a blur. "Could be," Sean replied, handing the picture back. "It was a blur and the snow was coming down pretty good. What do you think we can do?"

"I'm afraid not much. Our agent in the North Cascades sent in a report. I think you know him, Adam Raines. He has requested assistance. We are authorizing a few more field agents to sniff things out, but we don't have a timeline for when they will be able to be dispatched. I have made the necessary resource moves, but there seems to be a buzz that resources will be diverted. I will keep looking into things for you. Oh, and you had asked about what? The McKenzies? Our system didn't really have much on them, nor did the FBI's - a couple of misdemeanor charges for Hal, Daryl, and Jeb. Small-time stuff. Received some fines and revocation of hunting licenses, though it turned out they never applied for any hunting licenses to be confiscated. As long as they stay small time, the consequences for these things just aren't that severe with our current laws. I'm sorry Sean, That is just all I have right now," Rachel said.

"I appreciate you meeting me and helping out with all of this. Can I keep the picture of Hasegawa?" Sean asked.

"Yes. It is just a printout from the file. I hope I come up with more for you. And Sean, it was nice seeing you again. Don't be a stranger, okay?" Rachel said with a smile, pushing the photo of Hasegawa closer to Sean.

"I'll try not," Sean said, giving her a shy smile.

"I'll call you, drive safe," Rachel said.

"Thanks." Sean gave her a quick hug and hurried out of the café. He wanted to beat sundown to minimize the potential for ice on the highway. He was also eager to get back to Miranda. He didn't like leaving her alone with everything that had been happening. He didn't like the fact that these people knew where he lived. He felt responsible for Charlie and would feel horrible if anything happened to Miranda. Tossing the file that Rachel made for him onto the passenger seat, he started up the Jeep. Through the increasing onslaught of fresh snow, he headed for home.

He daydreamed thoughtfully of sitting in front of the fireplace with Miranda. His array of skirmishes had left his body weary, and he longed for rest. The little Jeep zoomed along, the deep tread on the big tires handling the fresh snow with ease. Occasionally, he would see an abandoned vehicle on the side of the road, skid marks cutting a path through the snow on the slick asphalt. He turned up the radio and relaxed in the driver's seat. He was able to make decent time with most drivers opting to avoid the road during the harsh weather. His biggest obstacle was having to carefully pass a plow that was clearing a lane on I-5.

The exit for Highway Twenty beckoned a happy sigh for Sean; he was now about forty-minutes from home. He passed the turn off for the Ranger Station in Sedro-Wooley and headed towards the Cascade Mountains. As he left town, he noticed a truck pull out behind him. He didn't pay much attention to it, except that the height of the vehicle allowed for the headlights to shine in the reflection of Sean's mirror. The tall stance of the Jeep precluded most other cars from doing so.

Sean drove on, the lonely twists and turns of the North Cascades Scenic Highway, giving way to the curvy foothills of the mountains. Sean slipped the Jeep into four-wheel drive high to provide more grip on the pavement. As the last bit of civilization disappeared in his mirror, he noticed the truck that had pulled out behind him was closing in.

The men in the big four-wheel drive knew their mission. They had to deal with the city boy in the Jeep. They figured the twisty roads of the wintry Cascades would make an ideal setting. They saw the red Jeep pass by their spot, just east of the town of Sedro-Wooley. The driver, one of the men who had come to join the McKenzies from Idaho, pulled the pickup onto the road. Pressing down on the pedal, the truck gained ever-so-slightly on the targeted Jeep. He did not want to tip off the driver he was pursuing too early.

The two vehicles made their way into the Cascade foothills. Any traces of towns and civilization, slipped away into the darkness. The windshield wipers did their work, keeping the view of the little square taillights in sight. The driver pushed harder on the pedal as the truck slipped through the snow and up the hill. He was able to bring the vehicle rapidly towards the Jeep. Flipping a switch on the dash of the truck, he sent a row of powerful lights beaming through the night ahead of them, creating a spotlight around the Jeep. The passenger confirmed the license plate number and nodded to his cohort.

The driver grinned and downshifted as he stomped on the accelerator. The back wheels of the truck slipped slightly, but then bit into the road, lurching forward. The Jeep began to drift to the right as if to let the big truck pass. The driver cranked the pickup into four-wheel drive and kept its pace, closing in on the thin bumper of the vehicle ahead of them.

The hefty green pick-up menaced forward, its modified bumper fashioned of a three-inch-thick slab of wood attached to a pair of bars welded onto the frame of the truck acted as a plow. It barreled ahead, swerving just to the left as it impacted the back of the Jeep. The force rocked the truck, but the short-wheel based-Jeep faired a more severe, jarring blow.

Sean tried to mind his own business and not pay too much attention to the truck behind him. He tended to be a bit hot-head when negotiating traffic while he commuted in Seattle. Since his move to the North Cascades, he had tried to turn over a new leaf and not let ignorant drivers bother him. Occasionally, he would glance up in his rearview mirror. He swore the truck was closing in on him. "Idiot, he doesn't need to be driving that fast on a night like this. Frankly, I probably don't need to be going as fast as I am –

and he's gaining on me," he muttered to himself, "Fine Sean, if he wants to be a jackass, let him squeeze by."

Sean gently nudged the Jeep towards the side of the road, signaling to the other vehicle to pass him. He watched in his rearview mirror only to see the truck maintain its path directly behind him. He winced as his rearview mirror filled with blinding light. Six high-powered KC lights were powered on, filling the night with oppressive brilliance. Sean looked away, his vision distorted by the sudden burst of light; he tried to use the feel of the road to guide him. He blinked away the blurriness and found he was edging ever closer to the side of the highway, he quickly corrected. He could tell from the glare in his side mirror, that the vehicle behind him was closing in, still in his lane. Sean quickly downshifted and jammed his foot on the accelerator. Just at that moment, the Jeep was struck on the driver side of the rear bumper.

The Jeep launched into a spin, momentarily pointing the Jeep towards the woods. Sean, downshifted again, taking his foot off the accelerator, and steered gently back towards the middle of the road. He reasoned that the truck might have forced him entirely off the road had he not just been accelerating. The truck behind him, likely out of a brief lapse in courage, backed off when the vehicles made contact.

Sean stomped the accelerator, the four-wheels of the Jeep dug in and launched the light SUV forward. The truck behind him was putting on a burst of speed as well. Sean gunned the engine and shifted again. He was successfully widening the gap between him and the truck behind him. His heartbeat was thumping wildly against his chest, as he continuously traded glances forward on the curvaceous mountain highway and the assailants behind him. Navigating the North Cascades Highway during a winter storm was a treacherous undertaking by itself, never mind at high speeds and a maniac playing bumper tag with you.

Sean tried to keep the Jeep in top gear and up to higher speeds, but the slippery roads and the dangerous turns forced him to ease up a bit. It was enough to keep a little distance between him and the truck, but not enough to pull away completely. Sean came up to a curve, shifting down into third, hoping to accelerate quickly out of the turn. As the Jeep headlights swept in front of Sean, they caught the gleam of two yellow dots in the middle of the road – the frightened eyes of a bull mule deer! Sean used his gearing to slow the Jeep down, swerving towards the butt end of the frozen animal. Fortunately, the noise of the skidding Jeep startled the deer into action. The agile animal leaped forward, just escaping the front bumper of the four-wheel drive.

The avoidance maneuver was enough to allow the big green truck to catch up to Sean. It swung around the curve and accelerated, slamming into the rear quarter of Sean's Jeep. The crunch sent Sean's heart into his stomach as he gripped the wheel. He spun towards the edge of the road, his headlights flashing an indecipherable vista in front of him. He snatched the gearshift, slamming the Jeep into second, pressing hard on the brakes, hoping the mix of down-shifting, four-wheel drive, and anti-locks would gather control. The impact from the heavy truck was too much for the little red Jeep, it continued spinning over the edge of the road, towards the steep bank of the river, which lie a frigid seventy feet below.

Sean knew his location on the highway thoroughly, and knew he was in trouble. The treacherous turn opened up on a straight-away that transitioned from forest on both sides to a dramatic drop to the Skagit River on the right. The Jeep bounced down the embankment; Sean undid his buckle with his left hand and gripped the roll bar as he was thrown out of his seat and onto the roof of the car. The sides of the tires caught the deeper snow on the side of the road, momentum forcing the Jeep to roll over on its side.

Sean released the latch of the convertible top, as the Jeep was completing its roll. The contents of the vehicle, including Sean, were deposited onto the snowy bank of the cliff. The roll bars, slammed down onto the ground, inches away from slicing off one of Sean's arms. The Jeep continued rolling, minus its roof, down the bank until it plunged into the swift-moving current of the Skagit River.

Petrified, Sean dug into the snow, fearing the ejected roof would act as a sled and carry him into the river anyway. Sean rolled off the roof, his arms embedded in over a foot of soft snow. He lay there, listening to the sound of the Jeep crunch down the descent to its horrible conclusion. The fiberglass roof stayed where it was; the tumbling Jeep had made a trough, wedging the roof panel into the snow, saving Sean and his belongings.

Sean's heart pounded hard, streaming blood through his body. Every one of his senses was on overload. Satisfied, and amazed, that he was not going to make a very lengthy plunge into icy waters, he switched his concentration to listen for the pick-up truck. He heard the throaty growl of the exhaust about a hundred yards ahead. "They must have stopped to see what would happen, satisfied when the Jeep rolled down the slope and took off," he reasoned to himself.

"What do I do now?" Sean wondered as he collected himself. The stormy night did not allow a sliver of moonlight to reach the earth below. Sean pulled up the collar on his jacket to fend off the bitter cold. He felt the ground around him, searching for anything useful that may have fallen out the

Jeep. He checked his hip, the holster to his phone was still there, but the phone was not. The phone jostled loose, ejecting into the snow. Sean dug into the powder around him, knocking something hard. His wet, cold hand rose triumphant. Relieved, Sean opened his phone, casting the night with soft blue glow. He hopped up and dialed 9-1-1. Sean's brief elation was displaced disappointment – 'NO COVERAGE'. "Of course!" he cursed to himself. He clipped the phone back to his hip and continued his search on the ground, kicking the snow with his toe. He came up empty. He opened his phone again and scanned the area with the blue illumination afforded by the bright screen.

Neatly sitting on the ejected roof of the Jeep, lay his gloves and the packet of information he received from Rachel. He quickly donned the gloves on his icy fingers and grabbed the folder. Continuing to scan the area, he came up empty. He walked along the road. Relieved the falling snow had given way to a soft flurry, Sean reviewed his options. He was approximately halfway between Sedro-Wooley and Rockport. He could try and make his way to help or dig a snow cave to survive the night. The smartest option was likely to the latter, but Sean was determined to make it to safety tonight. Not taking the time to assess himself for injuries, he began the hike in the bitter cold, knowing it would be a long one. Sean's nature refusing to yield to reason, he began trudging along the road towards Rockport. These people tried to kill him, and he knew Miranda could be vulnerable alone at his home.

As the day gave into evening, Miranda knew she should not worry about Sean. The drive to Burlington was a long one, and in poor weather conditions, it was even longer. She built a fire in the fireplace and cooed at Sammy, who seemed to understand that Miranda was sad. He was not playful tonight, he just stuck by her side, a quiet companion accepting attention when afforded, but not pushing for it as he often would.

Despite her melancholy, Miranda decided to cook dinner for Sean. She wanted to repay him for all of the kindness that he had shown her. In contrast to her hardened resolve, she had not often been in healthy relationships. She had certainly never been treated the way Sean had treated her this past week.

Despite the feeling of sadness at the property, since they had to bury her faithful friend Charlie in the woods nearby, she felt an odd sense of home amidst its walls. Being around Sean's things made her feel strangely comfortable and safe.

She began poking through the kitchen, searching for what ingredients were available to decide her menu. She found some salmon to thaw along with some broccoli to steam. She pilfered through the cabinets until she came up with some flavored rice. She figured these items would create a fine start to a meal. Studying her ensemble and with a hand to her forehead, she sighed in disgust. What was she doing here? Sean could still be barking up the wrong tree in condemning her family. She pushed back from the counter. She would leave Sean a note and return to her family at the homestead.

Sean continued the hike along the highway. The night grew colder, and a solid hour ticked by without any sign of humanity. Sean strained his eyes in hopes of seeing a pair of headlights and listened intently for the sound of chains, tires, or a plow pushing through the snow. He was not greeted with any of them. His spirits sullen, but determined, he crested one hill after another, closing the distance to the refuge he sought in the little town of Rockport.

Miranda looked at the clock on the wall. She continued to debate with herself whether to stay or to go. Worry began to creep into her thoughts. Puzzled in her conflicting convictions – she held her keys in her hand, and a note explaining her departure was already resting neatly beside the telephone. Yet, she was hesitant to leave until she knew that Sean was okay. By her calculations, a conservative estimate would have had him home by now. She began to worry. She figured the salmon would be ready to cook in another half an hour. She would give Sean until then before she began seeking help.

A half-hour later, Miranda relented to her worry. Flipping through the phone book on the counter, she dialed the local county sheriff's office. They told her that they expected a patrolman who was on assignment to be back at any time. His last call took him away from radio contact, while they took great efforts to avoid that from ever happening, it was a reality of the remote, mountainous region. They agreed to send him out as soon as they could.

Miranda hung up with the sheriff's office and tapped the phone against the counter. Next to the cordless base, was a sheet of paper with a list of numbers on it. She found the number across from Adam Raines, Sean's wildlife officer friend. She dialed the phone and was both pleased and yet felt awkward at the receipt of the friendly voice. What if she was worrying for nothing?

"Uh, Adam, this Miranda Shaw, Sean's friend," she began, her voice sounding as if she was asking a question.

"Yeah, hi Miranda, what can I do for you?" Adam's voice offered.

"Well, maybe nothing. Sean had gone into Burlington to meet a friend today. I am pretty sure that worst-case scenario; he should have been back well over an hour ago. I am starting to get pretty worried," Miranda said into the phone.

"Well, the weather isn't the best out there, but Sean is a good driver. He very well may have stopped to help out a motorist. Pretty much like him," Adam told her. "I tell you what. I have some friends with the state police that patrol I-5. They can dispatch to patrols and to snowplow units to see if they happen upon his Jeep. If you want, I can drive up from Sedro if they do not report him anywhere on the interstate."

"I don't want to cause any trouble," Miranda said, the sense of feeling foolish, taking a strong hold over her mind.

"Nonsense. Sean would jump at anything to help me. If my friends have nothing to report, I'll give you a call and drive the stretch between I-5 and Marblemount myself," Adam said firmly, hanging up the phone.

The time seemed to drag on. No Sean, no phone ringing, just the light patter of the Greater Swiss Mountain Dog's paws on the floor of the otherwise silent house. Miranda was tempted to hop into her car and drive towards Seattle. She paced back and forth, finally picked up her keys and grabbing for her coat. The phone rang.

She jogged over to it, hoping to find Sean on the other end. "Miranda, its Adam. The patrol reports no sign of his Jeep on I-5. Between patrols and snowplow units, they have been spanning the area pretty well all evening. They have plenty of vehicles abandoned and stuck motorists to help out, but no red Jeeps. I will get into my truck and head on up. Worse case, and he shows up; you guys can let me crash for dinner," he said, trying to sound upbeat into the phone.

Heading out into the cold evening, away from his family, was not his number one choice on a night like this. Still, Adam knew how dangerous Highway Twenty could be during inclement weather. He hoped he was simply wasting his time driving up to Sean's house, and he would find the familiar Jeep parked in the driveway. Adam left the outskirts of town and headed east on the highway. He noticed tire tracks had left ruts in the road through the snow, at least some vehicles had made their way through the night. He cautiously drove along the mountain road, looking for signs of a vehicle spun into a ditch or otherwise.

He strained his eyes to catch every sign through the now light falling snow. He was about halfway to Marblemount, at a spot that had historically claimed several lives over the years, when he saw the tires tracks on the road swirl erratically towards the exposed cliff, just past the safety of the dense forest. He slowed the forest service SUV down and switched on the spotlight mounted to the passenger mirror. He toggled the lever and swept the light across the bank. It appeared that the snow was disturbed all the way to the edge. At first, the way the snow channeled, he thought that it was likely that a vehicle had skirted dangerously close to the drop-off.

Then he saw something. He couldn't make out what it was. Getting got out of the SUV, he grabbed his portable spotlight. He trained it towards the object. "What the…?" A large dark panel stuck out of the snow. He advanced closer to it. It was the formed plastic roof of a Jeep. The back latches sheared off, leaving jagged edges on its border. His heart sunk. Peering over the edge, he pointed the powerful beam towards the river below. It looked like a vehicle had crashed down the side, gouges of the hill had been recently disturbed, and a trail of rubble and mud streaked the upturned snowy ground into the water.

He scanned along the bank, searching for any survivors of the accident, trying to justify in his mind that this could be anybody's Jeep, not necessarily Sean's. The cliffside was too steep for Adam to attempt a descent. He rushed to his radio and called in for help. The closest responder was an emergency vehicle from Rockport. Adam returned to the cliffside, hoping to see signs of life down below.

Twenty Six

Sean's muscles screamed as he trudged along the icy highway. The myriad of bumps and bruises were tightening up in the cold. He was shivering, hungry, and dehydrated. The road heading east had its flat spots and dips, but predominantly led him higher in elevation. The abuse his body had been taking in the past week was taking its toll. His lips felt as though they were cracking and bleeding in the cold wind. His hair was wet, the snow melting as it warmed from his body heat, and then froze back in place on his head. He kept his focus and made methodical, even strides towards civilization.

Several times, he paused, thinking he heard an approaching vehicle. Each time he would be disappointed. No lights would appear, no cars would round the bend. The snow fell with a slant, flakes finding their way into his collar and his shoes. The same shoes that fought for grip with each step.

As he approached the next rise, he thought his ears were deceiving him again. He thought he could hear the rumble of a truck. He stopped in his tracks, craning his neck. This time, the sound did not stop. He strained his eyes. Flashing lights broke through the trees in a blur of white and red– a rescue vehicle!

Sean felt his anxiety rise. He figured the vehicle was en route to the site of his Jeep. A search and rescue team hoping to extract a survivor or recover a body. They wouldn't be looking for him two miles north of the crash site. He had to get them to notice him. He opened his phone, hoping the illumination would catch their eye. The vehicle came around the corner. He didn't dare stand in the middle of the road with the conditions as they were.

Standing as far off the shoulder as he dared, waving his arms frantically. He held the phone in hand closest to the oncoming rescue truck. The driver could not see him in the snow. Sean could tell that the truck was not slowing down. He gritted his teeth. He had to do something. They would look for hours at the crash site before they realized he was not there. He took the phone in his throwing hand. Just as the vehicle passed by, he hurled the cell phone into the driver's side window as though he was making a throw from center field to home plate. It hit its mark in a fantastic shower of shattered plastic.

Brake lights immediately lit up the night. As the truck slid on the icy road, Sean could hear the pulsing of the anti-lock brakes until the rescue vehicle finally came to a stop. The driver popped out of the truck. He seemed angry and shocked at the same time. "Hey, what the…", the driver started.

"A vehicle in the river, right?" Sean asked.

"Huh?"

"You are responding to a vehicle crashed in the Skagit, right?"

"Uh, yeah, was that you?" the driver asked, his eyes straining to make out the figure in the snowy night.

"Sean?" a voice from the other side of the truck called. It was a man that Sean had joined on Search and Rescues in the past.

"Hi, Dave, how are you doing?"

"Uh, fine, I guess. You?" the rescue volunteer asked, a little confused.

"Had better days myself. Can I get a lift?" Sean asked with sarcasm mixed with fatigue.

"Yeah, of course! Let me grab the medical kit. Are you alright? Come and sit in the back, let's check you out. Mike, call it in," the man named Dave said. He moved to the back of the rescue unit truck.

"Hey, wait, don't call it in yet. Who's at the scene?"

"Adam from Fish and Wildlife. He found the skidmarks and the Jeep over the side."

"Don't call him on the radio, call his cell," Sean said, his mind churning.

"Uh, alright. I think I have his number. I'll give it to Mike," Dave replied. He dug his cell phone out of his jacket pocket and toggled the screen until Adam's number appeared, and tossed the phone to the emergency vehicle driver.

Dave grabbed a gray wool blanket and laid it out for Sean. "Any injuries?" Dave asked.

"Nothing in particular. Just sore, tired, and *very* thirsty," Sean gasped.

"We can take care of that, let's check you out real quick," Dave said, surveying Sean's clothes for tears, signs of an area that could indicate injury.

"You're lucky. No breaks, a few bruises. Let's get you back to town and get some hot fluids into you," Dave said.

"Can you just give me a lift to my house?" Sean asked, weakly, his body sensing it could finally relax. Sean didn't realize just how tired and sore he was.

"Yeah, sure, but I have to think that you'll need to make a police report," Dave told him.

"Probably, I'll do it in the morning. I'll give Jim a call," Sean replied.

"Hey Dave, the guy who radioed in the call wants to know where we are transporting Sean," Mike said, as he hopped in the driver's seat of the rescue vehicle.

"Would you tell him that he can meet me at my house if he wants?" Sean asked.

"Yeah, no problem, now, you just lean back and enjoy the ride. With the snow, it will take us a little while," the medic answered, motioning for Sean to lie back.

The burly green pick-up rumbled down the bumpy road. The snow was deep as it closed in on the pass. The raised four-by-four with its massive knobby tires kicked up powder in its wake, but made it safely to the training camp. The two men jumped out and headed for camp. They were pleased with their duties completed. They had hoped that their success would lead towards favorable positions in the upcoming assault on the Free Trade Convention.

The men entered the main bunker, the group of trainees and instructors turned to face the entrance. "We did it. Man, that guy's Jeep flew off the road, flipped a couple of times, and launched right off the cliff into the river!" the first man exclaimed.

"You guys should have seen it. It was awesome! City boy is toast!" the second man whooped.

"Yes, nice work. We heard it all on the scanner. Still no reports over the wire on the missing deputy, either. They assume he went off shift and went home after his last transmission. Apparently, he doesn't start his next shift until the morning," Tug said, his voice sounding pleased, but very business-like. "Men," he continued, "We have twenty hours. Let's review the plan one more time. I want you guys to organize in your teams and stay that way until the mission is completed. I want you to eat together, sleep together, piss together. I need you to click like you are all parts of the same. Your lives and our success will depend on it."

The men all clamored excitedly. They teamed up as instructed. Each had a sheet of instructions that they had to memorize and recite on command. A diagram in front of each team detailed their intended target. Pathways through the structure highlighted their team's color. The men were percolating with excitement; their most significant moments, their mark on history was close at hand.

Twenty Seven

Miranda was waiting with the door open when the rescue vehicle made its way down Sean's driveway. Miranda and his warm house were as welcome a sight as Sean had ever seen. He thanked Mike and Dave and promised that he would take it easy.

Miranda welcomed him with open arms. "What am I going to do with you?" she scolded him, squeezing him tightly. She took a good long look at his weary eyes.

"It's good to see you too," he smiled weakly and started a shuffle to his sofa. Sammy came up to him and nuzzled his master. "Come on, buddy, I need some love right now."

"You need some food too! I'll bring you some tea right away, and then I'll put dinner on," Miranda called from the kitchen. She promptly returned with a steaming cup in her hand, offering it to Sean. "I was so worried about you. What happened?"

"I was on my way back when some truck came up on me and…" Sean started, but was cut off by a knock at the door.

"I'll get it," Miranda said, and took off for the door, but not before Sammy cut her off and let out a deep bark. She opened it up, revealing Adam standing in the doorway. Miranda waved him in.

Adam patted Sammy on the head and went to find Sean.

"I'll get some dinner started, but don't let him tell the story before I come back," Miranda said and hurried off for the kitchen.

"Well, buddy, I am relieved to see you. When I saw your Jeep…" Adam said, patting his friend on the shoulder. "Man, I thought you were gone."

"Ah, it takes more than being forced off of the road, rolling over in a Jeep that plunges over a cliff and headlong into a river in the middle of a snowstorm to get rid of me," Sean said, serving up a smile. The tea he was drinking was revitalizing him with each sip.

"So, Miranda said you gotta wait to tell the story 'till she comes back in. But one question, was it an accident?" Adam asked, a single eyebrow unconsciously raised.

"No. It was *not* an accident. It was almost like they had that drop off in mind. They wanted me over that cliff," Sean replied.

"Any ideas who?" Adam asked.

"Can't be sure. I didn't see much more than headlights coming at me. It was a jacked-up four-by with a powerful light bar on top. That's about all I can tell," Sean said.

"How did they know you would be there on the road tonight?" Adam asked. The men looked at each other and then at once, swung their heads in the direction of the kitchen.

Miranda was standing in the doorway, an oven mitt on her hand. The look on her face was one of sheer horror. The only people who knew Sean was going to Seattle today were her and Rachel York. But then Miranda let it slip to her family that Sean was going and she was going to be waiting for him at his place.

"Oh, no," she sat down on the couch across from Sean, the blue oven mitt still attached. "I told my family that I was coming here and I would be waiting for you because you were going to Seattle for the afternoon. I can't believe that…but…it had to be…," Miranda fought to put the pieces together.

"What *is* going on?" Adam asked sternly, not expecting an answer.

"I, I didn't want to believe you, Sean, but my family must be mixed up in this," Miranda stuttered disbelievingly.

"But what are they up to? Poaching?" Sean asked, swigging down his third cup of tea.

"I suppose. I'm not sure. Yesterday I kind of caught my Grandpa and uncle in a lie. I found some maps and a blueprint of a building in the workshop. They saw me and seemed pretty irritated that I found the papers. They told me it was for my grandparent's fiftieth wedding anniversary. When

I talked to my aunt, she said they are well past fifty, and there were no plans for a celebration," Miranda told Adam and Sean.

"What were the maps of?" Sean asked.

"Seattle. Which was a little weird, because I don't recall Grandpa Lucius *ever* going into town. He hates the city," Miranda said.

"What about the blueprint?"

"I don't know, some building. Looked like a hotel or something," she replied.

"What would poachers need with blueprints for a hotel in downtown Seattle?" Adam wondered out loud.

"Setting up a meet? Trying to make sure they are discreet?" Sean suggested.

"I don't know; it just doesn't make any sense," Adam said, shrugging.

"How about the Japanese freight guy? Just a buyer? And running me down - twice – is poaching worth that much?" Sean asked - none of the events of the past week fitting together in his mind.

"I guess if the haul is big enough. Poachers have been known to commit murder. Maybe what we know about is just the tip of the iceberg. What did you find from your nearly very costly trip?"

"Well, Rachel was able to come up with some info on the freight company - Hasegawa Industries. They have been under investigation for some time for a variety of violations. They have some influence in the Japanese government, though, and have always been protected. Apparently, they have been involved with a political movement to derail the One World Organization. Not sure of the connection, but I suppose opening up an agreement that would make smuggling enforceable by international law would bother a shipping company that was profiting by such a thing," Sean filled in his friends with his meeting with Rachel. He pointed to the soggy and crumpled manila folder on the coffee table.

"Free Trade Organization? I have heard my grandfather and uncle talk about it. They make it seem like we'd be turning our entire country over the United Nations or something. My grandfather was even in a book that I found. What was it, the Greys?" Miranda said.

"Yeah, I've heard about them. Hate just but everybody. Nobody ever cared much, because they were generally seen as just a bunch of belligerent old-timers with some stodgy beliefs and pent up aggression. Never felt like they could do much harm," Adam chimed in.

"Okay, let's get back to the real subject. Sean, what the hell happened to you out there?" Miranda said, almost pleadingly.

"Oh yeah, that little thing. I was on my way back and had just passed Sedro-Wooley. I noticed a pair of headlights pull out behind me. Didn't think much of it at first. I noticed that it was a truck, and it began to close the distance quickly. Eventually, they flicked on their light bar and started playing bumper tag with me. I thought I was about to get away, when I came around that curve, the one just before the drop off near the power station. I saw a deer in the middle of the road and slammed on the brakes. By the time I was able to get moving again, the truck caught up to me. Hit me just right on the quarter panel, causing me to spin. The tires hit a deep rut of snow and sent the Jeep end over end over the cliff. I unbuckled and hit the latch for the roof, just as it was coming down for the second time, right before it went over the edge and into the Skagit.

I didn't know if it was going to work, but the roof panel broke away, dumping me and my stuff on to the ground as the Jeep went over. I tried my cell, and when it didn't work, I just started walking towards Rockport. Figured that no one might come along all night, but I was hoping. About two hours into the hike, I saw the flashing lights of the rescue truck, and here I am," Sean concluded, giving his friends an abbreviated story of the harrowing incident.

"These guys are serious. I can't believe my family is mixed up in this," Miranda said sadly. She looked at Sean, his color slowly returning to his face. She couldn't help but think about the pounding he has taken since he met her. "What can we do?"

"Well, we need to find out what these guys are up to. At this point, we have no evidence beyond poaching, and we know the government is not going to respond swiftly to those charges. We need to dig and find out exactly what is going on. Can you get back into your uncle's garage and find those papers? That could be our best link," Adam answered.

"I think I can. I will show up for breakfast tomorrow. They will expect me then," Miranda replied.

"Rachel is hoping to have a little more information for me as well. Hasegawa is the worldly link that we are missing. So far, the amount of poaching doesn't add up," Sean said.

"Maybe this is a goodwill meeting about future business. Or, more likely, this is just showing a wealthy hunter a good time for profit," Adam said. "These days, that is the most common method of poachers. Rather than quantity of kill for trade, it is the quality of the experience for a hunter after illegal game."

"What about the high powered weapons?" Sean asked.

"Oh yeah, that doesn't quite fit. Might just be a hunter who got a hold of something and wanted to play. Jim had said something about a depot shipment disappearing from various National Guard installations, but also a freighter," Adam replied.

"Our link. But for what?" Sean asked. "I'll see if Rachel can find out which freighter the weapons disappeared from. If it was Hasegawa's, we might have something."

"Guys, dinner is ready," Miranda called from the kitchen, "I know you want to continue this, but Sean needs to eat and go to bed."

"I could eat a whale right now," Sean admitted, his energy slowly returning.

"Salmon will have to do," Miranda replied and dished up their plates, "I need to keep the whales in the ocean, it would be bad for business if I began serving them."

Twenty Eight

Sean awoke to the smell of coffee, snaking its way into his bedroom. Light footsteps soon followed the aroma as Miranda appeared with two cups in hand and Sammy in tow. "Good morning," her voice sang. It sounded like a chorus of angels to Sean's ears. He looked at the woman bringing him coffee. She wore one of his blue button-down shirts.

Sean tried to stifle his reaction to her. Adopting his shirt as sleepwear was startling appealing to him. She was indeed, a vision.

"Yes, I suppose it *is* a good morning," Sean replied, sitting up, his cheeks flushed. He smiled at her and accepted her offer of the coffee cup.

Miranda slid in bed next to him, "How are you feeling?"

"OK, I'll hit a few Advil before I get too ambitious today. I need to call my insurance company and get a rental. I don't imagine they will salvage much of the Jeep worth keeping," he shrugged.

"Are you going to stay out of trouble today, or do I need to call for a babysitter?" Miranda asked, one eyebrow raised. She leaned in as she awaited Sean's answer.

"Will she be as sweet as you?" Sean asked, his face exhibiting a mischievous smile.

"Oh, no. I'll make sure it will be a militant, old school teacher with a mustache asking you to rub the corns on her feet," Miranda said with a scowl and planted a kiss on Sean's neck.

"Well, in that case, I'll do my best to stay out of trouble. Unfortunately, trouble seems to be finding *me* lately. Actually, wait a minute. I have an idea to help out that category today. I am supposed to be dead, right? When you go to your aunt's house this morning, be upset. Let on that I was run off the road and killed last night. You stayed with Adam as they tried to extract the body. I am beginning to have a plan," Sean said thoughtfully.

"What are you up to?" Miranda asked, now moving her lips along his chin.

"I am not sure. But somehow, I am going to use this to our advantage. Just don't let on that I am alright. In any case, it will keep them off of my back for a while," he replied.

"Okay, but you feel pretty alive to me," Miranda purred as she nuzzled into his shoulder.

The hot shower felt good on Sean's sore muscles. He rotated his neck so the stream of hot water could find its way all around his entire upper body. When he was through, he shut off the water and grabbed his towel. He made the first swipe across his body when he heard the phone ring. He quickly hopped down the hallway, toweling feverishly as he went, leaving a series of puddles in his wake.

He checked the caller ID and picked up the phone, "Hello?"

"Sean, you're okay…" the voice on the other end gasped, "I heard you had been killed in an accident on the way home last night."

"Far as I can tell, I am still very much alive and kicking. Sorry to worry you, Rachel," Sean said, forgetting that he was supposed to be dead.

"What happened? I heard the reports. Your car slid off Highway 20 into the Skagit. The wire said you were trapped inside and died. I made a few calls and got a hold of a guy at the city coroner's office. They have you logged, but he said nobody was actually stored there. A few more persuasive calls and I reached your friend Adam, I guess his name is…he didn't exactly say anything, but said to try your house and see if anyone answers. I am so relieved that you did," Rachel exclaimed exasperatedly.

"I should have called you. I got home, had to give my friends who were waiting for me the lowdown, and just crashed," Sean replied.

"I guess I can appreciate that. What happened?" Rachel asked urgently.

"On my way home, some goons forced me off the road. I knew I was headed for the drop-off, so I ejected the canopy of the Jeep, and fortunately, the canopy spilled on the roadside as the rest of the Jeep tumbled down the embankment. I have a few new bumps and bruises, but I am otherwise alright," Sean said, retelling the story one more time.

"What is up with the fatality reports?" Rachel asked.

"I thought it might buy me a little time to figure out what was going on without another assassination attempt," Sean answered.

"Maybe it is time you left this one to the feds. An attack on your life is grounds for a little more investigation," Rachel suggested.

"No, they'll leave it to the locals. There is not much manpower out here, and what few local guys are available are working on the case anyways. My friend Adam says that it is being held up from your office," he replied.

"I okayed his initial request, but was superseded. There has been a freeze on reallocation. Coming from D.C., our hands are pretty much tied. Hey, I found out a little more about Hasegawa. His freight company was enlisted to carry a container of supplies from the Philippines to the Port of Seattle for the military. The contents list was classified, but some friends in intelligence said weapons were among the payload. They use ghost invoices that have the interim contents blacked out; only the original sender and receiver have the completed list. Unless, of course, you hold a high enough security clearance. He said he wasn't sure if anything was missing from that particular load, but those shipments can sit around for weeks before they are taken to their final destination and inventoried. I called in another favor and got the ghost invoice that included the contents. It was a weapons cache," Rachel told Sean.

"Good work. You always were able to get what you wanted," he approved.

"Well, *almost* whatever…," the deputy director cooed.

"Sometimes, timing can be a factor, even for the most persuasive and worthy. Can you get me a list of the weapons that were in the container?" Sean requested, getting the conversation back on track.

"Already done. You have a fax machine I can send it to?" Rachel asked.

Sean gave her his fax number and thanked for her help. He returned to the task of getting dressed, Sammy, as usual, following him from room to room. By the time he had donned a comfortable t-shirt and pants, the facsimile of the shipping invoice was sitting in the tray. Grabbing it, he read through the document as he shuffled towards the kitchen. He would send it on to Adam as the actual weapons listed meant very little to him. He poured a fresh cup of tea, snatched a handful of Advil, and plopped on the couch. Turning on the television, he flipped randomly through the channels as he picked up his latest whitewater magazine. Settling in, he refuted his instincts and impulsivity to continue sleuthing to follow Miranda's instructions demanding that he rest and take it easy.

He concentrated on an article describing the latest in flip-lines and rescue gear for rafting. His attention broke when the announcer on the television said uttered the words 'Seattle' and 'Free Trade Conference'. The words strung together jarred him. Miranda had said something about her family and their anti-government notions. Rachel's discussion played in his head regarding Hasegawa's family and their support to thwart international free trade agreements. The pieces had been so random, with insignificant connections. Now they suddenly slammed into place. Miranda's uncle and grandfather had plans for a building in Seattle. They were up to something involving this conference.

Sean jumped off the couch and dashed to the phone. He tried Miranda's cell phone, but the message came back that she was out of her call area. Probably at her relative's house, he reasoned – well out of reach from the cell towers. He dialed Adam's phone. He would get Adam and Jim over right away and come up with a plan to finally get some answers.

Miranda returned to her relative's home in the quiet, snow-laden woods of the North Cascades. It felt wrong not to have to let Charlie out of her SUV. Thoughts of Charlie and a general lack of sleep from the night before made a sullen expression very natural on her generally bright and doll-like face. She swung open the door to the foyer, greeted by the familiar smells of the wood-burning stove and breakfast consisting of homemade sausage and biscuits and gravy.

"Miranda dear, you're okay?" Mrs. McKenzie asked her niece.

"Yes, aunt Helen, I am fine. I didn't get much sleep last night. My friend, Sean, he…he was killed in a car accident. On his way home from Seattle, I guess he seems to have lost control, and his Jeep rolled down the steep embankment and into the river. They aren't sure which killed him – hypothermia or the crash itself. Oh, Aunt Helen…" Miranda sobbed. She drank in the thought of losing Sean for real and the pain from seeing Charlie take in his last few breaths before he died, causing tears to stream down her delicate face.

"I'm so sorry, dear. Come in, and let's fix you some tea before breakfast. I have no idea what Hal and Lucius are up to, and the boys won't be back for a couple of days. We can sit and talk," the McKenzie matriarch cooed softly as she gently squeezed Miranda's shoulders.

"That sounds nice. Let me freshen up real quick. Where did you say Uncle Hal was?" Miranda asked.

"I don't know, he and your grandfather were up at the crack of down. I think they went to check the traps. I should be back soon. They know I don't wait for breakfast," Helen McKenzie snapped.

"I need to grab some things from the car, I'll be right back," Miranda said and hurried back out the door.

She scanned the meadow adjacent to the house. It led to a series of trails in the woods where the McKenzies would set out traps for wildlife. They would catch mink, bobcats, and foxes in the traps to sell their furs or make things around the house from their hides.

Nearly every wall had the head of some animal mounted on it. Pelt rugs were strewn throughout the house, even used as furniture covers. Her uncle had even fashioned a chandelier from an array of antlers that they collected from their many kills.

Miranda remembered being frightened, yet intrigued by the animal items crafted by her relatives. She was somewhat comforted by the fact that her family at least made us out of what they killed, not like the poachers who seemed to be executing for fun.

Focusing on the two sets of footprints led away from the house and workshop towards the meadow, Miranda reasoned that her uncle and grandfather did not appear to have yet returned. She hustled into the garage. She found the barrel near the workbench and pried it open as she had the previous day. This time, there were no papers inside.

Hastily, she inspected the workshop, looking for a new hiding place. She began opening cupboards and crates, shuffling through their contents until she ran across an old steamer trunk. The layer of dust revealed a set of handprints that marked recent activity. She tried to open the latch, but it was locked. She returned to the workbench and began searching for a key. Her search came up empty. She found a thin screwdriver and began picking at the old lock. She thought that she felt it almost catch once, but was disturbed by a blast of cold air accompanied by a horrible shriek of hinges that sent a chill down her spine.

"Miranda!" a voice called.

Startled, Miranda dropped the screwdriver, wincing as it bounced and clanged on the concrete floor. She turned to face her uncle and grandfather for the second time in this precarious position. She tried to think of something to say, but no words came to her lips.

"What is it this time?" Hal asked his niece, gruffly. "Looking for more memorabilia?"

"Yes. I was thinking about the anniversary celebration. I thought I could find some of Grandpa and Grandma's old pictures and whatnot…"

"You know that stuff isn't stored out here in the workshop. Ain't no pictures or bric a brac in here," Lucius snapped.

"Miranda, what are you up to?" Hal asked. "Is it that city feller again?"

"Uncle Hal, Sean is dead. He was in a car accident last night. He didn't make it," Miranda spat back and bursting into tears, pushed her way out of the garage.

The McKenzie men just stared at her, stunned. They were irritated that their niece was snooping, but they never intended to hurt her. Had they known about her friend, as much as they didn't like the idea of him, they would have been a little easier on her. She was the only girl in the family, and they shared a soft spot for her.

"Adam. I know what they are up to. Well, I don't actually know what their plan is, but I think I know the general target for all of this activity," Sean said excitedly into the phone.

"Huh? What are you talking about? Sean, did you get another blow to the head?" Adam asked.

"Funny. Listen, the McKenzies, and their cohorts. Monday, in Seattle, a One World Organization convention begins. Delegates have been filing in over the past couple of days. I heard it on the news this morning, and it just clicked. Their objective is the convention," Sean said.

"Hmmm. I guess I can see that as a viable target for these backwoods radicals. But how does a group of unorganized, country rebels think they can pull off something like a coup in the middle of a highly guarded convention center in downtown Seattle?" Adam asked.

"I don't know. They get a hold of some new toys – 'i.e.,' high caliber military weapons stolen off a Japanese freighter owned by a foreign sympathizer. Maybe they have gotten themselves some other outside help. Tough to say," Sean surmised.

"Maybe…," Adam agreed and added, "Let's go ahead and give Jim a call. Maybe we can make a little road trip and check things out. I think you are on to something. You hear from Miranda?"

"No, not yet. I hope to hear from her soon. I don't trust her family," Sean admitted.

"Alright. I'll call Jim and call you back," the US Wildlife Officer said and hung up the phone.

Sean rubbed Sammy behind the ears and returned to his morning coffee. He figured they would rendezvous with Jim and Miranda and seek out the One World Organization convention. Maybe there was no poaching ring at all. It was just a way for them to test their weapons and maybe get in a little practice. The sound of the phone ringing disrupted Sean's thoughts.

"Hello?" Sean said.

"Sean..." Adam's voice began.

"That was quick, where are we meeting?" Sean asked enthusiastically.

"We have a problem," Adam informed his friend, "Jim's missing. He hasn't shown up for his shift. He never reported back in after his last transmission yesterday evening. The base figured that he was in a dead spot for the radio. It sometimes happens out here. He usually calls in when he is back in the area. Never checked in and didn't show up for the morning shift."

"There a search on?" Sean asked.

"They were going down the reserve list and were about to call us. Yeah, they have the sheriff's department, and some of the ski patrol search and rescue combing his last known whereabouts," Adam replied.

"Where was that?"

"The McKenzies," he said grimly.

Miranda bought herself some time with her news about Sean being killed. The McKenzie men followed her into the house. They told Mrs. McKenzie to take care of her and went shuffling off to the back room. Miranda was a little surprised at how the men reacted. She excused herself from her aunts, telling them that she had to go to the bathroom.

She tiptoed passed the bathroom and paused at the closed door of the den. She heard her uncle speaking excitedly about Sean's death, "One more nuisance out of the way and the plans can proceed."

Miranda turned her head in disgust. Her family *was* involved. Her uncle's voice actually sounded happy with his report. Who *was* he talking to, Miranda wondered. What can she do? How involved are they? She leaned against the wall near the door. Her head was spinning – the barrage of thoughts were making her dizzy.

Afraid she would once again get caught snooping, she hurried back to the kitchen. Her aunt had her sit. Miranda was visibly disturbed. Her aunt had naturally assumed Miranda's distress was over the news about Sean. Even she would not fully comprehend the drama wrapped around her husband and her father-in-law.

Twenty Nine

Adam picked Sean up at his house. The Search & Rescue helicopter had spotted the Sheriff's Deputy SUV near the trailhead for Hidden Lake Peak. The search party had begun to arrive, abandoning their prior positions at the several "last knowns" that Jim had been. "We got lucky," the search and rescue crew leader, Charles Grisham reported as Adam and Sean joined the group forming at the trailhead. "We were able to see the truck before the pilots had to eighty-six with the new front moving in. He was returning to base from an area near the McKenzie compound. He took a pass south of the peak and saw the SUV. He put the call in, and I decided to abandon the other posts. Concentrate on this area before the storm sets in."

"I hope we get luckier. How bad is the next storm?" Adam asked, looking over the crew leader's shoulder at Sean, who was examining Jim's police truck.

"It is a gonna be a doozy. Should drop about twelve inches of fresh snow in the next twenty-four hours. Clear after that, but if Jim is in trouble out here, or if conditions change…" Grisham replied.

"I get it, we better get to work," Adam said. He walked over to Sean. "What are you looking at?"

"I don't know. I just wanted to see if anything looked out of the ordinary or if any signs might suggest which trail he went up," Sean replied.

"Find anything?"

"Not really. His stuff was all sprawled out in the back. Looked like he was in a hurry or something. Either that, or his gear was in serious disarray," Sean told his best friend.

"Doesn't sound like Jim. Every time I have climbed with him, he was well organized, almost painfully so. He was much more cautious than you or I usually are," Adam replied.

"Quite a few tracks up here," Sean said, surveying the area, "With all the search volunteers running around, tough to tell who left what."

"On the radio, the crew chief said there weren't many tracks to follow. Most footprints had been covered by fresh snow," Adam filled Sean in.

They grabbed their packs and began their assigned search positions. The two men knew this particular site better than most. They took the higher approach, the one that in the summertime, was a beautiful hike with incredible vistas. This rough path, nearly impossible to follow in winter conditions, led to the saddle that separated Hidden Lake Peak from Hidden Lake Lookout. This spot was a mere couple of miles from where Sean had spotted the dead wolf. Sean and Adam knew this when they began their climb. On the south side of the mountain, radio traffic was difficult to pick up. Jim might have followed a lead that took him up the slopes and was unable to communicate his intentions. They had hoped to find him huddled inside the small lookout cabin on top of the eastern pinnacle of the twin peaks.

The search crew had set up a radio command at the vehicle parking lot, hoping to break through the rough terrain and inclement weather. They used the same frequencies that Jim would have dialed in on his radio. There was no contact since the previous afternoon.

The first leg was easy, starting through an evergreen forest. The snowpack was considerably lighter in amongst the trees. Sean and Adam listened in on their radios that they had clipped on their jackets. They listened to the progress of each of the half dozen search teams. At every outside edge of the switchbacks, the men trained their field glasses across the divide, scanning the forest at the far side of the canyon. They looked for any sign that could lead them to Jim.

The hopeful rescuers pressed on. They heard on the radios that a dog team had been brought in. They would have a couple of hours at best, particularly in the higher elevations, to search before they would postpone it until the storm had passed. Sean and Adam knew that it would take more than a couple of hours to reach the lookout, especially with the slow and tedious nature of a search. They had figured that since they were following other teams, they would speed their ascent and not double up on areas that had already had eyes upon them.

Their determined pace took the two experienced hikers quickly up the side of the mountain. As they had the day they examined the wolf, they made a direct and steep ascent to speed their journey. The climb forced the men to swap several times between bare boots, snowshoes and crampons to aid their traction. The reports crackled intermittently over the radios as teams ran through their assigned coordinates. The searchers were scouring the terrain, but reported no results.

Sean looked at his watch. The altimeter alerted him that they were at 4900 feet, nearly a vertical mile short of their ultimate goal. Visibility had become very poor, so the combination of compass coordinates and altitude gave him a pretty good idea where they were. Adam's GPS was, of course, was their relied upon tool for navigation. At this point, Sean figured that they were approaching the saddle, far higher than any of the other search teams. Their scheme had been destination minded - get to the lookout, pray they found Jim and then work their way back down. The radios crackled their final message as the weather, altitude, and terrain swallowed up their reception. The communication was a call for them to abort the search. The storm front was looming directly upon them, and conditions were beginning to worsen.

Sean and Adam paused at this last transmission. "What should we do?" Sean called out above the wind.

"Well, I figure we are about an hour from the lookout, and about two from the base. Our best bet is to push forward. If we can navigate to the saddle, we can pick our way up the North Face of Hidden Lake Lookout. If we head down, the white-out could lead us into more trouble," the Wildlife officer said.

"Alright. We'll have to be careful at the saddle. That'll be a deadly slide to Hidden Lake," Sean replied. He thought of the steep drop to the lake that sat at 4800 feet, halfway down the north side of the twin mountains.

The two-man search team was experiencing the brunt of the storm. The searchers were able to see no more than ten feet in front of them. Scurrying up the steep slopes was treacherous enough in good weather, whiteout conditions made the ascent harrowing. Adam, the more experienced climber, took the lead. He carefully made steps in the snow for Sean to follow. His left hand gripped the head of the ice axe, ready to plunge into the ice and snow to prevent a fall. His right hand kept vigil on the GPS. The howling winds and blinding snow of the whiteout made the piece of equipment essential for making it to the saddle instead of getting lost themselves, or over an unseen cliff.

The wind had picked up dramatically. Sean's slender body had to fight both gravity and now strong gales trying to rip him off the face of the mountain. They traversed Hidden Lake Peak, towards the saddle. This area was avalanche prone and very open to the elements. A slip would mean a fall of at least a thousand feet and probable death. With each step, Sean dug the tip of the axe about six inches into the snow. While he couldn't see below him, he knew the drop of off was dangerous. Adam's footsteps provided a solid trail up the side of the mountain for him to follow. Sean barely kept him in view between the freshly falling snow and the snow that was being continuously swept up by the sixty mile an hour winds.

He felt his face being chapped raw by the cold and wind. He squinted as he pushed on, step by step. Studying each footprint that was left by Adam, he took care to stay on course. At one point, he almost ran into him. "We're at the saddle!" Adam called. The wind at the saddle was monstrous. Sean leaned forward to keep from being blown entirely off the mountain. To the left was Hidden Lake Peak. To the right was the jagged trail that led to the Lookout. Directly over the edge of the saddle, nestled about a thousand feet down, was Hidden Lake. When visible, the lake almost glowed an unnaturally brilliant blue. In the winter, it was an innocent-looking white plateau of ice and snow.

Cautiously, they moved to the eastern edge of the saddle. The steep ascents had separated the two men from the rest of the search party. In the now blinding snow, Adam felt they had to press on towards the northern ascent of Hidden Lake Lookout, nestled atop the eastern peak. The path to the top was buried in months of snow, turning a trip with good visibility a challenge into one of treachery. In the onslaught of wind and snow, it felt suicidal to the very mortal feeling Sean Kendall. Adam maintained the lead position, as his experience in the mountains far superseded that of Sean's. They attached crampons to their hiking boots and dug into the side of the mountain.

With great caution, Adam swung his ice axe into the thick ice and snow. He would give a tug with his arm, to ensure that his hold was secure and raise a leg to propel his body forward. A length of rope secured the two climbers as it flowed through its weave of carabineers and d-rings. The hopes were if one climber fell, the other would have enough grip to stop a full-face fall. Sean had fortunately never experienced such a climbing incident, but under the conditions, he was glad to have the extra security.

Progress up the windy north face was difficult and slow. The northern side of the Cascade mountains traditionally caught the brunt of storms, and this one was no exception. There were times when Sean was sure his light body would be blown clean off the route of ascent. Despite a small distance between him and Adam, he was barely able to keep Adam's boots in sight. Not only were they obscured by snow, but they had entered the lower bank of the clouds that were pushed along by the storm front.

Adam kept his attention on heading towards the summit lookout cabin. He relished the times when the degree of the slope softened, and the fight with gravity was not so severe. In the summer, it was easy to pick the route up to the peak, but in these conditions, Adam was struggling.

Focusing on the shortest path by making a bee-line straight up, he swung his ice axe into a block of snow. He gave it the usual tug and pulled his foot up. As the tip of the blade bore more of his weight, an entire chunk of ice and snow ripped out of the mountain. Desperately, he clawed with the axe and his free leg to get a bite of the mountain; he failed. Adam's entire body slid entirely off the face and into midair, his mind raced, he knew the fall was several thousand feet with nothing to impede it. "Fall!" he screamed desperately, hoping Sean would have enough time to brace himself.

Sean heard the chunk of ice and snow in time to see it break through the fog. He yanked his shoulder in, just enough for the blow to glance off harmlessly. He reacted swiftly, at the same time, hearing Adam's scream; he braced himself. Nervous that his weight would not sustain that of Adam's, especially with the additional force of gravity, he searched desperately, spying a horn of rock that poked out of the mountainside. He made a frantic loop out of the rope and swung it around the rock horn. At the same time, he felt Adam's body "whoosh" down the mountain. The line caught, and the coil tightened with Adam's weight around the rock. The impact wrenched Adam's back as his body slammed to an abrupt halt, but he was relieved to feel the mountain smack into him as he swung in the air.

The force of the rope pulled Sean out of his positioning and flung him into the air. His descent was brief, as the length of free line that he was able to snare around the rock left little slack. For a few seconds, he and Adam swung on either side of the underbelly of the stone as though they were opposing pendulums of a grandfather clock. Sean's heart rate slowly returned to normal, and he was finally aware of his surroundings. He looked down at Adam, who hung a few feet below him. He surprised himself as he let out a small, nervous chuckle. "Let's not do that again. Are you okay?"

"Yeah, I think so," Adam replied, and in response to Sean's chuckling and the immense relief that he was not a pile of broken bone and flesh at the base of the mountain, began laughing himself.

The two hung there, each with their ice axe and at least one toe of their crampons dug into the hillside laughing hysterically. Adam finally composed himself and began thinking about how to get out of their predicament. Since he had more slack in the rope, he decided that he would start climbing up the hillside to the horn. He dug in; with great caution, he worked his way up to the horn. When he reached it, he tossed a leg over the side, as if he were jumping into the saddle of a horse. He leaned back and grabbed the rope in a belay position. He instructed Sean to make his ascent. When Sean poked his head over the edge of the horn, Adam pulled him up and gave him a chance to catch his breath. Going back to work himself, he untangled the rope from the rock and repositioned themselves for the final ascent. Adam figured they were not far from the top and would reach the summit soon.

They made their way carefully up the snow-covered scree and boulders. Finally, they reached the summit without any added drama. Sean dove onto the snowy ground of the pinnacle, relieved to be back on terra firma. He hugged the ground for several seconds. Adam had untied their rope and coiled it around his shoulder. He helped Sean up, and the two inspected the lookout cabin. The storm door was frozen shut behind a shield of snow. Adam hacked the obstructions away with his ice axe until it was free to remove from its position. Eagerly, they sprung through the interior door and launched themselves inside. Quickly shutting the entrance to the hut, they locked out the wind and freezing precipitation. Adam collapsed on the bed, and Sean crumbled to the floor on top of his gear, both elated to be safe and out of the elements.

Unfortunately, the empty cabin meant that they did not locate their friend Jim on their ascent. They also knew that this meant his likelihood of survival was low. The storm outside was not hospitable to sustaining life for very long. They hoped that the search crews further down the mountain had had better success. Taking a brief assessment of the conditions of the cabin, they were thrilled that a volunteer in the fall had stocked a few provisions. Adam located the can opener and quickly got into two cans of chili. A small wood stove stoked to heat the little cabin and they placed their cans of chili on top of the propane stove to warm up their meals. Flopping onto the wooden floor, Sean used his pack as a pillow as he stretched out, feeling the stove begin to heat the small ten-by-ten cabin.

Adam assessed his injuries. The fall torqued his shoulder and the impact of the rope breaking his fall left a deep bruise on his side where he had bound it around him. Overall, he was pleased with the mild toll his body had taken.

"You alright, Bud?" Sean asked his friend.

"Yeah," Adam laughed, "I think your lassoing that rock saved my life. I think I would have pulled you off that face and we both would have bit it. You know, that wasn't protocol, you shouldn't have even had time to hit that rock before we were toast. Nice work, cowboy. We may just make a real country boy out of you yet."

"Yee-haw," Sean laughed and turned his attention to the little camp stove. The chili was ready, and he eagerly began scooping it out of the can and into his mouth.

Thirty

Miranda returned to Sean's house and found herself oscillating between childhood memories and the realities of recent events. She would remember fishing with her grandfather, uncle, and cousins along the rivers in the North Cascades. Miranda recalled holidays with the family and her Mom laughing with her brother. She even now remembered her uncle picking on her mother for the choices that she made – the decisions to leave the serene country where she grew up and head to the city. Her Mom loved her family, but always had a sense that she needed more, spending most of her adult life in Seattle, where Miranda was born.

She thought of her teenage years. The large family holidays ceased as her parents had become increasingly intolerant of their relatives' conduct and apparent lack of respect for other cultures. Her parents were staunch supporters of freedom of thought and preservation of the wilderness. A serious rift developed when Miranda was in the later grades of elementary school. Her parents decided that the family differences were too significant, and they didn't want their children to be influenced by the McKenzie family's misvalues.

When Miranda's parents were killed in a car crash two years ago, her need for family drove her to rekindle her relationship with the McKenzie relatives. Her estranged relations was overjoyed for Miranda to rebuild her ties. They immediately accepted her and made her feel as if the rift with her parents had never occurred.

Now, all that had changed. Miranda was beginning to understand her parent's notions that drove them away and created the wedge between the families. Though shocked, the pieces of the puzzle were sliding into an unfortunate fit. Her relatives were not the sweet and simple people that her childhood memories had conjured. There was, perhaps, something wicked in their nature.

She checked her watch – it was getting late, and she had not yet heard from Sean. The last time she did not pursue her concerns, Sean had nearly died on the highway. She picked up the phone and dialed the number for the Skagit County Sheriff's Department.

She was able to reach the dispatcher. Reluctantly, the dispatcher revealed to Miranda that the search had been called off due to weather. Sean and Adam were stuck on the mountain and presumably in the lookout cabin. Miranda thanked the woman and hung up the phone.

This news was another in a long series of bad information that Miranda had to endure. She reached down to pat Sammy. The Swissie had become quite affectionate with her over the past few days. In Sean's absence, he shadowed her around the house. Miranda felt secure with the big dog at her side and enjoyed his affection. She bit her lip as she watched the snowfall outside. According to the weather forecast, it would continue through the night. She let out a worried breath obscuring her view as it fogged a patch of the frosty window, she would worry about Sean Kendall on this stormy winter night.

The compound was busy - almost twenty-four hours before launch. The group had been training non-stop for a solid week. Tug kept each man's task very simple. Each had a specific job, and fortunately, precision was not a necessary factor for this operation. He sat in his tent and picked up the scrambled satellite phone.

"This is Rhinehart," the meek sounding voice said into the phone.

"Rhinehart. The operation is nearing D-day. I want to ensure that everything is set. I expect the agreed-upon sums deposited in the two accounts in the Caymans. I also expect for your boss to put an end to this Free Trade Organization. It will be his responsibility to make sure that this does not create a sympathetic public for these anti-American liberals to rise even further," Tug informed the congressional aide.

"Yes, of course. Everything is in place as soon as we here about the tragic incident in Seattle, the money will be wired. And trust me, this mission will squelch this whole international market scheming. My boss will return the focus of America on America," Rhinehart replied to the mercenary.

"I hope so, now just sit tight and stay tuned into CNN," Tug said.

"What will you do when this is over?" the aide asked.

"I intend to disappear for a while," Tug replied curtly. "Goodnight, Mr. Rhinehart, I have work to do. Oh, and Mr. Rhinehart, if you cross me, I *will* kill you."

Tug hung up the phone and listened to the wind blowing outside. He remembered his days in Central America, all of the hidden wars that the government loaned the military out to. Most without any knowledge bestowed upon the American public. It was after a long night of fighting that he had received word about his wife's death. A botched burglary claimed her life and the life of their unborn son. If he had been home where he belonged...he shook the thoughts out of his head. He was a soldier. He carried out his orders. It was after the news that he began to enjoy his job with a new vigor. When his commission was completed, he stayed in Central America and joined a group of mercenaries. He had nothing to go home to, and all he had ever trained to do was develop, lead, and carry out offensives.

His thoughts turned to the Sheriff's Deputy. The reports of the Search and Rescue operation had been closely monitored. He wasn't pleased to hear authorities found the truck He hoped for more time bought by the diversion. In retrospect, the trail was a little too close to home. It could lead to luring investigators to probe along the Highway Twenty corridor. His plan would take his men south to Highway Two. Maybe this could work in his favor, after all. If his crew took a southerly route, they would, in effect, execute an end-around, traveling right by any police activity. The snow, he surmised would keep the search going long after the mission would commence, and by then, it would be too late.

He allowed his lamenting thoughts to subside. The Greys dolts will be fingered for the transgressions. Their fights in town, mishandling of the exchange with Hasegawa, and their local reputation would paint a target on each of their backs. Meanwhile, he had his escape plan well ironed out, and his backers were tucked away safely in their ivory walled homes.

Lyndon poked his head out of his tent. Most of the crew had hunkered down to wait out the storm. Tug had ordered the troops to sleep through the afternoon, as soon as the storm had passed; they would run through the training scenarios once more. Lyndon snuck out of the tent. He had to get the word out. It had been days since he was able to break cover and reach headquarters. He wasn't sure what this mission was to entail until the past couple of days. When he agreed to work with Tug, he had assumed this would be a training exercise or at least have more preparation time involved. Tug and his backers were intent on hitting the target early in the convention, using the country boys as the fall guys.

When Tug killed the police officer, he knew that timing would be escalated. He would never have taken such a risk if he thought the authorities had enough time to trace it back. Now, after this morning's meeting, he knew he had less than twenty-four hours to prevent an enormous tragedy.

His people knew that he would be in deep. They knew that he had gone to Washington state, and was sure that they would figure out the convention angle. The last transmission let them know that he was heading to the convention site with Tug, and the hotel was the intended target, but the details and time frame were unknown. They did not anticipate that anything would happen so soon after the Colorado incident. No one would see this coming. He grabbed his equipment and headed for higher ground. The storm was a perfect opportunity for him to sneak out and make communication. The reception was spotty in the dense backcountry, however. He had to get somewhere where he could get a better signal.

He crept behind the tents and began to head for the road. He hoped that he would not have to walk very far to at least get one bar of reception on his mobile. When he thought he saw a faint blip of LCD on his phone, he pressed the first few numbers of his director's phone.

"Special Agent Lyndon," a voice called from behind him. "Who are you calling?"

The hair on the back of Lyndon's hair stood up. Tug! He turned to face him, as he did, the stock of Tug's rifle knocked the phone out of his hands. "What am I going to do with you?" Tug hissed at the federal agent.

"Tug! What are you talking about? I was just trying to see if I could get a little more information on that Search and Rescue," Lyndon stammered.

"Hmm. How good of you," Tug swung the barrel of the gun at Lyndon's midsection, causing him to double over. "I had my doubts about you from the beginning. They intensified as you seemed so desperate to spare the Deputy's life. I did a little follow up on you. Everything had checked out so nicely. But you see, I have some friends in the government too. They can extract information from the most interesting of places – even the FBI or ATF, is it? Are you impressed Special Agent Lyndon?"

"Tug, I…," Lyndon started before he was struck with the 9mm round from Tug's handgun. He fell to the ground, a small hole neatly placed in the center of his forehead.

"I've heard enough." Tug reached into the Lyndon's pockets and produced his wallet. He shuffled through it. Everything seemed benign at first, but he noticed a colored thread that was loose from the seam. It was a slightly different color than the rest of the stitching. He yanked at it, and the seam unraveled. It revealed and identification card. Tug pulled it out. There was a photo of Lyndon – Special Agent Lyndon, Federal Bureau of Investigations.

Thirty One

The search and rescue crew chief, Charles Grisham, had all hands in camp, all but two – Adam Raines and Sean Kendall. Most of the North Cascades was under a fresh blanket of late winter snow. He hoped his two missing volunteers had found shelter, and his crew wouldn't have three bodies to locate.

Grisham studied the maps of the area. The crew had searched the known trails and slopes that a fall might occur. All had come up without any sign of the young deputy. He gritted his teeth in his cigar as he planned the next stage of the search that he would direct as soon as the weather broke. He would have his men start with the ravines at the outer edge of the trails. Maybe something lured the deputy into taking a closer look, and he took a fall. In the meantime, he had his second-in-charge continually cycling though the FRS channels to try and reach Sean and Adam. He knew Adam pretty well, and knew he could handle the mountain, what he knew of Sean is that he was strong and athletic, but he also felt that he was too much a novice for the brutality of withstanding a Cascades squall.

Adam and Sean slept away their aches and pains, content with a fire in the stove and full bellies. Sleeping atop a mountain in a squall in a small cabin perched on massive boulders made Sean uneasy at first. The stresses of the high winds hitting the aged wooden walls and the subzero temperatures causing the trusses and high tension wires that secured the building's corners to the rock made eerie groans and popping noises. Sean imagined the structure being carried away in the wind. Fatigue hit hard, and the sounds were masked with Adam's snoring, allowing the battered climber to collapse asleep

Sean was the first to awake. It took him a few seconds to register where he was and another few moments to recognize the sore muscles and bruises abused by the hard sleeping surface. He tried to peek out of the frost and snow obscured windows. Through the white haze, he could make out sunlight trying to poke through. The wind still howled by at the cabin's elevation, but it appeared that the storm was finally breaking.

He looked over at his friend, who was starting to stir.

"Rise and shine, buddy!" Sean called to his friend, a little too loud for first thing in the morning.

"Oh, jeez! Did you roll me down the hill? I don't know if it was how I slept or getting yanked during the fall yesterday," Adam groaned sleepily. He sat up gingerly, with every ache and pain that his body had endured over the past days climb screaming at him.

"Yeah, tell me about it. Good news though, the snow has stopped falling. Visibility is still isn't great, but it's not like it was," Sean gave the weather report as he continued to peer out of the cabins frosty windows.

"Any luck on the radio?" Adam asked.

"No, not yet. The signal is weak, and I am not even picking up broken static," Sean replied.

"Let's grab a little chow and start heading down," Adam sighed, grabbing a couple of cans of corned beef hash off of the small storage shelf, "Signal will get stronger as we head down. The southwest ridge should get us a channel to base."

The two men devoured their ad hoc breakfast. The meal, which looked to Sean eerily reminiscent of the canned food that he gave to Sammy as a treat, tasted like Sunday brunch he was so hungry. The warm food was just what his body needed to re-energize for the haul down the mountain.

They cleaned their utensils and put their food containers into sealed baggies and stuffed them into their packs. Leaving any food items out worked quickly to promote pests, even at elevation. Most visitors to the lookout took great caution to leave it as it was or better than how they found it when they arrived, leaving behind books, games, or cookware to the group that maintained the lookout. Sean dug through his pack and left a set of his titanium silverware for future visitors in the dishware bin.

Making a brief entry in the cabin log, Sean noted the lookout's role in saving them during the brutal storm.

Bundling up and slinging their packs over their shoulders, the climbers headed out of the lookout. They boarded up the storm door and began planning their descent. The trip back down the steep face would be even more harrowing than the trip up.

Adam suggested that they rig a rappel line from the edge of the one of the summit boulders. He strung together several bands of webbing and had Sean carefully circle a rock that protruded over the northwest face. With the strap secure, he threaded their two sections of rope through a D-ring and began their descent off of the mountain.

Sean played king's taster and was the first to lower himself over the edge. The brisk wind blew him sideways, feet flailing in midair. His firm grip on the rope was the only thing preventing him from being tossed completely airborne. His feet clawed in the air to remain feet first, but the wind was too strong, and Sean's light frame blew horizontal to the landscape below him with each gust. He figured; eventually, he would end up on the ground and just maintained his slow, steady course of feeding the rope through his lead and brake hands until he reached the bottom. Occasionally, he would sway harshly against the sharp rocks, but most of the descent spent in midair. To his dismay, the rope didn't stretch but about halfway down the peak. Sean hung precariously in the air, determining the best course of action. Finding a small rock ledge within reach, he swung toward the side of the mountain. Detaching himself from the rope, he allowed himself to free fall towards the rock face, barely landing on the ledge below.

Waiting for Adam to repel down after him, Sean prepared a safe spot for him on the thin ledge. When Adam got to the end of the rope as Sean had, several feet short of the landing, he let out a muttered curse, "I guess we were a little short, huh?"

"Just a little bit," Sean called to his friend.

"Uh, how'd you get down?"

"Swing and release!" Sean replied with a childish grin.

"Nice pal, really nice," Adam cursed and began pumping his legs to get the rope to swing closer to the face.

Sean reached out and grabbed at Adam, catching part of his pack and reeled him onto the narrow perch.

"You're crazy," Adam scowled at his friend.

"We're here, aren't we?"

Scoffing, Adam set to work maneuvering the rope down from the rigging and set up a second repel section. Fashioning a second ring of webbing around a little stub of rock, they draped the line over the side, and

Sean, again, was the first to continue his journey midair down the mountain. Still fighting the winds, he maintained a secure grip on the line. Finally, he reached the end of the rope, but again it was too short, hanging fifteen feet from the surface below.

Sean tried to get on to a rock to climb his way down, but the pitch they had chosen to fasten webbing did not allow for a landing. Sean released his grip. Curling into a ball, he rolled to the terra firma below. Meeting with the fresh snow in a harsh collision, sending powder spraying into the air. His landing site was just off of the saddle, forcing him to roll down the steep embankment. Sean furiously tried to use his hands to stop, but momentum was working against him as he tumbled helplessly down the hill. He turned his feet forward and assumed what was basically "river position" for whitewater rafting. He stuck his feet in front of him as he slid on his bottom and used his arms behind him in a backstroke to help steer and slow him down. Eventually, he reached the apex of the bowl and tumbled headfirst into a six-foot trough of snow.

Collecting himself, he righted his body up and crawled his way out of the trough. Perching himself up on a snow-covered rock and looked up to see Adam begin his descent. He looked on as his friend hopped over the edge of the summit rock.

Adam, a little more adept, rappelled his way down the mountainside. He was able to collect himself at the end of the rope. He bound his leg in a loop to allow himself to hang hands-free. Pulling some carabineers and webbing from his equipment sling, he made a makeshift extension to the length of rope. He was just able to reach a rock outcropping with his toes and dance his way to safety. Once stable, he retrieved the rope by feeding the line through the D-ring and allowing it to fall the length of the peak to the ground below. He found Sean climbing his way up to help him coil the rope; silently, they began their hike to base.

Charles Grisham had his crew gathering their gear for an early assault on the mountain. He had several men cycling through the frequencies on the radio. Arranging his teams into sub-specialties, he instructed a squad of four mountain rescue specialists to head straight up, the path that Sean and Adam had taken. If they could get to the upper ridgeline, they should at least get a radio relay from base to cabin.

The rest of the men had their new search coordinates. The hunt would be further cast under a wintry veil of difficulty with another eight inches of fresh snow on the ground. The forecast called for the sun to peek out midday as it didn't take long for the weather to shift in the northwest.

It wasn't long before the radios began to squawk. At first, there weren't any distinct sounds, just a trading back and forth of frequency chatter. Still, it was a positive sign. Grisham paused with his duties, to cock an ear to the radio. Within a short time, he heard the sounds of Adam's voice. Grisham felt a huge sense of relief. He held his breath, hoping the report would include the find of the missing deputy.

"Base, this is Adam Raines. With me is Sean Kendall. Location is southeast ridge, all okay. No signs of Matthews. Over," the radio reported.

"Raines, this is base, glad to hear your voice. Request you return to camp, over," the volunteer on the radio replied.

"Roger that. Any reports on Matthews from your end?" Adam hoped.

"Negative. The search continued forty-five minutes ago. Four en route to you. Do you need assistance?"

"Negative. We are healthy. Call them back to rejoin the search, over and out," Adam replied over the small handheld.

Miranda woke up tired and weary. She tossed and turned all night. Being immersed amongst Sean's things felt natural and warm. She shook her head slowly. How could she think so much for a man so quickly? She was usually quite guarded when it came to men. She had more as friends than dates or lovers. Sean made her feel different - safe, warm, and yet, very feminine. Sean listened to her; he genuinely wanted to hear about her and share her thoughts. This was a distinctly different experience for her.

Unfortunately, amidst all of these new feelings came the worry that was becoming all too familiar with Sean's antics. Of course, she had to admit that much of it was her family's fault. "Family? They barely feel like family. I don't even feel like I know them anymore," she muttered to herself. She looked at the phone that had been silent all evening, not yielding a single ring. No word about Sean's safety. She sighed and shuffled into the living room with Sammy keeping pace. She looked out the window, relieved that the snow had stopped. Looking down at Sammy's soulful eyes looking back at her, with a seemingly worried expression, "I know Sammy; I hope he's okay too."

Tug reviewed his situation. He knew that Lyndon had leaked information out. He just did not know how much. He had to assume enough to do his operation harm. Fortunately, it was not in Tug's nature to be trusting. He had the training set up for an assault on the hotel several blocks away from the convention center. The hotel was a site where most of the delegates were staying while in Seattle. He also had provided false timetables out to the group. There would be added security throughout the entire convention, and with the misinformation leaked out by Lyndon and Tug's devious plotting, he was still confident that the mission could be a success. Besides, he would never be identified for this mission, The Greys or whatever these rednecks call themselves would be the blame for the impending attack.

Still, he wanted to make sure things came off without a hitch. With that thought, he had another idea cross his path. He needed a distraction that would lead attention further away from the convention center. He picked up the map of the area, studying the geography surrounding the convention center. He wanted to find something close enough that the Trade Center detachments would feel compelled to respond, but far enough away that his team would have time for clear ingress/egress.

His eyes widened, finding something amongst the office buildings, shops, and synagogues that fit the bill perfectly - a small private school sat eight blocks away from the convention center. The school took up an entire block and was a popular institution for some of Seattle's more affluent families. It was also notoriously left-winged. Tug smiled. What would bring the cops running from their posts quicker than a bunch of rich kids getting picked off by a high-powered weapon?

Thirty Two

Sean and Adam broke through the trees finding that they had reached the base camp. Rescue workers collapsed around the men, providing them fresh fluids and warm blankets. Sean dropped his gear, welcoming the resources, in particular the hot coffee.

Grisham, the crew chief, tried to get EMT medics to check him out, but he brushed them off. Borrowing Adam's cell phone, he quickly dialed Miranda's number. He knew that she would be worried sick by now.

"Hey, beautiful!" he called into the phone as heard it pick up on the other end.

"Sean! Where are you? Are you okay?" Miranda gasped into the phone, not sure whether to be angry with him for putting her through more worry or thrilled that he was okay.

"I'm fine, I'm fine. We got stuck up at the top of Hidden Lake when the storm hit. We were able to make it to the lookout, but we didn't have any radio access up there," Sean filled her in.

"You *have* to stop doing this to me! When are you coming home?" she pleaded into the phone.

"I'm coming home now. The chief won't let us go back out today anyways. He promises to call when they know something," Sean replied.

"Good. Hurry!" Miranda urged.

Sean hung up the phone and turned to Adam, who was still negotiating with Grisham to let him stay. It appeared that he lost the argument as his arms flopped to his side, and he made his way over to Sean.

"Well, we're kicked out for at least twenty-four hours. Grisham thinks we need rest before we tackle another assault on the mountain. I tried to tell him that we are fine, but he wouldn't listen," Adam told his friend.

"Well, let's go. We have other work to do anyway," Sean said, picking up his gear and heading for the SUV. "Did you call Laura yet?" Sean asked as they climbed into the rig.

"Agh, she's gonna kill me!" Adam said and quickly dialed his home phone to reach his wife.

When they reached Sean's house, Miranda threw the door open and gave them each a hug and planted an extra-long kiss on Sean's lips. "I am so glad to see you two!" she exclaimed.

"Trust me; we're glad to see you too!" Sean replied.

"Ah, your boy was in good hands with me," Adam scoffed casually.

"Yeah, right up to the point you tried to pull me off the mountain," Sean retorted.

"Adam started to retort but never finished, grinning at his friend. "I'm gonna make a few calls. You two do what you got to."

Miranda followed Sean into the bedroom as he selected some fresh clothes and a spare outfit for Adam. She hung outside the shower as Sean cleaned himself, and he retold his adventures from the previous day. Miranda secretly wondered if she could handle the worrying that seemed to be associated with caring for this man. When he told her that they had fallen on the ascent to the lookout, her stomach felt physically sick.

Adam, meanwhile, got busy on the phone, requesting additional resources. His conversations seemed to get more and more heated, "What do you mean not for a week? I requested these resources three days ago! What do you mean by other priorities? It isn't just a bunch of dead animals. I have a missing sheriff's deputy, and he happens to be a friend of mine! Well, who is your supervisor? Oh, it just came from above. From who? Well, find out!" he slammed down the phone with disgust. He looked up to see Sean and Miranda looking in at him. He felt a little embarrassed for them to see his tantrum.

"Sorry about that, guys. I don't know what the deal is. I have never had this much trouble getting a little help. Something big must be going on somewhere," Adam said sheepishly.

"Or *someone* big doesn't want you to have any help," Sean suggested.

"What do you mean?" Adam asked, furrowing his brows.

"Remember my conversation with Rachel? There seemed to be some interest in political levels. Maybe someone has some pull and is blocking your requests," Sean proposed.

"Maybe. I'll get some answers," Adam said with determination and returned to the phone. He dialed the state headquarters for Fish and Wildlife. He persisted and worked his way up the leadership chain, each time being told the same thing, "other cases are taking priority".

Sean, overhearing Adam's conversation, decided to give Rachel a call. He sat on the sofa in front of the fireplace, his shoulder nudging Miranda's. "Rachel, it's Sean. Hey, I have another favor to ask. Adam Raines, of Fish and Wildlife, has been denied requests for resources. Do you have any way of knowing who is doing that and why?"

"Yes, actually, I do. The requests run through my office, and generally, I have a say in the approval of allocations here in the northwest, that is unless D.C. steps in. They have authority over my office. We received a command to send most of our available agents out to Idaho. I'll be honest. I haven't even heard reports, aside from the typical complaints from ranchers about mountain lions. I tried to push back, but they say it came from a congressional oversight committee," the alluring government employee replied.

"Any idea who on that committee may have put it through?" Sean asked.

"Well, generally, I would say it would be someone on the committee itself, but in D.C., it could be a favor in trade from someone not even on the committee," Rachel said, thoughtfully.

"Like a senator from Idaho?" Sean asked.

"Like a senator from Idaho," Rachel agreed, and then added, "It would make sense that someone from Idaho would request to pull resources to that state."

"Can we be sure?" Sean asked.

"Not likely, if it were a favor from another politician, it wouldn't reflect in the tracking. We can check the records on who made the recommendation and the orders, but those people may not have been the ones concerned. They may have made the orders in response to a concession on a bill from another committee. It is possible to ferret it out, but it is your basic needle in a haystack," Rachel said, outlining the likely scenario.

"When can the agents be recalled from Idaho?" Sean pushed on.

"Well, the whole thing is pretty suspicious. Like I said, the complaints out of that area haven't been anything out of the ordinary. Yet, the team sent there has orders to be very cautious and take their time setting up covers. They are slotted to be there for several weeks," the assistant director responded.

Sean thanked his friend and hung up the phone. Adam was still cursing at one of his superiors on his cell. Sean gave him the slash to the throat gesture, indicating that he could give it up. Adam relented and ended his phone conversation. "What's up?" he asked Sean.

"You have been road blocked. Rachel says she was ordered to send all of the available northwest team to Idaho, something about mountain lions. Came from D.C. Any additional requests are to be vetoed until further notice," Sean filled his friend in.

"Did she know who made the order?" Adam asked.

"No, it came down from an oversight committee of the Department of Interior. The actual person behind putting the wheels in motion may have been anyone in Congress," Sean answered.

"Great. Well, I guess we are on our own," Adam said grimly.

Thirty Three

Tug lit his cigar and watched the team leaders of his mission flow through the script with little plastic figures around a cardboard model of the convention center. Admittedly, he was less interested in the actual retention of details. As long as the point would get across to the nation, and he could slink away into the crowd, he would be satisfied.

Once the point men demonstrated proficiency in their tactics, he worked with the new group he selected - two men to take on the school. It didn't matter how well this side mission was carried out either. As long as the school created a distraction, it would be a success.

He picked up his scrambled satellite phone and dialed Senator Small's number. He let out a puff of his cigar while the conspirator answered the phone. "Small," came the reply.

"Small, this is Tug. We are battle-ready. Are you prepared to make the fund transfers?" Tug asked.

"Yes, Mr. Gaskill. We have three offshore accounts to disperse the money. One of them will deposit Monday morning. The remaining two will transfer Tuesday evening when you complete the mission," Senator Small replied. "This will be quick and quiet..."

"From my standpoint, it will be. The Greys will either be arrested or eliminated. None of them have ever heard about you. I am your only link. If you cross me or come after me, you will have a problem on your hands. If you don't, you can sit back, relax and enjoy the evening news," Tug replied.

"I think I would like our business relationship to continue, Mr. Gaskill. You have proven yourself quite competent," Small admitted.

"We can entertain future engagements later. Let's remain focused on what is at hand. This operation has not exactly gone smoothly," Tug reminded the senator.

"Yes, and some of that has been your group's doing - bar brawls, poaching, failure to manage nuisance townspeople. Those hicks should never have been allowed out of the camp!" the senator bellowed.

"Yes, this is true. But babysitting was not part of my contract either. Fortunately, the whole focus has been on the McKenzie family and their connections. This has shaped up to work in our favor. It removes the focus from anyone outside of Washington state. The weapons appear to be stolen and not financed, leaving less inclination to search out folks such as yourself. For me, I don't even exist," Tug said, rubbing his chin.

"Have faith, Tug. I think you have handled the situation well. What about that sheriff's deputy?" Small asked.

"The search is still on. A late storm dumped a ton of fresh snow on the ground, but the conditions are improving. I think we will be in and out before they find anything," Tug said. "Oh, one other thing you should be aware of. I am planning a diversion. It won't be pretty. I am not even sure you will want to have any knowledge of it."

"I agree. Just do what you have to. I'll catch it CNN or Fox News like every other good citizen," Small concluded.

"Good choice. I am out. I will contact you when the operation is at a close, and I have extracted," Tug hung up the phone. His teeth gritted the cigar as it circled his mouth. He almost had butterflies in his stomach as he thought about the plan commencing.

The mercenary returned to his troops and called them into position. He laid out the plans for the assault on the convention center – this evening was the first time that they had seen the genuine plans. The tasks for each person were similar to those laid out for the hotel across town. The Feds, courtesy of Lyndon, would be patrolling the hotel. Many would-be diverted and would respond to the diversion. Entry and exit to the convention center would then be relatively simple. He readdressed each man's role in context of the convention hall.

Weapons checks were in place. Most men carried an MP4 fully automatic assault weapon. Lead assault teams were given Steyr assault rifles with 1mm rounds and grenade launchers. Snipers were outfitted with PSG-1 silenced barrel rifles with distance scopes. Sidearms adorned their hips. The McKenzie brothers also had eleven-inch hunting knives that remained attached to their ankles. Tug's little army was fortified and ready for combat.

Headset radios were distributed with the proper instructions delivered. They were tuned to the pre-selected frequency and tested. An upwelling of excitement swelled throughout the camp. Tug looked upon the group with almost a sense of appreciation. The very rough and unrefined hooligans had assembled themselves very quickly into a decent team of combatants. "Too bad none of them would return to their normal lives when this is finished," he thought to himself.

Adam's cell phone rang and he answered it promptly. He anticipated a call from his superiors, telling him why he was not allocated additional resources. Instead, he heard the familiar voice of Shayne Matthews, the North Cascades Park Ranger.

"Adam, any word on Jim?" the Ranger asked.

Adam relayed there was no word on the missing deputy.

"Hey, I got news from the ballistics lab. A single bullet did not shoot the wolf, but a mass of several bullets one after another," Shayne said.

"Someone unloaded? What at close range? The hole was consistent, not Swiss-cheesed," Adam questioned.

"Well, that's the kicker. Multiple bullets, rapid-fire. This was from a ten caliber fully automatic weapon. Ballistics says it was likely a Streyhr or OIWC assault weapon -probably from more than 30 yards away. Great shot from that distance, bullets come out so fast. They are not impacted by recoil. It was probably a burst of eight bullets hit square – one after another - and blew the hole out. That is why it was small in, big out. On route, the bullets strike at nearly the exact site, once they impact, they stray a bit and blow out as a big hole. Definitely a military weapon," Matthews replied.

"Can they verify that the weapons matched the shipment stolen from the Hasegawa freighter?" Adam asked.

"No, at least not conclusively. The shipment documents were missing, but a copy is held by the unit that sends the weapons. They report that Steyhr assault rifles were among the contents," Jim reported.

"Still think it is just a hunter with a toy?" Adam asked, his eyebrow furrowed.

"Honestly, it is still possible. You'd be surprised what gets used out there. Just go to one of those gun and ammo shows at the convention center and see what they have. It's crazy," Jim admitted.

"Hmmm. Well, thanks, Shayne. We'll call you if we hear anything about Jim," Adam hung up the phone and turned to Sean. He filled him in on the ballistics report and the other information shared by the North Cascades Park Ranger.

"So, he thinks it could still be just about poaching?" Sean asked.

"Yeah, he says just go to one of those gun shows at the convention center, and you'd see all sorts of stuff," Adam remarked.

Sean froze, *convention center*, the words circulated through his mind. The news mentioned the World Trade Conference at the convention center in Seattle. The plans that Miranda had found - they weren't for a hotel, they were for the convention center.

"Remember the blueprints? What if they weren't for a hotel, but the convention center itself?" Sean asked his friend.

"Well, I think if I was going to make a statement, that comes out a little more clearly than the hotel. I mean, except for a reception held there, where else are you going to have them massed together like you would at the convention center," Adam agreed.

"What do we do?" Sean asked.

"Well, if it weren't for the roadblocks I have been getting, I would say let's go to the feds. Now I am not sure. What about working through your friend Rachel? She might know somebody who will listen," the Fish and Wildlife Officer suggested.

"Good idea," Sean said, picking up his phone redialed his friend. "Rachel, its Sean. Any new information?" he asked into the phone.

"Well, I was just about to call you. I don't have anything new on the political front, but I did just receive a call from the Port of Seattle police. They have your delivery guys in custody," the attractive Department of Interior employee said, "Maybe this will connect the dots to Hasegawa. Nothing on who is blocking the allocation of agents. I have requested updates from the field in Idaho. They are settling into their covers, so that can tie them for weeks with no word on progress. Our best chance is to catch suspects ourselves and bring them in for questioning. You want to come down and observe the interrogation?" Rachel asked.

"Yeah, we were just talking about a trip to Seattle. Where should we go?" Sean asked.

"Well, they are being held at the dock security in Port Angeles. I can request them to be transferred to a field office in Seattle, that will buy you some time," she replied.

"We are on our way," Sean said. He turned to Adam and Miranda, "You ready for a road trip?"

"Yeah, but I'm driving. I remember your last trip to Seattle. I don't want to be in the bottom of the Skagit," Adam laughed.

The three grabbed their things hastily. Adam called his wife and told her that he was headed for Seattle. Sean whistled for Sammy to follow, and they left for Miranda's SUV. They agreed that her vehicle might provide a little more discretion than Adam's Fish and Wildlife SUV. Their first stop would be at Adam's house so he could get some fresh clothes, and Laura Raines could look after Sammy.

The snow had subsided, and the sky was beginning to clear. The winter sky revealed a clear view of millions of twinkling stars. Sean held his arm behind Miranda's hip and gave her a quick kiss as she climbed into her truck.

Turning west towards Interstate Five, they entered Sedro-Wooley and stopped by the Raines residence to let out Sammy and grab some fresh clothes, Adam had Miranda swing into the vacant North Cascades Ranger Station Headquarters. Adam made a beeline to the storeroom. Flipping on a light revealed a series of large steel cabinets. He unlocked one of the units and exposed a cache of weapons and gear. He grabbed a Colt .45 pistol, a shotgun, and several boxes of ammunition. On another shelf, he packed three pairs of binoculars, handing Sean and Miranda one each. He strapped the federal issue handgun to his waist and handed Sean his personal Glock 18 pistol.

The trio glanced at each other and silently made their way out of the office. Adam locked up the building, and they returned to the truck. Adam tossed the shotgun and extra gear into the back hatch of the SUV. Noting the late hour, Miranda suggested that Adam and Sean enjoy some shuteye. It was going to be a long night, and time to sleep might be a premium.

Thirty Four

The Port Authority building lie adjacent to one of the larger shipping yards in Seattle. Miranda drove her SUV to the gates and stopped at the security booth. She gave her information, and the attendant checked a list on his clipboard. Rachel had called ahead and placed them on the approval list. The guard waved her through, and Miranda slipped the SUV forward. The parking lot was a ghost town in the late evening hour. A small handful of cars were parked directly in front of the building, including a pair Port of Seattle police vehicles. Miranda suggested that she would try to secure some hotel rooms in Seattle while Sean and Adam went into the interrogation.

When the two men entered the building, Rachel was quickly there to greet them and whisk them away towards a meeting room. Inside, several uniformed officers and civilians in suits gathered around a large mahogany table. In the middle, facing the door, were two men in jeans and Port of Seattle polo shirts. As Rachel and her new arrivals entered, she shut the door behind them.

"Thank you all for coming. I remind everyone that these two are not charged with a crime, and this is not a formal interrogation. This is a discussion to determine the facts regarding some recent incidents alleged to occur in transit from Hasegawa Freight Corporation. Gentlemen, you are under no obligation here, and this is not a legal proceeding. I am Rachel York. I am the Assistant Director of the Department of Interior Western Region Field Office. Here with me are colleagues from my office as well as the Port of Seattle, and these gentlemen who arrived with me are with Fish and Wildlife out of Skagit County," Rachel informed the two sullen men.

Sean gazed around the room as Rachel made her brief introductions. He saw two men in navy blue suits, each with neatly pressed white shirts and esoteric ties from their necks. Two other men were in casual clothes and sported five o'clock shadows that had matured well past five o'clock. Of course, the two men in the Port of Seattle polo shirts stared uncomfortably at their Styrofoam cups of coffee.

"Okay, guys. We brought you here to discuss a couple of incidents involving Hasegawa Freight. We have witness of the Port of Seattle cargo van being used in the area of Diablo out off of Highway 20, where a hit and run occurred. More importantly, involved in a possible exchange. We need to know what you two know about this. Please understand, we assume you were merely transportation. It isn't you that we are after," Rachel said, her demeanor very cold and calm. She turned to the first man, "Would you like to begin?"

"I, uh, sure," the man began to scramble for words, and then lowered his head in realization that he might as well come clean, "Me and Shep here, were on the docks making preparations for our usual deliveries. We were approached by a man who works for the Hasegawa company. He said he had an urgent pick up for us. This was the second time in a couple weeks that we had been approached for something like this. They gave us an envelope with some cash in it and told us to be quick and quiet about it. This was pretty much setting up like the same deal. We were to drive out to Diablo and pick up a cooler that would need to ship to Japan. The weather kind of sucked out that way, but otherwise, it was an easy extra few bucks."

"Yeah," the man identified as Shep chimed in, "it was all stuff that we normally did, we just didn't have the shipping invoices to go with them. But they came down from the shipping company, so we figured they could do with their stuff what they wanted. Didn't think much of it."

"I see. What was this shipment, Max?" Rachel asked the first man again.

"Well, like I said, it was all supposed to be quiet. We were curious, though. It turns out the cooler was filled with ice packs and some containers containing what looked like the stuff you throw away from the Thanksgiving turkey, only bigger. Pretty gross stuff, but frankly, we ship a lot of weird stuff to and from all over the place."

Rachel shot a glance at Sean and Adam and continued, "Shep, what about this other delivery you mentioned. Earlier in the week?"

"Oh, yeah. Well, like Max said, we were approached by some guy from the freight company to make some easy money. Just make a late-night shipment. We figured they screwed up and just wanted to make up for it. Slip us a few extra bucks and call it good," Shep answered.

"So, what was this shipment?" Rachel asked.

"Uhh, don't know. It was marked, but it looked like whatever was on the crate was blacked out. Sometimes these things get recycled. Some people are lazy and don't properly remark them."

"How about you, Max, any idea what was in the crates?" Rachel asked.

"No, it was just as Shep said. No identifiable markings," Max replied.

"You didn't get curious this time?" Rachel asked, her tone very pointed.

"Well, yeah. We were told if the package was tampered with, it would be dangerous for us," Max answered sheepishly.

"Where did you take this delivery?" Rachel asked.

"To Burlington. Some guys were there in a big pick up. We helped them get the crates transferred and covered them with a tarp. There were about four guys. Country guys," Max replied. "Same guys at the cooler pick up."

"Who all was at the cooler pick up?" Rachel asked, her eyebrows raised, and her head cocked slightly.

"Well, like I said, the guys from the previous shipment, at least two of them and a Japanese guy. I have seen him somewhere before. Middle-aged. It was kinda cloak and dagger. A red Jeep showed up as we were leaving. That's all we know," Shep said, fielding this question.

"Alright. That is all I need. Sean, Adam, any questions?" Rachel concluded, turning the questioning over to Sean and Adam.

"These men you met with in Burlington, can you describe them a little better?" Sean asked.

"Well, they were big. Two of them looked sort of alike, brothers maybe, I don't know. A bunch of good ol' country boys," Max replied.

"What was the truck like?" Sean asked.

"Big, green, jacked up. Had a rebel flag on it," Max said.

"How about the Japanese man in Diablo? Did he look like this?" one of the Port of Seattle men asked, sliding a black and white photo of a man.

"Yeah, that's him. You agree, Shep?" Max said, nodding his head.

"That's the guy," Shep agreed.

"Mr. Hasegawa," the Port of Seattle man told the group.

The men in suits looked over their notepads and concluded that they had no further questions at this time.

"What happens to us now?" Shep asked.

"I think we are done here. You, gentlemen, have been very cooperative. I don't believe we are interested in pressing any charges based upon the information that we have. I think you two might have some issues to iron out with your employers, but I think I would stress that you have been accommodating with a key Department of Interior investigation. Just remember, sometimes easy money might be just a little too easy," Rachel said. She got up from her chair and motioned to Sean for him and Adam to wait for her outside.

Sean and Adam went into the hallway. Sean looked back and watched Rachel walk over to the two gentlemen in suits. They exchanged a few words, and she returned to meet them. The dockworkers, Max and Shep, were led out by the Port of Seattle men and turned over to the uniformed security men who were also waiting in the hallway. Sean overheard that they were free to go, but they would need to report to the security office the next morning. Their foreman would be there as well.

"Well, that confirms a few things," Rachel whispered as she came face to face with Sean and Adam. "We know Hasegawa himself is mixed up in this, at least in the transportation of the bear parts. We also know that there is a link to the McKenzie boys you two told me about. We can also assume that their first delivery could have been that of the weapons cache that came up missing."

"Okay, so it confirms some suspicions, now what?" Adam said.

"We have some work to do. You guys think this has something to do with the Free Trade Convention, right? The delegates and lobbyists are already starting to arrive. If they are planning something there, the clock is ticking fast," Rachel reported.

"Well, we are in Seattle now. Let's see if Miranda was able to snag a couple of hotel rooms and get some shuteye. Let's meet at 7 am tomorrow and get started," Sean suggested.

"I have several morning briefings. My office is involved in the convention. Though, my superiors have not been in support of anything other than an observatory role. Historically, protecting US resources has been a big part of these talks, led by my department. Signs of the coming times, I guess," Rachel said. "Keep your cell phone handy. I'll be in touch. Maybe I can meet you guys around lunchtime."

The lights of Miranda's SUV swung through the parking lot as she drove up to the curb of the building. Adam and Sean said goodnight to Rachel and piled into the truck. "My, she's pretty," Miranda said as Sean sat next to her.

"She's a very good friend. Can we go to bed now?" Sean replied sleepily.

Miranda put her hand on Sean's knee and shifted the SUV into gear. She was able to get two rooms on the outskirts of downtown Seattle. Most of the city center hotels were booked with the convention. As she pulled up to the hotel lobby, Sean tipped the valet, and the three sauntered inside.

"So, what's the plan?" Adam asked his friends.

"Well, I think we know something is up, and it revolves around this free trade conference. Let's see what we can dig up by snooping around the convention center. See who doesn't belong. Put ourselves in a mercenary's shoes. How would we pull off some type of stunt? What do they have to gain?" Sean answered, shrugging his shoulders.

"Sounds like a plan to me. Maybe by noon, Rachel will have something more concrete for us. See if there is a particular dignitary that they might target," Adam agreed.

They walked up to the counter. The attendant recognized Miranda and handed over two sets of keys. "I put it on my card. You can pay me back later," she said to the two men. She turned to Sean and held up one key. "I think having you owe me one could be very advantageous," she said with an impish grin.

Max climbed into his small, rusted yellow pick up. He put the truck into gear and left the shipyard. It was late, and they had to report early the next day to plead for their jobs. He was just glad that they were not in any trouble with the law. They were paid well, though, for their discrete deliveries.

He turned the beat-up truck onto the old highway 99 that led to the northern outreach of downtown Seattle. The streets were empty. He lit a cigarette and drew in a big gulp of air. Home was going to feel good. He was so tired; he didn't see the headlights behind him. A big black Hummer H1 with a massive steel brush guard barreling along the highway catching up to the little import pick up.

Max nearly choked on his cigarette as the truck lurched from the initial impact. The little yellow pickup careened out of control, bouncing off a curb and into a bus stop, the small glass building shattered, pouring its contents onto the sidewalk. The truck slammed to an abrupt halt next to an empty brick warehouse.

The Hummer came to a stop right behind the pick-up. Two men instantly jumped out and ran up to the cab of the vehicle. Each held a high-powered, silenced SOCOM assault pistol.

Max, stunned from this rude interruption keeping him from the warmth and safety of his home, grabbed for the door handle. Before he could yank it open, a bullet from one of the high-powered SOCOMs delivered a fatal blow, piercing his skull.

The men who had jumped out of the Hummer shoved Max aside and rolled the import pick up into the road. The truck started and slammed into gear. The quiet street was a ghost town at such a late hour, providing the men plenty of time to work. The new driver lurched the truck into gear and began to guide it towards the roadside. The driver's door still open, the man jumped out of the cab as the truck reached the road's end. It continued to roll along, just as it teetered on leaving the pavement, one of the men tossed an incendiary device into the cab of the truck. It made its way over the embankment and towards the dock of the Elliot Slough. As it toppled over the edge, towards the water, the little truck exploded into a ball of white flame. The brilliant glow descended into the murky waters of the slough. The remnants of the vehicle and its inhabitant slowly sank to bottom, leaving only a ring of ripples to signal its liquid entombment.

Shep arrived at his home, yawning sleepily. He parked his car in his driveway and called on every last ounce of energy to propel himself out of the driver's seat and towards his front porch. He was so tired; he couldn't remember how he got there. He hated it when that happened when he drove. In his sleep-starved haze, he didn't see the black Hummer parked just down the street. He walked up to his doorstep, grumbling because his porch light had gone out. He fumbled with his keys and dropping them once before he was able to get the door open. Relieved to be home, he tossed his keys on the kitchen counter. In his haste to finally crash into bed, he almost didn't notice the smell.

He walked towards his bedroom, passing through the kitchen. He paused. All he could think of was bed, but what *was* that smell? He sniffed, the sent familiar, but in his groggy state…it was gas! The light in Shep's head finally went on. In weary panic, Shep looked around the kitchen. He checked the stove. It was off. He shrugged, maybe the pilot light had gone out. He sighed; this was not what he needed right now. All he wanted was for his head, which had begun to feel so heavy, to hit the pillow. He bent over and pulled the front panel of the stove open.

Before he could check the pilot light, he heard the kitchen window shatter, and a small bottle with a fiery rag found its way to the kitchen floor. He stared at this intrusion with horror. Helpless, he stood wide-eyed as the room exploded into a fiery blaze. Shep barely had time to dive to the floor. He crawled towards the door but the subsequent explosion ended his life in a skin-searing blaze as it ignited the rest of his house on fire.

The man in the black Hummer down the street started the engine and calmly drove away.

Thirty Five

Special Agents Dick Steinmetz and William McCallum sat in their early morning staff meeting. No one had heard from Special Operation Field Agent Joe Lyndon for nearly a week. This was not an unprecedented incident with an agent that had gone covert. The problem here was, the group in Seattle did not know what facility to protect. When Lyndon was last able to report, the practice assaults had been designed around the prestigious Olympic Hotel - one of the premier hotels in downtown Seattle set to house many of the top dignitaries for the Free Trade event.

The FBI team assigned to this event was reviewing the protective and surveillance layers that followed protocol for the operation. Based on Lyndon's phone call, the concentration of agents would be around this crucial hotel. A sprinkling of agents would patrol the convention center, and even less would be spared to the other area hotels and spots that might be vulnerable to a terrorist attack.

"Well, gentlemen, today is day one of the convention. The kick-off is this evening. If an attack is planned on the Olympic, it could be this evening prior to the opening dinner event. Folks will be milling about at several cocktail receptions and preparing in mass to head to the dinner. Most of the day's events are scattered throughout the waterfront district. Everyone has their assignments. Keep your eyes open. We are hoping that Agent Lyndon will make contact soon. We are working with the hopeful assumption that he is either in a dead spot, or he must remain dark in deep covert status at this time. We will update you as we can. Any questions?" Steinmetz asked his group of highly trained FBI field agents.

As usual, the Bureau had been ridiculously thorough in their briefings up to this day, and each agent was well aware of their duties over the upcoming week. Those that worked closely with Lyndon reserved their concerns. They held each briefing with eager anticipation that word would come of his situation, but remained silent in their disappointment and fears that rose from Lyndon's continued silence.

Tug had his team holed up in an abandoned warehouse on the outskirts of Seattle. Pleased with how quickly and deftly they performed last night with the disposing of the dockworkers, he felt a slight surge of hope that this operation might unfold favorably. He was concerned that if things went awry, his other sniper for cleanup was buried under several feet of snow. Too bad, S.A. Lyndon was a pretty good shot.

He looked at this group of hicks and was actually impressed with their progress. He motioned the two men he had selected for the prep school detail. "Alright, I want you guys in and buckle down. Take a couple of shots, wing a few kids – I don't really care- just get the attention drawn. When you are sure that you have been effective, I want you – Dewayne, to head back and join the group, but only on my call. Take a sniper position from the fire escape in the hotel adjacent to the convention center. You will be exposed, so you will want to be quick. Makes a sweep and clear and get the hell out. You, Tubby, I need you to stay at the school. Keep it interesting for at least a half an hour. From the spot I mapped out for you, you can also see the Olympic Hotel, the same situation. I'll call you, and if I am not pleased with the presence around the convention center, I want you to take some potshots at the Olympic. Don't really care what you hit as long as there is confusion and plenty of attention drawn. That will give the team time to get in the convention center, raise hell, and get out of dodge with a minimum of activity around them. We'll have a clear back door for extraction. You will need to lay low until I advise you to move out," Tug declared.

"Uh, won't that make me kinda, uhh, stuck?" Tubby stammered.

"Everyone in this mission is vulnerable. You will be pinned down. I planned your access and extraction points very precisely. If you follow my command, I promise the law will not be a problem," Tug snapped.

"Yessir," Tubby replied meekly, his head hung low for being called out.

Tug turned to address the rest of the crew. They were buzzing about excitedly, sharing their perspectives on how the exercise would go. An incredible sense of anticipation had been building among the men. "We are about to make history boys, nut up, it's time to go to work," Tug declared, clapping his hands together for emphasis.

He ushered Dewayne and Tubby off to the prep school to take their positions and turned his attention on getting everyone else geared up and ready for the assault on the convention center.

Sean woke up, feeling the warmth of Miranda's leg sandwiched between his. He could smell her hair on the pillow and he drank it in. He gently rolled over and kissed her on her forehead. She responded with a small, low purr. The bed was comfortable and rolling away from Miranda was the last thing he wanted to do. He would love to take advantage of the hotel room and some quality time with Miranda. Unfortunately, his head was buzzing with what they might or might not find today.

He gently prodded Miranda awake. Her lips parted into a welcoming smile as she opened her eyes and looked at Sean.

"Good morning," she grinned, stretching her whole body out like a cat.

"Good morning, beautiful, I hate to say it, but we had better get going," Sean whispered.

"Ugh, that is indeed a shame," Miranda said, her eyes twinkling.

"You're telling me," Sean said, as he dialed Adam's phone to make sure he was awake and arranged to meet him downstairs at the Starbuck's at seven.

"You want the first shower?" Sean asked.

"Excuse me? I do believe a good conservationist would be looking to save a little water. Why don't you join me?" Miranda said with a wicked smile as she slithered into the bathroom.

Sean tore off his shirt and darted after her.

The coffee shop was abuzz with the rush hour mayhem that signaled the start of every business day along the Seattle streets. Men and women in business suits grabbed their coffees and ran out the door, casually dressed patrons sleepily took their coffees to little tables to read the morning newspaper or catch up on gossip. Through the crowd, Sean poked his head up, spying Adam bouncing through the entrance.

"What can I get for you?" Sean called out.

"Venti Mocha and a coffee cake!" Adam replied above the crowd.

Sean and Miranda soon appeared with three coffees and breakfast pastries. They snuck through the crowded entrance and out on to the sidewalk.

"Good morning Adam," Miranda said.

"Good morning, you kids sleep okay last night?" Adam asked, a mischievous grin on his face.

"Sleep? Oh, right, sleep. Yes, of course. And you?" Sean asked in return.

"Great, I don't often get a bed to myself. I have to admit, it is once in a while," Adam replied, "At least it turned out to be a nice day." The sun was shining and even in this early hour, the trio could feel it slowly warming the spring air.

"Good day for hunting bad guys," Sean shot back.

The three began making their way, the seven blocks to the convention center. They were very unsure of what they would find. Aside from the McKenzie brothers themselves, they were uncertain of what they were even hunting.

The brisk walk, despite the cool morning air, was making Sean warm enough that he wished he could take his jacket off. He knew he had to keep it on to conceal the Glock that rested in its holster in the small of his back. He rarely carried a gun, and it was only with the urging of his friend Adam that he had gotten his concealed weapons permit. Considering the encounters of the past week, and the assumed arsenal that the men they were seeking had, a handgun was at a minimum a necessity.

Adam himself packed a large Colt .45 strapped around his shoulder and rested at his side, and a smaller H&K pistol strapped at his ankle. He had considered giving it to Miranda, but without a license to carry, they might all be detained if they happened to be questioned by the authorities. Adam began wondering if they were indeed doing the right thing. Maybe they should have tried harder to get someone to listen to them. But he quickly cast the thoughts aside as he recalled the fruitless hours spent on the phone trying to get his superiors to deliver more field agents. Someone was blocking them, and they were on their own with this one.

The trio made their way past Pike's Place Market and towards the Elliott Bay waterfront. The streets grew more crowded as they closed in on the Bell Street Pier 66 Conference Center – the site of the One World Organization summit. The bayfront center shared its structure with the cruise ship terminals that launched out of Seattle and up to the Canadian Islands and Alaska. The convention center sat directly across the street from the Seattle World Trade Center, a nondescript building nestled between the Alaskan Viaduct and the main road lining Elliott Bay.

The sidewalks near the convention center were overflowing with pedestrians scurrying to get to their offices on time in the nearby buildings. The businessmen and women clung to their coffee mugs and briefcases as they entered their cubicle labyrinth riddle lairs. Others were streaming from hotels and adjacent coffee shops to make their way to register for the convention. Adam had noticed the security detail in the area was tight, especially around one of the fancier hotels. He took note thinking that it was odd that the hotel, which was five blocks away from the Bell St. Pier 66 Conference Center where most of the events were to be held, garnered so much attention. Regardless, they agreed to focus on the convention center itself. They studied the security detail, seeing. Metal detectors screened each entrance of the convention hall. Those carrying bags had to hand over their belongings to be searched by the attending security detail.

"Unless they have a connection to get inside, they are certainly not going to get through security without being caught," Adam mentioned.

"Unless they don't care about security. What if they were just going to take potshots, or run a van with explosive into the building?" Sean asked.

"Shots from one of the nearby buildings make the most sense. A van, like the one used in Oklahoma in the nineties, was pretty common for terrorists worldwide, these days, most of these buildings have some protection around them," Adam said, pointing to concrete pilings placed strategically around the building to prevent a vehicular attack against its infrastructure.

"So, we take a peek and see what buildings would provide you access, cover, clear shots, and an escape route," Sean agreed, surveying the nearby buildings. Most of them were hotels and office buildings.

"Well, I guess we should divide and conquer. Stay sharp and don't make a move on your own. Let's keep cell contact about every half-hour. I'll take the building adjacent to the convention center. Sean, how about you take the hotel across the street. Miranda, there is a little café in front of the Marriott. It gives an ideal vantage point to the area. Would you set up camp there? Buy a book and look like you're leisurely enjoying the morning. That will give us the necessary pulse on the street," Adam directed, looking over the area.

Sean and Miranda agreed, and the trio set off in their assigned directions. Miranda crossed the busy street and entered the little café. She selected a novel about a romantic mystery in Louisiana from the many books and magazines on display. It had been thumbed through quite a bit and looked like she may have already been several chapters into it. Walking to the café, she grabbed a vanilla Frappuccino that she could sip on for some time. Miranda found a table in front of the shop that gave her a view of the convention center as well as the main thoroughfare.

She pulled out her sunglasses, opened her book, and began to scope out the area. Many convention-goers bustled past. She recognized a few congressmen and businessmen that she had seen on television, but no one who didn't fit in with the crowd. Most of the traffic was heading into the center. The café itself was full of people getting their caffeine fix for the day before heading across the street for meetings.

Scanning the buildings surrounding the convention hall, each had a clear view of the center, but she could not discern anything out of the ordinary. A large ferry boat passed by on the Sound, the sun's rays sneaking through the gray clouds gleamed off of the captain's windows. Many pedestrians strolled by the café, some with cups of coffee in their hands, others with the morning's newspaper, none of them appeared inherently sinister. She settled in, assuming that she may be there for a while before anything, if anything, happened.

Adam tried his best to blend in with the crowd at the convention center. Many mirrored his causal dress, though business attire was the norm. He kept his empty coffee cup in hand and picked up a portion of a newspaper that was lying on a bench to tuck under his arm. The building next to the convention center was a northwest cuisine and seafood house, sharing the block with the cruise line slips. The entrance lacked security monitoring its access. Adam circled the block, turning down the other side of the building to an alleyway. He wanted to determine if the ingress of the building was worthy of using as an attack point. Accessible rooms with a clear escape would be critical criteria.

The alleyway was a key entry point used by several vendors delivering goods to the patrons of the building. The street front restaurant was receiving crates of produce out of a gray van. Again, no discernible security was in the area. A UPS van pulled into the alley and parked next to the produce truck. Adam walked around the brown van, just out of sight of the busy produce delivery man. The gray van was neatly marked "Seattle Produce" in green lettering. There was no phone number underneath the moniker. Adam noticed that the front license plate was missing on the van. Adam circled the vehicle, looking for other traits to satisfy his growing suspicion. He was startled when a man carrying a box of lettuce noticed him and approached rapidly.

"Can I help you?" the man asked, he wore a pair of gray overalls with Seattle Produce embroidered on a patch that was on the back of his coveralls.

Adam, startled at getting busted by the deliveryman, paused for a moment. "Uhh, yeah. I am attending the convention next door. I own an import company that ships up produce from Mexico. I have been looking for distribution arms in the Seattle area. I saw your van. Are you new to the area?" Adam asked, trying to sound like he knew what he was doing.

"I don't know, I guess. I just started with them a couple of weeks ago," the man said, still holding the box of lettuce in his arms.

"You got a phone number for the company? I was hoping to find it on the van," Adam said, trying to figure out why a business would neglect a medium for new customers to get a hold of them for more business.

"I suppose somewhere. I'm a little busy right now, can you look it up?" the man said, getting impatient with his interruption.

"Yeah, of course," Adam said, his suspicion of the produce van growing. He didn't want to rattle the man too much until he knew what other entry points they might have. He about-faced and hustled back out of the alley. He reached into his jacket pocket and pulled out his cell phone. A few phone calls and he could prove the produce delivery was a fake and he could round up the troops to take them down.

He dialed information. He fully expected the operator to return with a reply stating there was no such business. He was mildly stunned when the voice read off the phone number for the company. He walked toward the main entrance of the building as the call rang through. A man at the other end of the phone answered. Adam asked him about the company and if a delivery was being made at this location today. The man confirmed that this was the case. He even described the truck and the man that was making the deliveries.

Still not convinced that the produce delivery was legitimate, Adam made another call. Asking his friend in the King County police department to look at the company's history, it tracked back eleven years, with the same owner. Receiving got the owner's name and phone number, he thanked his friend.

Adam dialed the produce company's owner. The man on the other line was very cordial and confirmed that he replaced a few of his vans recently. The detailer who placed the stencil on the truck left the phone number off and was going to fix it in the upcoming week. He also mentioned that managers made the assignments for deliveries, and no one made specific route requests for this day. Adam thanked the man and hung up the phone.

He was sure he had found an access point. The building held a perfect position to access the flank, side, and entrance for the convention center. Pacing in front of the building as he mulled over his thoughts. He had to resign to the fact that the produce delivery theory was a bust. Adam sighed, studying the waterfront area, spotting the office building across the street, the World Trade Center.

The Trade Center was positioned directly across from the Bell St. Pier and Conference Center, presenting an ideal vista for an assault on the center. The parking garage gave good external access, while the office spaces offered a more protective bird's eye view. Nodding to himself, he decided to check out the interior of the building. Dodging traffic, he weaved his way across the avenue and into the lobby.

Sean ambled to the hotel across the street from the convention center. Strolling into the grand foyer of the lobby, examined the scene. A huge centerpiece of flowers stood in a giant marble vase in the center of the floor, a ring of plush sofas encircled it, providing a noisy little meeting area for the hotel guests to convene. Patrons were patiently straightening out bills and checking in at the reception desk. The full shoeshine seats kept the two attendants working feverishly to keep the stock of high-priced footwear polished for the politicians and businessmen attending the convention. Sean didn't have a good game plan for fitting in at the hotel. If the McKenzie brothers and crew had rented a room and were holed up in it, he wouldn't have a chance to find them. His best bet was to explore the building as best as he could.

Swinging his gaze around the lobby, he spied an upper-level mezzanine that opened up to the 1st floor and lobby. Long green vines hung down from the terrace above. Illuminated elevators worked their way up and down the levels in their glass encasements, allowing the riders to act as spectators as they traveled the floors of the hotel. Sean thought about having his shoes shined, it had a great view of the lobby and mezzanine floor, but he looked down at his feet dourly. His leather walking shoes could handle a good buffing, but his casual attire would stand out like a sore thumb against the mix of DKNY and Armani suits.

He shrugged off that idea and waited by the elevator. He held the door open for a pair of well-dressed ladies who flashed Sean a big smile as they passed. As they shuffled into the elevator, Sean asked them which floor and pushed the button for them as he directed. He felt a twinge of imprudence when the elevator stopped on the next level; he made a habit of taking the stairs if he was climbing any less than five floors. He felt a little better when the two women got off on the same floor.

"Sorry, forgot this is where we were going for breakfast," one of the women said, she was an attractive blonde, dressed smartly in a navy blue suit accented by a light blue button-down shirt, it lapels pulled out. Her friend was a brunette, a few inches shorter, equally well-attired wearing a well-tailored beige suit.

Sean nodded, "Yeah, me too."

The hotel restaurant was bustling. The clatter of clinking china and the buzz of early morning conversations roared from the dining room. The restaurant entrance overlooked the lobby and shared a view with the rest of the mezzanine. He could see traffic in and out of the lobby and the second-floor conference rooms adjacent to the dining facility on the mezzanine level. He reasoned that this location was an ideal vantage to assess the scene at the hotel. A line had formed at the hostess stand with a late breakfast crowd waiting to be seated. Not wanting to strap himself into a lengthy stay, Sean sauntered to the bar.

He found the women from the elevator seated nearby. They had also been put on the waiting list and were waiting for their brilliant flame-hued mimosas.

"Hey, did you put your name on the list? You can join us once we get our table if you want," the blonde smiled at Sean.

"No, I appreciate it. I didn't realize the wait would be so long. I am not sure how long I can stick around," Sean said, smiling back.

Sean felt a tap at his shoulder; he turned to see a waiter holding out a mimosa for him. "From the ladies, sir," the waiter said, handing the champagne flute to Sean.

Sean turned back to his new friends, "Thanks. I love these. My name is Sean, Sean Kendall." He held out his hand, smiling. Each of the ladies took turns shaking his hand.

The women introduced themselves. The blonde's name was Andrea, the brunette Britton. "So, are you attending the conference?" Andrea asked, casting a scrutinizing look at Sean.

Sean realized that she was studying his attire. Sean always tended towards overdressing, but he didn't think about the proper dress for the convention. He had planned comfort first for action. He had on a pair of khakis, a tight-fitting ribbed navy T-shirt and his black leather jacket.

"Yeah, sort of," he answered, "I used to go to these, now I am just in town to visit some friends." He looked at his watch, "They weren't sure when they were going to get out of their session, so I figured I would hang out for a while."

"Are you sure you don't want to join us?" the brunette haired Britton asked, as she saw the hostess making a beeline for them.

"No thanks, I'm not sure my girlfriend would appreciate it. Thanks for the mimosa, though," Sean smiled, raising his glass to them.

"Well, Mr. Sean Kendall, you enjoy your time here. Your girlfriend is a lucky lady," Andrea smiled as she and Britton followed the hostess to their table.

Sean looked around the room, sipping his orange juice and champagne, his cheeks blazing from the compliment. Focusing on his task, he didn't perceive anyone who didn't look like they belonged there. He walked casually over the railing of the mezzanine, and leaned over, looking down on the lobby. His arms rested on the rail, the champagne glass in his outstretched hands. Everything seemed business as usual – busy, but nothing arousing suspicion. "No big burly rednecks as far as the eye can see," Sean muttered to himself.

Continuing to study the lobby, he observed as bellboys scurried around, helping people with their luggage. Concierge staff attentively pointed out directions to guests on colorful maps of the city center Seattle. A UPS man hurried through the crowd, past the front desk, and back to where Sean assumed a service elevator was. He noticed that people were still checking in at the front desk - just a busy morning in a busy Seattle hotel.

Sean sucked down the last gulp of his mimosa and set his glass down on a nearby tray. He took one last look around the restaurant as Britton and Andrea waved goodbye. Sean gave a quick wave back. He walked into the heart of the mezzanine. The conference rooms were tucked away towards the back end of the hotel, opposite of the convention center. Sean could rule that area out. Most of the hotel with a view of the convention hall was in guest rooms.

He shrugged and figured he would take floors of the hotel and check them out one by one. Striding to the elevator, he decided to take it as high as he could and begin a methodical search of each level. Once he had cased each floor, he would then take the stairs to the next floor. In the elevator, Sean noticed that there were 20 floors and one penthouse floor, which required a key card. Sean punched the button for the twentieth floor and waited for the doors to open.

Miranda kept her vigil at the street café across from the convention center. She watched the general traffic pass by about their business. She strained to catch anything or anyone out of the ordinary. Most of all, she looked for her cousins. She was a little bit afraid of what was going to happen to them. She decided that it was up to fate now. Whatever they got themselves into, they did so on their own accord.

She shook her mind from the thoughts of her cousins and focused on her current task. She monitored the street and the entrances to the convention hall. Pedestrians in attire that ranged from the finest suits to slacks and dress shirts scurried about the sidewalks. She studied the building adjacent to the conference center, where Adam had entered. She tried to look at each window and balcony. She could see a little bit into the open windows, but the sun that was peeking through the early morning clouds cast a glare upon the closed ones. She traced the roofline of the building with her eyes. Ultimately, she came up with nothing. She sighed, wondering if they had embarked on a wild goose chase. For the sake of her cousins, she certainly hoped that they were.

Special Agent In-charge Steinmetz had his team of agents ready at the Olympic Hotel. Several agents were placed strategically throughout the lobby and several more scattered throughout the building. Snipers were stationed on the rooftops of three nearby buildings. They were unclear of the nature of the assault, but they had an idea of when it might take place. In the early afternoon, following lunch, a group of local politicians and business leaders were having a reception in the luxurious restaurant on the thirty-sixth floor. He had worked with the hotel to place a few agents in the restaurant as employees.

Several other smaller teams dispersed throughout the convention vicinity. Most were in positions near the security checkpoints. They monitored the searches of people entering the convention as well as video surveillance set up at a desk near the inspection area.

His team had spent most of the early morning sweeping the building for explosives and personally inspecting each delivery made to the hotel. Agents ran checks on the hotel guest lists and credit card vouchers. Special Agent McCallum joined Steinmetz in the command center they set up in a hotel room across the street. From their window, they had several high-powered scopes and cameras trained on the Olympic.

"Any hits on the list or credit checks?" Steinmetz asked.

"No, a lot of politicians, nobody who is on the radical watch list. So far, everyone checks out. We are also running checks on the employees of the Olympic," McCallum answered.

"Pay special attention to people hired within the past month," Steinmetz suggested.

"Right. So you still think the reception this afternoon?" McCallum asked his partner.

"Of all the events on the schedule here, it makes the most sense. Who knows? After the Colorado incident, we need to prepare for anything. This is the best information we have to go on. I sure wish Lyndon would get in contact with us," Steinmetz remarked.

"Roger that," McCallum said and issued the order to prioritize the checks of the newest employees first.

Steinmetz rubbed his chin as he stared out the window thoughtfully; he knew in his heart that agent Lyndon would not utter a sound to the team. Sighing, he quietly resolved that his field agent had been made, and the venerable Tug Gaskill had ended his life. Steinmetz had made a career of chasing rogue mercenaries and terrorists. He knew all too well when what men like Gaskill were capable of. Agent Lyndon was a top field operative, one of the best. Whatever happened here today, Steinmetz knew he had to keep his team prepared for anything.

Adam casually approached the entrance of the World Trade Center and walked in. He was still holding his coffee cup and newspaper props. He appeared as most of the occupants, hurrying along to their jobs. He paused briefly at the panel that listed the patrons of the building and their locations. Most of the businesses were lawyers, CPAs, and insurance brokers. The building lobby was a simple affair. It held a little desk to one side of the entrance marked "Security and Information". To the other side was a Starbuck's corner store, teaming with business on the busy convention morning. Across the lobby were four elevators. Beyond the elevators was the walkway to the entrance of the restaurant that was having its produce delivered.

Adam didn't see anything or anyone in the lobby that led him to aroused suspicion. He decided to case the individual fourteen floors of the building. First, he walked to the security stand and asked the attendant if there were any vacant or recently leased offices. The attendant admitted that on the seventh floor, an office had recently vacated. Adam thanked the man and began his sleuthing.

He started on the fourteenth floor. He tried to access the roof, but it had a double chain and padlock on it. It had obviously not been opened. The first few floors of the building held little of interest for Adam, just businesses that appeared to have been in operation for quite some time. Two offices on each floor had a clear view of the convention center. From their vantage point, they could see into the ornate glass roof of the entrance area. None of the top six floors gave Adam any notion that something might be wrong.

On the seventh floor, he stepped out of the stairwell. As the heavy steel door clanged shut behind him, he noticed that one of the offices with a view of the convention center had a "For Lease" sign in the window. He approached the office door carefully. The frosted glass did not afford a view of the interior of the office. He pressed his ear against the glass of the office door, trying to detect any noises coming from the inside, but the office was silent. He looked around the hallway. It was quiet and empty. Sliding a credit card out of his wallet, he slipped it between the door and the steel jam. He gently worked the card back and forth until he heard the triumphant click of the locking mechanism give way.

He took one final glance around the vacant hallway and slowly pushed the door to the office open. He grabbed his gun with his left hand and gripped it tightly as he poked his head around the door. The office was quiet and empty. The hardwood floor shone from the faint sunlight that was filtering through the window. Adam silently closed the door behind him.

Windows lined two of the outer walls. The south bank afforded views of the hotel next door. The north bank of windows, however, offered an unobstructed vista of the convention center. Adam silently glided across the floor, carefully checking every room, closet, and cabinet. Each was empty and silent, waiting for a new lessee.

Walking over to the windows facing the convention hall, he knelt beside one of the windows. He imagined himself in the pose of a sniper. He could take out entrances of the hotel next door as well as the convention center across the street. Rotating his field of vision to the rest of the convention hall, he observed that most of the grand foyer encased in glass. A NATO high-millimeter round could easily pierce the dense glass structure. Side service entrances to the convention hall could be seen as well. Several catering and florist vans, and large semi-truck from a staging company crammed into the tight alleyway.

This room offered a high vantage point, but certainly seemed undisturbed. Adam could not detect any signs that someone had spent any time there. He decided to continue his descent through the building. Each floor turned up as business as usual as the floors above. Adam reached the lobby without identifying anything that could be considered suspicious. He figured that much of their game plan was to be a waiting game. He just hoped they could react in time if they did discover something.

The Fish and Wildlife Officer again scoped out the lobby, seeing nothing out of sorts, he strolled back out onto the sidewalk. It was time for the three to make their next check-in, and he dialed their cell phones. Miranda reported that all was quiet from her spot. Sean reflected his Mimosa incident with the two ladies, but otherwise, he resorted to casing the floors one at a time. He had just completed the top level. Adam signed out and looked around the street. Lots of traffic cruised by; people hustled to and from meetings, all seeming to fit the mold.

Adam decided that he should complete his route of the office building and then would make a circuit of the convention center. He walked the opposite direction of the way he went the first time. He found a little service alley adjacent to the convention center. He ducked into it as casual as he could. There was no access for either building, until he reached the large bay doors of the convention center. He saw the trucks that he had spied from the office on the seventh floor. The alley kept going all the way to the gate that separated the road from the bay. Counting eight bay doors along the wall, he noted a pair of security agents checking all of the deliveries and trucks.

He walked out of the alley and onto the boardwalk that backed the office building and convention center. His thoughts persisted that it made sense for an assault to be initiated by a sniper from a nearby building. He turned left and walked along the rear of the building. Access to the restaurant was in the center of the building, manned by a valet. An expansive view of Puget Sound was enjoyed from this side of the building. Adam completed his circuit to the point where he went into the first alleyway he entered. The UPS van had been joined by a laundry service van. Adam assumed both were servicing the restaurant.

Again, he returned to the sidewalk, laden with no convincing evidence of anything sinister or out of place. He took another scan of the area; traffic remained constant. Taxicabs and even a few limousines pulled up to the curb to let convention-goers out. Two brown vans turned into an alleyway of the hotel Sean was casing.

Adam followed the sidewalk past the convention center entrance. He took the turn around the next block of the convention center, surveying each possible way into the building. At each point, he found security personnel manning each post. He found no clear route into the building, nor did he spy anything remotely suspicious or out of place. He waited at an intersection for a brown cargo van to pass by. "Man, these UPS guys are active today," Adam thought to himself as he walked back towards the office building. He was sure that the seventh-floor office made an ideal location.

Adam paused. He had counted four UPS trucks in the area. The UPS truck parked at the office building service entrance was still there even after he had spent two hours investigating the area. He didn't give it much thought while he was in the alley; his focus was on the produce van. He scratched his chin, what a better way to transport goods into a building without getting much attention? He picked up his phone to give Sean a call.

Sean checked out the entire twentieth floor. He found nothing, though he couldn't access most of the guestrooms. He walked over to the stairwell near the elevators. A yellow sign instructed him the staircase was closed as he opened the door. Peering over the rail and saw a man in coveralls and broom. The man looked up at Sean.

"I'm sorry, sir, the stairwell is closed. I should be able to reopen it in a couple of minutes. A guest dropped a glass," the maintenance man said, "You know, if you want to take the stairs, there is a second set. It is over by the ice machines. It isn't marked real well. Most people don't even know it exists."

"Thank you. I appreciate that. If I ever can, I choose stairs over the elevator," Sean remarked happily.

"To each their own," the man grumbled as he went about his work.

Sean turned and sought out the ice machine. He walked down the hall and past cart that was blocking the entrance to one of the many guest rooms as it was being cleaned. Near the elevators, was a sign that showed the range of rooms on the floor and which direction they were located. Underneath, was a sign that pointed towards the ice machine. Sean followed it to a little room. The dimly lit space was filled by the humming and occasional grumble of the big stainless steel appliance. Near the machine was a door that looked as though it might lead to a closet. Sean walked over to it and gave the handle a turn. It opened with a slight squeak. Sean immediately felt a blast of fresh air hit him. The stairs were partially open to the elements, in between the steel stairs and concrete walls; they opened up into gaps that allowed fresh air to rush in.

Sean peered through one of the open gaps. The view included the World Trade Center next door. He walked down a few extra steps to the first landing. The landing had gaps on two sides. On one, the same faceless side of the building next door could be seen. On the other, was a view of the convention center. Concrete rose to about waist high and then opened up to the elements. Sean gauged the view. He could see an angle of the front entrance, and an alleyway that housed several large trucks servicing the center.

He descended the concrete steps, stopping at the door for the nineteenth floor. He gave the door a yank. It didn't budge. Sean twisted the handle; it clicked back and forth only a fraction each way. He sighed disgustedly, "The doors must only open from the inside as a security measure." He sucked up his misfortune and began a slow jog down the stone steps. He would have to go all of the way down and back up again to search the upper floors. He wasn't very excited about it, since he wasn't likely to find much amongst the closed hotel room doors. He reached the seventeenth floor when his cell phone beeped.

Pulling the phone free from its holster, he spoke into it, "This is Sean."

"Hey, bud. I think I may have figured out their way in," Adam said. He shared his theory about the UPS deliverymen.

"Yeah, I have seen one at the hotel. He breezed right past the front desk. Now that I think about it, it did appear that the clerk expected him to check-in or leave the package there, but the UPS guy just cruised right along. I just figured he knew where he was going. Never even really thought much about the UPS guy," Sean admitted.

"Exactly, that's my point. Everyone is used to the friendly UPS guy running around, especially in a business setting. What a perfect way to sneak in," Adam announced excitedly.

"And, it's a perfect way to sneak weapons and supplies in, lugging around stacks of boxes," Sean added. "I'll go back through the hotel and try to find my guy, how about you?"

"Yeah, I have seen a van outside my building since we got here. I also just saw one pull into the convention center. Maybe we'll have Miranda move to that location," Adam said thoughtfully.

"I'd hate to lose the outside observer," Sean started, and then said, "Wait a minute, I may have the solution. I have a call from Rachel coming in. Hold on."

Sean switched calls and greeted Rachel.

"Hi, Sean. I have some news for you, where are you?" she asked.

Sean filled her in on his progress and about the UPS man theory.

"I like the theory. It's smart. Why don't I relieve Miranda and have her check out the UPS delivery at the convention center? I'll play observer.

She's been there long enough. But Sean, ...they found Jim Hall. He's been killed," Rachel informed her friend.

"What? How?" Sean asked, he felt his heart sink in his stomach.

"He was shot. Close range, apparently two days ago. They found him in a ravine nearby a....Hidden Lake?" Rachel replied.

"Hidden Lake Peak," Sean corrected solemnly. "Go relieve Miranda. I'll give her a quick call."

Sean hung up with Rachel York. He backed against the concrete border. He couldn't believe Jim had been killed. It was the first time that anyone that he knew had ever been murdered. "Oh God," he whispered to himself. He thought of the last time that he saw Jim. At his house with Adam. They were discussing his suspicions; his goose chase got his friend killed. Remembering that he had Adam on hold, he switched back shared the sad, disappointing news with his friend.

He shook his head, trying to clear his mind of his friend's passing. He had to get his thoughts clear. "These guys have to pay," Sean snarled. He picked his head up with a renewed ambition to get the people that were behind all of this. He dialed Miranda's cell phone.

"Hey, beautiful. How are things going down there?" he asked her, his voice trying not to quiver under the weight of his anger.

"Pretty benign so far. What's up?" Miranda asked.

"You get to stretch your legs a little bit. Adam came up with a theory that they might be using UPS vans and delivery uniforms to get into the buildings without scrutiny. He says he saw one turn into the convention center a few minutes ago. We need you to check it out," Sean relayed Adam's thoughts.

"Yeah, I'm ready to move around a little bit," Miranda agreed.

"Good. Listen; be careful. If you see anything, get on the phone with us immediately. Rachel is on her way to take your spot. I have a feeling we might be close," Sean said.

Sean hung up the phone, already restarting his descent. He had to find out where his UPS guy went. At the tenth floor, he paused, thinking he heard something. He craned his neck until he heard it again – "splat"! He froze in place. A few seconds later, there it was again – splat! He peered over the edge, but he couldn't see anything. Creeping down the staircase, he slowed when he reached each landing, bending around cautiously. Every few moments, he would hear another curious "splat" on the concrete below him.

As he rounded the bend of the ninth floor landing, he looked out across to the convention center. The view of the entrance was a clear shot from this vantage. The angle was much better at the lower floors, and he could see a trajectory well into the lobby of the center. He slowly stuck his head around the corner towards the eighth-floor landing. He didn't see anything at first, but as he proceeded cautiously down the stairs, he saw the undeniable form of an elbow sticking out from behind the concrete barrier.

Sean froze. He started to pull his gun out, but realized that he didn't want to fire a weapon at this point of the game in a public place. He stared at the elbow sticking out from the corner of the stairwell. It moved slightly, giving Sean the view of a gunstock. He tried to look over the rail for a better view, but the man was in a perfect position for obscurity.

Sean tiptoed a few steps closer. He stuck his fingers in a hole in the concrete above his head. He was two steps from the landing where the man was holed up. Sean let his weight fall on his finger grip by lifting his legs. He slowly worked himself into a swinging motion. As he built up some momentum, he lunged with an outward kick and swung himself around the corner of the stairs. Sean curved his body right next to the railing. His feet came in contact with a solid object.

He felt the soles of his shoes impact the side of the crouching man's head. The sniper sprawled to the ground, stunned by the hard hit. The Steyr rifle the man was holding clattered down the steps to the landing below. Sean let go of his grip and landed on the corner of the stairs in a crouched position. He was hoping there was only one man to subdue. He reached behind his back to grab his pistol just in case. Seeing only the man on the ground against the far wall, he relaxed his grip on the gun. Sean looked next to the man finding a black duffle bag stuffed with ammunition.

The man shook off the initial attack and lunged at Sean. The two men met, each with both hands on each other's shoulders. Sean braced his back foot and pushed forward, he felt the mercenary do the same. As they struggled for position, Sean gripped his assailant's shoulders hard and twisted with his entire body. The man stumbled back slightly and let go of Sean. Sean shoved him back and delivered a kick to the man's ribs, crushing him into the corner. The man reached down to grab his small revolver, but Sean quickly kicked it away with his foot, allowing to clank harmlessly to the ground.

The two men faced each other in a standoff. The man feverishly pushed a small button on his belt and called into the small headset he wore around his head, "Mo, it's Roy, we got trouble up on the stairs. Get up here quick!"

Sean charged the man again, ramming his shoulder into the man's mid-section. The impact of Sean's shoulders to the front and the unforgiving concrete wall to his back left the man gasping for air as he swung wildly to fend off Sean's attack. The man grabbed Sean's arms, but Sean had the leverage. He stuck out his foot and tossed the sniper over his leg. The man fell headfirst off of the landing and down the stairs. He landed at the bottom in a coiled ball with a horrible crack and a thunk.

Sean glided down the steps, and cautiously checked the man's pulse. He was alive, but he was unconscious. He had blood slowly trickling out of his mouth. Sean ripped off his headset and put it over his own head. He heard a gruff sounding voice calling into it, "What's that Roy? You alright down there? Sorry, I was on the crapper. Say again?"

At first, Sean was relieved that he wasn't going to have more company, but then, he realized that he spoke too soon. "Ahh, hell, I'll come down and see what's goin' on. Roy, are you there?" the voice drawled over the radio. Sean hustled back up the stairs and grabbed the handgun that fell and the black duffle bag. He hopped back down to the fallen gunman. Placing the pistol and the Steyr rifle into the canvas bag, he tossed the strap over his shoulder and began down the stairs.

He descended a couple of floors before he heard a door shut and footsteps coming down the steel steps towards him. He paused and waited for the footsteps to get closer. He heard them come down from the flight above. Sean assumed the person belonging to the footsteps was the man named 'Mo'. Sean tiptoed halfway down the flight of steps he was on. He saw a figure bound around the corner. Sean grabbed the step from the flight above him and held himself up with his arms as if he were about to do chin-ups. He drew his legs up the staircase and waited. He watched the man jog right past him. He coiled his legs as the man went by. The man was tall and thick, a scraggly beard encompassed his face. Strapped to his shoulder, he harnesses a rifle like the man in the stairs, strapped vertically on his shoulder.

Sean unleashed his legs into a powerful kick, catching the man square in the back of the head. The blow caused him to stumble back just as he tried to bring the gun around into a firing position. Sean followed him by leaping to the landing. Before the man could recover, Sean brought the rifle he carried and levied the butt of the gun into the side of the man's head. The lightweight metal stock met the man with a brutal crack. The man looked at Sean with a blank expression on his face. Sean watched the color drain from his assailant as the man turned pale, his knees buckling and, like his friend Roy, toppled down the flight of stairs, melting in a heap at the bottom of the landing below.

Sean bent down and added the second Steyr to his duffle bag. He checked the man for another weapon, but came up empty. He tore off the man's headset and tossed it in the bag. Looking over his shoulder, Sean turned to see if the first man had regained consciousness and was coming after him, but the stairwell was silent. Sean swiftly began jogging down the steps, simultaneously dialing Adam as he went.

Dewayne Miller and Steve "Tubby" Bauman nestled in their positions, on opposite sides of the school. Each kept vigil with their watches, instructed by Tug to be very precise with their timing. Tug estimated that it would take fifteen minutes for the agents and policemen near the convention center to react and converge on the school. Dewayne, the son of a rancher in Idaho, has listened to his father grumbled about the government for as long as he could remember. His family moved deep into the woods as the school that Dewayne and his siblings attended had accepted a black student. It was the first that their remote county to have entered their school. Dewayne's father was outraged and decided Mrs. Miller could teach the kids from their ranch. He and some family friends joined the Greys after they met a friend at church who was a member. Since then, Dewayne had been programmed to prepare for an uprising against the ever-growing liberal government.

Tubby's father swore that their family was descendants of Nazi militia leaders. He praised Hitler's cleansing efforts, and they enlisted as the Greys members in Washington. Feeling that they were one with the cause, they trained with the McKenzie family for years. Tubby had become a great shot with a rifle. Tug recognized his skill and quickly selected him for the sniper detail. He eyed his watch and raised his gun into position. Looking around his perch, an old water tank that sat on top of an old warehouse, he readied himself for the attack.

The old warehouse Tubby used for his position was a distribution center for a failed retail chain. The decrepit water tank hadn't been used for decades, but stood as an industrial symbol of days gone by. Under a ladder that ran to the top of the tank was a culvert, sealed off by a rusted mesh grill that hung precariously over its mouth. He had used a small electric screwdriver to unfasten three of the screws that held it in place. He was able to turn the grill up enough so that he could squeeze into the narrow opening of the conduit. It was a great hiding space that afforded him an eagle-eye view of the prep school, and yet kept him out of visibility. He wrenched the grill back into place, utilizing the mesh as makeshift camouflage.

Training his scope across the school and at the office building on the other side, he spied the roof access door ajar, propped open slightly with a small triangular piece of wood. Looking looked harder in the darkness, he could see just the tip of a rifle barrel sticking through the narrow opening - this gun belonging to Dewayne Miller. They were both set in position, ready for action.

Tubby returned his scope to position his eye at the commissary floor, where the last shift of students were finishing their lunch. Room monitors stood scattered throughout the room, tending to the children. He lined his crosshairs at one student, and then another. He watched them talking and laughing with their classmates. He thought to himself that he wasn't sure if he could bring himself to squeeze off the trigger, a bead of sweat forming on his forehead, sliding to his eyebrow until he smeared it with his sleeve. Adjusting his scope as he instructed, he glanced at his watch. Ten seconds to 1 p.m. Then he saw the Indian boy. He dressed in clothes typical of any other American student. Yet, his dark skin and dark hair belied his Middle Eastern heritage. Damn Arabs are taking over the country. Where would they be without their oil fields and the U. S. protecting them? This kid would make history, he thought.

Tubby Bauman's finger wrapped around the trigger and sent the noise-suppressed 10mm round into the air. He kept his scope focused on the boy. He saw a brief look of surprise on the kid's face, and then he crumpled to the floor. Monitors came rushing to his side, clearing away the horrified on-looking classmates. It appeared as though they didn't quite realize what happened, as they checked the boy's vitals and then finally found the hole just above his heart. The boy was dead.

The chaos that followed had the monitors clearing students away from the windows. The school bell rang, and teachers rushed out into the common area to rustle the children back into the building. Tubby rotated his scope around from child, to teacher, studying their moves, surmising that tug's plan was working.

When Special Agent In-Charge got the call, his heart sank. He called for two of the four teams of agents guarding the convention center to report to the school. He could already hear the sirens wail across the city. He spaced out his remaining unit at the convention hall to cover all of the access points. "Damn!" he cursed to himself.

Agent McCallum joined him. "I heard the call. A diversion?"

"That's what I was thinking. Just to be safe, I am keeping the hotel team intact. If something is going to happen, it will be within the next hour. Goddamn! A kid! We have to nail these bastards," Steinmetz said, a disgusted look crossing his face.

Thirty Six

Tug Gaskill listened through the scanner as the reports of the school attack came in. His men were right on time. He was pleased to hear that the convention center FBI detail responding. A wicked grin crossed his lips. His plan was coming to a head. He kneeled at the windowsill of the seventh-floor office. He had cracked the window three inches to get an unobstructed perspective of the area.

He trained his rose-tinted non-reflective field glasses at the convention center. He saw a dozen men in dark suits emerge from the convention hall and duck into two black Suburbans. The trucks took off quickly as soon as the last door shut.

"The security detail is breaking up," he said to no one in particular. He surveyed the entrances. Men in dark suits took positions at the entrance, two men at each access point. This was perfect. He trained his binoculars to the alley alongside the convention center. His eyes widened when he saw the woman walking up to the UPS truck. It was the McKenzie girl.

"What the hell is she doing there?" he demanded. He thought for a moment. He grabbed his gear and ran to the door. In fifteen minutes, the main assault would begin, and he could not have her alert the authorities prematurely.

Rachel sat, enjoying a caramel latte as she observed the goings-on around the convention center. She took Miranda's post at the café, sitting at a little bistro table next to a railing that lined the sidewalk. She leaned back as she watched the traffic pass by. Rachel didn't see anything out of the ordinary. At least not until she saw the men in suits bolt out of the convention center main entrance and the blacked-out Suburbans fly up to the curb.

Something had to be up. She dialed her office and asked them to find out what was happening. They very quickly replied with a report that a shooting had occurred at the Marshall Hall Private School, six blocks from her location. One student was confirmed dead. The convention center had the most available agents with the exception of the Olympic Hotel, where the FBI intel convinced them was a target.

Rachel didn't like this. It left the center vulnerable. She called Sean to fill him in on what was going on. She could hear sirens wail in the distance. Sean's phone was busy, so she left him a message. She relayed the shooting at the school and concerns about increased risk at the center. She got up from her chair and went into the little bookstore. She picked up a small map of the Seattle area. She asked a woman at the counter if she knew where the school was on the map. The clerk showed her. Then Rachel asked about the Olympic Hotel. They were within a few blocks of each other. Rachel thanked the woman and returned to her seat.

Rachel watched the area with increased vigor. Her instincts screamed that something was not right. The FBI received a tip on a hotel several blocks away from the convention center, now there was a sniper taking shots at kids at a school a few blocks from the hotel. The agents were being thinned out. Her pulse quickened, she had to get a hold of Sean.

Miranda approached the alley of the convention center carefully. There were several trucks parked at the loading bays. There was indeed a brown UPS van parked at one of them. She walked up to it as no one was in sight, continuing around the corner of the truck. The doors were shut and locked. She tried peeking in the window to see if she could see anything in the back, but the alley was too dark and what light did come in left a glare on the flat glass.

The door next to the loading bay opened. A man strode through and froze, stunned to see Miranda. He wore a brown uniform of the famous shipping company. Miranda was shocked with recognition.

"What the hell are you doing, Daryl?" Miranda confronted her cousin.

"Miranda! What are *you* doing here? You shouldn't be here! Get out of here, now!" Daryl yelled at his cousin.

"Daryl, I know what you are up to," Miranda admitted.

"This doesn't concern you, cousin. It is not safe for you to be here," Daryl pleaded. His eyes widened as he saw a man approach behind his cousin. The man grabbed her.

"This must be Miranda," Tug said. He had one armed wrapped around her arms and one hand over her mouth. Little squeaks were all that Miranda was able to get out as she tried to scream from behind Tug's hand.

"What are ya gonna do with her?" Daryl asked. He was afraid of what a man like Tug would do with his cousin.

"You said it yourself; it isn't safe for her here. We'll just make sure she gets somewhere safe. You go back to your work, and I promise you, I'll take care of your cousin," Tug said.

Daryl looked at him, unsure. He did not want to put his cousin in danger. He knew that in a matter of minutes, the convention center would not be a safe place. He also didn't trust Tug with her either. He felt like he had no choice, having Tug remove her from the area probably was the best choice. He nodded slowly and opened the back of the van to gather his last load. His team member was setting up their stash in the interior of the building, preparing for the attack. He grabbed the last two brown cardboard boxes and reluctantly left his cousin in the clutches of Tug Gaskill.

Tug and Miranda watched Daryl disappear into the convention center bay doors as he pulled the girl into the shadows. Tug would tow his piece of insurance with him. In his own pack, he grabbed a roll of duct tape. He shoved a small piece of cloth in Miranda's mouth and taped it in place. The mercenary then bound her wrists together, wrapping more duct tape. When he was pleased with his work, he ushered her into the back of the UPS truck. He radioed for one of his men to transport her to the warehouse, where they grouped for the operation. He shut the doors behind him and disappeared back into the shadows. He had an attack to oversee.

The clock ticked. Jeb McKenzie sat on a ledge just beyond the wall of the hot tub and sundeck of the hotel penthouse suite directly across from the convention center. A banner advertising the hotel bar and their big Fat Tuesday party shielded him from view from the street front. He had cut a small slit in the banner, allowing a hole for his weapon to peek through. He felt little beads of sweat begin to well up on his forehead. He was excited. He couldn't wait for the second hand to make its sweeps. Precisely thirteen minutes after the attack on the school, he would squeeze the trigger on his AT-4 rocket launcher.

The seconds swept by slowly. Ten, nine…he wondered if his brother was in position. He would be in the line of fire if he didn't successfully get to the interior of the convention hall. Seven, six…he thought briefly of the escape plan and wondered if it would really work. Tug was a little vague on it. Four, three…he knew this would be the most significant moment of his life. One…

Jeb McKenzie's finger squeezed the trigger on the AT-4 M136 rocket launcher. He jerked back slightly, the recoil from such a powerful weapon was surprisingly minimal, he felt the heat from the rocket radiate off of the wall behind him. He didn't mind as he watched the rocket hit the target. He grinned as he watched the glass roof of the building shatter into thousands of pieces that rained down on the crowd below. A brilliant flame leaped up from the building as the rocket found its ultimate destination. The ground around the building shook. People began to scream and scurry about in no logical manner.

Jeb couldn't take a lot of time to admire the handy work of the rocket. He had seen the FBI and security guards rise and scan the area as they tried to control the crowd. Jeb picked up his Steyr and focused on a man in a dark suit. He slowly brought the weapon up to the man's neck. He could see the small earpiece. FBI. Jeb squeezed off a burst round, and the agent crumpled to the floor. Another man in a dark suit knelt beside the man who fell. Jeb quickly fired another round. This man fell on top of the first agent. Methodically, Jeb swept the area with his scope and took out anyone who looked like security, police, or FBI.

Wendell looked out at the world seven floors below him. He watched the McKenzie woman approach the UPS van. She looked around the alleyway and turned the corner of the truck. He could see her try and look into the cab of the truck and was startled when the door to the building open. Daryl McKenzie stepped out and was equally startled to see his cousin staring back at him. Wendell, almost chuckled. He was a little nervous about what was going to happen. They had worked too hard and were in too precarious a position for things to go awry now. He saw Tug, the group's experienced leader, silently emerge from the shadows and subdue the woman. After a brief exchange, Tug pulled the girl into the shadows from where he came, and business in the corridor never skipped a beat.

Wendell grinned. It was almost time, and Tug was going to miss the start of his little mini-war. He trained his field glasses across the street. The

Fat Tuesday Banner gently waved in the breeze. He had to use full magnification to see the smallest tip of Jeb McKenzie's gun poking through the narrow slit he made in the vinyl fabric. He returned to the alley. His objective was the two FBI agents posted inside the bay doors, a mere fifty yards from where Miranda was abducted. Tug instructed him to eliminate any security detail that stepped foot in or out of the alley. Once he removed the visual targets out, he was to launch a small grenade assault on the bays of the loading dock.

It was time. His silenced PSG-1 sniper rifle came to life. The two FBI agents fell immediately off of the dock bay they were inspecting and onto the asphalt of the driveway below. Their dark suits splashed into stagnant puddles that had yet to evaporate in the shadow of the alleyway. Neither of them saw the attack coming. They had no time to report and no time even to draw a weapon. He swung his rifle to another bay where two security agents appeared, before he was able to line them up, he was hit from behind. He scrambled for his gun, but it was kicked away as a pair of strong hands grabbed him by the collar.

Adam felt in his gut that the vacant office was the ideal spot for an attack on the convention center, at least for an observation point. Even if not, he figured it would offer him a good view with Sean, Miranda, and Rachel at the other locations. He scrambled back up the stairs to the seventh floor. Again he pulled out his credit card and began to jostle the locking mechanism in the door. Silently, the door swung open. Adam didn't hear the click of the (lock parts) in place. Maybe he forgot to lock it when he left.

He walked into the room. He could feel a breeze coming from the corner office with the convention hall view. Adam walked carefully on the balls of his feet to avoid making noise on the hardwood floor. There was a man in a brown UPS uniform kneeling at the window. He had a black gun with a powerful scope in his hands, aimed at the building next door. He saw the man pull the trigger twice and cycle the scope through the dark corridor. Adam kept slowly pressing forward.

The faux-delivery man was pulling the gun back through the space between the sill and the window as Adam grabbed him by the shoulders. He had enough leverage and surprise that the man dropped his rifle. Adam spun the man away from the window and slammed his knee into the man's gut. The man's eyes were wide with astonishment as he was expecting Tug to rejoin in him instead of this intruder. Before he could react, Adam slammed his fist into the man's chin. His head snapped back, temporarily cutting off his air supply, causing him to fall unconscious.

Adam looked out the window to the alley below. He saw the fallen FBI agents. Scanning the length of the corridor, he found activity on the street was business as usual - until the rocket from the hotel across the street sent a rumble through the block. Adam traced its path and followed it with his eyes to the top floor of the hotel. It was the hotel Sean was casing out. He picked up his phone and called Sean.

"Hey, I was just about to call you. I found two men in the stairwell. He had a mini arsenal with him. I took him out and grabbed his bag of goodies. What the hell was that noise?" Sean said excitedly.

"That was some sort of rocket fired from your hotel. I figure it came from the top floor. It caused a pretty big explosion in the main atrium. I also caught a guy in the office building adjacent to the center. He had already taken two FBI agents. I guess this was a planned sniper location. Go check out the top floor. I am going ground to the convention center," Adam replied.

"Miranda! She was heading over to check out the alley. Do you see her?" Sean asked.

"No. I'll make a sweep of the alley. Maybe she heard the explosion and ducked back for safety," Adam suggested.

"I'll try her on the cell on my way up. If it was the top floor, then it came from the penthouse. There is no way in without a keycard," Sean said, his pulse quickening.

"Well, you better find a way. Good luck, and be careful," Adam warned his friend.

He found a cardboard box with UPS shipping instructions on it beside the unconscious man. Next to it was a large black duffel similar to that described by Sean. He gathered up the weapons and tossed them in the bag. He counted several boxes of shells, the PSG-1 silenced sniper rifle, and a rifle with scope and grenade launcher. He stuffed them in the canvas duffle and thought about what to do with the man. In the back of one of the offices was a storeroom. It was open. He dragged the man inside and dumped him in. He locked the door and heard it click behind him.

He hurried out the door; he had to get to the convention center and hopefully find Miranda. He turned a hard left towards the stairs and began bounding down towards the lobby. As he reached the lobby, he saw a large mail chute. He stuffed the bag of weapons down the chute and headed for the street.

Tug left his captive and ducked into the delivery entrance to the office building. He quickly bound up the steps as he heard the explosion at the center. The attack had begun. He was eager to get to his observation post.

He radioed to Dewayne Miller. "What's the status?"

"Man, FBI men are running all over the place," Miller whispered into his handheld radio.

"Well, it sounds like you have done your job. Now that there is a ruckus at the convention center, I need you and Tubby to up the ante. The center will become the priority. I need them pinned down at the school," Tug commanded.

"But sir, I don't feel comfortable in this position," Dewayne Miller stammered into his radio.

"Listen to me, Dwayne, you are gonna feel real damn uncomfortable with my Sig Sauer up your ass! You need to trust me. If you make a move now, you *will* be made. Sit tight and do as I say," Tug ordered.

"Yessir," Dewayne drawled and signed off his radio.

Tug assessed the situation. The attack on the center had begun. He could hear the explosion rocking the building next door. He had Miranda McKenzie as a bargaining chip, should he need it. He had the men at the school in a vicarious position, which would undoubtedly lead to their eventual demise. He was pleased with the current scenario.

Special Agent-In-Charge Steinmetz and S.A. McCallum stood at the command vehicle outside of the King's Pacific School for Boys. They blocked all streets within a block radius of the school. The school itself had already locked down, disallowing entry in or out of the building. No additional shots rang through the area. They still had no idea where the original shot was fired. Steinmetz was eager to get a forensic team to determine where the shooter may have been.

They had gained clearance from the schoolmaster to unlock the doors and let his team in. The child who was shot was removed from the building on a stretcher; he was dead on impact. The forensic team dashed inside with their gear and equipment. Steinmetz and McCallum stayed out at the command site. In the almost fifteen minutes that they had been there, his men had already set up communication links, and a central command with digital maps displaying the immediate surroundings of the private school.

The FBI Counter-terrorist Unit had links set up with the local police, FBI hostage negotiators, and local school authorities. They had the crowd outside under control about the time they heard the first explosion. People ducked any direction they could. The blast seemed to come from several blocks away. Slowly, a black plume of smoke took flight above the Seattle skyline.

Steinmetz was on the radio instantly, he called over the convention center security room, where the CTU had set up a security command post. "What is going on over there?" Steinmetz barked over his radio.

"Sir, a large explosion just shook the center. I am trying to get a hold of the agents upfront, but they are not responding. The cameras just show a shower of glass followed by an explosion in the atrium of the center. I think we need to call the guys back!" the voice of the agent in the security room said excitedly.

"We'll detach part of the unit back to you. Keep me informed. Find out what caused the explosion," Steinmetz ordered back. Steinmetz was reviewing the list of available agents in his team at the school. He had checked off several men to return to the convention center. He phoned in an emergency request for any available field agents in the Seattle area to convene on the convention center site. He was just about to call his men to return when he heard screams from around the corner.

"Steinmetz! There has been another shooting. A professor was shot as he was shooing some kids from a fourth-floor window. The shots came from the north side of the building," McCallum called as he jogged up to S.A. Steinmetz.

"Get some men posted at each corner of the building. I need a man patrolling each floor, protect those kids!" Steinmetz grumbled. He rubbed his chin with his thumb and forefinger. He would have to keep his men here and hope that the local field office would respond quickly to the convention center. He had his agent in the security office do status checks on each of the agents still at the convention center.

Sean turned around and hustled back up the steps ascending to the 21st floor. He arrived at the heavy steel door with a fading "Penthouse" script in the center. He tried the door. It was locked from the inside. The entrance to the roof access was also locked and secured with a heavy bar that required a special key to open. He knew he had to get in there somehow. Thoughtfully, he bounded down the steps to the twentieth floor.

He cautiously peered through the small wire-mesh reinforced window of the heavy steel door. He saw an empty hallway. Slowly he pushed open the heavy door. He could detect a faint smell of chlorine waft through the hall. He held the door to easy it back shut, avoiding it slamming.

The young retiree worked his way down the hall. He still had the bag of weapons slung around his shoulder. He slid his right hand under his jacket and felt Adam's handgun in the small of his back. He had to be ready for anything. He guessed that the penthouse took up the entire top floor. He had to figure a way to get up there. The Marriott along the waterfront is adorned with fabulous balconies attached to each room to allow their guests to enjoy the prime location along Elliott Bay. Sean had a crazy idea; he picked up his pace down the hallway.

Sean poked his head around the corner of the hallway. He saw a couple of kids being ushered out of their guest room by a lady, presumably their mother. He ducked behind a palm plant as they burst through doors. She was jostling them towards the elevators, urging them hysterically.

"I don't know Johnny. It was a loud noise. I am sure Daddy is okay," the mother tried to assure her children as they hurried down the hall.

Sean emerged from the camouflaging foliage and again jogged to the room that they had just vacated. Their door was just about to swing into its latch when Sean stuck his foot in its path. He looked down the hall at the frantic family, who were still fixated on the beeping of the elevators and pushed his way through and into their room. He could hear sirens wailing from the street below. He looked around the room. The beds were unmade and had towels and clothes piled up on them. In front of the television, two video game controllers sat in the middle of the floor.

He walked over to the balcony that faced the street. He looked down at the convention center where chaos was raining as people scurried in all directions, no one really certain of what they should do. He could see the glass atrium to the center was destroyed. Several legs and arms stuck out from the rubble. Two local policemen were trying to push onlookers away, so that they could tend to the victims and make it safe for the impending rescue vehicles. Sean was about to return to his plan for reaching the penthouse suite when he heard a click. He saw one of the officers across the street fall to the ground. The other officer paused and spun around, searching the area for the sniper that shot his partner. He had to hurry, before more shots were taken. He quickly stepped out on the balcony. He looked at the people out on Alaskan Way. All eyes were on the convention center and the stream of smoke and people that were emerging from the rubble. He noticed the balcony for the penthouse above, which sat directly overlooking the convention center, started above the next gallery over from the one he was standing on. Approximately twelve feet separated the two.

Without another thought, Sean dashed for the edge of the patio and leaped across the space between. He stretched his arms as far they could as his feet left the banister of the first balcony. He was surprised by how easily he made it, catching the railing of the adjacent room's patio with his forearms. Still, he was sweating what he had just done. Had he not made it, he would have fallen over 200 feet to his death. He locked onto the railing with the crook of his elbows and scrambled over the edge. He landed hard on the concrete balcony, crashing into an iron patio chair. He collected himself and peered at the sliding glass door that led into the guest room. To his relief, the curtains were drawn shut. He didn't want to explain himself to whoever was staying there what he was doing, acting like a flying squirrel outside of their hotel room.

He looked above him. The veranda for the penthouse was ten feet higher than him. He thought that if the stood on the rails of this balcony, he could stretch and grab the floor of the one above him. He hastily climbed on top of the iron railing, using the wall to steady himself. He reached up, able to put his hands on the floor of the penthouse veranda, he tried to reach over with one hand to see if he could grasp the edge. He couldn't quite make his fingers grip the floor above him. He rolled his eyes at himself and his hair-brained ideas and stood on his tiptoes.

The fingers of his left hand locked onto the concrete floor of the balcony. He tested his weight and tried to adjust his feet to allow his right hand to reach. His right foot slipped off of the narrow railing, and his entire body swung like a barn door into midair over the twenty-story drop to the sidewalk below. His left hand was the only thing preventing him from being splattered on the ground. As he swung, his back to the wall, he felt his feet touch the stucco side of the building. He pushed off and swung his body back towards the balcony. His body closed in, and he lunged upwards, nearly losing what little grip he had, but was able to lock his right hand onto the penthouse terrace floor. He hung there for a moment, allowing his heart rate to slow down and his muscles to relax briefly.

With all of his might, Sean heaved his body upwards. He let go of the floor of the balcony and, for a few seconds, was in midair with no contact of anything solid. He reached through the iron bars of the railing and locked his arms. His body curved around the concrete form of the terrace. With a solid grip, he was able to swing his legs over, his thick-soled shoes caught the edge of the terrace, he pushed his body over the side and onto the penthouse patio.

Sean landed on his feet, in a crouch position, quickly he reached for his gun and held it in front of him. The balcony was empty. He spun towards the room; no one was coming out after him. He looked back towards the street, the balcony was clear, but he knew it had an edge that ran along the front side. The hotel had plants on it to afford guests of the penthouse some privacy. It also allowed them to hang signage on it without detracting from the beauty of the room. As he peered over the edge of the waist-high wall, he heard another click, and the second officer across the street went down. Sean lunged his upper body over the side and pointed the gun towards the clicking sound. Landing on his knees, he held the gun in front of him. He saw Jeb McKenzie lying prone on the foot-wide ledge that skirted the building on the other side of the sundeck wall.

"Freeze!" Sean commanded, "If you move, I *will* shoot you."

Jeb McKenzie stayed in his position. He continued looking down on the convention center and sighed as if irritated, and he tilted his head towards this new distraction.

"Put the gun down," Sean ordered.

The big McKenzie man slid the gun through the slit that he made in the Fat Tuesday sign and looked at Sean, "Ah thought you were dead, boy."

"Back away from it," Sean continued. "I want you to get up slowly, place your hands on the deck wall."

Jeb did as he was instructed. Sean looked over onto the ledge. An open cardboard box sat next to a dark blue canvas duffle like the other Sean had found. In it was a cache of armaments.

"Step over the rail," Sean ordered.

Miranda's cousin glared at Sean, but reluctantly did as he was told. As he lifted his second leg over, the big man's foot snagged the top of the wall, and he tumbled towards Sean's direction. Surprised, Sean was slow to react. Instinctively, he brought the gun up over Jeb's head so he didn't accidentally fire. As he did so, Daryl allowed his momentum to ram Sean in the gut, knocking him over, the Glock 18 rattled across the patio flooring.

Jeb reached down and grabbed his hunting knife from its perch in his ankle sheath. He brought the blade down toward Sean's heart. Sean was just able to push his hands forward to block the blow.

"I've been looking forward to catching up with you pretty boy. I wanted to take you out a while ago!" Jeb snarled, pressing down on Sean's desperate grip.

"What did I ever do to you?" Sean said, trying to think away out of the situation.

"You think you're so smooth. Mah cousin needs a real man," Jeb drawled.

Sean struggled to keep the big man's hands from overpowering him. Jeb had a good eighty pounds on Sean's thin frame. His wiry opponent was quicker, though. Sean twisted to the right, pushing with his hands against Jeb and the knife. Jeb's force with gravity sent him sprawling onto the stone deck.

Sean backed away by kicking his feet forward and sliding backward on his butt. He searched for the gun that he dropped while he knew Jeb was gathering himself for another strike. Sean saw the gun resting eight feet away. He lunged in that direction. At the same time, Jeb dove across the deck after Sean. He was able to grab Sean's ankle.

"Come back here, you little punk," Jeb growled, locking his strong hand on Sean's ankle.

Sean stretched out, trying to get a hold of the Glock. It was just a little too far away. Jeb slashed down with the knife, trying to stick it in Sean's calf, Sean was able to deflect away the blow. His kick gave him enough momentum to get a finger on the gun. Jeb, feeling he was close enough to get to Sean, released his grip on Sean's ankle and took a big leap. Sean was able to kick out with his feet, catching Jeb in the chest, using the ground as support, Sean's thin but sturdy legs tossed Jeb back. He whirled around, grabbing the gun and jumping to his feet.

Jeb was able to collect himself and poise for another attack. Sean stood still, his gun frozen in position at Jeb's chest.

"Make a move, big fellow," Sean dared the big redneck.

Jeb took a chance, thinking the pretty boy would not keep true to his threat and skillfully tossed his knife at Sean. Sean reacted, ducking, the blade grazed his arm as hit whizzed by. The glanced of the knife was enough for Sean to lose his grip on the gun.

Jeb grinned. "I didn't *think* you had it in you, boy!" He grabbed a deck chair and swatted Sean away from the gun. The frame of the chair caught Sean in the head, sending him spinning towards the floor.

Jeb reached over the ledge and grabbed his duffle of gear. He poked his head in to retrieve his gun, but was interrupted when Sean smacked with the stem of a deck umbrella. Sean wielded the aluminum pipe in the center, allowing him to use both sides to keep Jeb at bay.

Jeb pushed the bag forward to shield the blows from the umbrella pole. Sean was able to hook one of the handles of the duffle. He swung hard with his left arm to tear the bag away from Jeb. He was successful, the bag and much of its contents spilled over the deck. When the bag slipped off the end of the pole, Jeb was able to grab the end. His superior strength wrenched the pole away from Sean. He hit Sean in the Head, swung back around, and caught Sean in the stomach. They circled each other, Sean feeling his head throb and the trickle of blood streaming from his arm. Sean tried to find a weapon to counter the attack, was unable to come up with anything. Jeb continued swinging the pole at Sean, connecting with the back of Sean's neck, sending him to the ground. Jeb grinned and at seeing Sean fall to the ground. Sean's body twisted, and he landed face down.

At Jeb's feet, was Sean's Glock. He bent down and picked it up. He stood over Sean, who was still facing the ground, though his body was still facing Jeb.

"You might not have the balls to pull the trigger boy, but Ah sure do," Jeb sneered.

Sean face down, his body twisted. He landed on something hard, sliding his hands under his stomach, he gripped Jeb's SOCOM .45 handgun. It spilled from the bag when it flung from the pole. He wrapped his hand around it and slid his finger into the trigger.

"Say, goodbye boy," Jeb said, cocking the Glock.

Sean spun with all of his might and squeezed the trigger of the SOCOM. It caught Jeb square in the chest, knocking him backward. Jeb was able to pull the trigger on the Glock, but the bullets flew harmlessly into the air. The big man fell to the ground with a big thump.

Sean got up and looked down on the McKenzie boy. Jeb stared up at Sean in astonishment; he tried swinging his arm up to fire back.

Sean squeezed the trigger on his own gun, "Goodbye."

Sean sighed and looked around the deck. His heart was beating furiously. He was so close to losing his own life, and now he was struck with the reality of taking someone else's. He was ready to leave the rest of this mess to the authorities and get back to Miranda. He started to walk away. He took one last look at Jeb McKenzie when he saw the small ball rolling away from Jeb's body. It looked like an avocado, rolling across the tile. Sean recognized it, it was a grenade, and the pin was out!

Sean looked to the doors of the sundeck, there was nothing to protect him from the blast of the grenade. Without any hesitation, he leaped off of the deck. His arms and legs stretched out as if to slow down gravity. He reached down as he flew past the ledge and grabbed onto the Fat Tuesday banner. The explosion sent a concussive shower of debris at Sean and, worse for him, knocked one of the pilings that held the banner off of its roost. The vinyl banner ripped, sending Sean swinging downward like Tarzan on a jungle vine. Sean swung helplessly, twenty-one stories from the ground. People on the street looked up to see him dangling from the giant banner. Swaying towards the balcony of a fifteenth-floor suite that was closest to him, Sean pumped his legs, getting the banner to swing him over to the balcony. As he hovered above the small porch, he let go of the banner, flinging him onto the stone terrace. Landing all fours, he paused, catching his breath relieved that he did not fall all 210 feet to his death.

He collected himself on the little balcony and assessed his next move. He leaned against the railing on the fifteenth floor, looking out at the convention center. The crowd was trying to figure out what to do. People were being pulled from the wreckage caused by the initial explosion. Sean heard vehicle engines charging down the street. He looked up, expecting to see rescue vehicles, instead saw two black HUMVEEs screaming around the corner. They drove right up to the steps of the convention center and into the damaged atrium. Several men jumped out of each Hummer. Each man was dressed in black and carried assault weapons.

Sean knew he had to get down there to help. Miranda could be down there. He knew Adam was there. He looked in the window of the suite. No one was in the bedroom. Some wet bathing suits were drying on the iron chairs on the balcony. He tried the slider. It pushed open. He danced quietly into the hotel room. The door to the sitting area was cracked open about an inch. He could hear the television in the next room. He moved through the bedroom and placed his gun back under his jacket before entering the living room where he heard the TV. Boldly, Sean just marched on through without really looking at the person viewing the news.

Nonchalantly, he just smiled as he reached the door, "Crazy day out there, huh?" The stunned person on the small sofa just stared at Sean open-mouthed as this stranger just strolled through his hotel room and out into the hallway.

Adam darted out of the office building lobby and out to the convention center. He was moving primarily against the grain. He knew he had to see if he could find Miranda. He figured she had ventured into the convention center. He hoped that she had gotten clear of the blast. He pushed his way through the crowd that was stunned by the events. He saw two policemen come up to the center and started trying to control the flow of chaos. He began walking up to them to fill them in on what was going on. Before he was able to get within ten feet of them, one of the officers collapsed to the ground. The second officer began to approach his partner, but he too was struck down.

Adam ducked away from the convention hall entrance. He stared up at the hotel across the street. "Damn it, Sean, get that guy!" Adam cursed under his breath.

He went around the corner and thought to himself for a moment. He didn't hear shots. He figured they must have a powerful rifle that could be silenced and still carry almost two hundred yards. He skirted as close to the wall as he could and slipped into the entrance of the convention center. He walked gingerly on the shards of glass and rubble. He balanced on a beam to cross over a shallow pit that was left by the rocket. He studied the atrium. It was a large glass entrance the could hold hundreds of people moving in and out of the main auditorium and conference rooms. The explosion trapped many of the attendees in the back of the center. They tried exiting through the fire exits, but doors had been barred shut from the outside.

Adam met the first of the convention goers that dared to seek a safe passage. They informed him of the bolted doors. He told a few of them to find someone on the outside to help them free the doors, and to be wary of the front entrance. Adam wanted to find the main security room and see if there was anyone there who could help. He passed the main entrance to the center, beyond the atrium. Opposite of the auditorium, I saw the business offices. He figured that he would find the security office in there. Down the hall, he saw a door that led to the alleyway that he watched from the office building next door. Halfway down the hall, he saw several large discarded cardboard boxes.

He was about to open the security office door when the first gunshots rang through the atrium. Adam heard the screams of the people that he had just passed. He snatched the gun from his side and began to head back towards the atrium. He heard the door to the security office swing open. Two men carrying assault weapons came jogging out. They were dressed all in black and were startled to see a man with a pistol in his hand. Adam wheeled around and landed in a firing position that was engrained into his mind when he was a Delta Force member. His right foot forward, his left leg tucked under him, both arms extended.

The men from the office began squeezing off rounds from their Steyr automatic weapons. Adam cleanly nailed the first man in the chest, knocking him to the floor. The second man rolled into the entry of the mailroom. The first man began to stir, patting his chest. Adam recognized the bulge of the Kevlar vest he was wearing and added a round into his forehead, dropping the man instantly. Adam didn't see the third man peer out of the office. The man had recently shed his brown UPS uniform for the black outfit of his comrades. He swung the MP5 submachine gun out the door and sprayed a series of rounds into the hallway. Adam dove out of the way, but caught a bullet in his left calf. He groaned and rolled out of the way, squeezing several rounds into the doorway of the office.

Big Daryl McKenzie motioned to his team member in the mailroom to roll forward as Daryl covered him with more rounds from the MP5. The man nodded and rolled into the hallway. Adam had backed away, scooting on his hind end with his good leg. He had positioned himself behind a fallen beam from the atrium explosion. The bullets from the assault team's guns whizzed harmlessly passed. Adam waited patiently for one of the men to make a mistake.

A shower of bullets continued to whiz by. Adam heard a familiar click that he recalled from his stint in the service. It was the click of the Steyr assault rifle transitioning into grenade launcher mode. Adam knew the man would temporarily have the gun pointing away as he slammed the lever into place. Adam briefly popped up from his protected position and delivered a bullet into the man's unprotected shoulder. He heard a grunt as he dropped back behind the beam. Amongst Daryl's cover fire, Adam heard the man he hit drop his assault rifle. Adam lunged to the left of the girder, seeing the man lying on the ground holding his shoulder. Adam squeezed off one more round from the Glock. He stared the man in the eyes as the bullet found its mark.

Daryl McKenzie eased his way out of the security office. He had swung his weapon over his shoulder and positioned it for grenade launch. He was going to rid himself of this nuisance. Adam scrambled to his feet as the "fump" of the grenade sliding through the tube could be heard. He sprinted into the atrium as the area behind the girder he was using for cover exploded into a fiery dispersion of rubble.

Adam's mad dash into the atrium ran him right into an assault team member that was charging into the convention center from one of the black Hummers. The collision knocked them both back. The man swung his assault rifle up to his new enemy. Adam grabbed the barrel and twisted it away. In one even sweep, he delivered the butt of the gun into the assailant's stomach. It was enough to knock the man over. Adam was suddenly aware of the seven other men with assault weapons that stopped what they were doing and turned their attention on him.

He remembered a small café counter on the near side of the atrium. He sprinted with the assault weapon in hand. As he heard guns going off in his direction, he blindly returned fire in a random spray at the assault team. He saw the counter ahead.

Daryl McKenzie entered the atrium. He saw Adam near the counter on the wall where the atrium met the main hall of the convention center. He joined his team in the lobby and pointed the grenade launcher in Adam's direction. Adam sprung over the counter as he could hear rain of bullets impregnate the wood of the café. He heard the cocking of the gun's grenade. He looked desperately around the small restaurant. There was very little room behind the counter. He saw two double doors and sprinted through them. The kitchen was tiny, just large enough to hold supplies and make sandwiches. On the back wall was a dumb waiter. Adam heard the "fump" of the grenade launcher and dove into the dumb waiter. His weight hit the small cabinet as he tugged the lever when he flew by, sending the manual elevator on a free fall downward. He could feel the heat of the blast that erupted the little café kitchen into flames and debris.

When the dumbwaiter found the basement floor, it slammed Adam's shoulder into the corner of the pressboard cabinet. He shook his head, as though to lose the stars that seemed to be spinning around it. He grabbed the assault weapon that he had slung over his shoulder and pointed it out of the little wooden elevator. He looked around the room. With the exception of a dim yellow light above the dumbwaiter, the room was very dark and very quiet. He fished his small Maglite out of its pouch and shone it around the room, following the beam of light with the point of the rifle. He stood behind a crate, exposing only his head and shoulders with the gun and flashlight.

He quickly realized that he was in the storeroom of the cafe. It was lined with shelves containing cups, napkins, and dry goods for the little café. Space on the atrium level was a premium, so it made sense to have this small room with access to the restaurant through the dumbwaiter. The flashlight further revealed that little storeroom was enclosed by a wood frame, with strong chicken wire strewn around the wood. In the middle of the far wall was a delivery door locked with a thick padlock from the outside.

Comfortable that he was temporarily safe, he took a moment to take care of his injured calf. He found some towels on a shelf in the storeroom. Using his pocketknife to make strips from the white terrycloth towel, he fashioned a bandage and tied it securely to his leg. The steady pressure alleviated some of the significant pain and stopped the bleeding.

He refocused on assessing his situation. Judging by where the café sat in the convention center, he figured that the basement led to the loading bay of the alleyway that he viewed from the office building. He assumed that there was a network of alleys that though the basement that would allow workers to move about without interfering with the conventions that took place above. He pulled out his cell phone, the signal was weak, underneath all of the concrete, but he was able to get a tone and dialed Rachel York's cell number.

"Rachel, it's Adam. I need a favor. I am in a basement under the convention center. Yes, I know, I haven't seen Sean or Miranda. It is pretty chaotic up there, so I could have easily missed them. So listen, I found a storeroom with access to the café that was just inside the lobby from the atrium. I was wondering if your office could pull up the schematics and find a path for me to get to the back convention rooms. That is where most of the hostages are. An assault team is en route to take them out, I need to get there quickly," Adam hastily informed the DOI Assistant Regional Director.

"Yes, I think they can do that. I'll patch them through, hang on…"Rachel agreed, as she clicked over to call her office.

Adam surveyed his options to get out of the storeroom while he waited for Rachel's instructions. He tried kicking the door open. The hefty steel lock gave no sign of wanting to break away. Adam eyed the lock and realized that he wouldn't be able to shoot it from his angle. He looked down at the combo-function assault rifle that had almost taken his life several times upstairs. He grinned and walked back behind the large wooden crate. He clicked the Stary into the grenade launcher position and let loose his way out of the storeroom. He was rewarded with a boom and the sounds of wood and wire flying across the concrete floor. A shower of drywall from the ceiling above rained down. Adam peered around the crate with his flashlight. The wood and chicken wire gate was completely clean off the frame wall.

Rachel's voice came back almost hysterical, "Adam, are you alright?"

"Yes, Rachel, I'm fine. I just needed a way out of the storeroom. I wasn't feeling very creative," Adam retorted.

"I won't even ask. Listen, I have the information you requested," Rachel said, and step by step, she guided Adam over the phone through the corridors of the convention center basement.

Steinmetz knew something was not right. He had still not heard from Lyndon, and at several key sites, his men were thin. Something horrible was happening and they were fed misinformation to get them pinned down in this situation. He was now sure that the hotel information must have been inaccurate. He placed a call to the lead agent at the hotel and instructed him to maintain critical security posts only and immediately send the rest of his team to the convention center.

The situation at the school oscillated from quiet and managed to chaotic when new shots were fired. The volleys seemed to come from everywhere; there were no discernible locations. The forensics team had minimal access to the sites where the shootings took place since those areas could not be confirmed secure. They had to get a handle on where the shots were coming from. Steinmetz guessed there were multiple shooters, and they were not stationary.

He had not been able to get an update form the convention center, and that was very disturbing. He had a sinking feeling about every move he made.

Tubby swung his gaze through his field glasses from the school to the Olympic Hotel. As far as he was concerned, this place was a sanctuary of hedonism for crooked politicians and businessmen that were sapping the strength from America. He trained his glasses at the front entrance. He saw the blacked-out Suburban pull to the front, and half a dozen men jog from the hotel and jump into the big SUV.

"Feds!" Tubby thought to himself. He grabbed his big Barrett Light sniper rifle and aimed it the roofline over the driver's seat as the big truck wrenched into gear. He squeezed the trigger on the 30mm gun and watched as the bullet pierced the sheet metal. He waited as the Suburban careened off the road and into a fire hydrant. One of the agents inside the vehicle hopped out and took a defensive position with handgun drawn, searching for where the shot came from. Tubby lined the agent up and sent a bullet into the agent's throat. The man clad in the traditional dark suit and tie dropped immediately out of sight. He saw two other agents hop out of the other side of the truck, but they were out of his scope, blocked by the bulky SUV. Tubby swung the Barrett in the direction of the Olympic Hotel lobby and fired a couple of shots into the busy room. He wanted to send a message to the agents that there was as much trouble at the hotel location as there was at the convention center.

Tubby continued searching for his next shot. Trying to find one of the men dressed in a dark suit. Hotel guests scurried for cover. Hotel security ushered people away from the street front and entry doors. Tubby could not have known that an agent that was sitting in a sniper position atop the hotel had triangulated his position from the shot that killed the second agent. Like the victims that he and Dewayne had slain, he had no idea his life was over when the bullet from the FBI sniper struck his left temple and pierced his brain.

Tug looked at his watch. He reviewed the plan. The rocket launcher hit its mark; the school and the hotel were being pinned down by his snipers, and the assault team had entered the building and were making their sweeps. This whole thing would all be over, right about the time when the back-up agents, SWAT teams, and perhaps even the National Guard would arrive. If all went well, a large shoot out would ensue, and all of the Greys "soldiers" would eventually be exterminated. This whole episode would key on this backwoods group, and further investigations would stall, leaving himself and senator Small and his backers wholly removed.

To be safe, he wanted to make sure that none of the Greys men were taken into custody. He wanted them eliminated, he had his sniper gun and planned position, but he also included Joe Lyndon in the plan, assisting in the cleanup. This posed several problems for Tug. To wait for the operation to be completed, would put his own escape in jeopardy. He also knew that his location in the office building had been compromised. Fortunately, he had a backup plan, and Ms. Shaw as a little added insurance.

He picked up his scrambled cell phone. He punched in the necessary numbers. He reached the man he needed who was nestled in between two large freighters that were in resting in their slips. "This is Tug. I'll need Operation Chinook in fifteen minutes at the pre-arranged location. The trail will be hot," he hung up the phone.

Sean ran across the street. People were fleeing in every possible direction, looking every which way to try and spy where danger was coming from. Many had now directed their attention up at the 21st floor sundeck of the hotel across the street. When Sean came running out, he heard people murmuring about him being the guy swinging from the penthouse balcony, barely escaping the explosion. He paused briefly to tie a piece of cloth he had torn from his shirt sleeve around his left bicep to hold off the bleeding from the cut delivered by Jeb's well-thrown knife.

He hurried across the street and past the two black Hummers parked on the front steps. He pulled the SOCOM handgun that he had obtained from Jeb out of his waistband and entered the atrium of the convention center. Smoke and dust still hung heavy in the air. Several bodies were strewn about the debris-filled floor. He clung to a wall to keep some semblance of protection nearby. At least no one was going to sneak out of the wall.

He moved forward, out of the atrium, and into the lobby. He followed the sounds of sporadic gunfire and screams. The sounds came from deeper in the complex. Sean hurried. He was hoping that he would catch them at their flank. As he came to an intersection in the hallway, he paused. Carefully, he peered around the corner, his nose following the snout of the gun. There was a man posted, protecting the rear of the little doom squad. Sean withdrew his head. The man was positioned with his assault rifle raised towards the ceiling, his back to the next hallway.

Sean dove to the deep burgundy carpet and rolled into the hallway. The gunman began lowering his weapon into position, but he wasn't able to get a shot off before Sean was able to deliver a bullet from his prone stance. He fired the weapon three times, until the man dropped to the floor. Sean stared in that direction to see if more shooters would appear, but none did. He got up and sprinted over to the man. He knelt and checked the man's pulse. There was none. Sean quickly rolled the fallen gunman over and grabbed the assault weapon. He also saw a handgun at the man's side and took that as well. As soon as he had the guns in position, he rolled back to the corner.

Sean continued down the next hallway. He could see men dressed in dark fatigues trying to get into a set of closed double doors. A gold plaque above the doors was marked the Cascade Ballroom. From his belly, he watched the frustrated assault team back away from the door.

One of the men hoisted his weapon and pulled the trigger. The door sprung from its frame in a mighty explosion as the projectile from the gun hit its mark. Sean heard a chorus of horrified screams from the ballroom. He leaned out and aimed at one of the assault team members who was hustling into the room with his weapon drawn. Sean fired the SOCOM and hit the man in the thigh. He fell, screaming while holding onto his leg. Another man next to him spun and saw Sean down the hallway. The man fired a violent burst from his automatic weapon. Sean scooted back as bullets peppered the corner he was lying in and the wall behind him.

Sean stood with his back to the wall, protected by the corner. He held up the assault rifle that he swiped from the first man he shot. He was afraid that if he just let loose with fire, he might hurt an innocent person. As he stood there trying to figure out what to do, he heard the gunfire escalate in the ballroom. Sean knew he had to do something. He looked at the strange weapon in his hand. A tube in the bottom held a grenade. He studied the little switches and found one marked grenade. He switched it over and reached his arm into the hallway. Without looking, so he could keep his body protected, he fired the shell into the ceiling halfway down the corridor.

The ceiling burst into an explosion of sheetrock and wood - smoke and debris filled the air. Sean used the cloud to charge into the hallway. He fired the assault weapon in the direction of the two men who were firing at him, he heard clicks, but nothing happened. Out of bullets, he dropped the assault rifle and pulled both handguns out of the waistband of his pants.

Sean burst through the debris with both guns drawn. As he emerged from the cloud, he saw the man who was shooting down the hall at him. He had ducked when the grenade exploded was just returning to position to resume fire where Sean had been. With the SOCOM in his right hand, Sean fired and caught the man in the shoulder; Sean could see blood and tissue fly in the air as the bullet ripped through his flesh. He spied the man on the floor that he had shot. He was sitting up with his legs outstretched. He had re-shouldered his weapon and was aiming it, Sean. A couple of wild shots streamed out from the unsteady aim of the assault rifle. Sean fired back with the gun in his left hand, catching the man in the throat, killing him as he choked on the torrent of blood filling his windpipe.

Sean heard shots to the right as he surveyed the room. Another gunman shot wildly into the crowd of convention-goers that were trying to flee through a back door. He saw Sean and spun in his direction. With the gun in Sean's left hand, he crossed his body and shot at the man. The first squeeze of the trigger missed and landed in one of the pillars lining the ballroom floor. The second and third found their home in the man's mid-section and collarbone.

Sean looked around the room. The room was chaos as panic-stricken convention-goers. Sean's heart rate was pounding in his chest, as the last several seconds had flown by with him reacting and working off of adrenaline with very little thought involved. Now he was able to take stock of the situation. The assault team had been thinned and they were trying to mow down an evacuating crowd but were stifled with shots that began coming from the back of the room.

Sean paused to figure out what was going on. He saw Adam ushering people through the door down a dark stairwell with his left hand while he was shooting cover fire with his right hand wrapped around one of the Austeyr assault weapons. Sean was aiming to help when the fire exit doors, which had been chained shut from the outside, burst open. Several men in face shields and SWAT team uniforms crashed through the door. They pumped several canisters of tear gas into the crowd.

Sean saw Adam pull his shirt over his face to avoid the caustic sting. He also saw a towering figure that looked like Daryl McKenzie slip into the doorway of the basement. The man paused. He turned and glared at Sean, his eyes briefly dancing with rage and then returned to the stairs and disappear into the crowd. Sean tried to cover his face and go after him, but he was instantly confronted by several SWAT team members, with weapons pointed at him. Sean dropped the two handguns to the floor and held his hands up in the air. One of the SWAT members pounced on him and pinned his arms behind his back. Sean looked up to see the last of Daryl's head bob away into the crowd.

Thirty Seven

Adam's eyes were still stinging despite his best attempts to conceal them from the tear gas. He continued holding the door open, with one eye out for trouble. Most of the patrons dropped to the floor and covered their faces in anticipation of the SWAT team, taking control of the situation. Many attendees scooted along the floor, looking for fallen co-workers and friends who were hit by the assault team.

Adam almost didn't see the police officer approach him; his vision was so blurry. He blinked away the tears and tossed his weapon on the floor. Two men grabbed him and spun him against the wall, wrapping his arms behind him and securing them with plastic zip bands immobilizing his hands. Adam knew the routine and awaited them taking him to a nearby holding facility. He was promptly marched out of the ballroom by the two SWAT team members and into the parking lot of the adjacent ferry terminal. The doors had recently been pried open, having been sealed by the thick chains that had been used by the assault team to trap the conventioneers.

A van was waiting for them, and he was pushed inside. Sean was already inside, urgently retelling about Daryl McKenzie slipping into the crowd that had escaped into the basement.

"Look, we don't have time for this. Go check it out! I'll show you. Arrest me later if you have to. I don't care, just don't let him get away!" Sean growled at the policemen who were ignoring him. They were jotting information down into notepads.

"Hey there, pal, having fun?" Adam grinned at his friend, who was still scowling at not getting his message across.

"Man, I am glad you're okay. Daryl McKenzie got away. I am trying to get these dolts to listen to me so they can do something about it!" Sean snarled.

"Look, sir, I am not going to tell you again to be quiet, we have our orders to follow," one of the policemen warned Sean.

Sean ignored him and asked Adam," Have you seen Miranda? I haven't seen her since she went into the alley."

"No, I haven't. We will," Adam assured him, and leaned back calmly in his restrained bench seat.

"We need to get the hell out of here," Sean said sternly, "Isn't there anything you can do?"

"Just wait," Adam shrugged against his bonds.

The policemen were closing up the van when a black Suburban screeched to a halt behind them. They both looked up, as did Sean and Adam. Rachel York strode out of the passenger seat, and one fluid motion produced her badge, holding it out in front of her. "I am Assistant Regional Director Rachel York, DOI. I have orders to release these two men."

"But ma'am…" one of the SWAT team men began, he had his orders and procedures to follow.

"Excuse me," Rachel cut him off, an eyebrow raised and snapped, "this is not open for debate. Do it now, officer."

Reluctantly, the SWAT officer exchanged a glance with his colleague, who just shrugged and complied. He released their bonds from the bench seat of the van and then cut off the zip bands around their wrists.

"You can retrieve the papers from my office or have your superiors contact me directly if you have any questions or issues. Gentlemen…," Rachel held out her arm towards the Suburban. Adam and Sean strode in front of her towards the Suburban and climbed in. As the last door shut, the driver stepped on the gas and zipped down the road.

Tug picked up his scrambled cell phone. He pushed in the buttons and waited for the other end to pick up. "Ajax," the man on the other end answered.

"Ajax, it's time. Begin with the hotel. Three missing, at least one assumed dead. Also, one missing in the office building, last known, the seventh-floor suite," Tug replied matter-of-factly into the phone.

"Consider it done," the man identified as Ajax responded and hung up the phone.

Tug radioed Dewayne Miller and Tubby Bauman. Dewayne reported that Tubby had been shot. Relaying what he saw through his scope. Tug ordered him to abandon his post and head toward the backside of the office building. He had repositioned himself in the roof access stairway, just inside the door to the roof of the office building. He glanced at his watch. He made a quick calculation of how long it would take Miller to get down from his position and make it to the street.

He listened to the police radio traffic, the attack on the convention center made a mess, there were only a handful of civilian casualties, and seven members of the assault team had been killed. One was missing. Jeb McKenzie was assumed dead. He had not responded in quite some time and he figured the explosion at the hotel claimed his life. He had Dewayne Miller coming to him. Aside from the one missing at the convention center, all of his ends were being tied up. He cycled through the radio checks until he finally got an answer.

"Tug! It's Daryl. Man, things went crazy at the convention center. Things got out of hand, I was the only one to get out," the voice crackled over the radio.

"Where are you now, Daryl?" Tug asked.

"I am in the basement of the building. When the SWAT team entered, I mixed with the crowd as they tried to escape. They are searching for a way out. I remember from the schematics you showed me a door leading to the alley," Daryl replied, whispering into his radio.

"Go with the crowd, by now, the building is surrounded and you will be made if you venture out on your own," Tug instructed.

"Yessir," Daryl agreed.

"Once you are clear, if you do not run into me, your instructions are to return to the warehouse for final extraction. Are we clear? You must get to the warehouse," Tug stressed.

Daryl agreed and tried his best to filter into the flow of the crowd. When they did find a door out, they burst through, with their new sense of freedom, fleeing from the horrific episode that erupted inside. While the police were doing their best to sort through the crowd, they had no details on who they were looking for. Daryl shed his outer layer of clothes, revealing a simple denim button-down shirt and a pair of dungarees. He squeezed through the crowd and mixed in with the traffic along the street.

His first order of business was to get somewhere safe. Second, he wanted to find his cousin. Lastly, he had already received word on Jeb being dead. He wanted revenge against the pretty boy once and for all.

"Ajax" finished his duties at the hotel and had moved onto the office building. He started with the office on the seventh floor. He surveyed the room. It appeared as Tug had said, it had been cleared out. He searched each room, coming up empty. He reached the corner office and tried the handle on the storage room door. The door was locked. Ajax put his ear to the door and swore he heard something barely audible on the other side. He knelt to the floor. The neatly polished floor had a very discrete trail leading from the convention center view office to this door. Someone with rubber-trimmed soles was dragged to this closet. He removed his lock pick tools from his jacket pocket and got to work. The tumblers clicked into place, and he yanked the door open.

He saw the man that Adam had encountered a little over an hour ago. He was barely conscious and lying on the floor. His wrists were bound with zip bands. Ajax nudged him with his foot. The man woke up startled, and looked up at Ajax with wide, frightened eyes.

"Oh, so you *are* alive," Ajax said. His suppressed SOCOM let out a faint sound as the bullet slid through the silencer, killing the formerly missing assault team member.

Ajax picked up the phone and called Tug once more. "Gaskill, this is Ajax. Both buildings are clean."

"Excellent. I have one en route to me as we speak. I have one more rogue, and I have the package at the warehouse. That is where you will conclude our business," Tug replied.

"And what do I do with the package?" Ajax asked, feeling like he knew the answer anyways.

"Bait, just in case the rogue doesn't feel like following orders. I think he'll want the package. We might hold onto it until we know the rogue is a historical fact," Tug answered. Pleased that the crew who could identify him were all but taken care of.

"Roger that, Ajax is out."

Tug hung up the phone and climbed the stairs to the roof access door. He pulled out a case that held a little wire. He gingerly wrapped the wire around the steel bar that barricaded the access door shut. He affixed a little igniter with small chewing gum sized wad of putty and stood back. A spark grew to a flash that traced its way around the wire until it burnt itself out. Tug reached out and grabbed the falling piece of steel before it clanked on the floor. He set it aside and pushed his way onto the rooftop.

Being sure to stay low and out of the line of sight, Tug made his way to the edge of the gravel rooftop. He set his gear out and covered himself with rust-covered wire mesh that match the rusty scaffolding that encircled the peak of the building. He leaned over the edge and sat with his Barrett Sniper rifle pointed in the direction of his unsuspecting assault team member.

The driver of the Suburban pulled over to the sidewalk outside of a café down the street from the convention center. "We took over this café for a command post. Let's check-in and share what we know. Maybe we can get an update on the situation," Rachel said, looking back at Sean and Adam. Sean was hesitant. He just wanted to keep looking for Miranda. Reluctantly, he shook his head, and he and Adam followed her into the café. The tables were cluttered with area maps, building schematics, phones, and laptops. Agents were hustling about getting updates from other agencies, providing their own intelligence, and agreeing on courses of action.

Rachel led them to the back of the room, where several men were sitting in high back chairs, watching an assistant plot marks on a blown-up map of the convention center area that was laid out on a coffee table. One of them saw Rachel and stood up.

"York, what the hell do you think you are doing?" the man growled.

"Listen, Ron; I am not sure you have the whole story. We have…." Rachel began before she was cut off.

"You have relieved a SWAT team of two men who need to be questioned about their connection to a terror attack. This one was responsible for blowing up the balcony at the Marriott. Several eyewitnesses saw him. The other one, *Agent Raines*, is nowhere near his jurisdiction and as far as I can tell, way out of his league! Whatever their connection, they have a responsibility to the disaster that has occurred hear. They are responsible for the loss of life of…" the DOI Regional Director yelled at Rachel, pointing and glowering at Sean and Adam.

"Chief, if it weren't for these men, many more people would have died. They prevented a slaughter out there. And where were you? Adam Raines of Fish and Wildlife had requested resources half a dozen times. Resources that you blocked! If anyone is responsible for what happened today, it's you!" Rachel snapped back, her eyes filled with fury at her supervisor.

"Well, look here, Rachel, you are out of line. You might be second in command, but I'll remind you who *is* in charge here…" Beckett spat back.

"Sir, with all due respect, Ms. York is right. Since the moment I got wind that something was up, I notified your office. I was shot down every time I asked for a resource, every time I tried to get someone in your office to respond to my suspicions. When I learned that the operation was going to take place, I again tried to get downtown to respond. Only Rachel took charge to assist. If it weren't for her help, Sean's insight and action, along with my breaking jurisdiction, we would have a lot more body bags to fill," Adam responded.

"What you did was illegal and will likely cost you your job!" Beckett snarled.

"What we did was save lives! If I lose my job for doing what I felt was right, so be it. As far as I am concerned, you and your office are negligent, irresponsive, and even at fault for derailing a federal investigation!" Adam said, his demeanor struggling to remain reasonable.

"My office had orders to follow and protocols to track, that you apparently are blind to, but maybe we should have reacted with a little more prudence on your requests," Ron Beckett began in a softer, almost apologetic tone.

"Look, sir, we don't have time for this. We still have a woman missing and several members of the assault team at large. We just need an update and take care of business," Rachel said.

"Well, if you think I am going to let these two go traipsing around…" Beckett started and then changed his mind when he saw the raised eyebrow of his assistant director, "Alright. How do you know more are at large? We are starting to collect a fairly large body count, admittedly, many of them bad guys. Who can you confirm is still out there?"

"Sir, if I may," Sean asked, and the Director nodded, "One man, Daryl McKenzie, got away when I was taken into custody. His cousin, Miranda Shaw, who was with us, has been missing for nearly an hour."

"I see. And we have at least one sniper at large from the school. Forensics was able to identify that at least two shooters were involved. We have massive cleanup at the school, the Olympic Hotel, the convention center, and the hotel across the street. You must realize the possibility that if your friend was in the atrium at the time of the attack, she might be somewhere in that mess," Beckett told the trio.

"I have to believe that she is out there somewhere," Sean said firmly, "as for Daryl McKenzie, he is a dangerous man. We need to find him before someone else gets hurt."

Tug took notice of the clouds that had taken over, just as the forecast had indicated. He was hoping it would rain. It would make slipping away into the Seattle traffic much easier in reduced visibility. He strode over to the edge of the office building and put down the case he was carrying. He sat down on the roof and opened the case. He examined the Barrett Light sniper rifle that he was holding and checked the magazine and sight adjustments one more time. He stretched out and leaned against the raised brick edge of the roof. He adjusted his scope again and began spotting individuals coming down the street as he had directed Dewayne Miller to do just minutes ago.

He saw the usual traffic, with people bustling around. A distinct ring of crowd formed at the fringes of the area where most of his group's activity had taken place. It was as if an invisible bubble had been placed there. Primarily only uniformed policemen and government agents in their dark business suits wandered through the area. Tug could have taken any one of them out. Anyone within one thousand yards could be prey to Tug and his Barrett sniper rifle.

Finally, he saw what he was waiting for. Looking nervous, turning his head every which way to see if anyone was looking at him, Dewayne Miller ambled towards the Trade Center. Tug thought to himself, "This idiot would be picked up by the cops any second."

He lined up his shot and let the bullet loose from its chamber. The pop from the Barrett echoed between the buildings. Tug watched through the scope just long enough to see a red spot form in the area right in the middle of Miller's eyes. He saw the man fall to a heap on the sidewalk as horrified and confused pedestrians slunk out of his way. Tug coolly turned away and whipped a soft rag out of his pocket. He began wiping down any portion of the Barrett that might have had his fingerprints on it. When he was satisfied, he tossed the rifle down and bean calmly walking towards the roof stairwell.

"Mr. Beckett, there has been another shooting!" an aide said, running up to the group, "I just heard it on the radio. Some man was walking between the school and here and was gunned down."

"Did they have a preliminary on who it might have been?" Beckett asked.

"No sir, they said the shot probably came from one of the buildings near the convention center," the aide replied.

"The office building next door, the convention center!" Adam exclaimed.

"How do you know that?" Beckett demanded.

"I was over there earlier. I took one sniper out. They got access by posing as UPS delivery drivers. There must have been another one I didn't run into," Adam replied.

"Let's check it out," Beckett said to his staff, "Hankins and Bales, you're in. Jessica, call the Bureau and see if they'll assist. You two stay here." Beckett pointed at Sean and Adam.

"Mr. Beckett, I was up there today. I know where to look. Earlier, they were using suppressed sniper rifles to keep the noise down. If they have gotten to the point where they aren't worried about noise, that means they are on the are way carrying out their exit strategy, or they just don't care anymore. We need to go now," Adam said.

"Technically, you do work for me, but I don't like the way this is all turning out. And you, I can't be liable for a civilian," Beckett said, discounting Adam's plea and dismissing Sean without a second glance.

"What about McKenzie, what about Miranda?" Sean asked.

"Another reason we need you here. I'll have you work with one of our agents to create descriptions and profiles," Beckett offered. He turned to one of the agents nearby, "See what they know, but keep an eye on them. As far as I am concerned, they are suspects."

Rachel stepped up to her boss and separated him from the rest of the group. In a low tone, she said, "Sir, they have knowledge that can help us get to the shooters. Raines has been all over that building today."

"Look, York, I'm sure you mean well, but I cannot be responsible for these guys. If you keep your head on straight, you might be the regional Director someday, maybe then you'll understand," Beckett responded.

An agent across the room called out to Beckett, "Sir, D.C. is on the phone; they want an update."

Beckett excused himself from Rachel and crossed the office to grab the phone and make his report, "Alright, the rest of you get your gear on and head to the Trade Center, report back what you find."

The small group of agents quickly gathered their equipment and left the office. Rachel took advantage of the opportunity, as Beckett was distracted. "Hey McCarty, would you please get me a SATCOM link with D.C.? I think there is a cell in the main van."

"Yes, ma'am," the young Department of Interior agent hurried off to comply.

Rachel glanced at Sean and Adam, "There is a door right back there by the coffeemaker, it leads to the back alley, move, now."

Without hesitating, the two men dashed out of the small café.

Adam turned the corner and saw the two agents assigned to the Department of Interior head to the World Trade Center building. Rachel gave Adam a radio and Glock 19 pistol in a holster. He strapped them to his shoulder and headed quickly for the office building across the street.

The agents split up. One circumvented the building to its flank, the other two headed into the freight elevator with a building security guard. Adam took the stairs that he went up earlier.

The agent on the freight elevator stopped on the seventh floor. He located the office that Adam had described to them. The door was unlocked, so the Fish and Wildlife agent strode through. The room was empty. He poked into each of the offices, about to leave when he paused in the doorway of the back corner office. The storage door was ajar. He walked over to the little room and poked his head in. On the floor, was one of the men that Adam had described. He was lying in a pool of blood; a single bullet wound to his head.

Adam himself cautiously bound up the stairs. He paused at the seventh floor, not detecting any activity, decided to continue up as high as he could. The word that reached Beckett was that the shot came from the roofline. Adam placed his foot on the step, but froze. He heard the faint sound of rubber-soled shoes softly hitting the stairs ahead. He drew his Glock that he received from Rachel and positioned himself to catch the person descending the staircase.

The soft footsteps reached the landing above, and a figure swung around. It was a man dressed in a maintenance uniform. He seemed startled when he saw Adam. He looked down the stairs with a curious look. Adam broke the ice.

"Have you seen anyone else in the stairway, sir?" Adam asked, studying the maintenance man.

"Uh, no sir, I got a call that the roof door was open, so I went up to check it out. Is everything okay?" the man asked nervously.

"Depends. What did you see up there?" Adam continued questioning the man.

"Nothing, sir. Just the door was open. I think sometimes people sneak out there for a smoke break," the man suggested.

"So it was called in. Do you mind waiting here a moment," Adam asked.

"Of course, sir. Does this have something to do with explosions across the street?" the man asked meekly.

"We'll see," Adam said. He picked up his radio and called to the agent in the lobby, "This is Adam Raines. I have a maintenance man in the back stairwell. He claims to have been called to check out the open door on the roof. Can you verify?"

"Raines? Boy Beckett is sure pissed at you," the voice on the other end said, but agreed to check into Adam's information. Adam looked up at the man on the landing; ten steps up. "What's your name?" Adam asked.

"Uh, Frank," the man said, looking down at his coveralls, he slid his finger nervously along the stitching on the "Frank" name tag sewn on to his denim uniform.

Tug waited on the seventh-floor landing, waiting for the call to come back over the radio. The maintenance man, Frank, patiently stood holding his toolbox.

The radio crackled, and the voice responded, "Raines, this is Stevens, the desk manager says that no calls have been reported to maintenance."

Before Adam could respond, he saw Frank flip the latches on the toolbox with his thumb. As if in slow motion, the events began to unfold. Adam raised his gun as the man grabbed the contents of the toolbox and allowed the steel case to fall to the floor. He brought his hand up, with a SOCOM firmly in his grip. Each man held stoically in a standoff. Before any of them could react, the door to the seventh floor flew open, and the agent who had just inspected the office began to burst through. Knowing that he would be in the line of fire, Adam delivered a powerful kicked into the agent's side. The agent flew back through the doorway he was coming through and onto the floor just as two bullets flew by and embedded themselves into the steel door. Adam fired off a couple of unaimed shots as he dove down the stairs. He reached out and grabbed the railing to arrest his fall. In the process, his weapon fell and clanged down the steps.

He looked around to find some sort of handy weapon. On the landing of the sixth floor, he saw a fire extinguisher. He dove down the remaining steps and punched his fist through the glass door that housed the extinguisher. He grabbed it from its roost and wielded it in his hands, not entirely sure how to use it to his advantage. He heard the door open on the landing above him.

He called out to the agent to be careful. Several shots fired from the landing above towards the doorway. Adam crept up the stairs close to the landing the "maintenance man was on. Firing several shots for cover fire, the man called Frank leaped down the stairs, his weapon in front of him.

As he rounded the corner, he saw Adam's silhouette on the steps below. He braced his foot against the door that shielded the agent and thrust is gun towards Adam. Adam let loose on the nozzle of the fire extinguisher, and a cloud of white powder shot into Tug's face. The gun fired, but with no real aim. Adam dropped the canister and was able to grab the wrist of the man and try to wrestle the gun away. Despite not being able to see very well, the man delivered a skillful blow with his foot to Adam's chest, knocking him down the steps.

Adam landed hard against the concrete landing and wall of the stairwell below, but he was able to take the SOCOM with him. The man at the top of the stairs picked up the canister of the fire extinguisher and threw it down on Adam. The Fish and Wildlife agent was able to roll out of the brunt of the blow, glancing off his shoulder and clanging loudly on to the concrete floor. Tug produced a sizeable military knife from his side and brandished it towards Adam, but the seventh-floor door swung open again. The maintenance man spun towards the door and slashed with his blade, catching the DOI agent across the chest, before he could strike a fatal blow to the agent's throat, Adam fired off a round from the SOCOM, catching Tug in the back. Tug wheeled around in pain, his flak jacket under the overalls catching most of the impact from the bullet. He raised the knife to throw it at Adam, Adam squeezed the trigger once more, catching Tug above the clavicle. Tug collapsed, and the knife fell harmlessly to the stairs.

Adam got up, taking stock of the new bruises he received. The door to the stairs flung open again, the agent's chest, spattered with dark, sticky blood. Adam was already calling on his radio for assistance. "Stay right there, I have help on the way," Adam said. He radioed to the lobby to the other agents.

He collected himself and walked up the stairs to Tug. He bent down and checked his pulse. It had slowed dramatically, but it was still present. He quickly patted him down for more weapons. Finding nothing, but his radio and earpiece, he moved on to the DOI field agent. He took the rag that the agent had pressed against his knife wound and tied it for him so it would be tight and remain in place.

Four agents from the FBI had shown up along with two medics. Each EMT took a position alongside each fallen man. They simultaneously asked Adam how he was, and the Fish and Wildlife agent quickly dismissed any concerns about himself. The FBI men approached Adam and began making quick plans for a thorough search of the building.

Daryl McKenzie mixed in with the crowd the best he could. Most of the convention attendees were wearing suits and business attire, though a few were more casual, none quite as informal as Daryl McKenzie. His size didn't help him avoid attention either. By the time they did surface from the basement, several medical crews, policemen, and government agents were milling about, attending to the people. The group was quarantined into a corner for a quick medical inspection and questioning.

Daryl looked around nervously. He was afraid that someone might have recognized him coming in with the assault team. He also knew that he did not fit in very well. He tried to walk as casually, but as quickly, to the street as he could. One of the policemen near the perimeter stopped him.

"Excuse me, sir, we need to verify a few things before you are allowed to leave this area. First, are you okay?" the policeman asked as Daryl nodded. "Were you part of the convention?" The policeman looked Daryl up and down, judging his appearance.

"No sir, I was just walking by when the explosion happened, I thought maybe I could help, but then these guys came in, and everything just got confusing. Look, right now, I just want to find my cousin. I lost her in all this mess," Daryl stammered.

"I understand. Before I can let you go, I need to ask you your name and how we may reach you. Do you have any ID?" the policeman asked.

"Uhh, sure," Daryl patted his pockets, "I guess I don't have my wallet on me, I'm, uhh Shawn. Shawn Kendall. My number is 555-503- 1224. Can I go now?" Daryl asked insistently.

"In a minute," the policeman started, but was distracted when an older gentleman nearby collapsed, clutching his chest. The policeman put his hand up for Daryl to wait and rushed over to the help the old man.

Daryl looked around the area. The man on the ground had secured the attention of most of the officers and medics nearest to him. He backed away until he felt he was past the last officer and began walking quickly down the sidewalk. The policeman who had been questioning him called out but, Daryl was already disappearing.

Rachel remained in the café and quickly began making some phone calls. She knew that they were going to need a little of politicking to get out of trouble unscathed. She kept vigil by the phones, hoping to hear about

Miranda or what was happening over at the Trade Center with Adam. She paused when a police report came in regarding a "Shawn Kendall". Rachel froze and listened to the report. The officer at the convention center debriefing corral described the account. A large man in denim was reported to have used the name Shawn Kendall with a bogus phone number. He was being questioned by the authorities when he took off. He mentioned needing to find his cousin. When given the description of Daryl McKenzie, the officer confirmed that it was a match.

Rachel quickly got on the phone and reached Sean.

"Well, Daryl is alive. It sounds as if he knows where Miranda is," Sean said.

"Well, it sounds as though he knows Miranda is around here, but it also sounds like he is looking for her, too," Rachel corrected her friend. She took a breath and added, "If he finds her first, do you know where he would take her?"

"I don't know. These guys are goons, but it has seemed like the brothers care about her. I don't think at this point, Miranda would go anywhere willingly with him," Sean replied.

"She *has* disappeared. Either she had been hurt and had not received help yet, or someone recognized her from the McKenzie homestead and has abducted her," Rachel said.

"So, what's the plan?" Sean asked.

Just then, the room came to life with the reports from Adam and the two agents at the office building. Agents scrambled and left their desks to join the efforts at the building. Aides picked up their phones and radios to ensure medical help was on its way.

Rachel filled Sean in and agreed to meet him across the street.

Adam was receiving medical attention when they walked up. An EMT was checking Adam's pupils for possible concussion with a small flashlight. "You don't need to worry about that, not much inside to hurt," Sean joked.

"Hey, you missed all the fun again. What, did you have another twentieth story balcony to jump off?" Adam asked his friend.

"Twenty-first, but who's counting. Besides, someone had to be planning the next step. With your head being used to stop forward progress down flights of stairs, I figured I was the default brains of this operation," Sean quipped.

"Well, what is the plan?" Adam asked.

"Good question. You didn't happen to ID Daryl McKenzie up there, did you?" Sean asked.

"No. Why? New Info?" Adam furrowed his brows.

"He was positively ID'd leaving the convention center. Wasn't sure if he was trying to hook up with his buddies in the office tower or not," Sean said, his face visibly concerned. Daryl was about their only lead now.

"Still no signs of Miranda, huh?" Adam asked, his voice sharing his friend's concern.

"No. I don't know what to do next. Beckett thinks she may have been in the rubble of the atrium at the convention center. I just don't know," Sean replied. He was pleased to see that Adam was okay. But he was visibly disappointed to hear that there was no additional information on Miranda and no ID on Daryl McKenzie.

"Don't worry, Sean, we'll find her," Adam reassured him.

Ron Beckett marched up to the trio. "What the hell are you guys up to? I thought you were supposed to be in custody!" he bellowed.

"Does it matter? The shooter from the Trade Center almost escaped," Adam said, rubbing his sore neck and back of his head.

"You were probably there in cahoots with him, but took him out when my agent entered into the scene," Beckett said and then turned to Rachel. "Ms. York, I am holding you personally accountable for these two. Be sure. Your job is on the line here."

"Beckett, why can't you pull your head out of your ass for one second to see that once again today, one of these men has done what you have been unable to do?" Rachel shot back at her superior.

"York, you are hereby under suspension, and your presence is no longer required here," Beckett growled.

"Suspended for what? For having a clue? For doing my job even if that means not hiding in your shadow waiting to say 'yes sir'?" Rachel continued laying into her boss.

"For insubordination. One more outburst and I will arrest you for impeding a federal investigation," Beckett snarled.

All of the Department of Interior agents in the area stopped what they were doing briefly as the two heads of their regional department squared off in front of everyone. They didn't notice the long, black limousine pull up. Several men in elegant suits emerged from the vehicle. These men two witnessed the exchange between Beckett and Rachel. One of them had heard enough and approached the group.

"What the hell is going on here?" the man in front of the small group demanded.

"Congressman Reilly, what are you doing here?" Beckett asked in surprise.

"I was in the convention center this afternoon. I came over to see how the intervention and investigation were going," Oregon Senator Ric Johnson informed the head of the Northwest Region of the Department of Interior.

"Well, sir, I am certainly glad that you are okay. We have things under control now. We have several suspects in custody, several more in body bags, and admittedly we're just about to process these two for questioning," Beckett said, motioning to Sean and Adam. He left out the friction that was occurring in his office between him and Rachel.

"It seems that you and Ms. York were having a bit of a disagreement. Would you like to tell me about it?" Johnson asked, his eyebrows raised slightly.

"Just a simple internal matter, sir, nothing to trouble a busy Senator who has endured a hell of a day," Beckett responded curtly. He put his hand on Johnson's shoulder as if to turn him back towards his vehicle, "Sir, for your protection, I must insist that you return to a safe area, this zone is still hot."

"I thought you said you had everything in control," Johnson said, a hint of sarcasm in his tone. He shook Beckett's hand free from his shoulder and continued, "Why don't you indulge me on your issue with Ms. York."

Beckett sighed and reported, "These two individuals have been underfoot all day, impeding the investigation, they have discharged their weapons in the convention center, been involved with an explosion at the Marriott. Ms. York seems to be intent on aiding them in their activities in which they have no jurisdiction."

"I see. These two gentlemen, excuse me, you are…" the Senator held his hand out to Adam and then to Sean, shaking each of their hands. "Well, Mr. Beckett, it seems that you *are* mistaken. I had the misfortune of bearing witness to the so-called antics of these men. If it were not for Agent Raines creating an escape route and providing cover fire and this gentleman, civilian or not, single-handedly taking down nearly the entire squad of terrorists, many more lives would have been lost today. If Ms. York were assisting these men, then I applaud her for her judgment and instinct in light of the grave incidents that occurred this afternoon."

"Sir, Agent Raines' activities out of jurisdiction are grounds for immediate dismissal, and Mr. Kendall's actions were criminal. They should not have taken the law into their own hands. Ms. York is just as responsible for helping them. I appreciate your views, but…" Beckett began, his temper gathering steam.

"But what Mr. Beckett? You gave the orders not to allow Agent Raines any additional resources. This could have been prevented if all of your agents responded as swiftly and decidedly as he had. And I can tell you that I personally would sleep better knowing the DOI in my region were run by someone as competent as Ms. York. I aim to see that you are removed from your post. I suggest you drop the charges on these two gentlemen, on the word of a United States Senator. I might also recommend that you immediately change your position on Ms. York. She may very soon be your successor!" Senator Johnson asserted to Beckett, his demeanor strong, but in control.

"Sir, I am not sure where you received your information. I assure you that if I had word on something like this occurring, I would have been on top of it. Agent Raines…" Beckett began before Johnson cut him off.

"Oh cut the bull crap Beckett," the Senator reached into his jacket pocket and produce several documents, "Five different overrides on resource requests in the last four days. All of them made by Agent Raines, initially approved by Ms. York and each overridden with your signature. Mr. Eley of the Senate Oversight Committee would like to have a conference call with you first thing in the morning."

"Yes sir." Beckett turned to the agents that he had tasked with processing Adam and Sean, "They are free to go. They can help provide any additional details they might have on their own accord."

"Tomorrow morning Beckett," Johnson called out over his shoulder to the division head as he walked back to his limousine.

As one set of EMT were finishing up with caring Adam, the other set sped away towards the hospital while working feverishly on Tug Gaskill. An agent accompanied them in the back of the ambulance. The wounds to Tug were not nearly as bad as they seemed. A bullet had pierced his neck, but had narrowly missed his femoral artery. The duo of medics were able to get pressure to stop the bleeding and began treating some of his less critical injuries.

"His blood pressure is returning to normal. I think he is going to make it," one of them said.

"Well, here's a catch twenty-two. Do we go ahead and give this something for the pain, or do we let him suffer?" the agent scoffed as one of the medics was preparing a syringe with a potent analgesic.

The medic tapped the needle, ensuring there were not any air bubbles in the chamber and leaned down to administer the needle into Tug's thigh. He swept the site with an alcohol swab and directed the needle into place.

He was so surprised by the swift movement of the knee; he did not have time to react. Tug's knee delivered a severe blow to the medic's chin, snapping his neck back, temporarily cutting off his airway. Before the EMT could fall to the ground, Tug swept his left arm up, ripping out the monitoring equipment that was reporting his vitals, and grabbed the syringe away from the blacking out man who was just helping him. The agent, sitting on the bench across the van from him was drawing his gun, Tug slashed with the syringe and caught the agent in the neck. The agent fired the weapon, but missed his target badly. Tug grabbed the gun away as the agent's hands went to his throat, which was losing an immense amount of blood. The mercenary swung the butt of the gun down and caught him the Bureau agent in the back of the head, knocking him out cold.

The ambulance screeched to a fish-tailing halt as the driver heard the shot behind him. Equipment and the occupants were jostled violently. The unconscious agent landed on top of Tug's leg. He pushed the agent off of him with his shoe on the FBI man's face and returned to an upright position.

The medic on the other side of the gurney that Tug had vacated just stared in awed horror. He paled as the gun steadied in his direction. The mercenary collected himself. The quick action took almost all that he had of strength. He eyed the EMT, "Is there anything I need to know about my injury?"

"Uhh, you might want to have the bandage changed every couple of hours until the bleeding stops for good. Steady pressure needs to be applied. No arteries were hit, you were lucky," the trembling man responded.

The driver poked his head back to see what was going on. Tug looked up and, without blinking, fired the trigger of the gun at the driver, shooting him between the eyes. The driver slumped to the floor of the van in between the cab and the work area.

The rogue mercenary returned his gaze to the medic that had been working on him. "Got any pain relievers that won't make me too drowsy?"

"Yeah, I've got an NSAID in a pill form. It will take the edge of the pain, but you'll stay alert," the medical tech replied.

"Put some in that duffle bag with some bandages," Tug ordered, using the gun to point to a medical bag next to the tech.

The terrified man complied and put the supplies in the bag. He lifted the bag and placed it on the gurney that separated the two. "We really should get you to the hospital."

"I appreciate your concern. What I really need now is a cell phone. Toss me yours," he nodded at the phone that was clipped to the medic's hip. The EMT again did as instructed and lobbed his cellphone at the gunman. "Thank you. Now, I am afraid that your services are no longer required." Tug raised the FBI agent's gun and once more squeezed the trigger. The horror on the medic's face was replaced with the blank look of death as the seconds of his claim came to a hasty end. Tug checked the FBI agent's pulse. Finding none, he picked up the duffel of supplies and burst through the double doors of the ambulance.

A crowd had begun to gather around the van, whose lights were still flashing, that had stopped abruptly. Tug waved the gun menacingly at the crowd that ducked erratically out of the way, making a path for Tug to escape through. He took a quick baring of his surroundings and dashed for the relative darkness of the alleys. He dialed the medics cell phone as he jogged west towards the riverfront.

"Chinook, this is Tug. The exit strategy needs to be changed. Be at the old dock across the street from Safeco. ETA twenty minutes," the terrorist team leader commanded into the cellular phone.

Daryl McKenzie was frantic. He knew he had to get uptown to the old warehouse. His heart raced wildly. He wasn't sure if the police would inherently be after him or not. He refused public transportation and kept to the back streets. Occasionally, a police cruiser would rumble by, and the big McKenzie boy would duck into a nearby alley. At this pace, it would take him all night. He wanted to get out of Seattle immediately. He came upon a taxi and flagged it down. He hopped in and told the driver the address of the warehouse.

As the taxi came within a block of the warehouse, Daryl had the driver stopped. He paid him his fare and hopped out. Maybe he was paranoid, or he was just going crazy, but he wanted to make sure that the police did not somehow track this location down. He looked up and down the street, but there were no additional vehicles in sight. The area around the warehouse was greatly abandoned, many of the structures awaiting resale for someone to renovate them. The momentum in Seattle's older neighborhoods was to turn these forgotten older stretches into trendy condominiums, but it had not yet reached this part of the city.

The warehouse typified the image of a forlorn industrial corner standing as an old red brick square with two large loading doors, and a sign so faded its words were a dim mystery on its façade. The warehouse sat adjacent to an alley, with a fire escape zigzagging down the side. The week's rain left large puddles in the dark and dingy corridor.

Walking up to the warehouse, Daryl peered inside one of the dirt-clouded windows. He saw a man that he did not recognize sitting in a chair opposite of Miranda. His first impulse was to charge in, but he saw that the man had a silenced handgun resting on the table in front of him. The man was tall and thin, dressed in a neatly tailored black suit. He sat back in his chair as if he were waiting for something. Whatever was going on, Daryl was not comfortable with it.

He had left his weapons at the convention center, rightfully fearing a police search upon exiting. Looking around the alley, he spied a rusty old pipe at the bottom of the fire escape. Daryl jogged over and picked it up. The pipe was about five feet in length and relatively heavy. It was the best weapon choice that he could come up with. Walking over to the window he was looking through, he saw that the parties inside had not changed. Miranda sat in her chair at the table across from the gunman, her face wrinkled in resentment. Satisfied, Daryl walked around the backside of the warehouse. Locating the back door, he tried the handle. It wouldn't budge. With the pipe, he went to work, prying it open. The old wood frame cracked, and the door opened.

Daryl knew the sound would carry through to the occupants in the middle of the warehouse. He darted around the corner. He didn't even hear the footsteps of the man who came to check out the noise. The man poked his head carefully around the corner, his gun poised in front of him. As he made his way around, he had his finger pressed on the trigger, but no one was there for him to fire on. He walked up to the rusty old dumpster that rested in the alley alongside the warehouse. He was almost close enough to peek his head into it when his shoe hit a puddle. This simple sound that otherwise would have been benign, sounded horrific in the silence of the dark alley. He paused, waiting for what seemed an incredibly long time and finally peeked over, his gun keeping vigil in front of him.

Daryl fought to remain still. He could swear that his heartbeat could be heard rattling out of the old dumpster. He was so scared and so anxious that he almost revealed himself to get the moment over with, as he listened intently but could hear no one approaching. Then he heard the foot hit the puddle. The soft little sound of displaced water almost caused Daryl to fall back. He readied the old pipe in his hands. The shadow of the hand crested the top of the dumpster. Soon, the tip of the silenced gun followed. Daryl let loose with the pipe, his big arms smashing it down into the gun-wielding hand with all of his might. The blow met the flesh and bone of the wrist with a nasty crunch, causing the man in the black suit to reflexively impulsively lose his grip on the weapon.

The gun clanked and rattled to the bottom of the steel trash container. Despite experiencing immense pain, the man who had so silently entered the alley, leaped to the top of the dumpster and skillfully produced a knife from his side. He turned it over and over as his good hand twirled it in anticipation of attack. Daryl swung the pipe again, trying to knock the man's legs out from under him. The man jumped and avoided the blow. Daryl's momentum swinging the big pipe, took him slightly off-center. The man saw this moment of weaknesses and dropped into the dumpster, driving the knife into Daryl's left shoulder. Daryl howled, dropping the pipe instantly. The man poised for a second blow. Daryl's arm met his as the knife repositioned for another attack.

Despite the man's superior skill, Daryl's strength became dominant in this arena of close combat. The man did not have enough room to avoid the clumsy but powerful Daryl McKenzie, in the tight confines of the dumpster. Daryl grabbed the man by the throat and began to squeeze with all of his might. The knife swept by Daryl's side, the big McKenzie boy's left hand grabbed his opponent's wrist and began bashing it into the side of the dumpster, the whole time maintaining his grip around the man's throat. The knife clanked to the floor of the dumpster, the man brought his knee up to Daryl's midsection, but the big country man endured the blow and continued the squeeze on the man's throat, crushing his trachea in the process.

The man in black collapsed with a thump in the belly of the steel dumpster. Daryl looked around the alley to see if any passersby heard the commotion, but this sleepy part of Seattle did not house many visitors or inhabitants, particularly after dark. He looked down at the man lying at his feet one final time, retrieving the gun and knife and climbed out of the dumpster.

Daryl made his way into the warehouse and found his cousin, bound and gagged, sitting at a table in the middle of the otherwise empty warehouse. Miranda's eyes widened when she saw her cousin. Striding over to her, he removed the gag from around her mouth.

"Miranda! You're alright!" Daryl said, obviously relieved.

"Thank goodness, that man was going to kill me as soon as you showed up. What have you gotten yourself into?" Miranda asked her cousin.

"Well, things didn't go the way that it was planned, but it was for the right cause," Daryl admitted sourly.

"You really believe that, don't you? It is okay that you were planning to kill hundreds of innocent people. You think it is okay that this *cause* of yours killed your baby brother!" Miranda spat at him.

"We learned from Grandpa that war is an admirable fight. I would have given my own life if we got America back. It is part of being a soldier. I am proud of my brother. We don't have time for this. We have to go," Daryl said with haste as he started to remove the rest of Miranda's bounds.

"We? You need to turn yourself in, every policeman in the state will be after you. I need to find my friends," Miranda said urgently.

Daryl stopped what he was doing and put the knife he was using to free Miranda on the table. "I was afraid you were going to be like that. I had hoped that you might appreciate me saving you - appreciate family. Maybe you don't know what family is," Daryl said grimly.

"I know what family is, I just don't know who *my* family is," Miranda said coldly.

"This will make things a little more difficult," Daryl said, basically to himself as he rubbed his prominent square chin.

"What are you going to do with me?" Miranda asked, suddenly realizing that reasoning with her cousin was not an option.

"I am going to take you with me. I am sorry, cousin, but if they are after me, I might need you to convince them to back off," Daryl said.

"Daryl, this is crazy," Miranda pleaded.

"Miranda, I am going to have to ask you to shut up. It is *your* fault that Jeb is dead. In my eyes, you are a traitor to this country. You are a traitor to this family," Daryl said. His voice was colder than Miranda could ever remember.

Sean started his search, where he last saw Miranda. Rachel had provided Sean with a DOI pass as well as had an agent call ahead to allow him access. The police and FBI were still processing the convention goers who had escaped through the basement. He searched the loading docks where Miranda was last seen. When he saw that the brown UPS van was gone, knowing that it had to have left prior to the melee, that she might have been packaged in it. They must have had someone else on hand to remove her from the scene. If she were killed on the spot, her body would be somewhere nearby. They wouldn't have been careful with a body so close to the time of the assault. They could probably take her and use her for leverage or bait.

He ran his fingers through his hair and wondered if they would take her to get to him. But, the McKenzies thought he was dead. Then bait for who? Maybe it was just to have a hostage to hold the FBI at bay. Or…. an idea evolved in Sean's head. The shooting of the sniper from the counter sniper on the roof of the office building, they were systematically eliminating the assault team once things went awry. Maybe Miranda was held to entice the McKenzies should either of them get away. Sean knew Daryl was looking for Miranda. He took off to find her. He had a head start and an idea of where she might likely be. Sean didn't know what Daryl knew but figured the big McKenzie boy would hide where he felt safest - the North Cascade Range, where he has spent his life hunting, tracking, and fishing.

The reports continued streaming into the DOI/FBI staging area. They were all recorded and transferred to the appropriate agents. One in particular froze Sean in his tracks. An agent debriefing from Swedish Memorial Hospital reported an abduction just as the attack began. The injured agent had witnessed the incident, but was shot by a sniper before he could respond. He shared his story as soon as he regained consciousness.

Sean felt his stomach tighten – could Miranda be the victim that the agent mentioned?

Thirty Eight

Daryl left Miranda tied up in the warehouse and went out into the back alley. Daryl's truck was parked in a vacant lot several blocks away. He stopped. He figured if anyone had identified him, they would put out a call on his truck. He looked around the nearby streets. Then he remembered the man in the black suit. He jogged back into the alley and looked over the side of the dumpster. The man in black lay in the contorted heap that Daryl left him in.

He hopped over the side and searched the man's pockets, pulling out a set of keys. It was for a rental car, a silver Ford. Daryl leaped out of the steel storage bin and into the alley. He walked around the close perimeter blocks, pushing the key fob at every silver vehicle he passed by. Finally, the lights flashed on one of the vehicles, a nondescript gray sedan. He hopped in the car and started it up. He shifted the sedan into gear and tires spinning, drove back to the warehouse.

The big McKenzie boy parked in the back alley, and got out, leaving the car running. He strode into the warehouse, and with the knife he left on the table, cut Miranda free from the chair, but left the bands around her wrists secure. Jostling his cousin towards the car and pushed her into the backseat. Daryl got back in the driver's seat, made one last check over his shoulder to see that his passenger was secure and drove away.

Special Agent in Charge Steinmetz had about all he could take this day. His team had finally secured the private school. The chaos of families reuniting with their students, the harried faculty, and the frenzy of media at the school was left to forensic teams and a handful of police securing the building. The Olympic Hotel had been evacuated and searched. The hotel was eager to get their guests squared away, and it was apparent the hotel was targeted just to throw the FBI off track. Steinmetz was also now painfully aware that Special Agent Lyndon was likely dead. He would have produced himself in the midst of the events downtown.

He refocused his teams to join the mass of law enforcement and emergency crews at the convention center. He was intrigued and annoyed by the DOI having set up an emergency headquarters nearby. That would be his first stop. He ordered his field agent to pull the Suburban over, and he got out. Despite the oppressive fatigue that was well on its way to setting in, Steinmetz rambled up to the café that was serving as the DOI headquarters. He flashed his badge at the door and walked into the room.

Some of his agents were already working with the DOI field team. He nodded at them as he passed by. Beckett looked up from his table and moved his gaze to the irate, very official-looking man storming into his work area.

"May I help you?" Beckett asked the man.

"Special Agent-in-Charge Steinmetz," the FBI man said, showing his badge for what seemed the thousandth time today. "Who is in charge of this operation?"

"I am," Beckett said sharply. Rachel smirked in the background. She was used to her boss constantly vying for superiority. "What can I do for you?" Beckett continued.

"We have been tracking this operation since the Colorado bombing incident, we had a man on this inside working it, but I fear the worst for my agent. What I want to know is, what the hell are *you* doing here?" Steinmetz asked pointedly.

"Well, we have been engaged after some activities in the North Cascades National Park raised some suspicions with my agents. My team was recently able to put the pieces together on the convention center assault. My team prevented a holocaust here today," Beckett boldly informed the G-man.

"Oh, and when did you decide to involve the FBI, NSA or Homeland Security who have jurisdiction in these matters, *outside* of the National Forest?" Steinmetz asked.

Rachel was about to come unglued with her boss' lines. She had tried to get him engaged in the threat since Sean called her, and he refused to allow her to put together even a small team until the first shots were fired. She finally had enough.

"Alright, Stan, first off, you wouldn't allow *your* team to commit to this threat. If it weren't for a Fish and Wildlife agent and a *civilian,* today would have been a catastrophe. Adam Raines of the North Cascade field office out of Sedro-Wooley has been calling in this threat for several days. It took stuff to hit the fan before you would commit. And you, I have already tried communicating with your office, Mr., what was it, *Special Agent-in-Charge*, and I was quoted some bureaucratic bullshit. Look, here's the deal. We all know that someone in D.C. had stalled us. We need to skip the nonsense and get down to business. We have more facts than you do on this, but you have the resources. Let's pull together what we have and see if we can't prevent a few more lives from being lost," Rachel fumed at Beckett, her voice heated, yet never wavering from strong and collected.

The room fell silent. All eyes cast on Rachel. The Department of Interior Assistant Regional Director stood waiting for a response from the crowd of egos and politically-agenda motivated government officials. Despite the very stressful day and her irritation with how the events were handled, she wore an appearance of grace and unwavering calm.

Steinmetz finally broke the silence, "She's right, Ms...?"

"York," Rachel replied evenly.

"Ms. York may be the only one here with concise, rational thinking. I do have several teams of agents at my disposal, and it does sound as though we each hold different pieces of an incomplete puzzle. Let's see what we can do. Mr. Beckett, you were working on a plan. Let's refine it with what information we have, and I will provide the agents to support your team," Steinmetz offered.

"Alright," Beckett shook his head; he was in limbo of having his ego stroked and yet feeling foolish just the same. "Let's roll out what we know. We have a group of radicals who call themselves the Greys, most of which have been eliminated. We have secured each of the attacked buildings. It appears as though we might have a hostage with at least one of the radicals that have escaped. We think the suspect is Daryl McKenzie. A guard at the center reported seeing a young woman believed to be Miranda Shaw, the suspect's cousin, being dragged into a van just before he was shot. McKenzie was last seen leaving an interrogation corral at the convention center. Someone, presumably one of the radicals, was taking members of his own group out. He is en route to Seattle's Swedish Hospital with a gunshot wound. With the areas secured, our primary objective is to locate the hostage and get her back," Beckett provided a synopsis of where the day had led them.

"Our agency has been tracking a suspected mercenary since the Colorado bombing. Our agent infiltrated the group and joined them in the North Cascades. His last report led us to put most of our team at the Olympic Hotel, which we now know was a red herring," Steinmetz added. "What do we know about this hostage?"

Rachel looked around the room for Sean to fill in what he knew, but he was nowhere to be seen. "Her name is Miranda Shaw, a relative of the McKenzies, the lead Washington contingents to the Greys. We presume that Daryl McKenzie is the radical member that got away. Our hunch is he had a pretty good idea where to look for his cousin."

"Is she part of this attack?" Steinmetz asked.

"Negative, she was assisting my department in uncovering the operation. She was last seen entering the alley between the convention center and the office building where the sniper was," Rachel replied.

"Hey, we have something on the wire," one of the aides manning the reports called to the group, "Here it is. We have a positive on the green Dodge pick-up. Air support found it in the old warehouse district north of town. A cruiser went out to positively ID, it was affirmed."

"Let's get a crew out there. Beckett, how would you like to divvy out the teams?" Steinmetz asked.

"Let's get a bird in here to pick up one of my men, three of yours, to check out the warehouse. We'll get the Seattle police to have the cruiser sit tight and assist when we arrive. I want an on-call team here to be ready to respond to new information. Can we get a local law enforcement liaison in here?" Beckett suggested.

"I can arrange that Beckett. Alright, team, you heard the man, let's go," Steinmetz said, appointing three men to join the DOI field agents.

Rachel pulled Adam aside. "Where is Sean?" she whispered.

"I don't know. He was just here. I thought he was going to hang out and see what the FBI had," Adam whispered. "He couldn't have gone far, Miranda had the keys to the SUV." He picked up his cell phone and dialed Sean's number.

"Yeah," Sean's voice came over the phone.

"Where are you? They found Daryl's truck. It is north of town in the warehouse district." Adam reported, his voice conveying his concern about his friend's solo actions.

"I just wanted to retrace where Miranda was and where Daryl was last seen. He must have had a ride waiting or acquired one somehow. The warehouse district north of town?" Sean asked.

"Yeah, it makes sense for a staging area. A lot of the buildings are abandoned. Been taken over by crack houses and the sort," Adam filled in his friend.

"Sounds pleasant. And they found Daryl there?" Sean asked.

"I don't know. They are sending a team out there right now. It sounds as though the truck is just sitting there," Adam said.

"Even he must be smart enough to know that it would be tracked," Sean said. "I think I know where he would go," Sean admitted.

"Let me tell the folks here, they can get out there start looking," Adam suggested.

"No, I don't want them to go busting in. If Miranda is there, that could put her in danger," Sean replied.

"We'll pick you up then. We can head to the warehouse. This thing could be over soon," Adam said.

"Alright, let's go. I'll be on the north corner of the convention center," Sean told him.

Adam hung up the phone and turned to Rachel. "Can we pick him up?"

"Of course. I'll get the car. We don't want to advertise our presence. Beckett has had it with us. There is only so much our charm will buy us," Rachel warned.

Daryl drove the gray sedan down the highway towards his family's home in the North Cascades. He felt like his whole body was overheating with stress. He was frantic to get back to the environment where he felt most comfortable. A place where he felt he could hide, or if he had to, win his own private war. Daryl constantly checked his mirrors and kept his speed perfectly on the set limits.

As he swung the car off of I-5 and onto the North Cascades Highway, he saw a police cruiser parked on the side of the road. Daryl felt his pulse spike. He felt as though his blood would come shooting out of his veins. He looked straight ahead and kept his driving precise. In his rearview mirror, he could see the patrolman standing outside of his car, watching the traffic roll passed. The officer's gaze did light upon Daryl's stolen gray sedan, but only for a moment.

Daryl breathed a sigh of relief as the officer's eyes lifted from the sedan he was driving and landed onto the vehicle behind him. Focusing on the road ahead of him, he was glad that he kept Miranda tied up in the backseat. If she saw the police cruiser, he knew she would try to attract attention. His desire to reach the sanctuary of the deep woods of the North Cascade Range intensified. Each mile that clicked by felt like one mile closer to freedom for Daryl McKenzie.

Tug Gaskill slithered silently through the back alleys of Seattle as he made his way towards Safeco field. With cat-like stealth, he avoided the helicopters and police cruisers that periodically passed by. He was cautious to steer clear of the busier streets and soon found himself outside of the gates leading into to Safeco Field. The ballpark that, in a few months, would hold thousands of fans cheering for their Mariners baseball team; it was also the ballpark that was the landmark that denoted Tug's freedom. As he passed through the street that stood between the baseball and football stadiums, he looked at his watch. He would be right on time. Bolting out of the alleyway, he crossed the very busy Alaskan Viaduct Way to the chain-link fence of the shipping yards.

He strode quickly across the sidewalk, following the fence line until it again turned westward. From this vantage, he could see the freighters nestled in their berths of the shipyard. He hurried along, staying in the shadows. The sidewalk came to an abrupt end as it ran into a levy that overlooked Elliott Bay. Tug took note of the razor wire that glistened atop the fence. Looking around, he spied a scrap of plastic culvert that had been carelessly left behind from the last batch of roadwork along the Viaduct. He found the seam, and with a few expertly placed jabs from the scalpel that he had liberated from the ambulance, he fabricated a protective cap for the dangerous fence. Slipping the conduit over the wire, he vaulted over the obstruction without a scratch.

The mercenary kneeled on the ground to survey that last remaining steps to freedom. The dock area was deserted, and he had a clear path to the water's edge. He jogged down the gentle slope to the rim of Elliott Bay. As he had prescribed, he could hear a zodiac, racing across the bowline of the freighter that was directly in front of him. He stood in the shadows and waited for it to pull up. Amidst the sounds of water lapping at the edge of the pilings and the purring of the outboard motor on the zodiac, Tug heard something else - the sound of keys jingling to the rhythm of someone's footsteps.

Like a cat awaiting its prey, he slunk down into the shadow of the dock as much as he could. This intruder's timing could not be any worse. He needed this step of his mission to be without complication. The jingling of keys grew louder until he could see the red glowing dot from the pedestrian's cigarette. As the individual crossed in front of Tug, he recognized the figure as a security guard. Gritting his teeth, he uncoiled his body towards his unsuspecting victim. With snakelike fluidity, he struck at the security guard.

His left arm wrapped around the man's head, his shirtsleeve stifling any sounds that might have uttered in his dying moments, his right arm delivered a sweep of the scalpel severing arteries, vocal cords and the security guard's trachea. Even as the man was falling to the dock, Tug had unsnapped the night watchman's holster and was holding the Colt .45 revolver in his hand before the thump of the guard's body could be heard crumpling on the wooden slats.

Over his shoulder, Tug saw that his ride was ready. A Coast Guard zodiac that would blend in with the variety of rescue, police, and other Coast Guard crafts that were by now clogging the downtown portion of Elliott Bay. Tug snared the security guard's pant leg and heaved the officer into the cool Pacific waters as he climbed gently into the zodiac. As his feet hit the floor of the small boat, the outboard came to life, streaking through the dark waters to Tug's freedom.

The commotion along the waterfront was remarkable. Helicopters circled overhead, their large spotlights sweeping over the area capturing the activities below. Boats of every size and shape were milling about the bayfront to aid in searching for additional victims and presumably, Tug and his crew. Most of the attention was directed at the convention center near the Bell St. Pier. Crews were still in the process of clearing the debris in search for more victims, wounded or dead.

Tug's little Coast Guard boat slid right by the others, their crews focused on their assigned tasks. The boat driver silently made his way through the busy waters and to the directed destination - The Ursa Major. A line was immediately cast down for Tug to climb up and the zodiac sped away. Hand over hand, Tug hauled himself up the line. With an attentive crew, Tug was quickly welcomed aboard the freighter that was just powering up its screws for its planned exit from Puget Sound heading for its homeport in Osaka, Japan. Tug stood under the placard designating The Ursa Major as one of the vessels under the ownership of Hasegawa Freight.

He watched as the city of Seattle began to slip behind him, foot by foot. The day was not exactly as he had mapped it out, but the results at the end of the mission were as they were supposed to be. The Free Trade Convention was in ruins, the delegation was scared beyond their wits, and the entire crew that was drawn from the deep woods of the Cascades, were dead. He turned away from the railing and went to find the stateroom that would be his home for the next few weeks.

Special Agent Steinmetz joined the men that had parked down the block from the abandoned warehouse. The DOI agent that was assigned to work alongside them jumped out of the car next to him. A small team of FBI agents had already taken a flanking position around the green Dodge pick-up. One of them carried a million candle-watt flashlight and trained the big beam on the passenger compartment of the tall truck. Another agent rushed the vehicle and stuck the gun to the window as he peered into the cab of the truck using a small mirror affixed to a telescopic wand. The cab was empty and he signaled the all-clear.

"Alright, let's spread out. I want the warehouses canvassed. Go two by two and be very careful. If you note anything suspicious, wait for back up before you enter. I will call for more bodies to help the search," Steinmetz called to his team as they gave him the report from the truck. He scratched his head. This whole day was giving him a headache.

He joined the search as his team began block-by-block inspecting the warehouses. He took the third building on the right. It was one of the few that had a light on. He stole up to the building carefully, drawing his gun and holding it up as he peered into one of the dusty windows. The FBI agent saw an empty room with the exception of a single table surrounded by half a dozen chairs. Continuing his way along the alley of the building, he walked past the rusty steel trash bins, shining his flashlight along the grimy concrete. As he rounded the corner of the building, he shut off his flashlight

The door to the back entrance was creaking as it swung in the breeze. He raised his handgun and pointed it out in front of him. Slowly, he kicked the door open with his foot. It swung wide enough to squeeze his body through. He reported his position to the team and walked inside. The building was eerily quiet. The loudest sound was the wind whistling through the open back door. Creeping slowly down the hallway to the room that had the light on, S.A. Steinmetz felt his heartbeat quicken. As many times as he has entered a suspicious building in his career, he could always count on the familiar jitters that would accompany the potential for danger. This trait had undoubtedly kept him alive throughout his career.

Hearing his fellow agents enter the door behind him, he pushed on into the room. He swung his gun in each direction, just as he was trained to about twenty-five years ago. The room was empty, and he was able to feel his heart rate to return to normal. He had the agents that were following him hold their positions. Steinmetz studied the room. Surveying the table and chairs in the middle of the vacant space, he studied each piece of furniture carefully, as if each had a story to tell him.

One chair, in particular, caught his attention. There were rub marks against the wooden back slats that made up the back of the chair. He knelt by the chair. Under it lie several green plastics pieces. Picking them up, he realized that they were plastic tie- bands, similar to those that many law enforcement agencies use in place of handcuffs. He held the shards up to the agents. He ordered some of them to resume searching the rest of the warehouse. To those still in the room, "I think we have a hostage."

"Special Agent in Charge Steinmetz! We have a body. In the dumpster in the alley," one of the agents searching the exterior of the building called to him.

Steinmetz followed his men out to the alley. Several powerful flashlights were exposing the interior of the garbage bin. The contorted body of a man in a black suit adorned the rusty, dank bottom of the steel container. An agent had plastic covers over his shoes, so that his own tread didn't disrupt the evidence. He wore plastic gloves on hands that were checking the man's non-existence vital signs.

"DOA", the agent called from inside the bin.

"Check him for ID. Doesn't look like the McKenzie boy's description," Steinmetz said.

"We have a wallet," the agent called out. "It's not the McKenzie we were looking for. John Smith, original. It appears as though he died from asphyxiation. Major bruising around his throat. Pretty good struggle, he has cuts and bruises on his hands, knuckles and face."

"Call in the coroner and forensics. Alright, let's piece this together. We had a missing person, an assault team member ID'd, and left the scene, presumably looking for that same person. There are signs of a struggle, forced entry, and of an abductee. Just a guess, but I would say that cousin Daryl knew where to look for Miranda, the missing person. Didn't like what he saw or wanted her for his escape. Confronted the assault team member who was tasked with holding her until the siege was completed. And now they are gone again. Get Rachel York on the phone, I want to hear what that friend of hers has to say," Steinmetz said, rubbing his chin, looking up into the night sky that was starting to fill with clouds.

Rachel's leather and burl wood-clad SUV thundered north on Interstate Five. Rachel had kept her radio on receiving reports from the field and would alternate between the radio and her cell phone. On one of her phone calls, a friend in the department told her that Beckett had been asking about her. He rambled that she was not a field agent and had no jurisdiction to be poking around in these matters. She urged her friend to keep it quiet until the time was right. She would report in when it was appropriate.

Adam sat in the passenger seat, assisting Rachel with directions once they turned off onto Highway Twenty towards the Cascade Range. In the intermittent light that filtered into the truck, saw Sean tending to the gun that he was given. His silent friend loaded the chambers of the black assault shotgun and clicked them into place, his face offering nothing by way of expression. This sight was a mild shock to Adam. Sean's cold attention to the weapons in the backseat was an ominous foretelling of events to come.

Sean himself was thinking about the events of the past week. Finding the dead wolf in the woods, its life ripped out of it from a high-powered weapon. Meeting this amazing woman at the bar - in his opinion, one of the unlikeliest spots to find someone. The chance run-ins with her following that first evening. The feelings that have grown so quickly with the time that he had spent with her. The friction with her family, the various bruises which resulted from that friction. He thought of the McKenzie family and their twisted dealings. Being run off the road in his Jeep. His mind reeled off the unreal events that unraveled at the convention center in Seattle, like a movie. The image of Jeb McKenzie lying on the ground after the bullet fired from Sean's hand found it's mark – the explosion and the terrifying leap of faith from the 18th-floor balcony – and finally, the cataclysmic melee at the convention center seared in his mind.

Now he was ready to risk his life once more for Miranda. He wasn't sure what he was going to find out in the North Cascades. He wasn't even sure if Miranda would be there and, if so, if she went willingly or had been forced by her cousin. One thing was for sure; he was going to find out and see to her safe return. He slammed the cartridge in the butt of the gun that he was holding. The click of the metal parts created an unusually satisfying feeling for Sean. He had moved to the North Cascades to escape the drama, and now he was on his way to confront one of the biggest dramas of his life.

Miranda struggled against her bindings. She had been transferred from the silver sedan to one of Hal McKenzie's four-wheel-drive ranch trucks, and then finally straddled onto the back of a snowmobile. A long and bumpy ride through the cold night air had brought her to a discrete valley sheltering a little cabin nestled in its core shrouded in a deep cloak of snow. She looked around the dark cabin. She had never been here before. The trails to get there were narrow, rough, and barely navigable. She assumed it one of the family's hunting cabins. There were animal skins strewn about the one-room cabin, no windows, a small cast iron wood stove, and no running water. Knowing her relatives, they were the only ones to know about this bungalow tucked away so deeply in the woods.

"Daryl, what are you going to do with me?" Miranda asked at her big cousin, who had just returned with an armful of wood from behind the cabin.

"I don't know, cousin. I need to let the heat of all this blow over. Maybe I can let you go then. It will be up to the elders. I am sorry I had to do this to you, but you shouldn't uh got in the way," Daryl responded, his voice pitched like a parent scolding a child.

"This whole thing to blow over? This might not blow over for years," Miranda started before being cut off.

"Who knows?" Daryl snapped, "Like I said, in the morning, Grandpa and Dad will join us, and we'll talk about it. Damn it, cousin, you shoulda stayed out of this. You and that damn city boy. I hope he was worth it."

"It has nothing to do with Sean. I cannot believe what you have done…all of those innocent people. Their blood is on *your* hands!" Miranda exclaimed, her eyes cast in a disapproving stare.

"Casualties of war cousin. 'Sides, there weren't nobody innocent. We did what we had to do for America. You'll see – someday people will look back and hail Jeb as a hero," Daryl defended.

"No, Daryl. All they'll see is a criminal. Whatever veil of righteousness you want to place on your actions can't hide the fact that what you did was murder. Pure and simple," Miranda disputed.

Unfazed, Daryl studied his cousin between bits of jerky. "I guess that's why we menfolk need to tend to such matters. Women are too soft. I'm sorry you can't understand."

"Well, can you untie me, at least? We're miles away from anything. I need to go to the bathroom. I'm going to have to eat at some point, Daryl," Miranda pleaded.

"Alright, I guess that'd be alright," Daryl reached down and pulled out his long hunting knife and swiped through the binding that held Miranda's wrists together. "Here," he tossed his cousin a Ziploc bag of elk jerky.

Miranda looked at it for a moment, but realized, this might be the closest thing to nourishment that she might get for a while. She reached for a piece and began chewing on a strand of jerky. She remembered her uncle giving her all sorts of smoked meats from his hunting spoils. A strange feeling that the life that she knew was utterly changed forever had begun to sink in. She had an odd amalgamation of nostalgia and disgust coursing through her. She looked up at the cousin that she used to swim and fish with, play cards with all night long. The cousin that would play dolls with her when no one else was around, just to make her happy, was the same sick man that stormed a convention center full of innocent people and opened fire on them. He was the same man that kidnapped her and now held her for who knew how long. She wanted to cry, but for some reason, no tears would come. Instead, her emotions were replaced with anger and compulsion to survive. To right the wrongs that her family had unleashed.

The silence of the SUV was broken with the ringing of Rachel's cell phone. The call came just as the reception was waning. "York," her voice called into the small phone.

"Hey, I wanted to give you this information that just came in. The sniper from the office building, he was in transport at the hospital, but he escaped. He killed three EMTs and an FBI agent. An all-points has been issued, but no word yet. Thought you should know. And Rachel, Beckett is having a cow wondering where you are, what do I tell him?" the aide from her office asked.

"Tell him I am following up on something, I am out of cell range. I promise I will call when I can. Just keep him off my back for a little while longer. But can you do me a favor? Will you let me know if you hear anything about the missing assault team member? His name is Daryl McKenzie. He has a small rap, minor stuff. See what contacts he has in the area near his home," Rachel requested.

"Yeah sure, but is that where you are headed? Is that where you think he has gone? Back home?" the aide asked.

"Tony, just give me a little time to get out there. I want to allow my friends to get the girl back safely, before something happens, or he goes deeper into hiding," Rachel told him.

"Okay, I'll do what I can. Just promise me you'll be careful," Tony asked.

"I promise. Thanks, Tony," Rachel hung up the phone and slowed the vehicle down as the curves of Highway Twenty set in.

"Diablo is coming up. The McKenzie homestead is tough to find. It is a right on a hidden curve, with some overgrowth camouflaging the entrance," Adam warned.

"Man, these people want their privacy," Rachel said, she couldn't remember seeing another home for miles.

"They are a little wacky, always have been. We always thought that they were pretty harmless, though. I guess now we know different," Adam admitted, he was lost in his thoughts briefly, until his eyes widened. "There, it was right back there."

Rachel slammed on the brakes, and the SUV slid to a stop. She shifted the truck into gear and backed up to the barely noticeable driveway. The driving lights of the truck picked up the opening in the brush. The driveway sunk slightly, leaving an even more deceptive view from the road. The undergrowth was just enough to let a vehicle squeeze by with a branch or two scraping alongside.

As Rachel's SUV descended the driveway, Sean felt his pulse quicken. Whatever pain or fatigue had set in during the recent events, had been wholly overridden with adrenalin, rage against the McKenzies and their inhumanity, and his concern for Miranda. He holstered the handgun and held the shotgun in his right hand. The long drive to the homestead was killing him emotionally, and the wraps he had on his feelings were fraying and about to be unleashed.

Adam checked his weapons and devised a plan with Sean. He wanted to check the perimeter of the buildings. He had understood that the McKenzies had a small house and a large shop. Each should be cleared before they entered. He also urged Sean to allow him to make the first moves. Adam knew without a warrant; his career was at stake.

The SUV rolled to a stop and instantly, Rachel shut off the lights. A quick survey revealed a ramshackle house and large shop about twenty yards away. A new gray sedan was parked beside the shop. She looked to Adam for his instruction, but before either of them could speak, Sean had leaped from the truck. He scurried across the lawn towards the house.

"Oh no. Get back to the highway and call for back up. Tell them we have probable cause that a kidnap victim is detained inside. Hurry, this could get ugly real quick," Adam said urgently and jumped out of the SUV after Sean.

Rachel backed the vehicle up and made a hasty three-point turn to head back to the highway to find cell coverage. She was very concerned and now thought that maybe they had made a mistake. Perhaps they should have gotten help sooner. It would take a helicopter forty-five minutes to reach this location. It would take land traffic a couple of hours. She would call all of the local support that could respond as well. This was going to get messy and she would have a lot of explaining to do.

Sean jogged up to the side of the McKenzie screened front door. The old orange-stained windows did not afford much of a view. He crept along the edge of the house towards what appeared to be a kitchen window. He looked across the way at the shop. All of the lights were out, and the building seemed to be empty. Adam came running up beside him.

"You were supposed to wait for me," Adam whispered.

"We need to find her. Our biggest ally is surprise, unless they heard us come up the driveway," Sean hissed back.

"Well, let's do this right," Adam said and gingerly peeked his head into the kitchen window. "There is a lady doing the dishes. A second older lady is at the table, all wrapped up in blankets."

"Her aunt and grandmother," Sean said and whirled to the front door that was nearest to the kitchen. He kicked his foot to the knob of the door, and it flung open. Sean burst inside.

Adam cursed and followed his friend into the McKenzie house. Sean had rushed to the woman doing the dishes and grabbed her by placing his arm around her shoulders. He held the shotgun up and leveled it at Grandma McKenzie's spot at the table.

"Mrs. McKenzie, is Miranda home?" Sean asked in an almost sinister voice.

"What are you doing? Who are you?" Helen McKenzie asked, her voice trembling.

As Sean suspected, and hoped, the two elder statesmen of the McKenzie family came running in the room at the sound of their front door being kicked in. Sean swung the shotgun in the direction of the two men.

"Who the hell are you? You unhand my wife!" Hal McKenzie bellowed.

"I'm a ghost. How about you gentlemen have a seat next to Grandma there. Mrs. McKenzie, I am sorry to have startled you, but I have some serious questions to ask you. Grandma McKenzie, I am sorry I have to trouble you when I know you need your rest. Can we get you anything?" Sean said, motioning the two men over to the kitchen table. The McKenzie grandmother shook her head. She just stared in her feeble silence.

"Sean, this is not the way to do this," Adam started. Sean cut him off.

"Go check the rest of the house for Daryl or any other of their Greys house guests. I don't need any of them sneaking up behind me," Sean ordered and returned his attention to the McKenzie family. He directed Helen to the table with the rest of her kin.

"Listen here, you beast," old Lucius McKenzie started.

"No, you listen here, old man. I don't know what goofy backwoods cause you think you stand for, but you started a little war in Seattle today. It cost you a grandson. It may have cost you a granddaughter. I want to make sure that the latter doesn't happen," Sean snapped.

"What are you talking about? Where's Miranda?" Lucius asked.

"She came to Seattle with me. When the heat came down, I believe your grandson abducted her," Sean informed the elderly McKenzie.

"Daryl wouldn't hurt her. He loves his cousin," Helen declared.

"That may be, ma'am, but I believe he is using her for protection from the law. He probably isn't real happy about her being involved in spoiling the day in Seattle, either. Now I need to know where he may have taken her," Sean replied. He looked up as Adam returned and gave the "all clear" sign.

"We ain't gonna tell you nothin' boy," Hal McKenzie glared at Sean.

Sean ignored him and appealed to the women. "Miranda is in trouble, and I need to find her. Where would Daryl have taken her?"

"I said boy, we ain't gonna tell you a damn thing," Hal continued his rant.

"The silver sedan. He was here, wasn't he, Mrs. McKenzie?" Sean asked, looking into Helen's eyes.

"He was. But he didn't bring Miranda in with him," she admitted.

"What did he come for?" Sean asked.

"To switch vehi…" she started.

"Shut up, woman. Or so help me I'll," Hal spat at his wife.

"Oh, Hal, shut up!" Grandma McKenzie growled at her son, "You and Lucius have caused enough trouble for our family today. I don't know what you two are up to, but I want to get my grandbabies back in one piece."

The room went silent as the feeble old matriarch commanded her son to be quiet. Adam almost laughed at the scene. She turned to Sean and continued, "Daryl was here. He came to switch vehicles. Where he needed to go, that car that he drove home wouldn't make it."

"Can you tell me where it was that he was going?" Sean said, his voice calm and sweet to the sick older woman.

"One of the hunting cabins that Lucius and Hal built years ago. Lucius, please tell the boy what he needs to know," Maude McKenzie.

"But…"

"No buts, Lucius. Tell him *now*," Helen demanded.

Lucius looked pitiful, exchanging his glances from Maude to Hal and back to Maude gain. Finally, he looked up at Sean. "Out on Diablo Ridge. It is very difficult to get to. Probably used a snowmobile to get to there. The last trail bit of trail you gotta do on foot. Even if I told you how to get there, you'd probably never find it. No one but this family has ever been there. I don't expect a city boy like you to be able to make it," Lucius sneered.

"Tell me what peaks you see from the cabin," Sean requested. Lucius looked tight-lipped, and Sean just glanced over at Maude. She glared at Lucius.

The old man relented, "Fine. You can see Diablo Peak, the Pickets, and Mt Challenger through two clefts in the valley. But you still ain't gonna find it, boy," Lucius cackled.

"Thank you. It was a pleasure meeting all of you. Ma'am, I assure you I will bring your granddaughter back. I wish I could promise the same for your grandson," Sean shot Grandma Maude a pleasant look and swung the shotgun back in the direction of the men one last time, "You boys behave now."

Sean looked up at Adam, motioned for the door, and began walking out. On the kitchen counter, in a fruit bowl, he saw keys for a rental car. He snatched them up and walked out the door.

"Damn it, Sean. We can get in big trouble for this," Adam uttered to his friend sternly.

"We are already in trouble for what happened in Seattle. It will all work out once the facts are presented. Come on," Sean motioned for Adam to get into the silver rental car parked near the shop. He slid in the keys that he had pilfered out of the fruit bowl and started the car. He backed up and hit the accelerator, launching the sedan down the rough dirt driveway. The rental car bounced up and down over the ruts and potholes of the crude little road.

As Sean reached the highway, he paused. He looked both directions searching for Rachel's SUV. He saw her taillights to the east, just in front of the next curve. He pulled the vehicle out of the driveway and sped towards the waiting SUV. He pulled the sedan alongside the truck.

"What's going on?" Rachel asked urgently.

"We think Miranda is being held at a hunting cabin deep in the Range. The McKenzie women were a little more forthcoming than the menfolk," Sean said.

"Did you call the cavalry?" Adam asked.

"Yes, I have a team of feds via cooperation with my department, and local sheriff's deputies on the way. Where should I direct them?" Rachel asked.

"Send a squad to the McKenzie house. And then have Adam give you the approximate GPS coordinates when he maps it out," Sean suggested.

"Beckett and Steinmetz aren't real happy about us taking off. They further believe you two should be in custody until they piece everything together," Rachel warned the men.

"Well, I guess we better take off now, huh?" Sean said.

"Sean, let the experts handle this now. They are used to hostage situations. We can't even be sure that Miranda *is* with Daryl," Rachel pleaded, trying to urge her friend with reason.

Sean looked at Adam, as if for guidance. "It's your call, bud. I am with you all the way," Adam answered.

"Call the troops, Rachel. We are going hiking. Oh, can we ask for one more favor? Can we borrow your truck?" Sean asked, the first time in hours that he cracked a little grin.

Rachel rolled her eyes, "Why not, I've practically given you my career at this point. I suppose I wait here to direct traffic?"

"Yeah, I don't know what the situation is going to be like up there. And you have done enough. I don't want you in any more danger," Sean replied.

Adam finished plugging in the approximate coordinates using the peaks that can be seen from the cabin as waypoints, coming up with approximate longitude and latitude coordinates. It is some pretty hairy country. If the skies are clear, you can chopper in along the Diablo ridgeline. We'll need to call Hall and have him bring out some packs of equipment and snowmobiles."

Adam got on the phone with Shayne. Sean walked up to Rachel as they switched vehicles. He stopped and hugged his old friend. "I can't thank you enough for your help."

"You always were the guy to do the right thing, even when the rest of the world encouraged you to do the opposite. And apparently, you can kick a little butt along the way," Rachel managed a little smile for Sean and planted a light kiss upon his cheek. "Now go take care of business. I'll handle the political end."

Rachel watched her friend get into her SUV and drive east towards the deep woods of the North Cascades. She remembered old feelings that were never allowed to be nurtured or kindled. She shook the nostalgic thoughts away and began thinking of a way out of the trouble that she and her friends had mired into.

Beckett received the call from the Department of Interior aide. He summoned Special Agents Steinmetz and McCallum over. "All right, I know you have some investigators out in the Cascades of Washington looking for your lost agent as well as the looking for the attacker that got away. We have a potential hostage situation out there. I got a call from my Assistant Director, Rachel York. You met her earlier, she and those friends of hers tracked down the whereabouts of Daryl McKenzie, the suspected attacker. We need to divert your team to respond to the coordinates that Ms. York has provided," Beckett said, his voice denoting his tired irritation.

"If he is the man responsible for the loss of my agent, I am all for it. What about York? Is she and her friends, what a wildlife officer and a civilian, going to keep their noses out of this until my men can get there?" Steinmetz asked.

"That's what I told her, but apparently her friends have already left. It also sounds as though they know the region pretty well. I am afraid our job will be to go up there and clean up the mess," Beckett informed the FBI agents.

"Well, I am not happy about this, but if that is the case, I wish them luck in the meantime," McCallum commented.

"Okay, so let's get the team at Marblemount to Diablo. How soon can we get a couple of birds in the air?" Steinmetz said, switching into action.

"I can get two with men from Boeing Field in the air within fifteen minutes. They should get there first. I also have a chopper down the street that I will divert to transport us to the scene," McCallum replied.

"Beckett, when this is over, your office has some explaining to do," Steinmetz said firmly, but without malice.

"I understand. Let's try to save a few lives today," Beckett agreed.

McCallum's cell phone beeped, and he answered. When he concluded his conversation, he turned to the two men that were busy strategizing. "That was a call from the regional office. They ran prints from the man apprehended in the hotel. His name is Tug Gaskill. He is a former special-ops commando. He had a falling out after getting written up on charges in the Middle East six years ago. He was accused of abusing POWs that his group was taking in. He argued with his superiors and just vanished. He has since been linked with various mercenary activities in Central America."

"Great, we have a bunch of rednecks led by well-trained soldiers. That's a nice trend," Steinmetz muttered. Overhead, the whir of a helicopter's rotors could be heard.

Thirty Nine

Miranda had holed herself up in the corner of the small, dingy cabin. Years of storing staples, tired and sweaty hunters, and blood-stained clothes from gutting kills left the cabin with a very rank aroma. Despite that, she had arranged herself into a ball, tucked in with a blanket that Daryl gave her. She did her best to fall asleep. She wanted all of this to be over as soon as possible. Arguing with her cousin only seemed to make her situation worse.

She shut her eyes, and her mind drifted to an image of children playing in a creek, swinging from a rope that her uncle had tied to a tree limb. The mental picture of kids splashing and laughing, the way that kids are supposed to flashed briefly through her mind. She never guessed the brainwashing that was occurring behind the scenes. She now understood why her parents had decided to remove themselves from her relatives. She thought it was something that her parents should have worked through, but now she knew what they were protecting her from. What they were disassociating themselves from.

Her thoughts switched to her Grandma Helen. She was so excited to have Miranda come back into their lives. She was so sweet and full of love. How could that same sweet woman be married to a bigot like Lucius? How could she have raised a son and two grandsons so full of hate and unrest that they would attack innocent people? She could remember racial jokes and slurs from time to time. Each one made her cringe. But she could never imagine this.

She peeked through her closed eyes and saw Daryl sitting in a chair. His head slumped in his hands. A half-dozen empty beer cans littered the table. She thought about her options. In the chilly night, could she survive long enough to find help? Could she sneak out while her cousin slept? Did she have a clue how to find her way back? She felt that she had to take a chance. She thought that removing her from her cousin's grasp would give both of them a better chance at survival.

Miranda slowly slid out from her blanket, keeping an eye on Daryl the entire time. He even let out a slight snore as Miranda got to her feet. She crossed the wood plank floor to the door of the tiny cabin. Her right foot had just accepted the weight of her step when the wood beneath let out a creak. Miranda's heart stopped. Daryl let out a big snort and opened his eyes. Miranda lunged for the door. The click behind her made her stop.

"Don't do it, cousin. I can't afford to let you go," Daryl said, he had his favorite hunting rifle raised towards her.

"I will just slow you down. You can move more easily without me," Miranda pleaded.

"Sorry cuz. I told you, I will let Dad and Grandpa determine how to play this out. In the meantime, let's make this easy on ourselves. Give me your shoes," Daryl said, holding his hands out.

"What?" Miranda asked, looking at him like he was crazy.

"Your shoes. You won't get very far in the snow without them. It will encourage you to stay here with your good ol' cousin Daryl," the eldest McKenzie boy said.

Miranda relented and handed over her shoes. Daryl took them and tied them around a leg of the chair he was sleeping in and resumed his position. Miranda slunk down in the corner of the cabin, bundled back up in the blanket, and laid her head against the wall. She allowed herself to drift to sleep with alternating reflections in her mind of a happy childhood and the events of the past week, including Charlie.

Sean and Adam arrived at the trailhead closest to the coordinates that Adam had calculated from the description that Helen McKenzie had solicited from her husband. Sean was frustrated that they would have to wait, but without any gear, they would be doubtful to find the cabin, much less survive. He decided to rest for a minute and bottle up whatever energy reserves he could scrape out of this horrific day. He awoke startled when there was a tap at the window. Adam grunted next to him. He, too, had fallen asleep.

Sean was relieved when his eyes adjusted and saw a familiar face outside of the window.

"Hi, ladies," Shayne beamed into the truck.

"Oh jeez, I guess we fell asleep," Sean yawned.

"Are you sure you are up to this? It sounds as though you guys have had a hell of a day," John said.

"Yeah, we did, but we're ready. Let's go," Sean said. He gave Adam a little shove. His friend stirred and yawned while stretching his back into an arch like a cat. "You ready, buddy? It's time."

Adam looked at Sean, "Let's do it."

"Alright guys, I have two snowmobiles, two of us will have to ride tandem, the other can tow the gear. Oh, and I brought along some help," Shayne said, walking to the back of the Park Service Search and Rescue truck. He opened the back, and a deliriously happy Greater Swiss Mountain dog bounced out of the truck.

Sean knelt to accept his dog's affections. "How're you doing, buddy? You remember Miranda? We need to find her tonight."

"This is going to be a long haul. Think he's up to it?" Shayne asked. Sean nodded.

"Thanks, Shayne, I appreciate this," Sean said.

"No problem, man. Hey, we lost one of our own this week, I don't want to lose another," Shayne said.

They quickly went to work unloading the snowmobiles and securing the gear onto the back of one of them. Sean selected the one with the gear, leaving Adam and Shayne to tandem the other. Sammy plodded happily along. The Greater Swiss Mountain dog's legs were made for travel in rough terrain. His stamina in the mountain range was virtually without parallel versus other dog breeds. What seemed arduous to his two-legged companions was a treat to the do that had been cooped for the past two days.

Sean sped the snowmobile up the slopes. Old forest service and logging roads made the path for them to travel. Sean's lighter machine plowed up the trail a little quicker than the one that Shayne and Adam shared. Sammy brought up the rear, but he was able to stay close enough to hear the sounds of the engines as they roared up the hill. Sean knew that there was limited terrain for the snowmobiles and that Sammy would catch up once the men continued on foot. The night was cold, but not like it had been. Clouds had rolled in obscuring the moon, but Sean didn't mind. He just wanted to find that cabin.

Almost three-quarters of the way up the forest road, Shayne's snowmobile headlight was flashing behind Sean. He let go of the accelerator and stopped his machine. He turned back to face Shayne, who stopped in the middle of the narrow road. He flagged Sean down. Sean killed the engine on his snowmobile and quiet filled the valley.

"Engine stalled! Hold up!" Shayne called to him.

Sean looked back. He was dead set on getting to that cabin. They were closing in, and he wanted to get up there as soon as possible. He looked at his watch. It was a little after midnight. He figured Daryl would have reached the cabin at least three hours ago, probably four. By now, he would be settling down to sleep. Sean could hope to catch him by surprise.

He cupped his hands to his face and called out, "I'll see you up there; I am going to check it out!" He started and revved the motor of the snowmobile before either Shayne or Adam could respond and took off up the trail.

"Wait! Damn it, Sean!" Adam cursed and looked at Shayne, "Let's get this thing started before Sean gets himself killed!"

Shayne shook his head and tapped the spark plugs trying to get the motor restarted. A tiring but consistent paced Sammy strode by after Sean, looking at Adam and Shayne as he trounced passed.

Sean focused on forging ahead. They had only about a mile left on the snowmobile, and according to Adam's calculations, another mile or so on foot. As Sean drove the snowmobile forward, he could feel the all of the rage that had built up over the past week boil up and intensify. He ignored the calls from Shayne and Adam on the FRS radio and drove on. In minutes, he reached the abrupt end of the trail. He hopped off the snowmobile and paused to check his GPS. According to Adam, the hunting cabin would be about one mile up the slope.

He lowered his shoulder, allowing his pack to slide off. He opened it. The black sawed-off shotgun stuck out through the opening. He took a swig of water and re-slung the bag over his back. Sean began to make his way up the snowy slope of the hill. As he looked up, he saw the gray clouds part and give way to shards of moonlight, allowing him to climb without turning on his flashlight.

The slope was very steep and passed through dense brush. Like the entrance to the McKenzie homestead, there was little trace that this direction led to anywhere. Sean plunged ahead, at each ridge, pausing to scan the area. The moonlit snow afforded great views of the land. Despite the awe-striking beauty of the terrain, Sean hardly noticed and merely went back to focusing on reaching his destination.

It was on the third ridge that Sean began to smell the smoke from the wood-burning stove. He focused in his binoculars, hoping to see whiffs of smoke in the air, but the translucent white streaks were too subtle for him to pick up. Assured that he was heading in the right direction, Sean continued his trek up the next ridgeline. Occasionally his FRS radio would crackle, but the ups and downs of the mountains would only allow broken static to travel through.

Sean reached the peak of the fourth ridge. He scanned with his binoculars, hoping to see a cabin. At first, he didn't see any buildings in the little trough of a valley. The smell of the wood smoke was strong here, though. Sean began slowly combing each square yard of the valley when he finally saw a wisp of smoke from a little brown chimney. The cabin was completely covered with snow from nearly every vantage in the area. The location was handpicked by the McKenzies not to be seen from any of the nearby peaks.

Sean scanned around the little hump that was attached to the chimney. He focused through his glasses and saw a set of footprints leading up to the eastern side of the building. There was one way in and one way out. Sean put away his field glasses and began descending the slope to the cabin. The moonlight had poked a large hole into the clouds, and the entire area surrounding the cabin was illuminated with the spectacular glow off of the crusty snow. Sean became acutely aware of the crunching of his footsteps as he descended into the valley. He was halfway down the bare slope when he was surprised to see the cabin door open.

Pausing as he hunched down, Sean scanned the area around him. He was completely exposed on the face of the treeless slope. He watched Daryl McKenzie, in untied boots and disheveled clothing stumble out into the night. Sean checked his watch. It was three a.m. Daryl walked to the side of the cabin and unzipped his fly. Sleepily he began spilling his urine onto the snow. Sean tried to slip the shotgun out of his back, but it was stuck. Slowly he slipped the backpack off his shoulders and opened up the pack. Daryl was just finishing when Sean's radio crackled.

"Sean, it's Adam. We are at the end of the road. We are proceeding on foot. Wait for us. There should be a ridge about a click or two uphill. I am guessing the cabin is nestled there," the voice carried over the radio and seemed to fill the small, snow-insulated valley. Sean scrambled to click off the volume as quickly as he could, but Adam's entire message was out before the radio went silent.

Daryl, just zipping up after finishing his business, wheeled around, looking all over the valley for threats. Sean pressed himself down into the snow, but Daryl quickly spotted the green backpack Sean was wearing. The big McKenzie boy dashed for the entrance of the cabin. Sean tried to pick up the shotgun that he dropped to turn off his radio, but was too late to get a shot off by the time Daryl disappeared into the little wooden hut. Sean gathered his gear and turned his radio back on.

"Adam, it's Sean. I found him just beyond the third and fourth ridge. I caught him with his pecker down, but he got back inside the cabin before I could get to him," Sean said, breathily, as he jogged down the hillside.

"Sean, just pin him down, we'll be there in a few minutes!" Adam called into the radio, but he knew Sean well enough to know that was not going to happen.

The door to the cabin flew open, and Daryl, carrying a barefoot Miranda by her neck in the crook of his arm, appeared. He held a Steyr in his other arm and began unleashing a violent torrent of bullets at the wide-open Sean.

Sean dove for a snowbank. He could hear the bullets plunk into the ice, rock, and snow. Sean knew with his weapons; he had no chance of taking out Daryl without risking harm to Miranda from the distance he had to cover.

"Come on out, boy," the McKenzie brother called.

"How about you leave Miranda out of this, or do you have to hide behind women to protect yourself?" Sean called back.

"You little turd, it's shameful, but I need Miranda to help me out of this situation. I let her go, you and your friends can just fire on me until you get lucky and hit me," Daryl drawled.

"We just want Miranda, Daryl. Let us take her, and we will let you and the authorities take each other on. Otherwise, I *will* kill you," Sean replied.

"No deal, pretty boy. I say back off, or cousin here gets one in the ear," Daryl threatened.

"I don't even think a thug like you would do that to your cousin. Look, there are more men on the way. And Daryl, *I* was the one who got Jeb. He was easy. Not real bright that brother of yours," Sean taunted the man holding his cousin hostage.

"What? You?" Daryl stammered.

"That's right, Daryl, little brother Jeb dying at the hands of the scrawny pretty boy. I wonder if you'll squeal like a school girl when I kill *you,* Daryl," Sean continued prodding the ego of the huge country boy.

"Ah'm gonna tear you apart, boy," Daryl snarled.

"You can get your chance, Daryl. Let Miranda go, and I guarantee you, it's on. You and me, one on one. What do you have to lose? If you get me, you take vengeance on your brother's killer. You get to take off deeper into the woods never to be seen from again. If you don't let her go, we wait you out until we get at you anyway, and you have no chance. It's up to you. Or are you afraid your redneck ass can't handle a little pretty boy from the city?" Sean called out.

"Deal. Ah'll put her back in the cabin, you and me'll head north on the ridge. Give me two minutes in the cabin. If anyone comes while I'm in there, I will kill her," Daryl said. "Ah suggest you use that time to get yerself a head start. One other thing, toss yer weapon over that ridge," Daryl said.

"What? Am I supposed to take you on defenseless?" Sean said.

"You got a knife?" Daryl asked.

"Yeah," Sean said.

"Ah, do too. All Ah need is my bow for huntin'. Ah'm gonna gather my things, and when Ah come out, Ah'm gonna kill you and keep heading into the woods," Daryl said.

"Toss your gun first," Sean said, "You have Miranda to shield you."

Daryl paused and reluctantly tossed the gun over the ridge, in one quick motion, he drew his large hunting knife from its sheath and held it to Miranda's throat. Satisfied, Sean threw his shotgun over the edge.

"Handgun," Daryl called and tossed his own over the ridge to the snowy bank below. Sean followed suit with his own. He watched Daryl disappear into the cabin.

Sean pulled out his radio and called to Adam, "Hey guys. Wait at the ridge until you see Daryl exit the cabin. Don't let him see you. Miranda will be inside. I am going to lead Daryl away from the cabin and away from Miranda. Once she is safe, I don't care what you do," Sean said.

"What is going on? We are almost to the ridge right now," Adam told his friend.

"I was able to get the dolt to chase after me, one caveat, I had to toss my gun over the edge of the canyon," Sean told him as he was striding across the canyon to the next ridge.

"What do you mean?" Adam asked exasperatedly.

"Mano y mano," Sean replied flatly.

"Are you crazy? He will kill you," Adam said.

Sean saw the door to the cabin open up, and a winter hunting suit donned Daryl came out and onto the snow. He had a large pack strapped to his back, a green hunting bow tied to the back, and a nine-inch hunting knife in his hand.

"Boys, I've got to go," Sean said and replaced the radio into its holster at his side. Sean knew his athleticism would get him any distance that he wanted against the bigger, dangerous Daryl. Daryl's advantage was that he was very knowledgeable about the area. Sean just maintained a steady pace, leaving the cabin further and further behind.

As soon as the back of Daryl's head disappeared beyond the next ridge, Adam and Shayne broke for the tiny hunting cabin. Adam let go of the collar he was holding, and Sammy raced down to the tiny hut. Adam arrived behind him and first and pushed the wooden door open. Miranda was gathering clothing that she could put on to escape.

"Adam!" she exclaimed as Sean's friend burst through the door.

"Are you okay?" Adam asked.

"Yeah, I'm fine. Daryl is after Sean. Sean told him that he was the one who killed Jeb in Seattle, and Daryl lost it. He agreed to trade me for an opportunity to go after him," Miranda hurriedly filled Adam in.

"You and Shayne take one of the snowmobiles back to the truck. Try and direct traffic as they arrive via radio," Adam said, "I'll go after Sean and Daryl."

"Adam, bring him back. This wasn't his fight," Miranda said.

"As you get to know Sean better, you'll realize this *is* his fight," Adam said. He checked his weapons and headed back out the door and into the snowy canyon.

Sean gained considerable ground and had plenty of time to observe Daryl trying to keep up. "Come on country boy, you can't beat a little pretty boy in the forest?" Sean taunted.

"Just keep running pretty, Ah'm comin' for you!" Daryl growled.

Sean was looking for a spot where he might be able to utilize his speed to neutralize Daryl's strength. Most importantly, he wanted to get more distance from the cabin. Sean figured that by now, Adam and Shayne would have reached the cabin, and Miranda was safe. He took a side switchback. He knew that the tougher the terrain, the better his nimble body could maintain distance. He didn't realize that the last turn he made led to a cliffside overlook of a blind canyon, a grand view, but a dead end.

Sean looked over the edge of the cliff. It was a sheer drop, all rock, about seven hundred feet to the ground below. He looked further up the trail; it led right into an inverted rock wall. Each direction he looked was another dead end. He would have to double back down the trail. He sprinted to the bend, but saw the big Daryl McKenzie stomping up the path. He wasn't as quick as Sean, but his powerful body marched up the trail relentlessly. Sean returned to the spot at the rock face, just a few yards from the drop off of the cliff. Studying the rock above him, he was able to find minute little finger holds, about as big as a nickel. Sean wrapped the first digit of his fingers around a pair of these tiny holds and hoisted his body up. He scrambled with his feet to get just the slightest bit of traction. He was able to groove his toe onto another nickel-sized rock. He looked above him, he could see a thin ledge about four feet up, with no holds in between.

Sean could hear the crunching of the snow as Daryl approached. He could think of no better plan than to dyno, or lunge for the ledge above him. With every bit of finger strength and grip that he could muster, he vaulted himself up the rock face. He slapped down with his left hand first, his fingers grazed the ledge, but could not hold on. Slamming his right hand against the rock, he was just able to get three of his fingers to drape the edge. Sean hung there, his feet dangling, the momentum of his bodyweight swinging him like a screen door, so that he faced outward instead of at the rock. He could see the top of Daryl's hat surging up the path. Sean swung himself back to the rock and pulled himself up to the ledge. The rock shelf was about four feet wide by four inches deep. He had just enough room to place his heels squarely on the ledge without falling off.

He stood there frozen. Amazingly, Daryl did not see his final lunge to the ledge and continued facing the end of the trail at the cliff. Sean figured that Daryl knew the area well enough, but he big hunter assumed that Sean had trapped himself at the edge of the drop-off. Sean waited until Daryl had passed just underneath him. He bent his knees slightly and dove off the ledge. He wrapped his forearm around Daryl's head as he let gravity drive him into the big man. Sean pulled with all of his strength, trying to wrench Daryl's neck to break it.

Sean was successful in knocking the big man to the ground, but the burly Daryl McKenzie was solid enough to prevent Sean from causing any real harm. The collision with the ground knocked the wind out of both men. Daryl was the first to recover. He knelt up and whirled to face Sean. Sean, knowing that close quarters was death for him, rolled on his shoulders and flipped up onto his feet facing Daryl. From his knees, Daryl lunged towards Sean's legs, trying to wrap him up. Sean steadied his weight on his left foot and kicked out with his right, catching Daryl in the head, just above his nose. The big man reeled back. Sean backed off and began slowly turning the man's fighting circle with Sean's back to the path. He knew he would need to beat a hasty retreat if they locked up.

Daryl saw this and countered, moving to his left, drawing the large hunting blade out of its sheath. He swung the knife at Sean taking wild strokes, to position Sean where he wanted him. "Come on, boy, I thought you were the big man. I don't believe it was you who took out Jeb, not unless you shot him in the back," Daryl growled.

"Oh no, I got to see those brown eyes with their 'oh shit' expression in them right before he blew up into little pieces," Sean baited Daryl. Sean took a big sniff of his jacket, "I think I got some of his stink on me."

"Why you little bastard," Daryl screamed and took a wild lunge at Sean, slashing with the knife.

Sean used Daryl's size and momentum against him, sticking his right foot out as he grabbed the arm that Daryl thrust at him. The result sent Daryl cascading to the ground with a large thump. Sean immediately followed with a kick to the back of Daryl's head. The impact almost made Sean sick as his sole cracked against the skull of his attacker. As he drew back for another kick, he hesitated slightly, trying to plan his next move when Daryl's hand shot up and grabbed Sean's ankle.

Sean tried to pull away, but was unable to break the bigger man's firm grip. Daryl lifted himself and yanked Sean's leg, sending the smaller opponent to the ground. Daryl began to twist Sean's leg, trying to break it, but Sean was agile enough to twist his body to keep pace. He was able to save his knee from popping, but wasn't able to get away from severe pain in his ankle. Daryl realized that he had dropped his knife. As he bent over to pick it up, Sean swung his other leg around, kicking Daryl hard in the back of the head.

The blow was hard enough to make Daryl release his grip slightly, and Sean pulled free his aching ankle. He pushed himself back along the forest floor while the hulking Daryl McKenzie, knife in hand loomed above him. Sean inched back through the light snow, but found himself backed up the certain death of the drop-off. His hand brushed by the loop of the backpack that his foe had dropped during the struggle.

Daryl grinned at having backed Sean up to the cliff edge. He took his time, slowly approaching Sean, so that he didn't get taken by any of his surprise antics.

"Ah'm done with you, boy," Daryl spat, coming at Sean with the knife.

Daryl sprung at Sean with the knife, lunging his entire body to land on him, so he could pin him and strike a fatal blow with his blade hand. Sean caught Daryl with his knees and grabbing the backpack, swung it to deflect the oncoming blade. The knife sunk into the pack, and Sean rolled out from under Daryl, but the big man grabbed Sean by the collar. He drug his enemy's flailing body to the edge of the drop-off and swung Sean out into the air, high above the seven-hundred-foot fall. Daryl let go of his grip as Sean grabbed desperately at the sleeve of the big man's jacket. Sean hung there as Daryl tried to shoo him off as though Sean were a pesky bug. Daryl dropped the knife, with his backpack still stuck on it, and grabbed Sean with his now free hand. He tried to wrench Sean off, who had a death grip around the sleeve of the jacket. Daryl slowly started removing his coat, hoping to slip free from it, allowing Sean to plummet to the bottom of the canyon.

The big McKenzie boy was startled when he felt the tugging at his pant leg. "What the…", he looked down to see a powerful dog pull back on the cloth in its mouth, dragging big Daryl crashing down to his butt in the snow.

Sean locked his grip around Daryl's arm and used it to help swing his body back on terra firma. The irritated terrorist kicked at Sammy and caught the big dog in the jaw with his boot. Sammy reeled back for a moment and lunged for another attack, but Daryl was able to grab the end of his bow and swung it like an axe down on the dog. The blow struck the back of Sammy's head, knocking him unconscious. Sean positioned himself to attempt a counter-attack, but another swift swing of the bow golf club-style careened him into the rock wall. Sean hit hard, his back crushing into the rock. He could feel sticky wet liquid meandering down the back of his head to his neck.

Daryl walked over and freed his blade from the backpack. Brandishing the weapon, he approached Sean menacingly. He walked over to Sean, who was still trying to collect himself after being thrown into the rock wall. Daryl kicked Sean in the head, causing him to again fall back to the wall, sliding to a stop on his hindquarters. The big McKenzie boy held the blade in both hands and prepared to drive it into Sean's midsection, "Ah'm gonna gut you like an elk," Daryl snarled.

As he came at Sean with the huge knife. Sean quickly unsheathed his own knife and swung his whole body into an arch, driving the blade into Daryl's ankle. The big man let out an enormous howl chorusing through the forest, dropping to the ground as the blade slid through his tendons.

Sean popped up and began hobbling down the path, searching for a large branch to use as a weapon. He knew he would never get close enough to an area on Daryl to inflict a mortal wound with a knife. If he came within arm's reach, the big man would grab him and slice his throat.

Daryl temporarily ignored his excruciating pain and rose to his knees. He released the bow from his pack and steadied an arrow aimed directly at Sean's back. "Time to die, boy!" he exclaimed, drawing the bow back. Sean froze, the image of Daryl's camouflage green bow behind him. In his final seconds, he knew as good of a hunter as Daryl was, he was unlikely to miss his mark.

As Sean leaped to the ground, he waited for the arrow to pierce his back, but was instead greeted with the crack of a rifle. Sean wheeled around to see Daryl fall to the ground, and the arrow drift harmlessly into the tree branches. Across the valley, on one of the switchbacks, was Adam, resting the Steyr rifle on his extended left leg, eying the scope, making sure that Daryl was not moving.

The burst of fight or flight adrenaline gone, Sean winced as he got up on his feet. He grabbed the branch he was heading for and broke off a few of the twigs sticking out. He used it now instead of as a weapon, but for a crutch as he made his way back up to the cliff face. He poked the bow away from Daryl's hand with his walking stick. Daryl laid on the ground, his body in a fetal position, his skin pale.

Adam came running up the trail. He had his gun drawn and pointed at Daryl, for safekeeping. "You alright, pal?" Adam asked.

"I thought I was done for. I'm glad you came along when you did," Sean said, kneeling to check the pulse on Daryl's carotid artery, "He's alive."

"Sean, your head is bleeding pretty good, why don't you sit over there," Adam said, pointing to a spot by the rock with the inverted face, "I'll get help on the way." Adam placed a call into the radio. His call reached Shayne, and he had him relay it to the FBI helicopters.

"How is Miranda?" Sean asked, tending to his woozy, but now conscious dog.

"She's fine. A little cold, very tired. Very worried about you, buddy," Adam replied, his face sharing the concern of Miranda.

"I am fine. I guess, I thought that I had tapped into his ego enough, that he would stick with hand to hand and not use the bow," Sean said.

"And what were you going to with him hand to hand. Even if he didn't get a hold of you, you couldn't chip away at him enough to do any real damage before he got lucky and snagged you," Adam said disapprovingly.

"I don't know. I just wanted to take care of this. I didn't know if he was crazy enough to hurt Miranda, I just wanted to separate them the best I could," Sean said.

Their conversation was interrupted by the sound of helicopters closing in over the mountains. Two men rappelled down on a pair of lines. A rescue basket was sent down after them. The first man checked over Sean and his injuries as the second man prepared Daryl for medevac lift. Sean assured the man that he was okay once he was given a bandage to hold against the cut on the back of his head.

"We need to get this man to the hospital. We can take you to a spot where one of the FBI helos can pick you up. Can you guys rappel?" one of the rescuers asked. Both Sean and Adam shook their heads, and one by one, they ascended the winch driven rescue lines. Sean went first, with his arms wrapped tightly around his heavy and terrified dog. Adam followed, and they were swiftly carried down the hillside.

The rescue chopper slowed to a halt hovering above the McKenzie compound. Several black helicopters rested on the ground amidst a dozen SUVs, vans, and cars from various law enforcement and government agencies. A small crowd gathered to watch Sean and Adam rappel down to the McKenzie grounds, and the Greater Swiss Mountain dog lowered via a sling. As soon as they touched down, the medevac helicopter retrieved the rescue lines and took off heading west.

Several people rushed out to the two men, including Shayne and Miranda. They were quickly whisked inside the McKenzie shop that had become the new headquarters for the task force. A section of the large shop was roped off with police tape as the contaminated crime scene area that was being used by the investigators and officials.

"Can we get you something to drink? " Beckett asked the two as he motioned them towards a pair of chairs.

"Water, would be great," Sean nodded, and Adam agreed as Special Agent in Charge Steinmetz sat down with them.

"Well, gentlemen. I am trying to understand whether you two are serious pains in the butt or heroes. You have broken half a dozen laws, discharged weapons, assaulted people, and been responsible for several deaths along the way. Yet, you have saved countless lives, found people that my agency was trying to track and ultimately foiled a plot to kill hundreds of people, including several senators and a handful of congressmen," Steinmetz said looking at the two men with a frown, "On that note, I would like to introduce you to Senator Johnson from Portland. He was one of the people that you saved at the convention center today."

Senator Rick Johnson turned to Adam and Sean, "What you two, Ms. McKenzie and Ms. York did today was nothing short of heroic. I was in the ballroom when things unfolded. We were in the room and would have surely all been killed if it had not been for this man," the Senator said, looking at Sean.

"I saw you through the debris cloud," the senator continued, "I also understand that you two prevented the attack from completing their ultimate goal, which was the extermination of the entire attendee roster of the conference."

"Yes sir," Adam and Sean chimed together.

"Ms. York tracked me down. She informed me of everything that you two had been up to over the past week. She told me it is you two that I have to thank for being alive as we stand here. She further elucidated that you two are potentially in a lot of trouble. I have already spoken to Mr. Beckett of the DOI and Mr. Steinmetz of the FBI. They have agreed that no charges will be brought upon you, though you will be asked to participate in legal and oversight committee hearings," Senator Johnson said.

"Thank you, sir," Sean and Adam again said in unison. The senator shook each of their hands and produced two business cards.

"If either of you need anything, please do not hesitate to give me a call," the Senator assured the men and left the room.

All eyes fell upon Adam and Sean. "What is up with the McKenzies?" Sean asked.

"The entire family is being held for questioning. Lucius and Hal will both be charged with conspiracy to commit a terrorist attack and aiding and abetting a fugitive," Steinmetz replied. "The forensics teams will be here, the convention center, hotel, and school for several days, making sure every scrap of evidence is picked up and accounted for."

"Mr. Raines," Beckett said to Adam, "I would like you to report to my office tomorrow morning. I will need you to surrender your weapon and badge as protocol for any officer that has discharged his weapon. You will be on leave with pay until further notice. And Mr. Raines, you should feel very proud of what you prevented today."

"Thank you Mr. Beckett. I apologize for the methods that we had to undertake," Adam said, reaching his hand out to Beckett.

"I am sorry our hands were tied. Just bad timing, I guess. No hard feelings," the Regional DOI Director stated flatly. "We are going to need to print and process your friend. We will need to match up the prints on any weapons you two fired versus the terrorists."

"Of course. Sean…," Adam turned to his friend, but Sean wasn't there. The Fish and Wildlife agent turned to the porch steps where he saw Sean and Miranda huddled together, a vigilant Sammy at their feet.

"I can't believe all of this happened," Miranda said, the shock from the day's events wearing off and the horrible realities sinking in.

"I know. It is crazy. Do you know what they are going to do with your Grandmother and your aunt?" Sean asked.

"They both have been cooperative and were not privy to anything that had gone on, at least not until Daryl came here for supplies. Grandpa and Uncle Hal will go to prison. I guess the ladies of the McKenzie household are going to have to fend for themselves. Aunt Helen is already talking about moving Grandma to Idaho. I just don't know…," the toll of the day sapping every of iota out of the young biologist.

"I'm just glad you're okay," Sean said as he squeezed her tightly.

"I've certainly had better days," she sighed, scratching Sammy's head, "I've had better days." Somberly, she turned to watch the commotion that had taken over her relative's ranch. The Senator's helicopter lifted off of the ground, sending a spray of powdery snow into the air, making the scene of flashing lights and busy agents even more surreal.

Forty

S ean and Miranda walked along the bank of the Skagit River. The early spring sun glistened off of the little ripples that were making their way downstream. Sammy frolicked ahead of them, his nose working overtime to gather in every delicious scent that wafted through the air. Several days had gone by, their stories told hundreds of times to dozens of people along the way. Grueling sessions with NSA and FBI personnel left them exhausted before they were finally allowed to return to Sean's home. Even then, they were faced with mourning Jim Hall's death. A service at the National Park Observatory did little to supply the fallen deputy justice. Sean, Adam, and Shayne paid their respects and promised to create a memorial in the park that would continue to pay homage to his service and friendship.

Miranda had the unpleasant task of helping her aunt and grandmother plan their immediate futures. Deciding the ranch was too much for them, they agreed that the two McKenzie women would travel to Idaho to live with their relatives. Following the investigation, the assets of the ranch would likely be turned over to the government for reparations for the family's involvement.

"So, how is your Grandmother?" Sean asked, his arm interlaced with Miranda's.

"She's okay. All of this stress was not what she needed, but she is pulling through. Aunt Helen will take care of her. I don't think our relationship will ever be the same. She seems to blame me a bit for Jeb's death and her other son being sent to prison, well, when he gets out of the hospital anyway," Miranda replied as Sean gave her a little squeeze.

"I'm sorry to hear that. I suppose it goes with the territory of only being comfortable with what you know and have been told all of your life. I guess they feel that the rest of America, yourself included – perhaps especially so, should have the same warped mindset," Sean suggested.

"I guess, but it doesn't make me feel any better about it. It is kind of weird. I am torn in this world of feelings for my family, and yet I walk away from them, feeling very ashamed of the whole lot. It's so heartbreaking. I understand what my parents had gone through with them. But, it's all over with now," she shrugged.

" So, what now?" Sean asked, "Back to counting whales?"

"Yeah. It is going to be sad without Charlie coming home with me. I am sure my life will never be the same after this," Miranda said. She quit walking and turned to face Sean. She looked up into his bluish-green eyes and pulled herself out of her gloom to offer up an exceptionally warm smile.

Sean looked back at her, everything about this woman oozed kindness and sincerity. "No, I guess life never will be quite the same. I guess my heart never will be either," Sean leaned in and gave Miranda a deep kiss.

She curved her palm around Sean's chin and kissed back. "You are amazing, Mister Kendall," Miranda said, her eyes never leaving his.

"Do you suppose I could get frequent flyer miles between Marblemount and Anacortes?" Sean asked a little smirk on his face.

Miranda smiled and hugged Sean. She giggled as Sammy poked his nose in between the two. "I think there could be a plan in the works. Maybe you could come for a visit, an hour drive down Highway Twenty's not so bad... Maybe even own a spot in the toothbrush holder...".

"Toothbrush holder, huh? Boy, that sounds serious, Ms. Shaw," Sean drawled, his heart and head battling over the thought of being serious with a woman again - a thought that he had abandoned for quite some time.

"Oh, I think you'll be alright," the young marine biologist grinned, "I'll be gentle on you."

Sean struggled for a reply. His mind flooded with how much he cared for her and how good he felt, yet also with the fear that rose. His quandary of a comeback was cut short as a crew cab pick-up pulled up.

Adam leaned out of the passenger window, "I thought that was you two. I've been calling Sean's cellphone number. Anyways, we thought you might want to be a part of this. We are releasing those two bears you saved back into the wilderness. They received a clean bill of health and would be waking up from hibernation any day now anyway. The folks at Northwest Trek think they will be just fine. We'll set them up right where you found them. It's a great spot with plenty of resources."

Sean looked at Miranda, who just nodded at him, "Great, let's go!" They climbed into the backseat of the truck and had Sammy jump in after them. Adam introduced them to Mark Henson of Northwest Trek.

"So, how are you recouping?" Sean asked his friend.

"I'm doing good. All the bumps and bruises are healing, just have to wait for my suspension to be lifted. I have to go into Seattle for some psych eval. I'm not allowed to carry a weapon 'till I'm cleared," Adam replied.

"So basically, you have been a thorn in Laura's side, and she pushed you out of the house," Sean chided.

"Yeah, pretty much," Adam chuckled.

The big Ford truck rumbled along the network of old forest roads until they reached a logging road that came to an abrupt end in front of an old clear-cut meadow. "Here we are," Henson declared, "This spot is only about half a mile from where Adam said you guys found them. They will know this territory and have an easier time adapting without their mom."

They hopped out of the truck, with a forlorn Sammy left in the cab. They didn't want the dog's presence to stress the young bears any more than they already were. They were given a mild tranquilizer for the trip that would wear off within the hour.

Sean helped Mark and Adam lift the cage from the bed of the truck and carry it to the middle of the meadow. They found a leeward side of a large boulder that offered a patch of snowless ground. They carefully placed the cage on the soft grass. Mark lifted the door open, and the foursome retreated to the truck. With cameras and field glasses ready, they waited for the bears to wake up from their drug-induced slumber and re-enter their homeland.

The young female stirred first, startled about being in the crate. She looked around for danger and cautiously slunk through the door of the cage. She sniffed the air and made a few grunts, staying close to the cage to keep vigil over her still snoozing brother.

The male's snout began to twitch, as though he could smell something familiar. He opened his eyes and, like his sister, appeared tentative and nervous about his situation. Seeing her outside of the crate, he quickly followed suit. The siblings nuzzled each other briefly and took stock of their surroundings. They communicated with little grunts and bleats, then with a concerted movement, headed for the forest rim, towards the ridge that Sean had found their mother.

Mark smiled at his crew and patted Sean on the back, "You did good, Kendall. You did real good."

Senator Timothy Small grumbled on the porch of his Virginia townhouse, his home while Congress was in session. Jerry Rhinehart and Harold Billings sat opposite of him, sharing his tension as they swirled their cognac.

"Never should have used that bunch of rednecks. And what happened to Gaskill? He was supposed to handle the situation! Now he is missing, and one of those country boys is in custody," Small growled.

"Tug was highly recommended. He handled the Colorado situation perfectly, sir," Rhinehart replied.

"Well, this is a bunch of horse pucky, now I understand that this whole thing is under review from the DOI Oversight Committee. Those blocks we put on that cowboy Fish and Wildlife agent might come back to haunt us. We should have handled him differently," Billings roared.

"Maybe, fortunately, Gaskill is the only one who can finger us. We need to get to him before he decides to get around to doing just that. Jerry, what are our options?" Small asked his aide.

"Well, sir, I see it one of two ways. We either take him out, or we make sure that he is unequivocally unable to speak," Rhinehart said.

"Do you have someone who can do either?" Small asked.

"I think we can come with something," Rhinehart replied, sitting back comfortably, blowing smoke from his cigar out towards the ceiling.

"You had better, Mr. Rhinehart. Tug knows you the best. He is going to want to do one of two things. Kill those individuals that can identify him or strike up another deal that makes him invaluable to the cartel. If he decides the former, Mr. Rhinehart, I would not want to be you," Small said thoughtfully.

Rhinehart's arrogance flew out of him as he knew that Tug Gaskill's talents and pension for killing was a near unstoppable force. He shook his snifter of cognac solemnly. His boss was right. He needed to get to Gaskill if he ever wanted another peaceful night's sleep again.

With the weather breaking, and Spring looming ever nearer, the Alpha carefully guided the pack further south along the Cascade range. Food was plentiful, and the female of the Alpha pair was already showing signs of coming into heat. The pack had not felt danger for weeks and was becoming more comfortable settling into their Washington habitat. Reaching the top of a ridgeline, not far from where they lost their packmate, they enjoyed their unencumbered view of the valley below them.

The alpha started the procession with a very soft, low sound that slowly escalated into a piercing howl. One by one, the pack members joined the chorus, one final song for the brother wolf that had once been part of their family. Their sonnet wafted through the range, signaling a return of the wolf to the Cascades of the lower forty-eight.

"That really was wonderful today, seeing those bears released," Miranda said over the steam of her coffee cup. She enjoyed their afternoon together, but she was intent on getting back to Anacortes before dark.

"Yeah, it was rewarding. I was surprised that they were able to return so quickly, but I guess the least amount of time in captivity the better," Sean replied. He looked out his window towards the marker that designated the resting place of Charlie, the dog.

Seeing where his gaze had landed, Miranda slid her hand on Sean's shoulder, "It wasn't your fault, you know. None of this was. It was my family. We should all be glad that you stood up for what you cared about, for me." "Thanks. I guess in my head, I keep trying to redo the things that went wrong and try to figure out how I could have done better," Sean said, shrugging his shoulders.

"You? You were terrific. You did so much more than anyone could have asked of you. How about me, my own family...I never saw it coming," her hand pressing against his shoulder, causing him to face her. "I certainly never saw *this* coming." She opened her mouth slightly as she met his. Their kiss, like so many between them, sincere and passionate.

"Are you sure you don't want to stay a few more days?" Sean realized that he didn't want her to go. Without the pressures of the past week hanging over their heads, the thought of a couple of days never leaving the house, clothes being little more than a trifling option, sounded very appealing to him.

"Oh, I am sure I *want* to, but I don't have the advantage of an extraordinarily early retirement. And I love my job. I need to get back to it. Maybe you could visit me some weekend. You could, you know, help me count a whale or two...," Miranda grinned mischievously.

"I do know a nice bed and breakfast that has a suite right on the Pacific. It even has a Jacuzzi that overlooks the water," Sean admitted.

"Oh, Mr. Kendall, you do have a little devil inside, don't you?" the young marine biologist cooed.

"I assure you that I *am* an angel Ms. Shaw," Sean smirked.

"Then that has got to be the most tarnished halo I have ever seen! Very well. Until next weekend my love...," Miranda declared, carrying on the air of an overacting thespian until the word "love" came out.

They both paused in shock, but then as if it were just a part of the act, Sean concluded, "Then I shall get your things, madam." He whisked off her to grab her suitcase and duffle bag. Walking her to her SUV, he stooped as they shared one more kiss before the woman that had been a stranger less than two weeks ago, backed down his driveway.

Watching until her taillights disappeared into the trees, he leaned against his front porch scratching Sammy's ear. Sighing, he felt like he missed her already. Sammy let out a small whimper as if he knew what his master was thinking.

Sean could not deny the intense feelings that had developed with Miranda Shaw. Maybe it was the intensity of the circumstances that surrounded their meeting, or perhaps they would feel the same if they met in a coffee shop and never had been pulled into such drama. The word "love" continued ringing in his ears. This was a word that he had disassociated himself with for so long.

He shook these sober thoughts from his head and just smiled. He enjoyed his time with her. They had fun. He didn't need to apply a label to his feelings; he just had to like being around her. Ushering Sammy into the house, he shut the door behind him. His home seemed warmer and more alive for some reason. But then again, maybe cheating death had a way of making one appreciate what they had just a little bit more. Having an alluring, charismatic woman around helped as well.

Snatching a beer from the fridge, he settled in front of the fireplace with Sammy. He flipped on the news to see pictures from the convention center that were recorded earlier in the day. Turning up the volume on the television, he heard the reporter say, "...and with the quick and decided action of the Department of Interior task force led by Regional Director Ron Beckett, a major disaster was averted. He played a hunch with his team and turned away a sinister terrorist attack at the Free Trade Organization Conference. Several armed men were placed into custody, while several others had been shot during their failed attempt. Mr. Beckett said that all information and would-be assassins had been turned over to the FBI as they had been running a parallel operation. Seattle sleeps better tonight, knowing that its citizens are under the safe protection and watchful eye of our government agencies…."

Sean flipped off the television and decided to watch the flames leap from the wood as they danced their way up the chimney was a much more redeeming and honest close to his evening. With men like Beckett and the politicians that block the resources of agents like his friend Adam, the country was a much more dangerous and hostile place. He took a final swallow of his beer. Amidst the calm and comfort of his peaceful home in the North Cascades, Sean got an eerie feeling in his stomach that somehow, all of this wasn't quite over.

Blood
in the
Water

A Sean Kendall Thriller

An activist is found slain on the beach inside the Makah Indian reservation in Washington state, home of the very people he was protesting. The murder weapon, an ancient Makah spear, and tensions over the tribe's defiance of orders to cease their whaling ritual, the case looks like a slam dunk.

Detective Joe Woodfeathers calls in for help from the outside - Wildlife Officer Adam Raines and Sean Kendall. Finding not everything being what they seem, Sean and Adam follow the investigation to Portland, Oregon. The pair quickly find themselves uncovering an international conspiracy, one that has ties eerily close to home.

Before they can unravel the entire mystery, a call for help aboard the Portland Spirit river cruise sends Sean on a daring rescue in the swift waters of the mighty Columbia River.

* 9 7 8 0 9 8 5 4 3 8 9 0 6 *